Tree-House Comix Proudly Presents

CAT KID COMIC CLUB
PERSPECTIVES

WRITTEN, ILLUSTRATED, AND COLORED BY

DAV PILKEY

AS GEORGE BEARD AND HAROLD HUTCHINS

WITH DIGITAL COLOR BY JOSE GARIBALDI

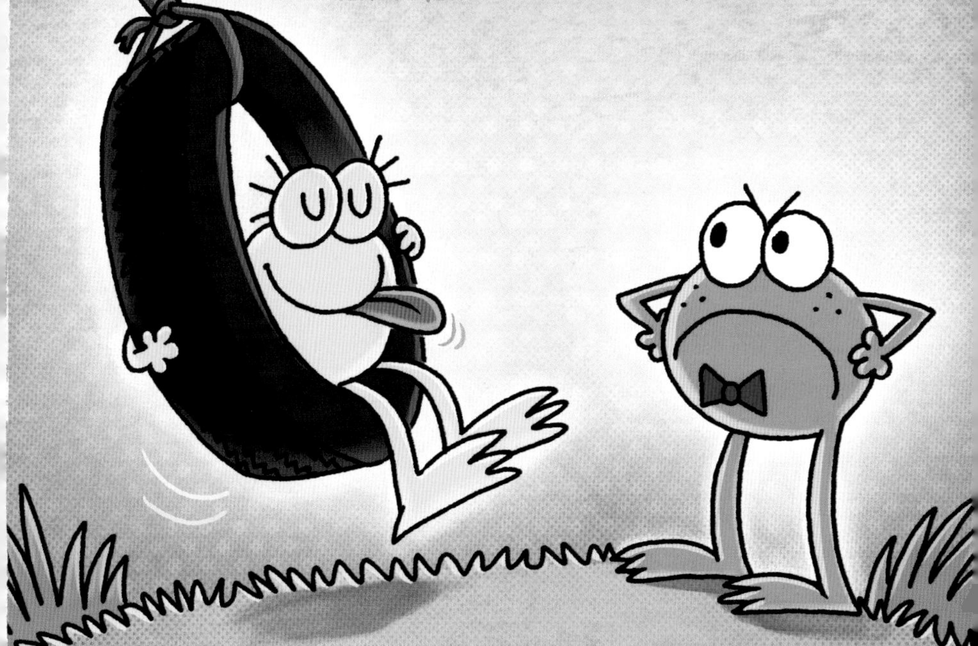

graphix

AN IMPRINT OF

SCHOLASTIC

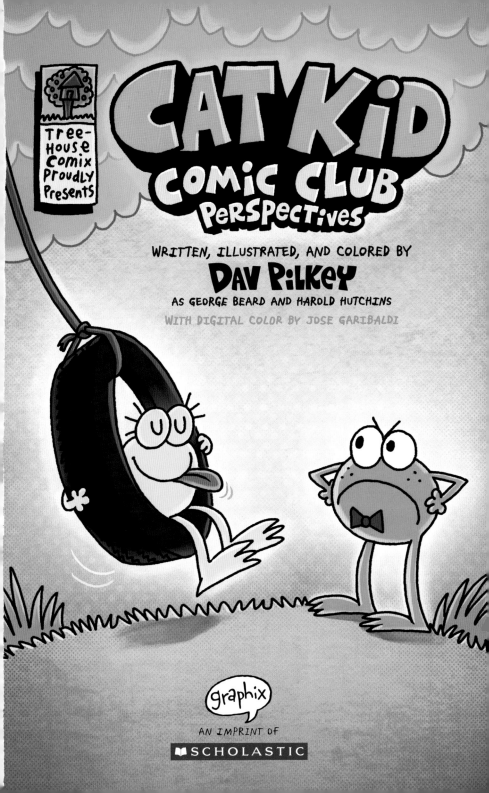

Library of Congress Control Number 2021932630

978-1-338-78485-5 (POB)   978-1-338-78486-2 (Library)

10 9 8 7 6 5 4 3 2 1   21 22 23 24 25

Printed in China   62
First edition, December 2021

Illustrations and hand lettering by Dav Pilkey

Clay and paper models, Japanese calligraphy, photography, poetry, and paper cutouts by Dav Pilkey

All mini comics (except BABY FLIPPY) colored by Dav Pilkey using acrylic paints, colored pencils, ballpoint pens, markers, crayons, gouache, and watercolors.

Digital Color by Jose Garibaldi | Flatting by Aaron Polk
Special Thanks to: Arcana Izu and Asaba Ryokan

Editor: Ken Geist | Editorial Team: Megan Peace and Jonah Newman
Book design by Dav Pilkey and Phil Falco
Creative Director: Phil Falco
Publisher: David Saylor

CHAPTERS & COMICS

Chapter 1. Time Wasters 5

Chapter 2. More Goofing Around 29

Comic: Time Wasters: Wasters of Time 33

Comic: Chubbs McSpiderbutt 43

Chapter 3. New Day, New Perspective 61

Comic: Supa Fail 2: Old Lady's Revenge 63

Chapter 4. Big Trouble for Little Melvin 83

Chapter 5. The Next Day... 91

Chapter 6. Sister Stories 97

Comic: Skelopup 99

Comic: Baby Flippy 113

Comic: Shodo Gardens: Photos, Poems,
and Calligraphy 129

Chapter 7. The Inspiration 141

Chapter 8. The Saddest Friday of All Time 159

Comic: Squid Kid and Katydid 167

Comic: Baby Frog Squad 181

Chapter 9. Naomi and Melvin Redeem
Themselves (sort of) 197

Comic: My Sister Naomi 199

Comic Preview: The Under Werewolves 209

Notes & Fun Facts 221

To my Mother, Barbara Pilkey,
and my Okaa-san, Yayoi Chiba

With two perspectives...
Warming sun and cooling rain
many flowers bloom

- D.P.

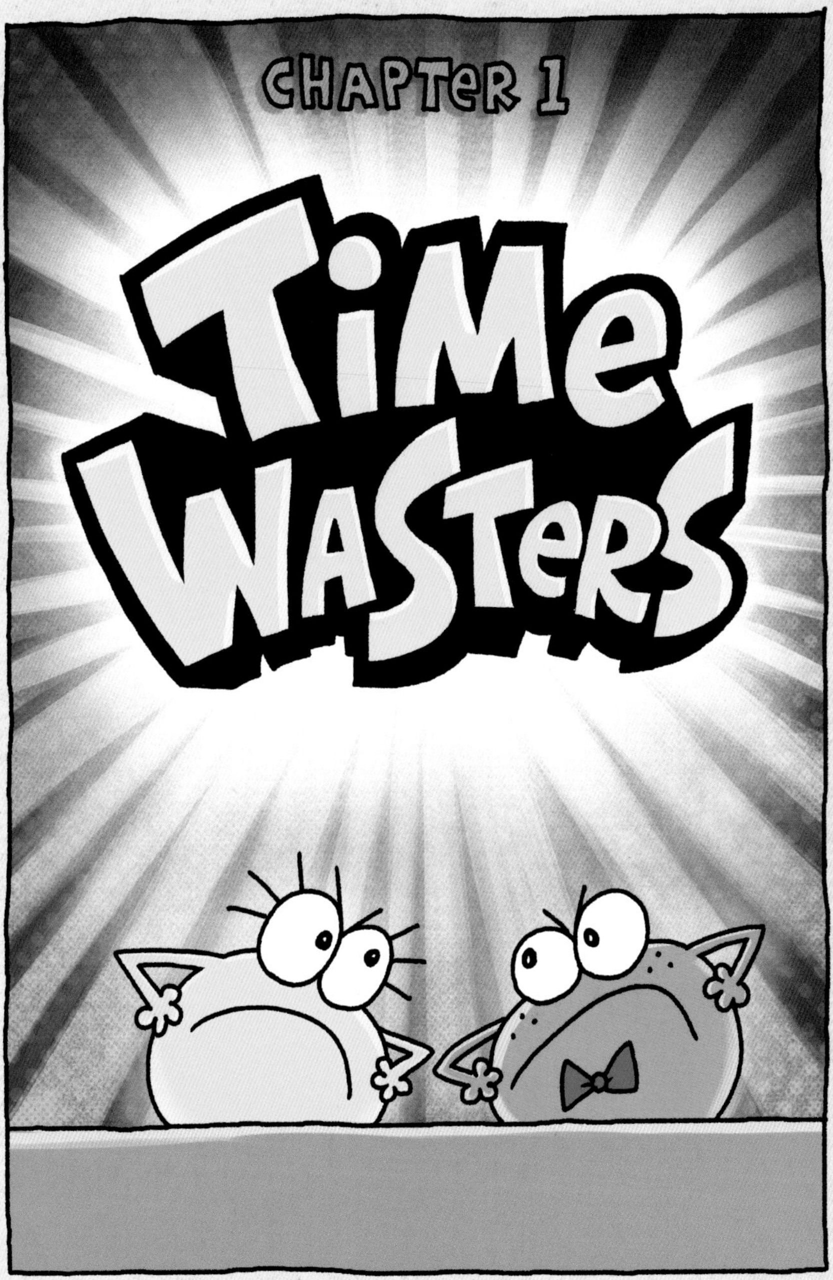
CHAPTER 1
TIME WASTERS

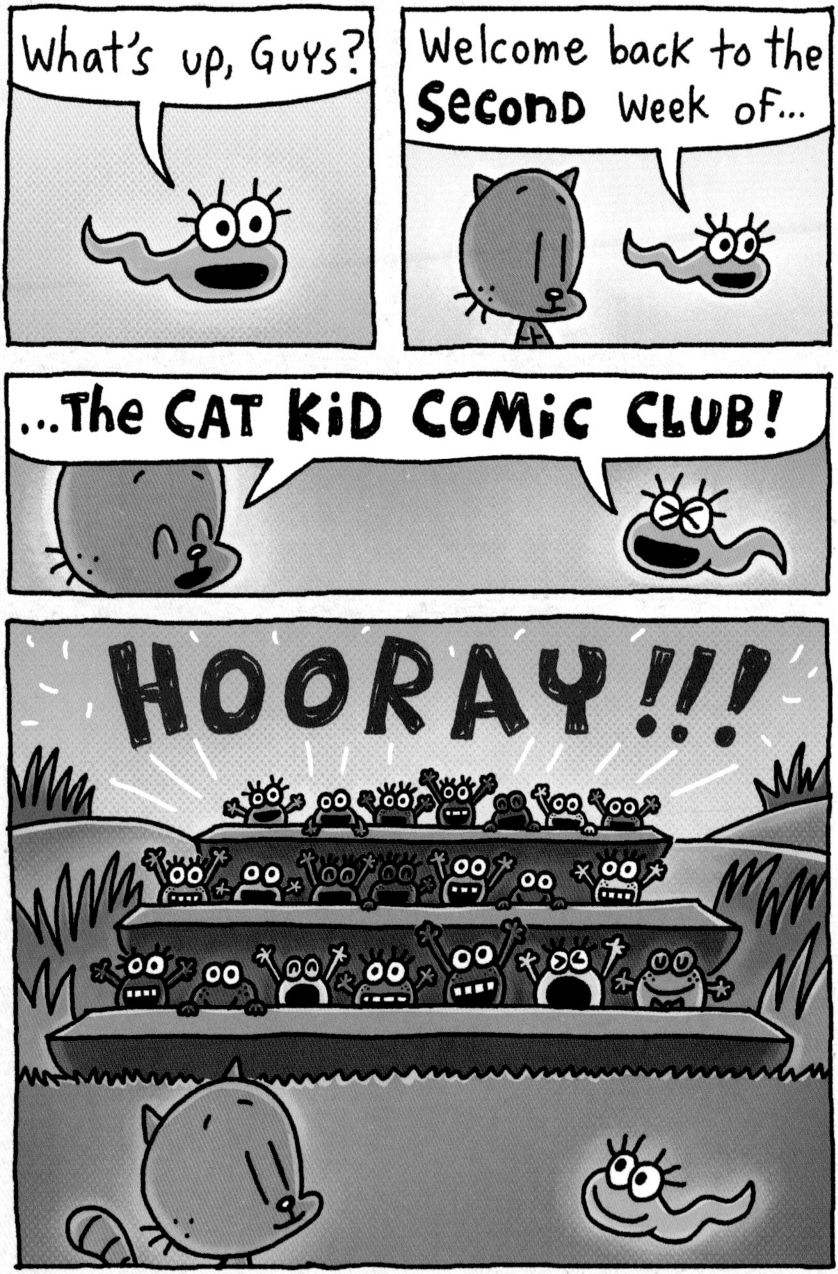
What's up, Guys?
Welcome back to the Second week of...
...The CAT KiD COMiC CLUB!
HOORAY!!!

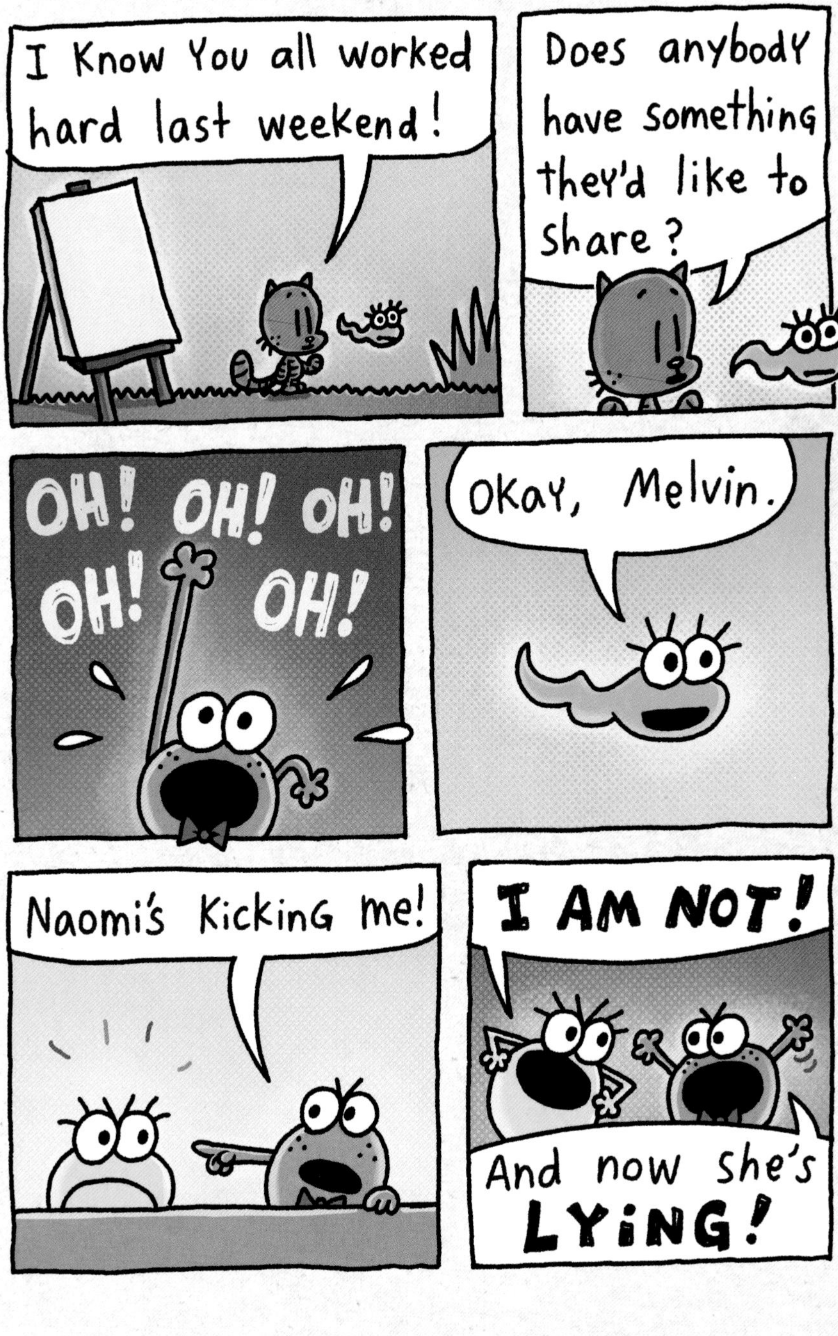
I Know You all worked hard last weekend!
Does anybody have something they'd like to share?
OH! OH! OH! OH! OH!
OKay, Melvin.
Naomi's Kicking me!
I AM NOT!
And now she's LYING!

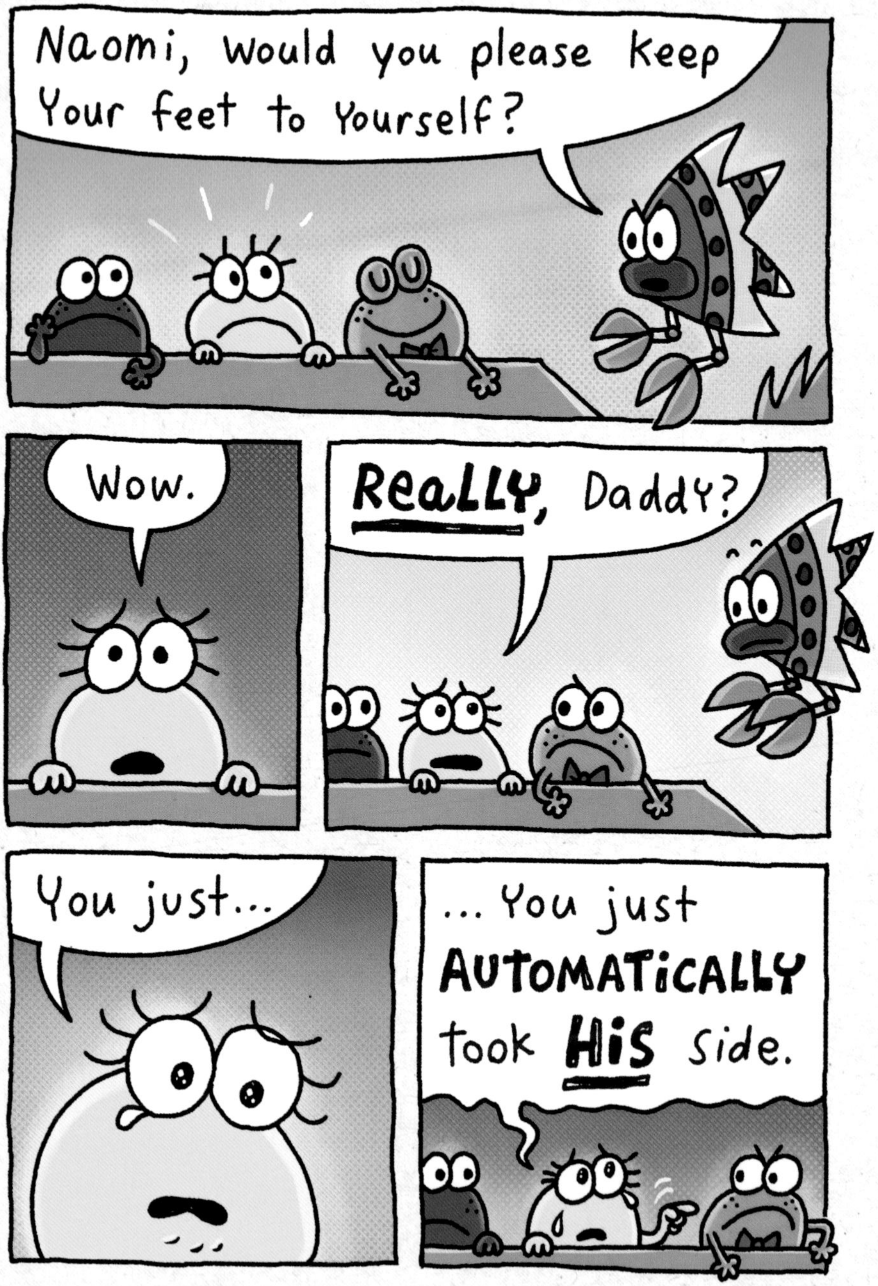
Naomi, would you please keep your feet to yourself?
Wow.
REALLY, Daddy?
You just...
... You just AUTOMATICALLY took HIS side.

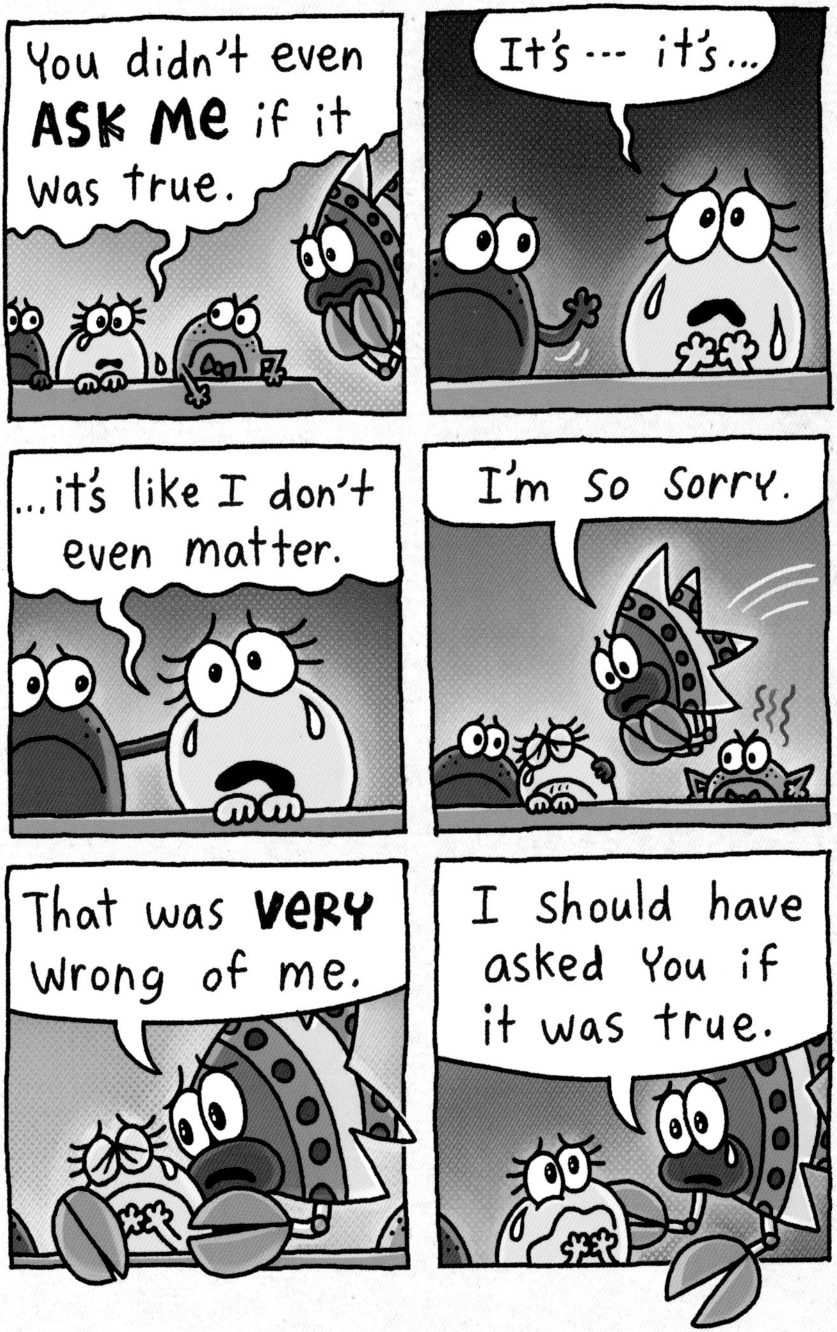
You didn't even **ASK ME** if it was true.
It's --- it's...
...it's like I don't even matter.
I'm so sorry.
That was **VERY** wrong of me.
I should have asked you if it was true.

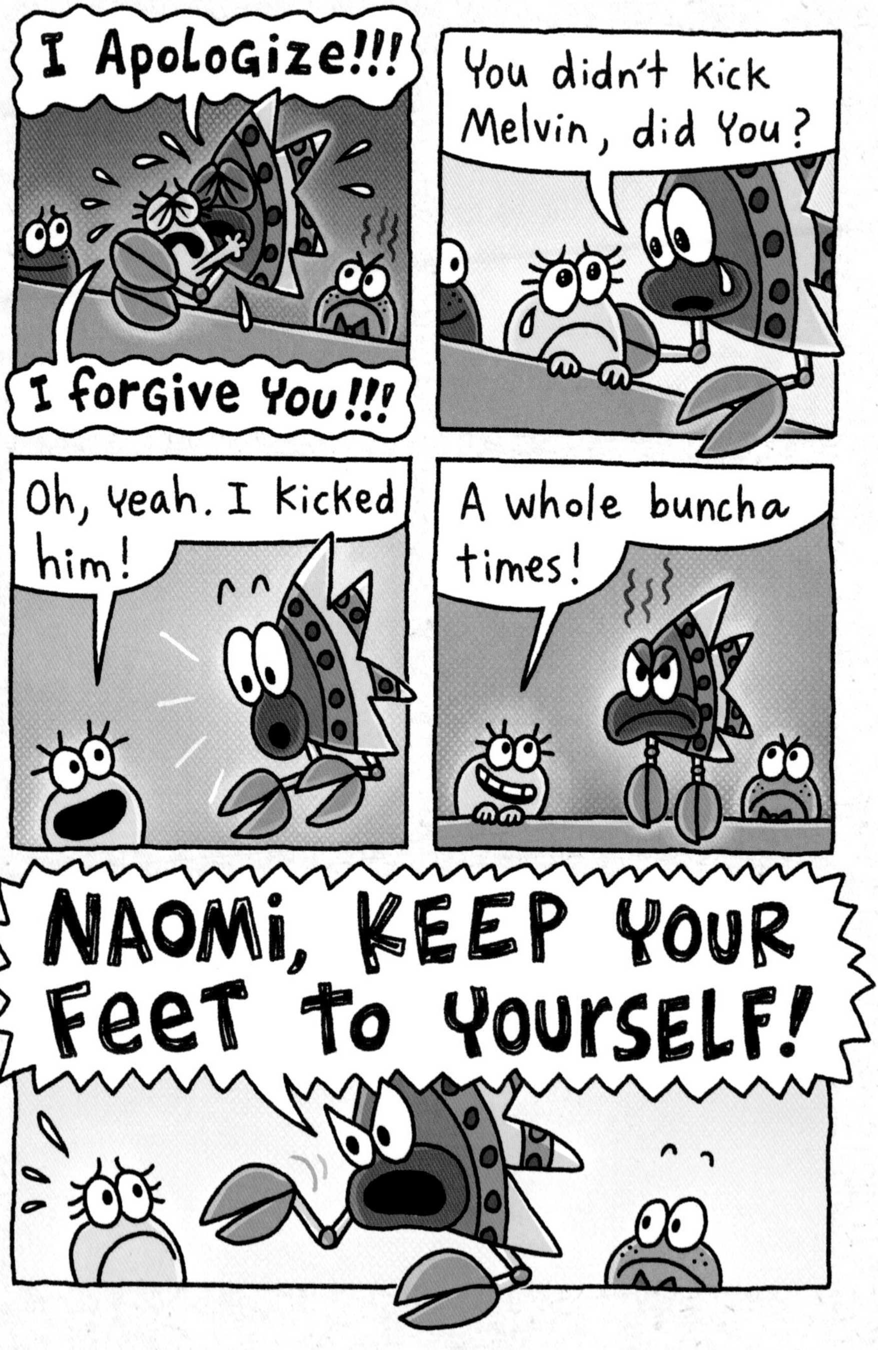
I ApoLoGize!!!
I forGive You!!!
You didn't kick Melvin, did You?
Oh, Yeah. I Kicked him!
A whole buncha times!
NAOMi, KEEP YOUR FeeT to YourSELF!

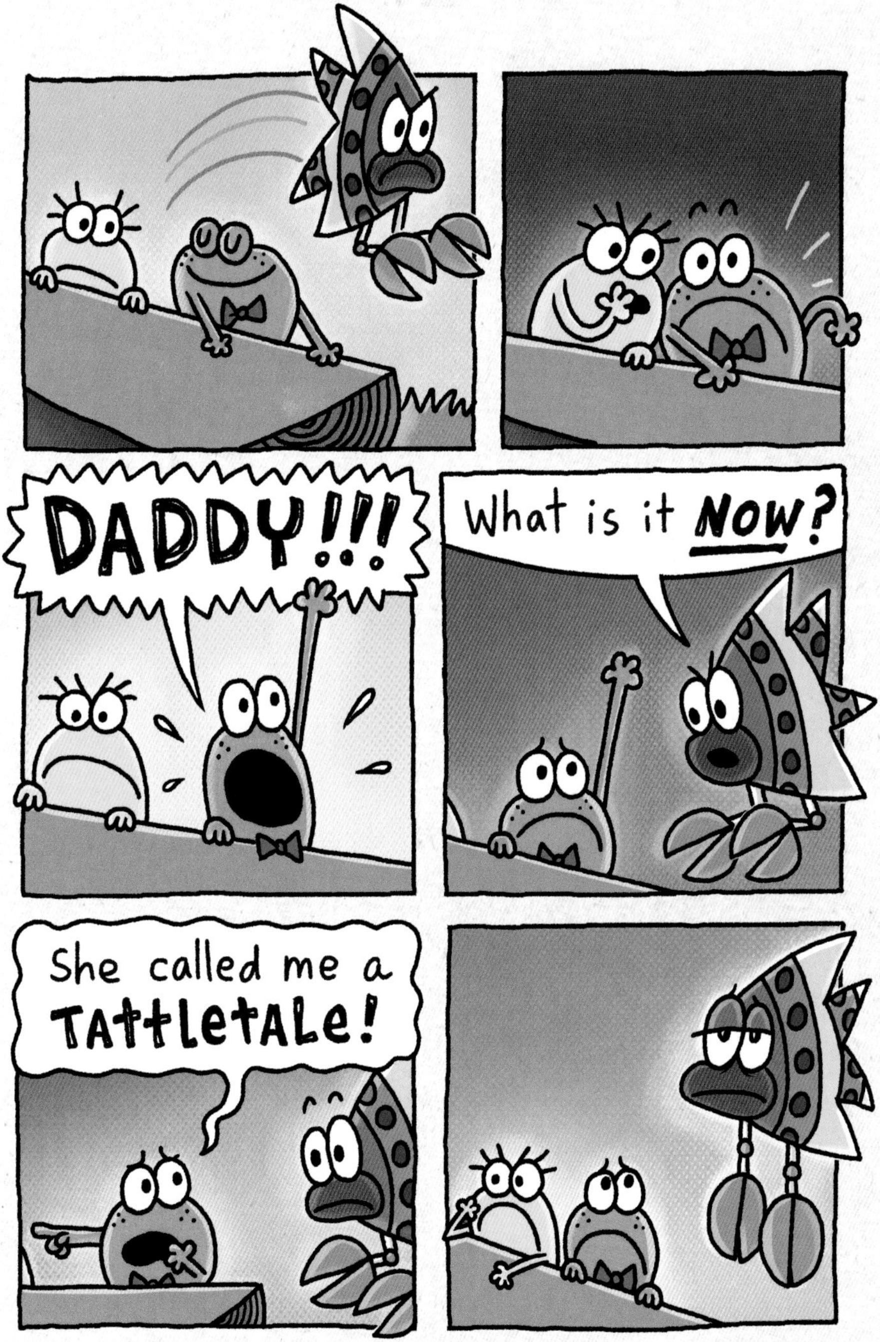
DADDY!!!
What is it NOW?
She called me a TATTLETALE!

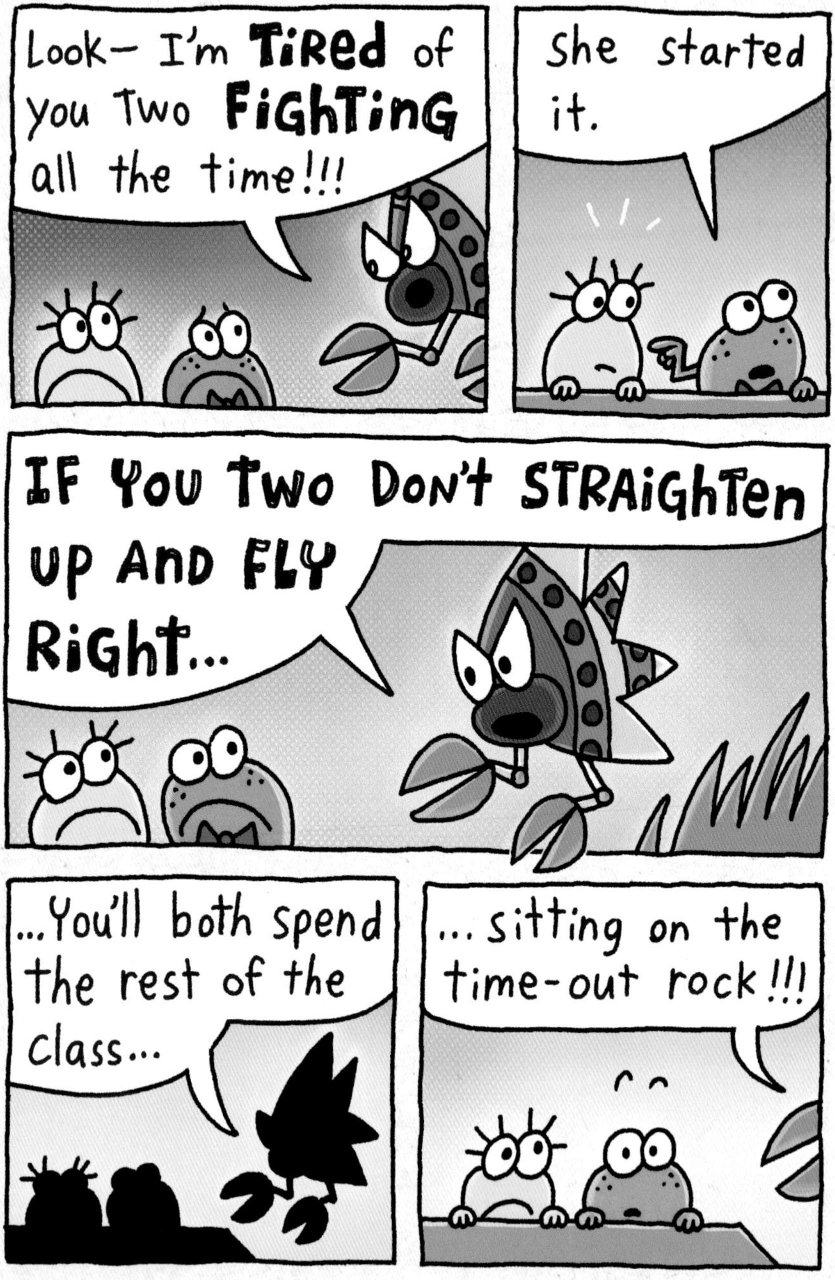

Look– I'm TIRED of you Two FIGHTING all the time!!!
She started it.
IF YOU TWO DON'T STRAIGHTEN UP AND FLY RIGHT...
...You'll both spend the rest of the class...
...sitting on the time-out rock!!!

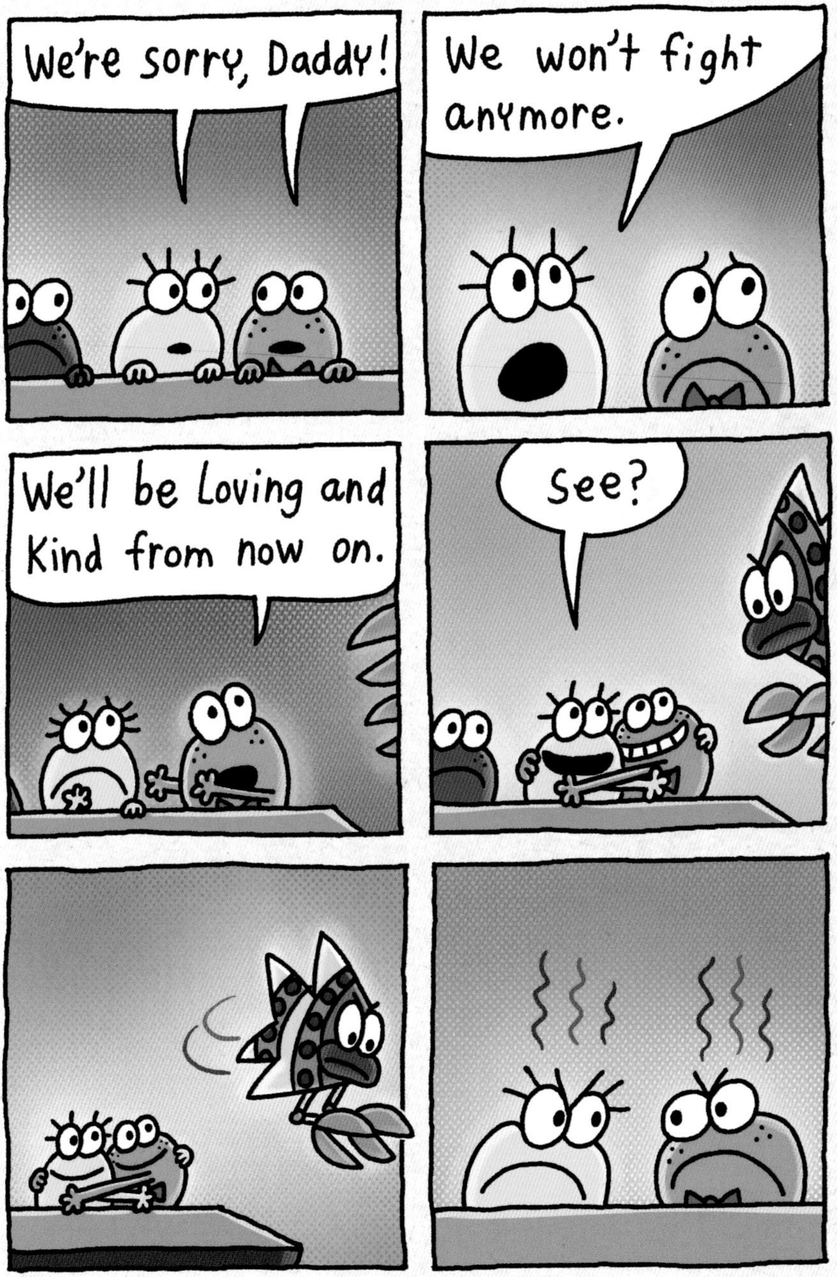

We're sorry, Daddy!
We won't fight anymore.
We'll be loving and kind from now on.
See?

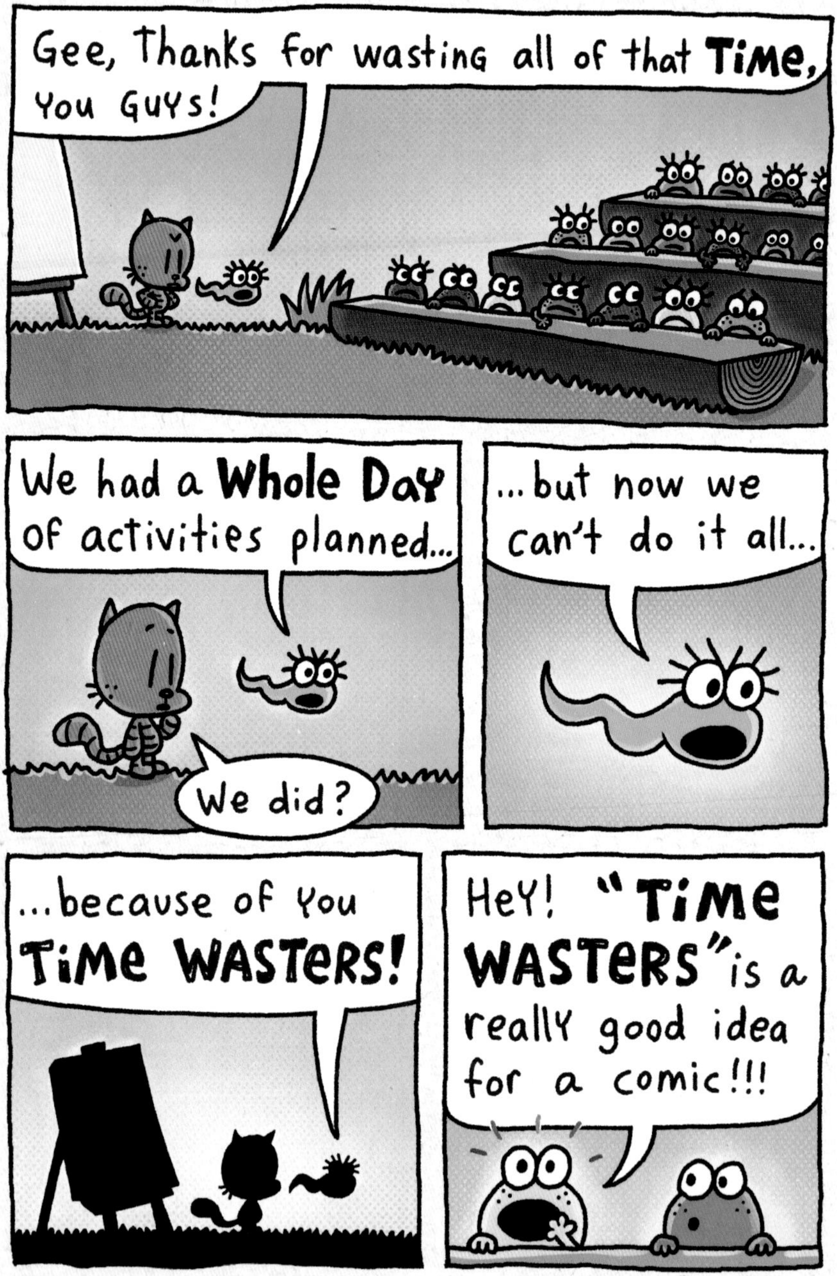
Gee, Thanks for wasting all of that TiMe, You GUYS!
We had a Whole Day of activities planned...
We did?
...but now we can't do it all...
...because of You TiMe WASTERS!
HeY! "TiMe WASTERS" is a really good idea for a comic!!!

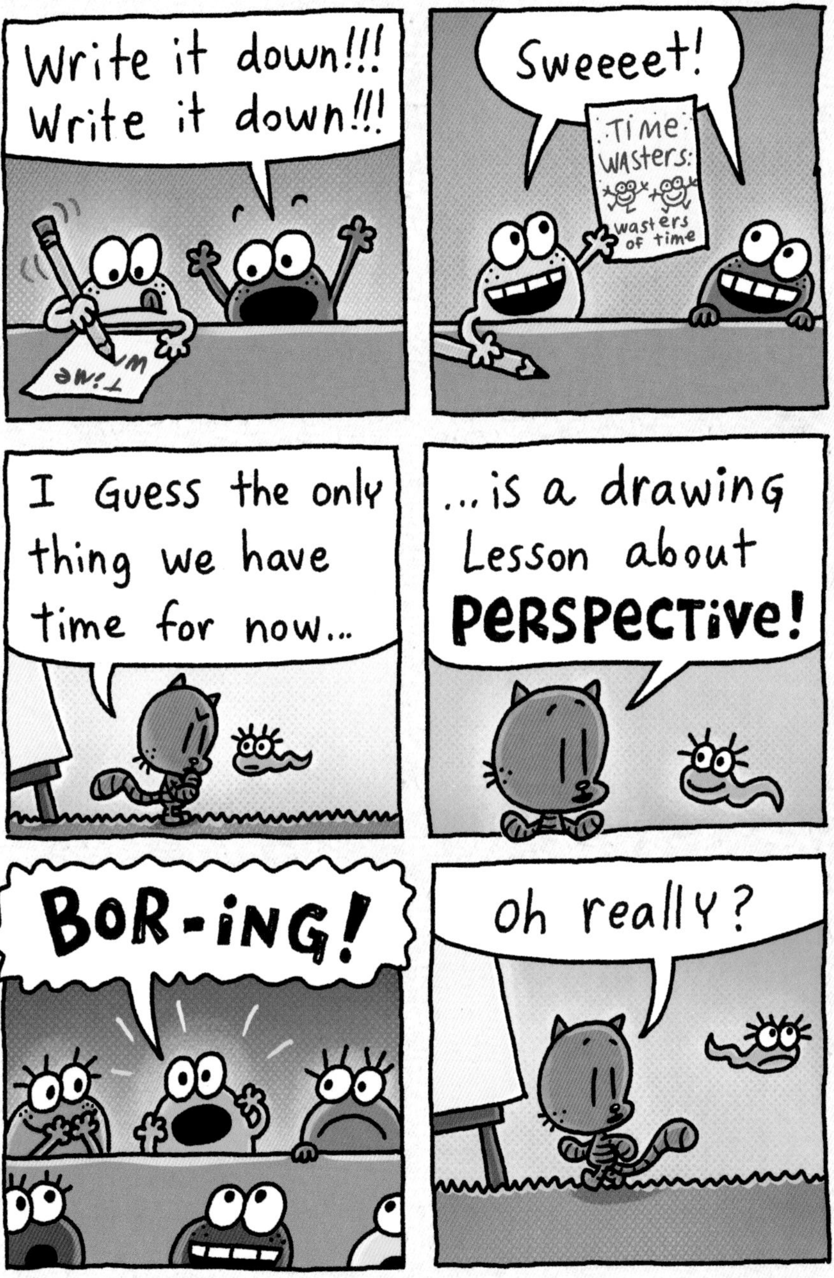

Write it down!!! Write it down!!!
TiME W
Sweeeet!
TiME WASTERS:
wasters of time
I Guess the only thing we have time for now...
...is a drawing Lesson about PERSPECTiVE!
BOR-iNG!
Oh really?

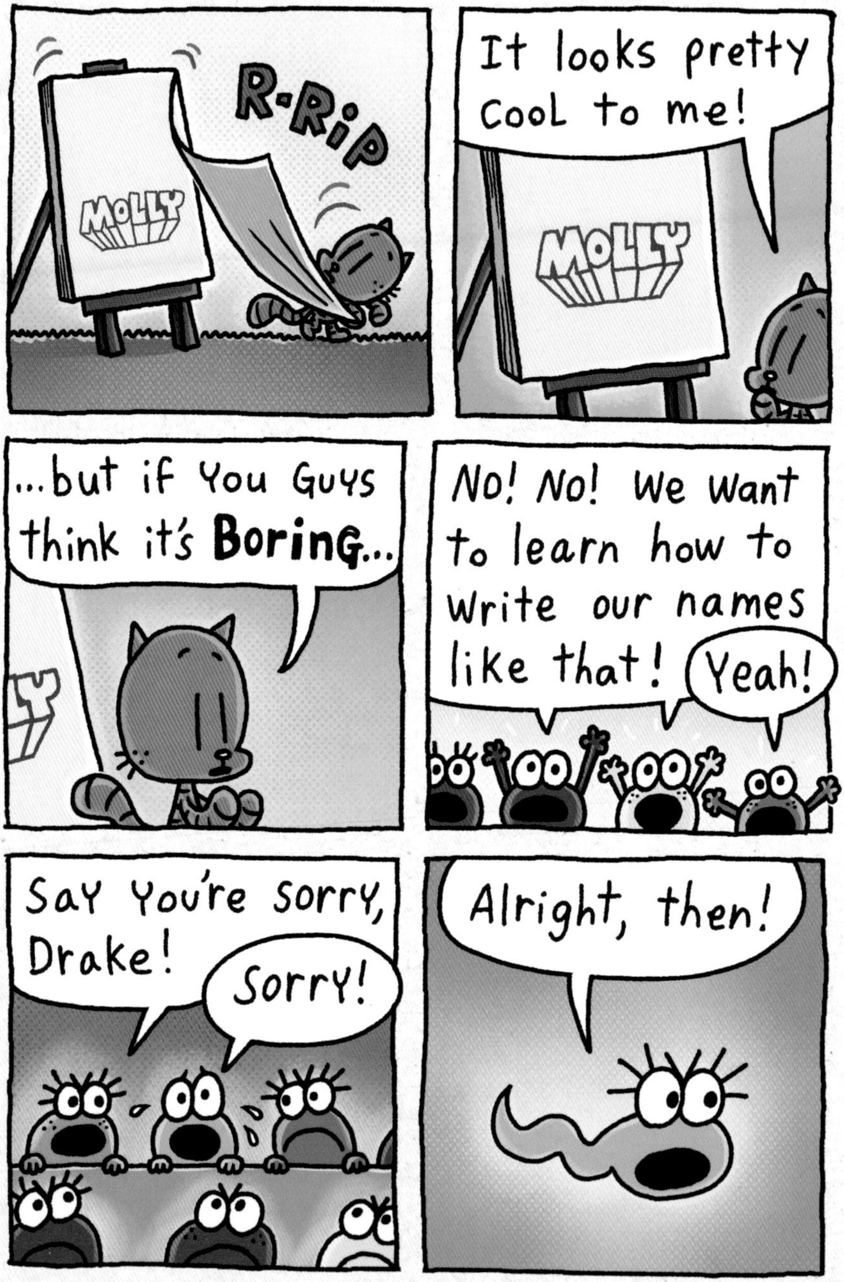
R-RIP
It looks pretty cool to me!
...but if you guys think it's **Boring**...
No! No! We want to learn how to write our names like that!
Yeah!
Say you're sorry, Drake!
Sorry!
Alright, then!

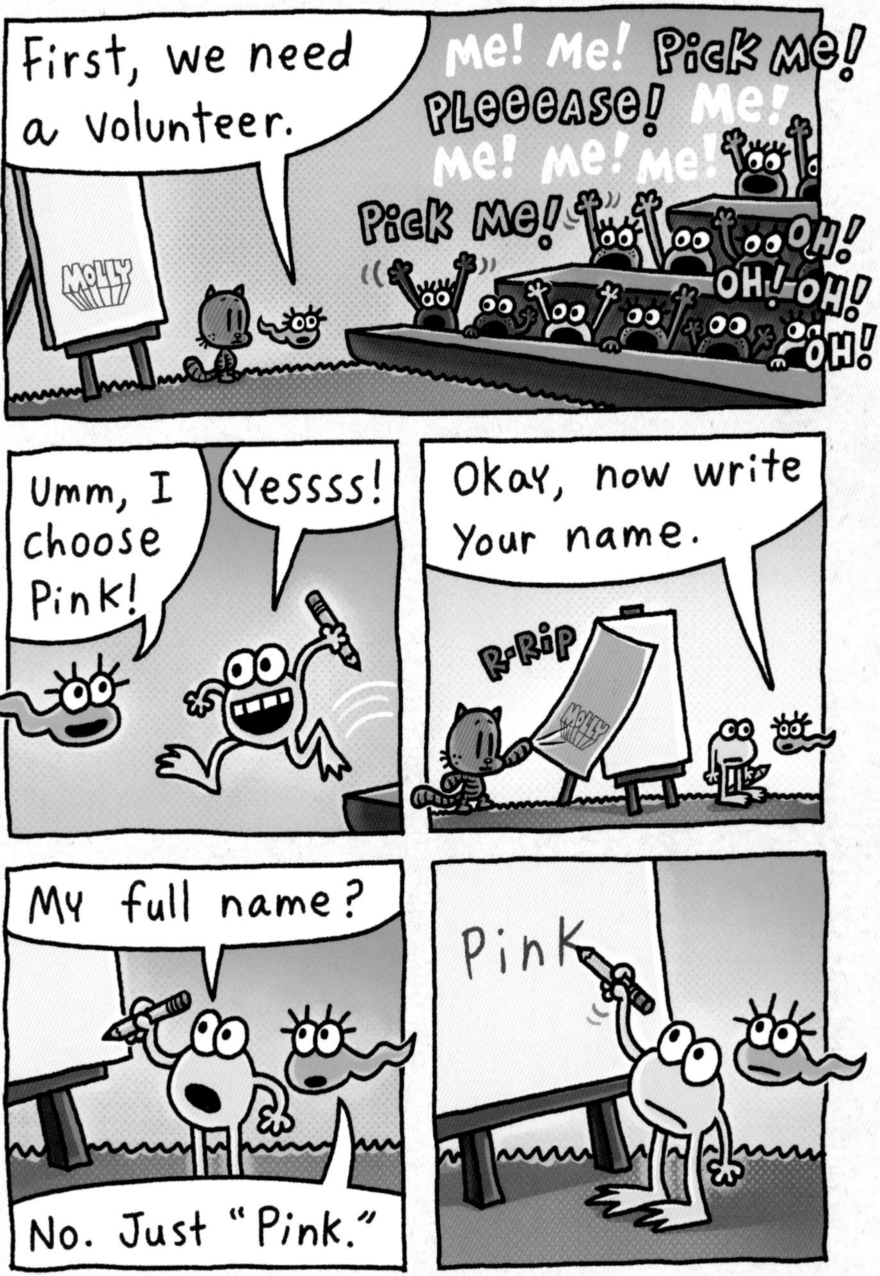
First, we need a volunteer.
Me! Me! Pick me!
PLEEEASE! Me!
Me! Me! Me!
Pick Me!
OH! OH! OH! OH!
MOLLY
Umm, I choose Pink!
Yessss!
Okay, now write your name.
R-RIP
MOLLY
My full name?
No. Just "Pink."
Pink

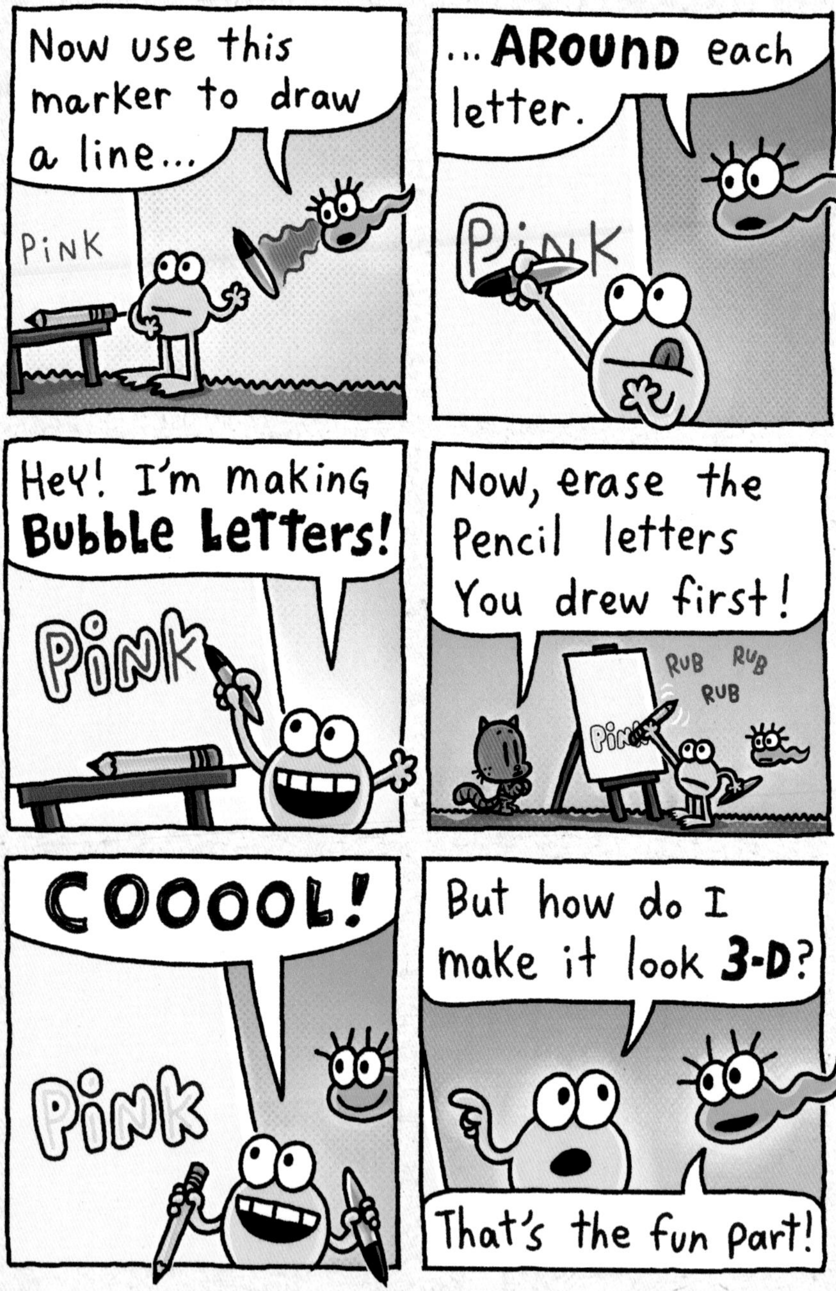

Now use this marker to draw a line...
PINK
...AROUND each letter.
PINK
Hey! I'm making Bubble Letters!
PINK
Now, erase the Pencil letters You drew first!
RUB RUB RUB
COOOOL!
PINK
But how do I make it look 3-D?
That's the fun part!

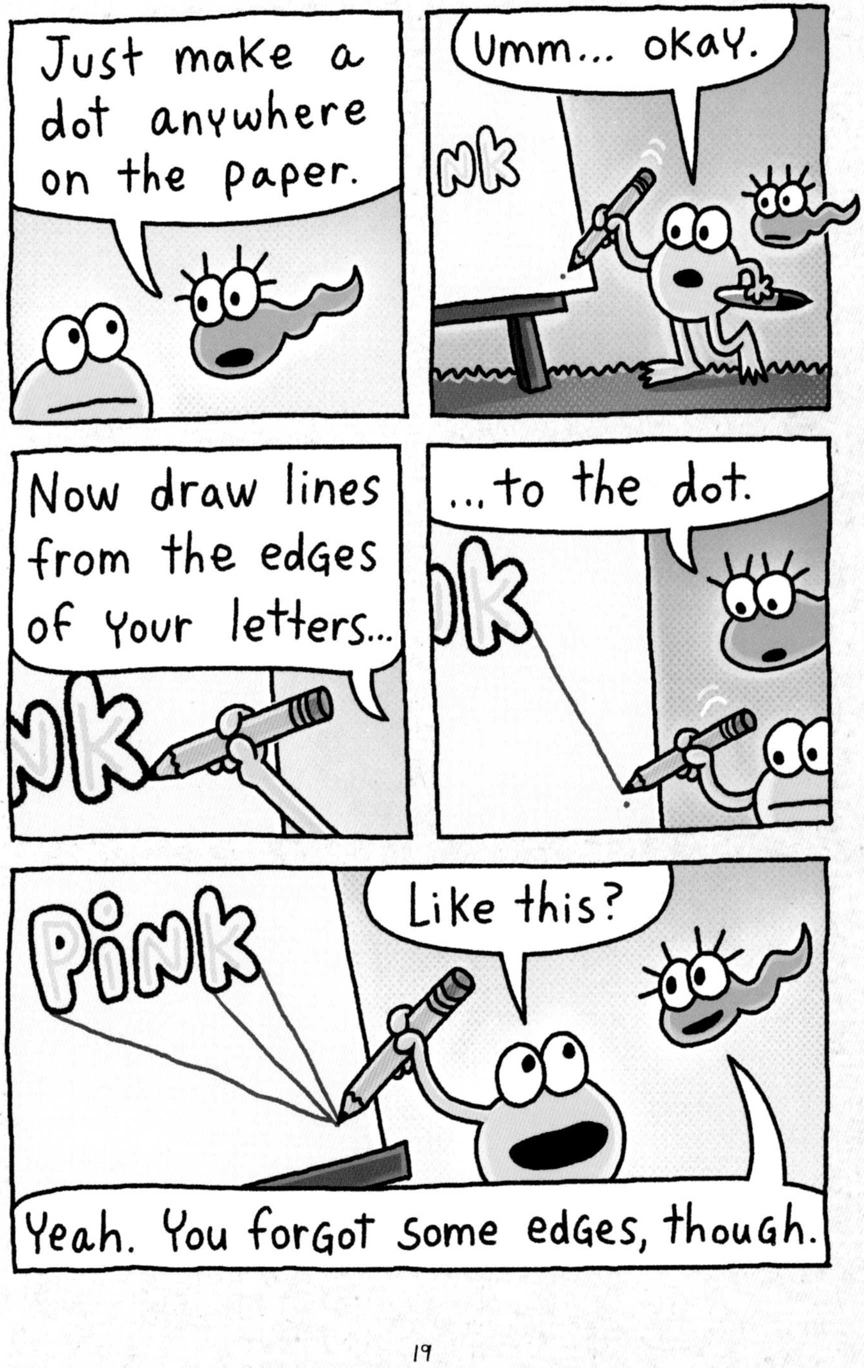

Just make a dot anywhere on the paper.
Umm... okay.
NK
Now draw lines from the edges of your letters...
NK
...to the dot.
K
PINK
Like this?
Yeah. You forgot some edges, though.

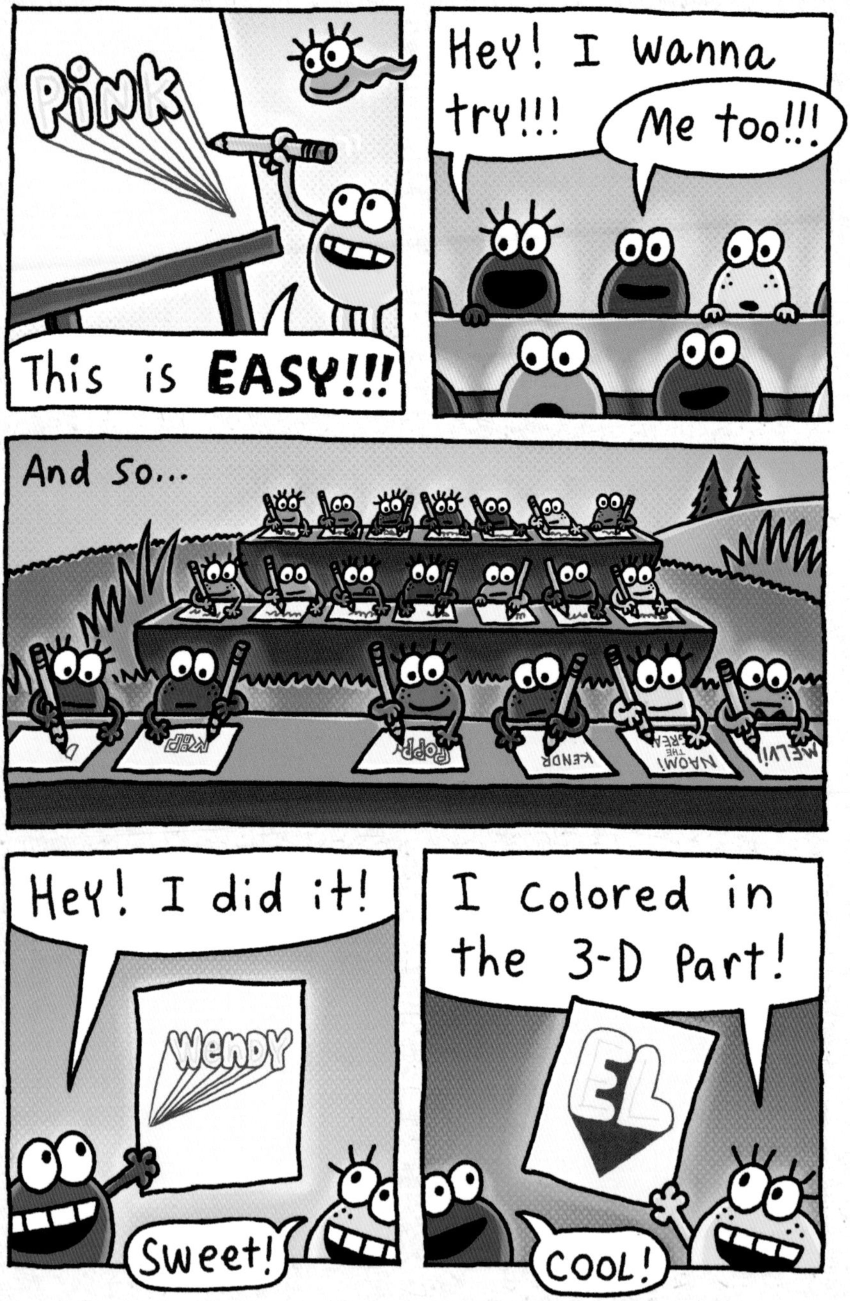
PINK
This is EASY!!!
Hey! I wanna try!!!
Me too!!!
And so...
Hey! I did it!
WENDY
Sweet!
I colored in the 3-D Part!
EL
COOL!

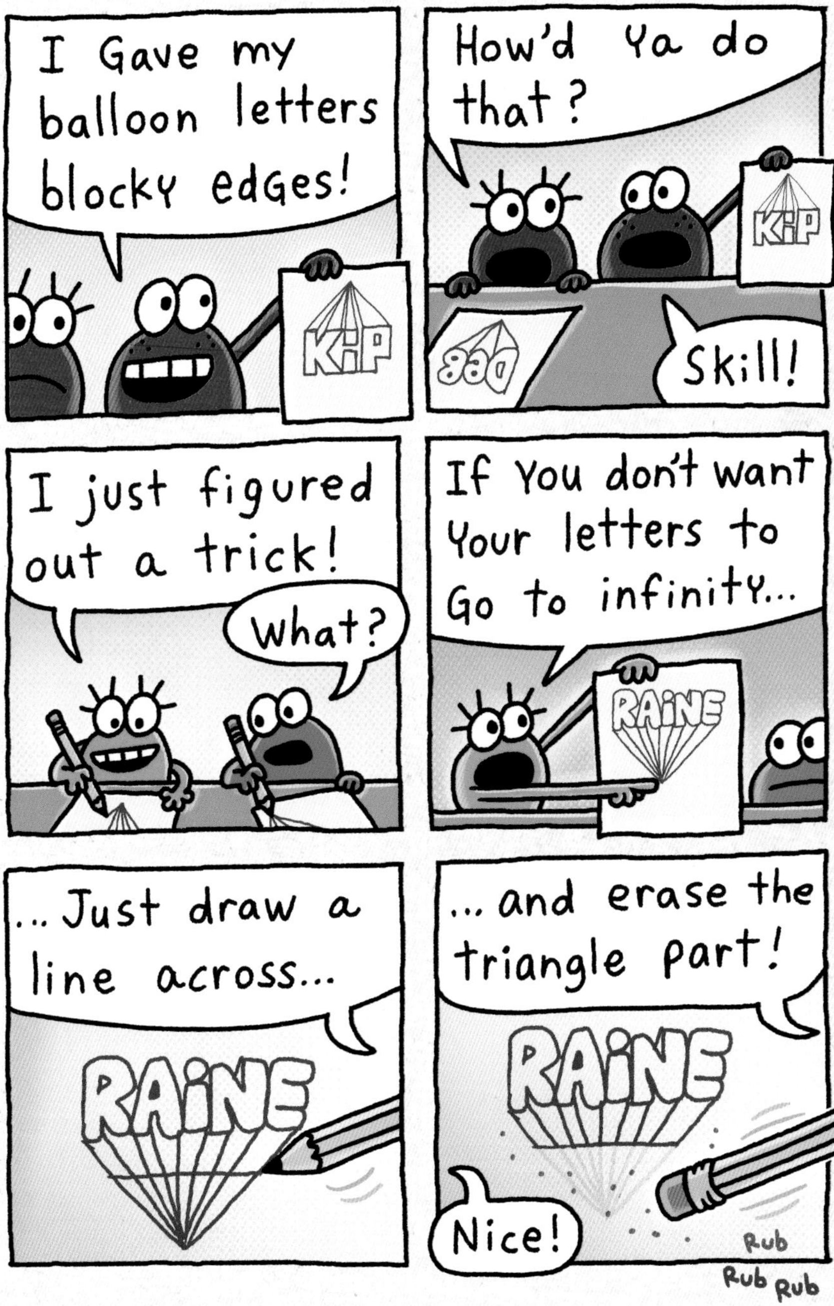
I Gave my balloon letters blocky edGes!
KiP
How'd Ya do that?
KiP
DEB
Skill!
I just figured out a trick!
What?
If You don't want Your letters to Go to infinity...
RAiNE
...Just draw a line across...
RAiNE
...and erase the triangle part!
RAiNE
Nice!
Rub
Rub Rub

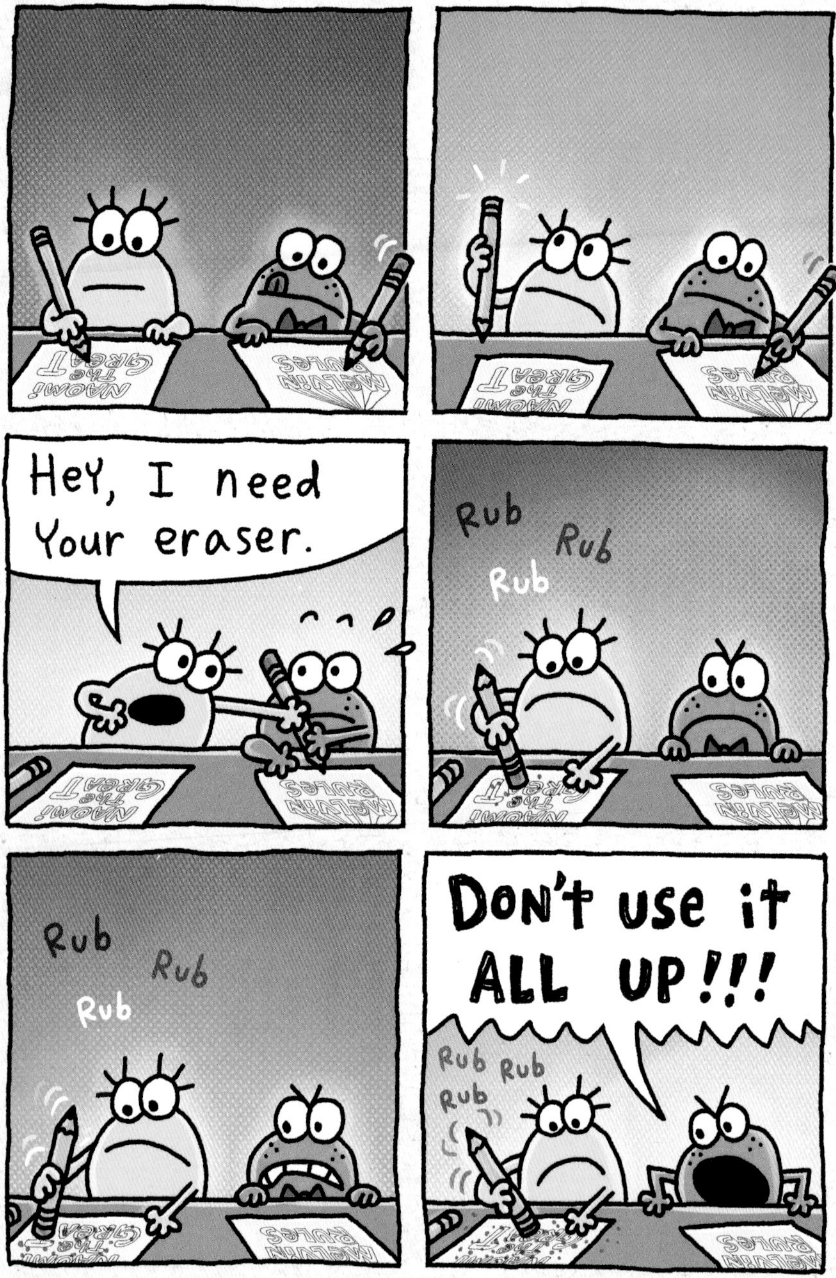
Hey, I need Your eraser.
Rub Rub Rub
Rub Rub Rub
Don't use it ALL UP!!!
Rub Rub Rub

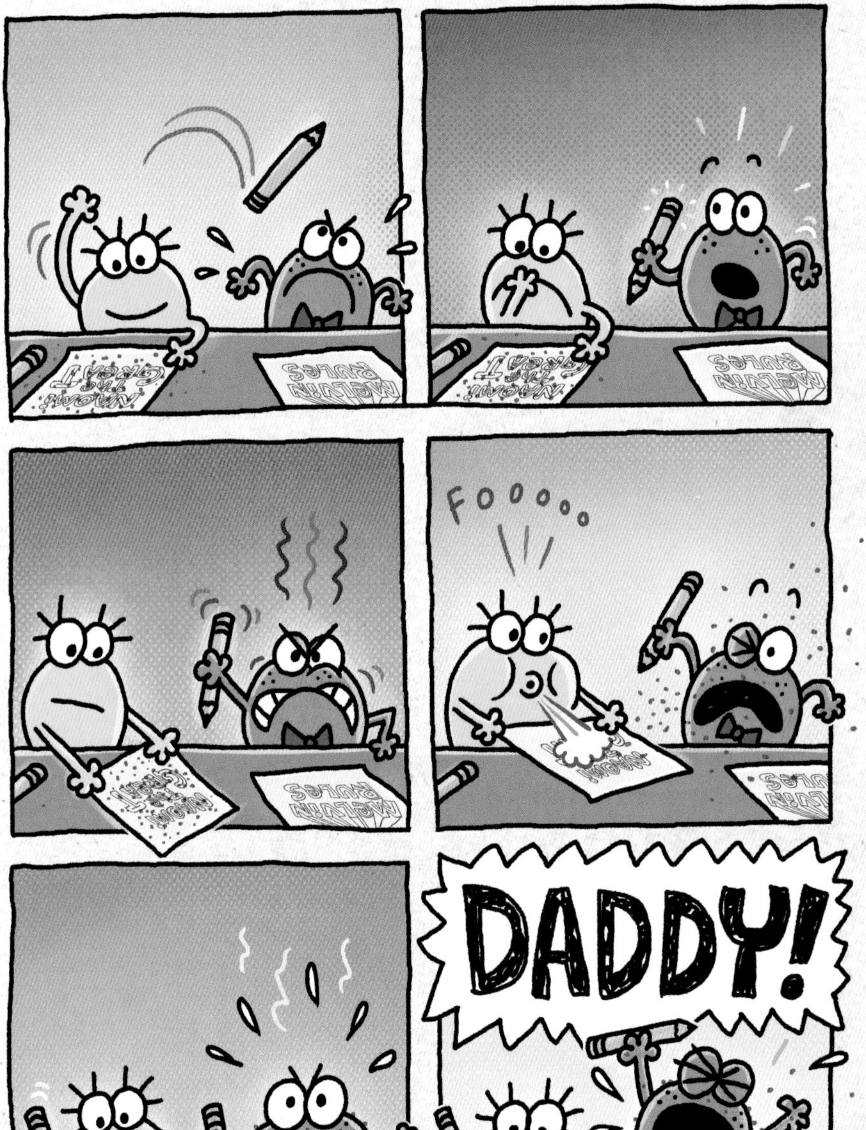
FOOooo
DADDY!

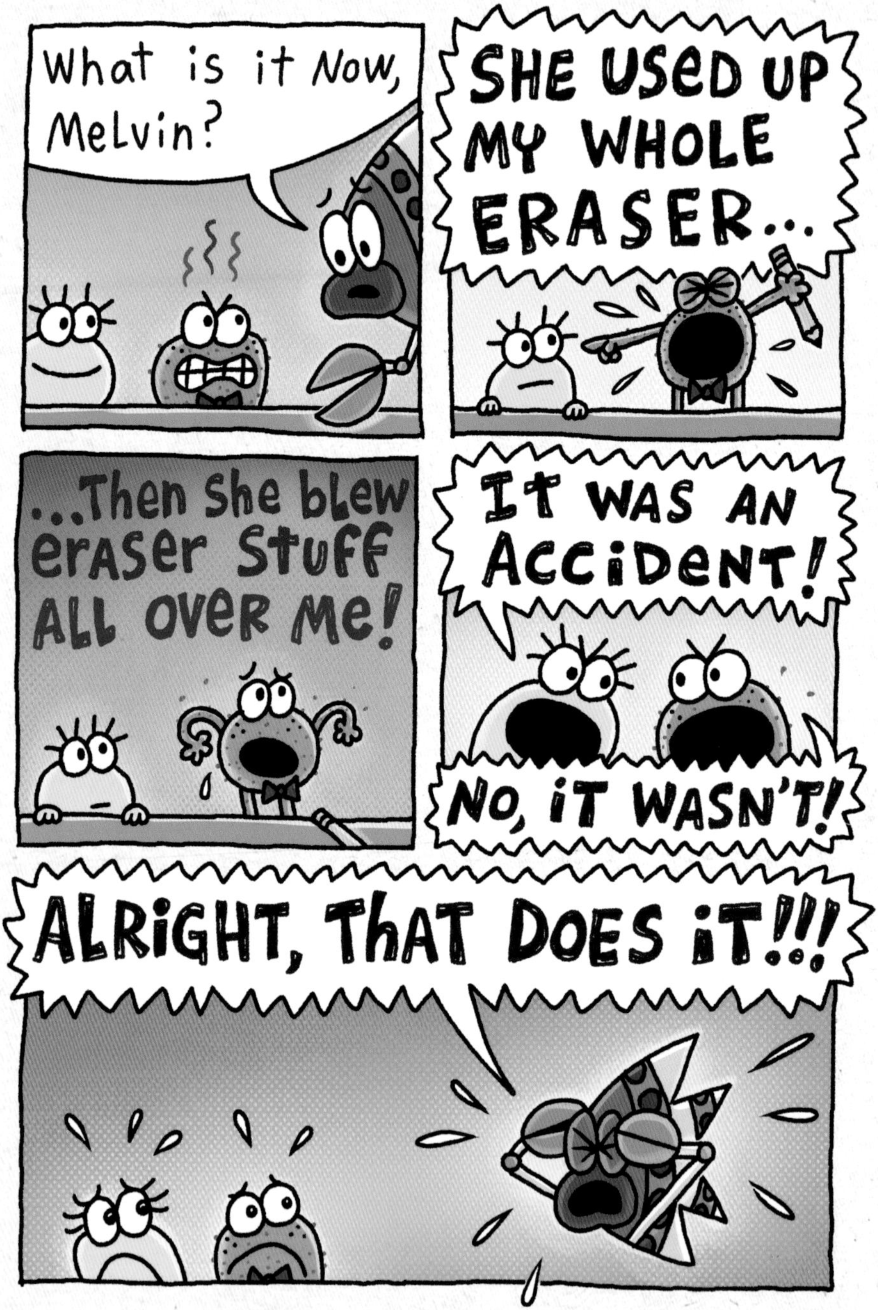
What is it Now, Melvin?
SHE USED UP MY WHOLE ERASER...
...Then She blew eraser Stuff ALL OVER Me!
IT WAS AN ACCIDENT!
No, IT WASN'T!
ALRIGHT, THAT DOES IT!!!

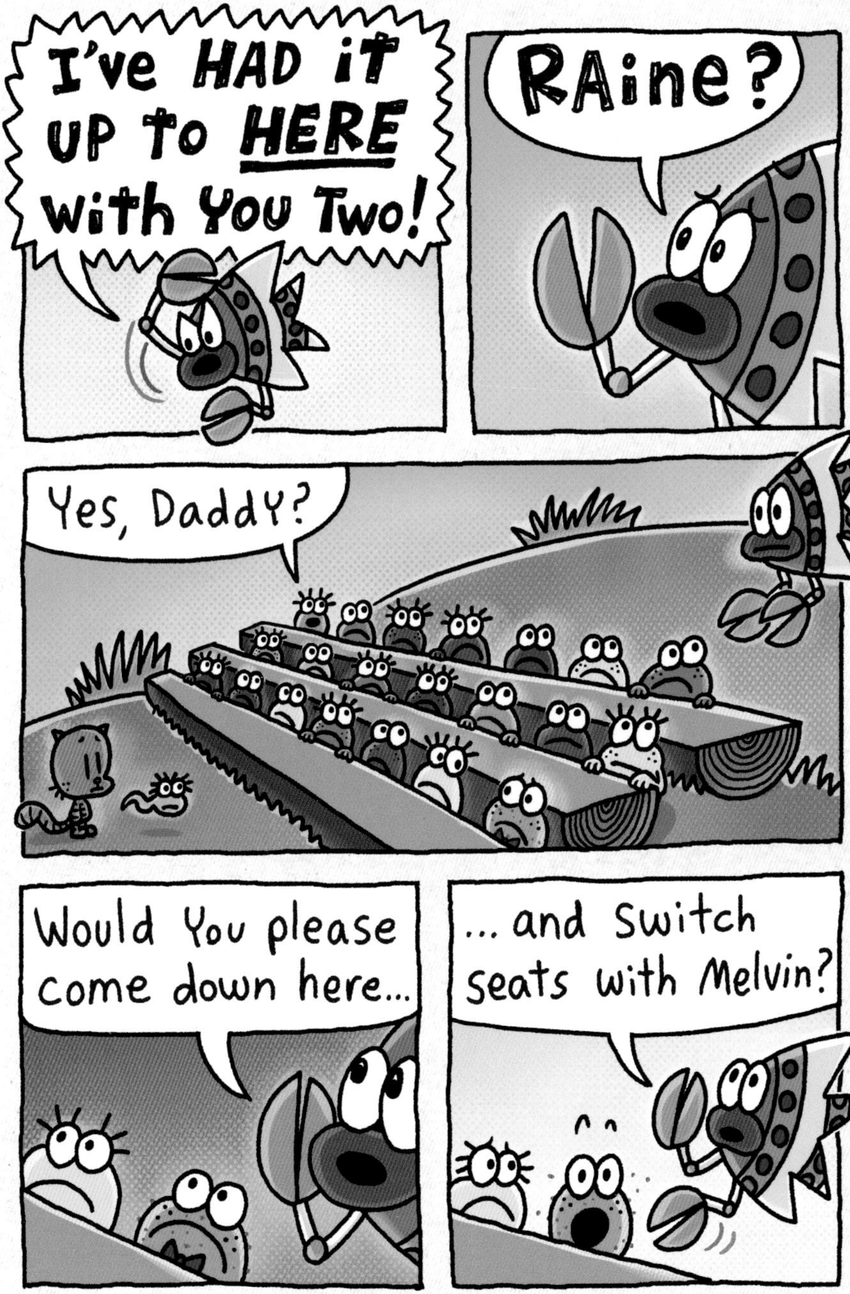
I've HAD it UP to HERE with You Two!
RAine?
Yes, DaddY?
Would You please come down here...
... and Switch seats with Melvin?

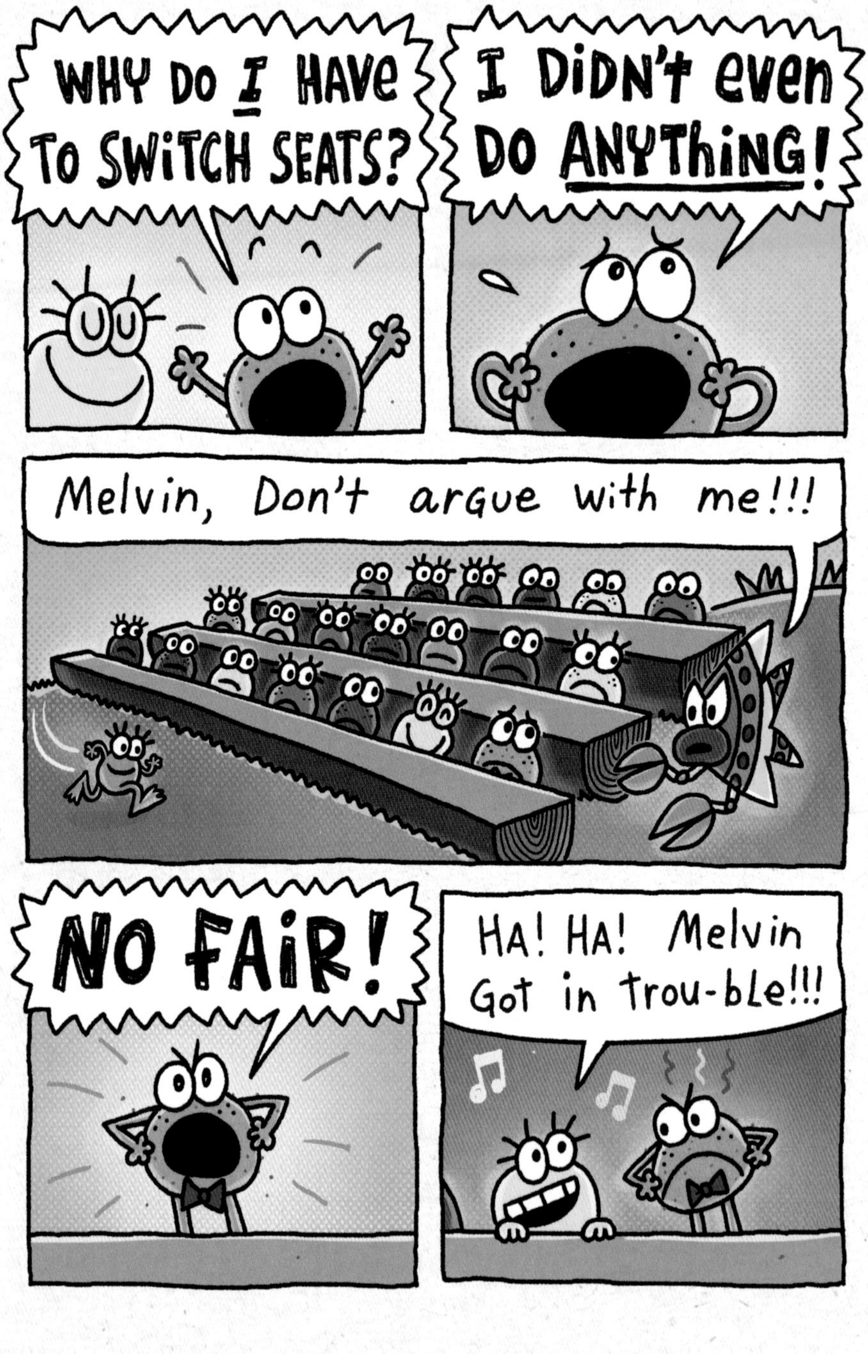
WHY DO I HAVE TO SWITCH SEATS?
I DIDN'T even DO ANYTHING!
Melvin, Don't argue with me!!!
NO FAIR!
HA! HA! Melvin Got in trou-bLe!!!

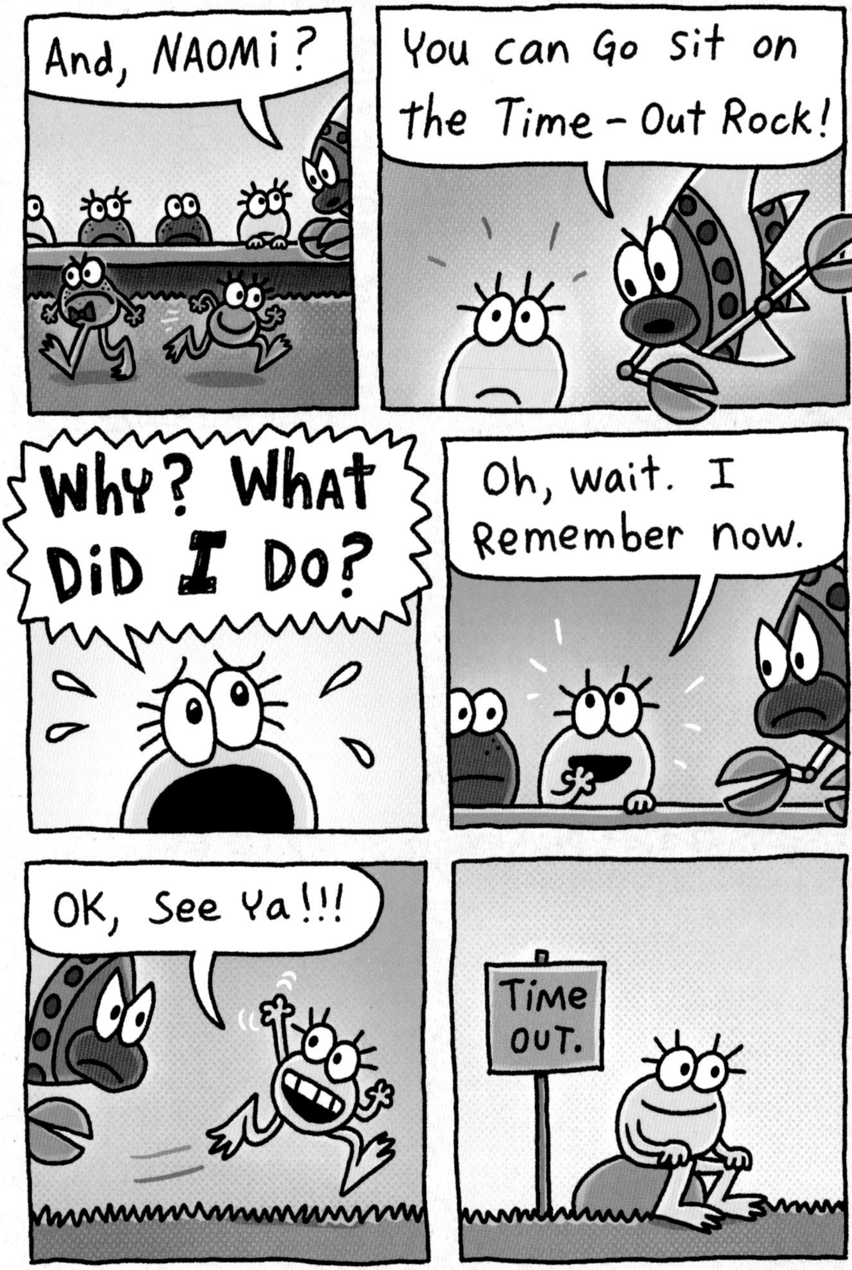
And, NAOMi?
You can Go sit on the Time-Out Rock!
WHY? WHAT DiD I DO?
Oh, wait. I Remember now.
OK, See Ya!!!
TiME OUT.

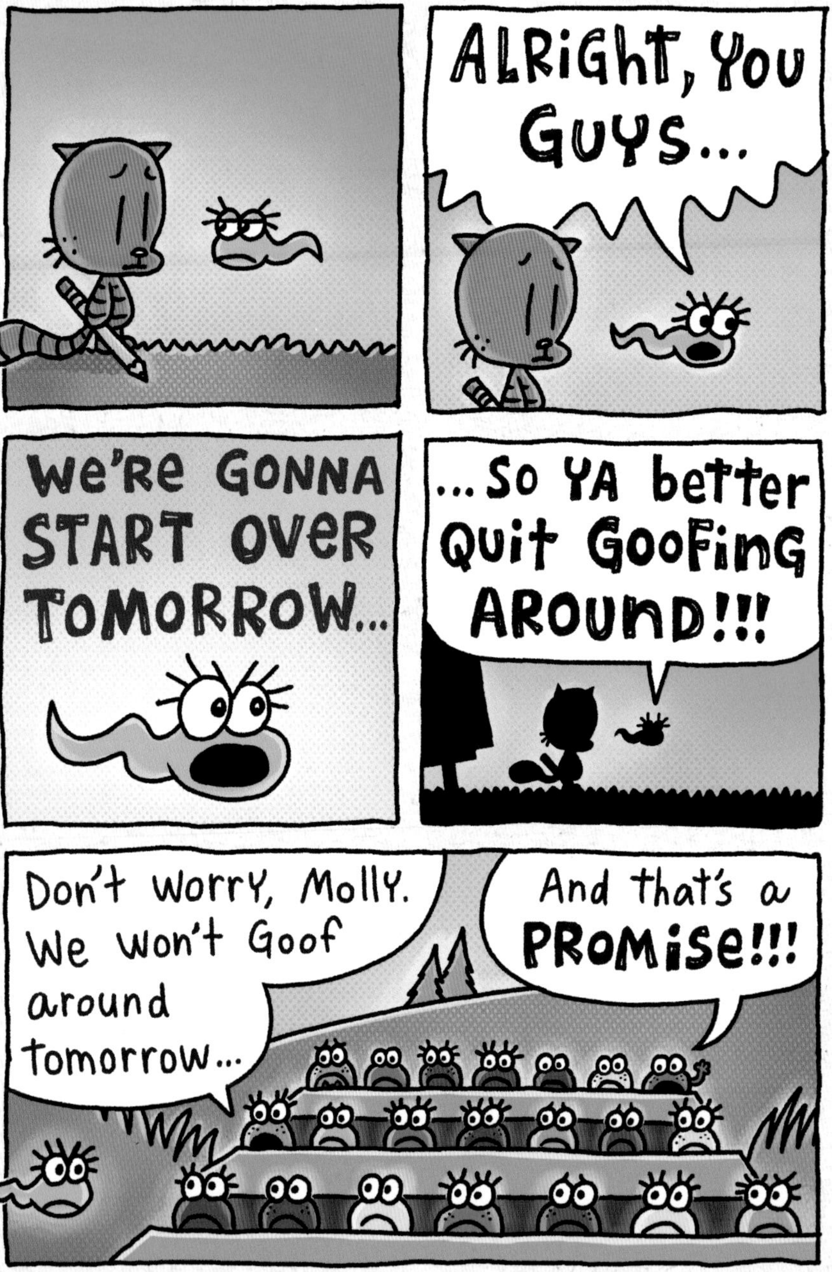
ALRIGHT, YOU GUYS...
WE'RE GONNA START OVER TOMORROW...
...SO YA better QUIT GOOFING AROUND!!!
Don't worry, Molly. We won't Goof around tomorrow...
And that's a PROMISE!!!

Chapter 2

More Goofing Around

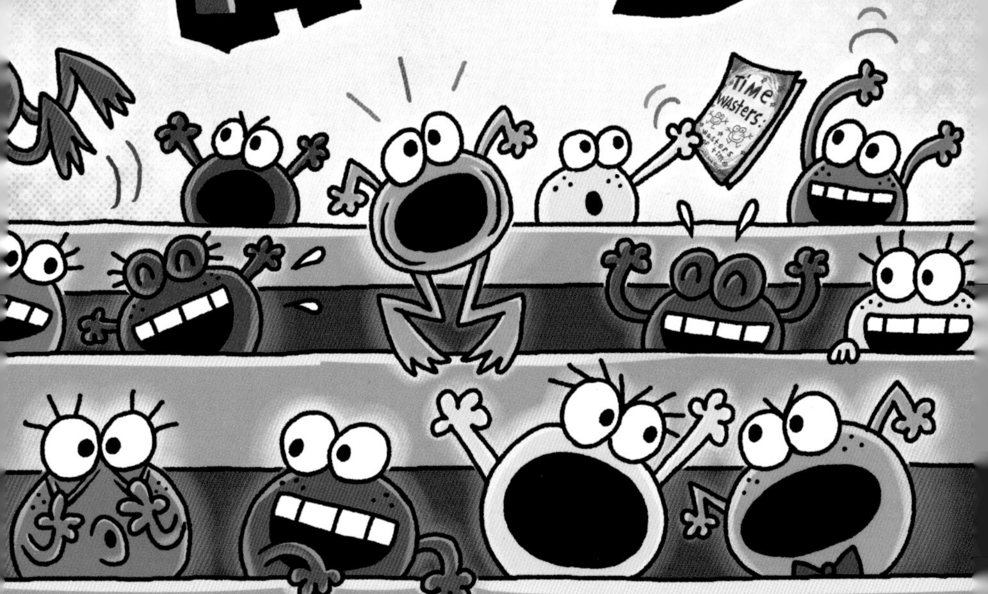
Time wasters:

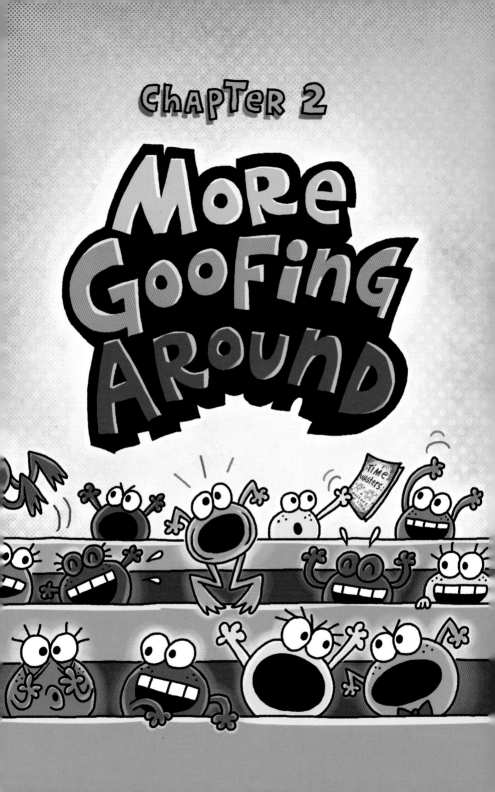

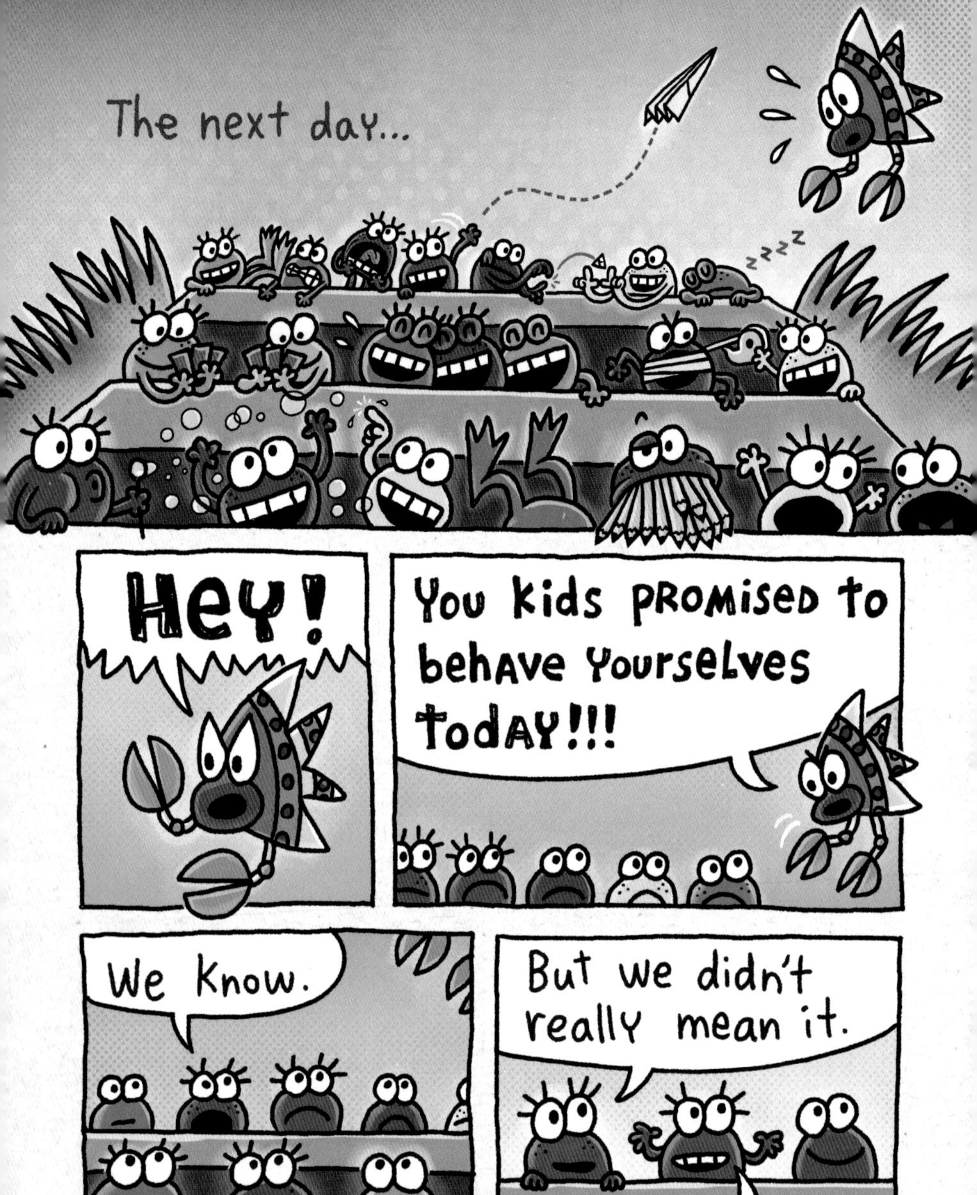
The next day...
HEY!
You kids PROMISED to behave yourselves TODAY!!!
We know.
But we didn't really mean it.
Yeah. We just say stuff sometimes.

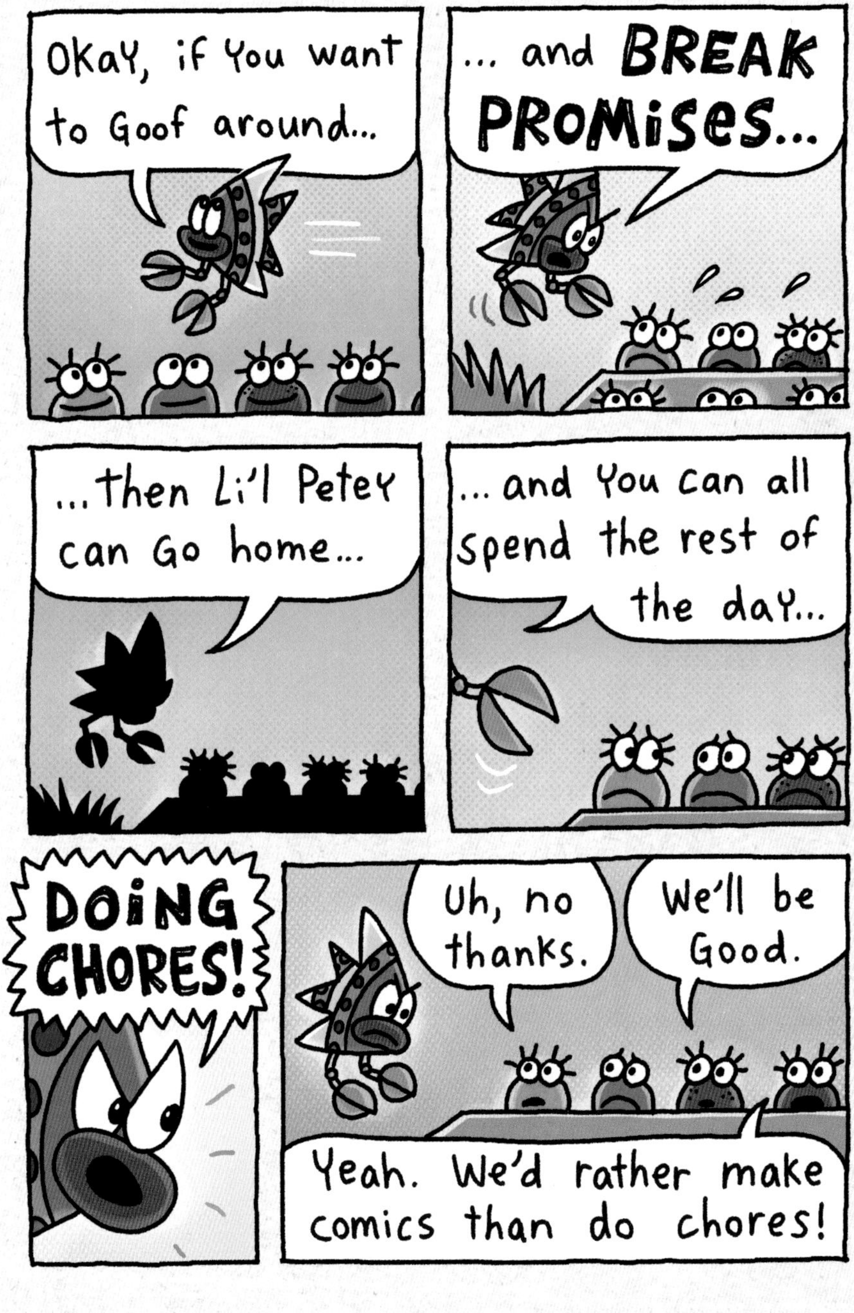
OKAY, if You want to Goof around...
... and BREAK PROMISES...
...then Li'l Petey can Go home...
...and You can all spend the rest of the day...
DOING CHORES!
Uh, no thanks.
We'll be Good.
Yeah. We'd rather make comics than do chores!

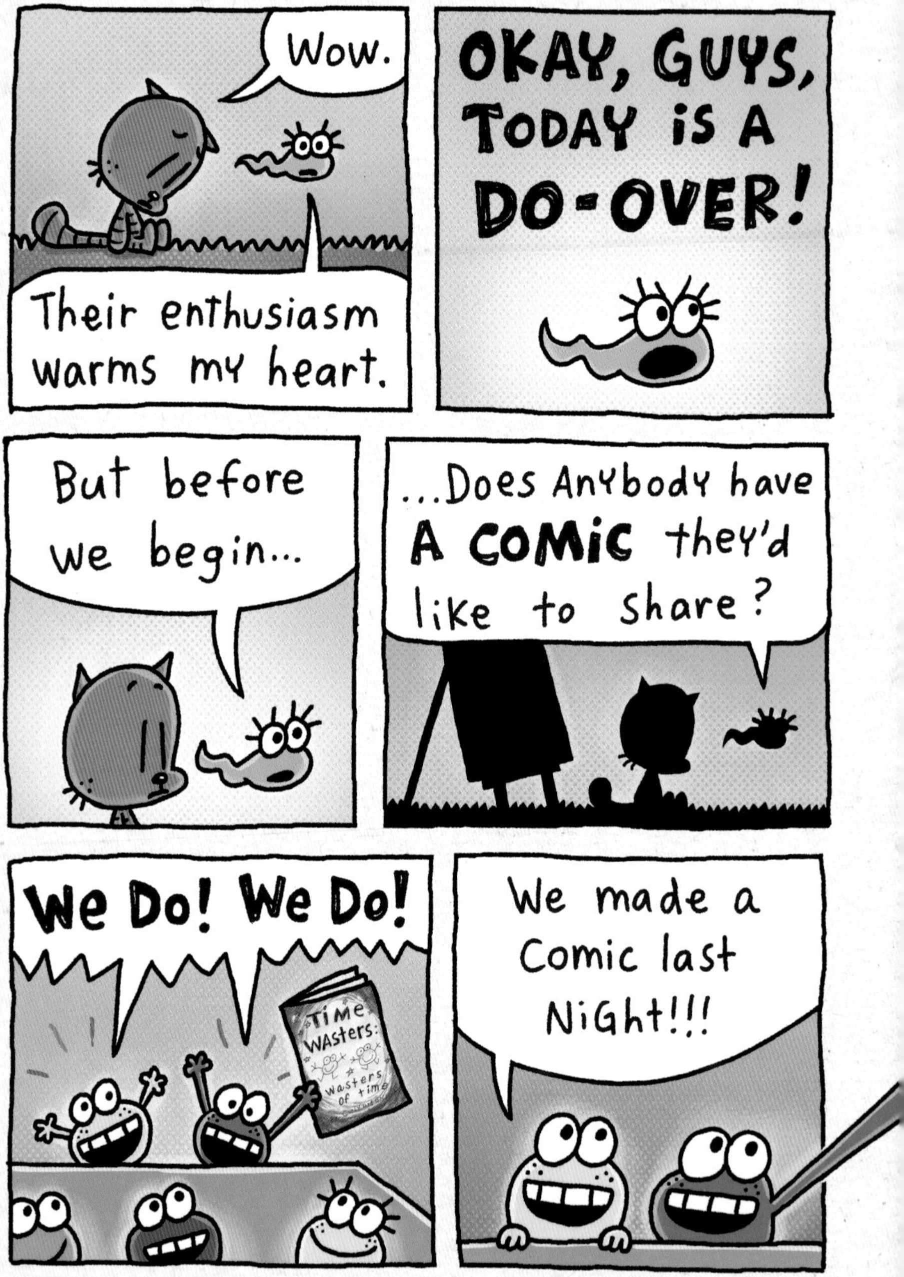
Wow.
Their enthusiasm warms my heart.
OKAY, GUYS, TODAY IS A DO-OVER!
But before we begin...
...Does Anybody have A COMIC they'd like to share?
We Do! We Do!
TIME WASTERS:
Wasters of time
We made a Comic last NiGht!!!

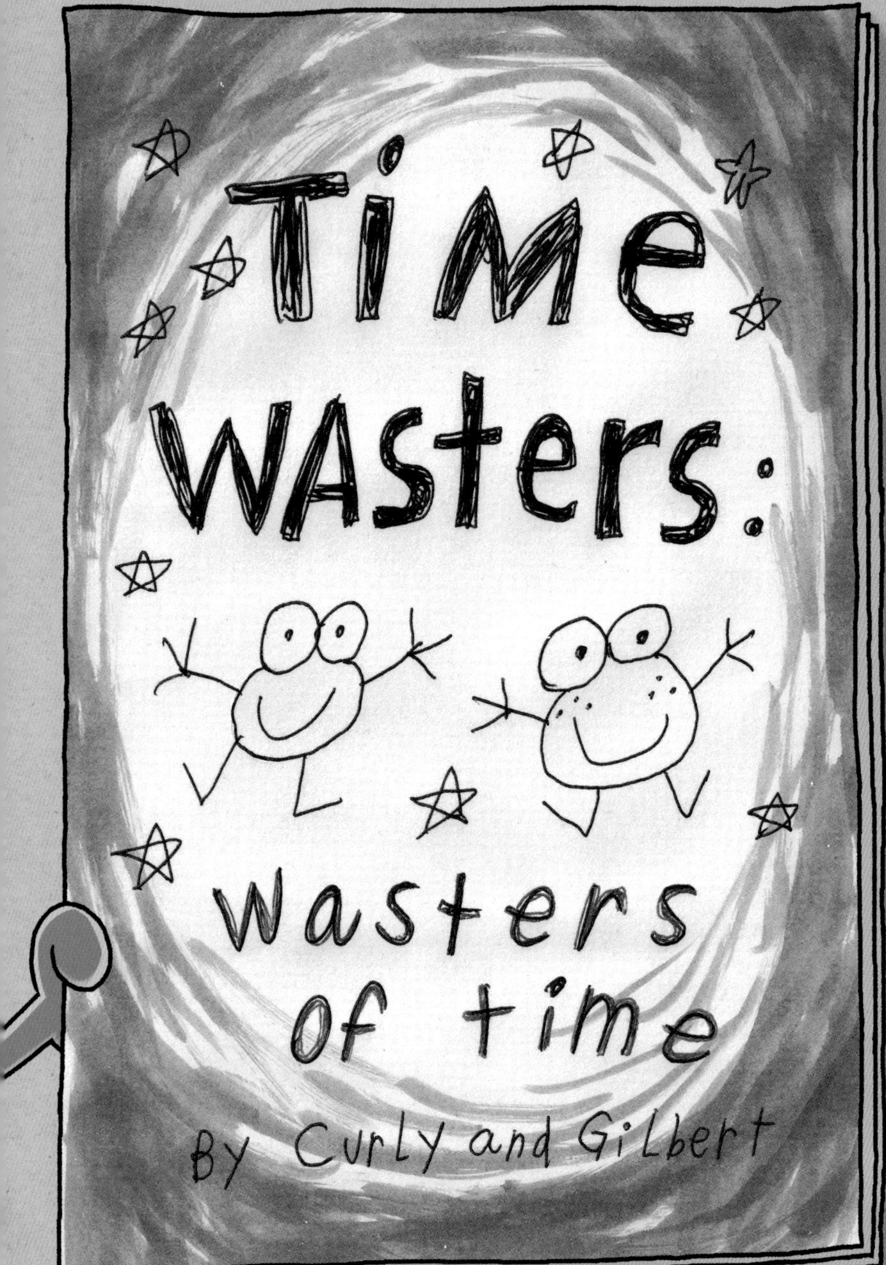
Time Wasters:
wasters of time
By Curly and Gilbert

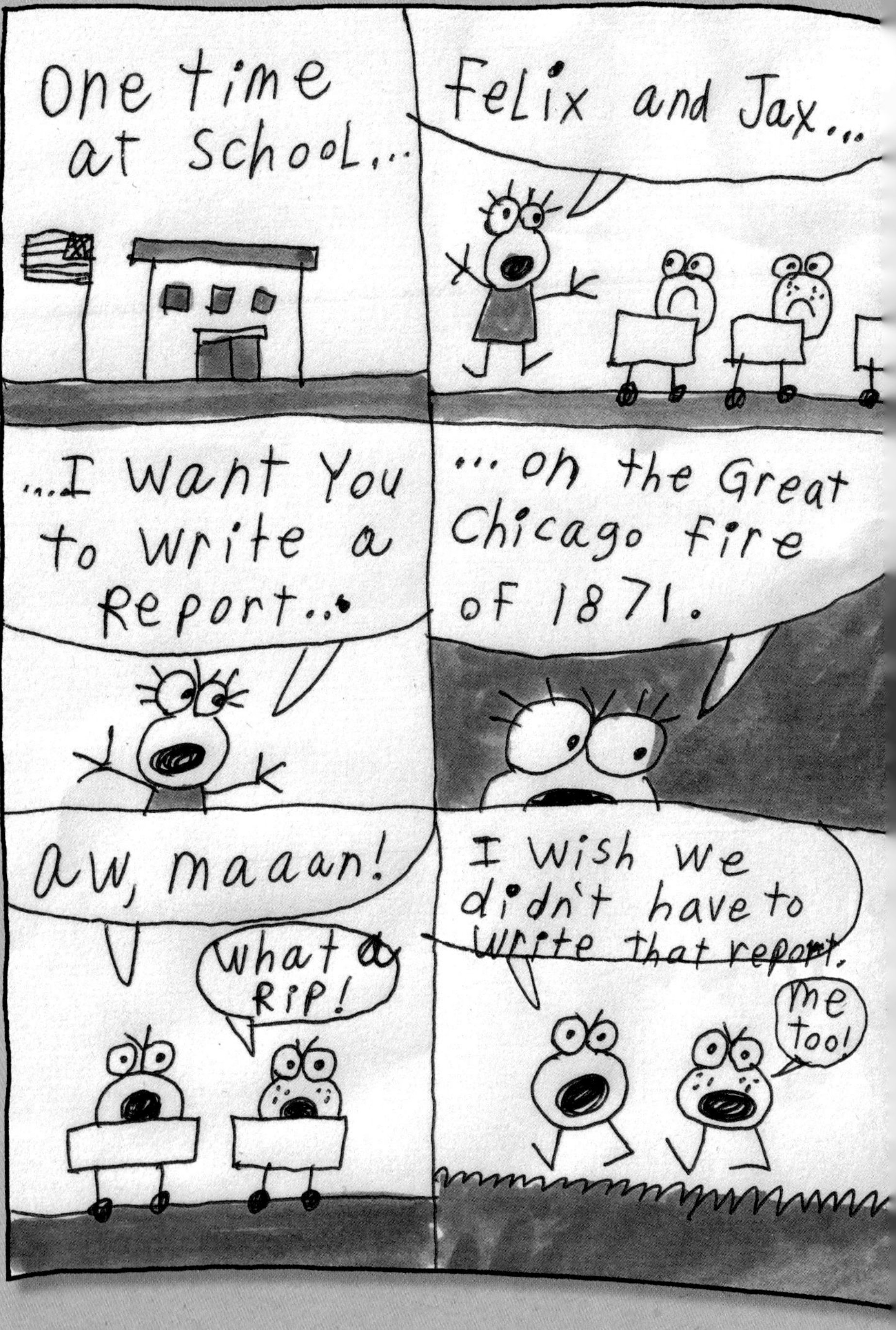
One time at School...
Felix and Jax...
...I want You to write a Report...
...on the Great Chicago fire of 1871.
aw, maaan!
What a Rip!
I wish we didn't have to write that report.
Me too!

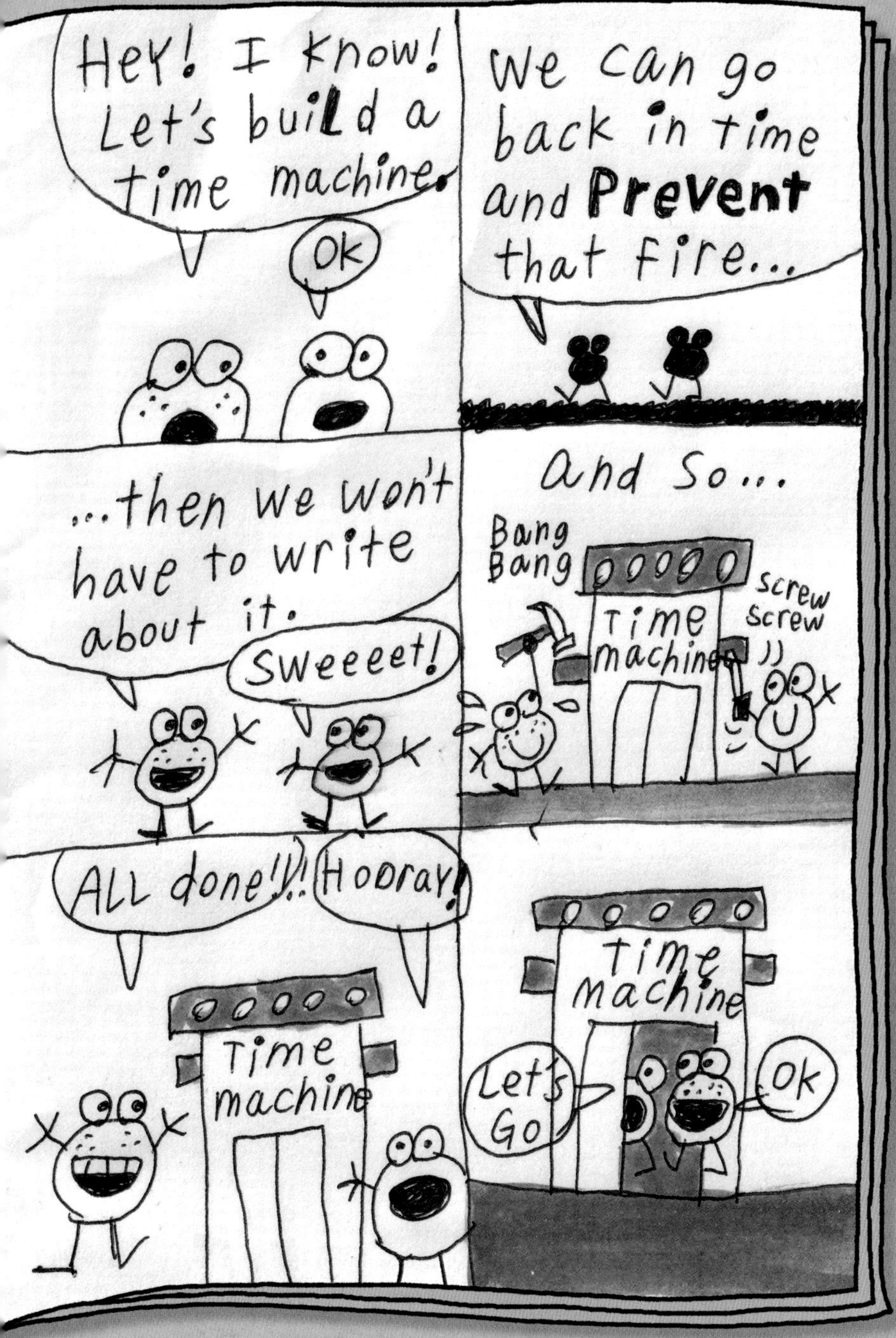
Hey! I know! Let's build a time machine.
OK
We can go back in time and Prevent that fire...
...then we won't have to write about it.
Sweeeet!
and so...
Bang Bang
Time machine
Screw Screw
ALL done!!
Hooray!
Time machine
time machine
Let's Go
OK

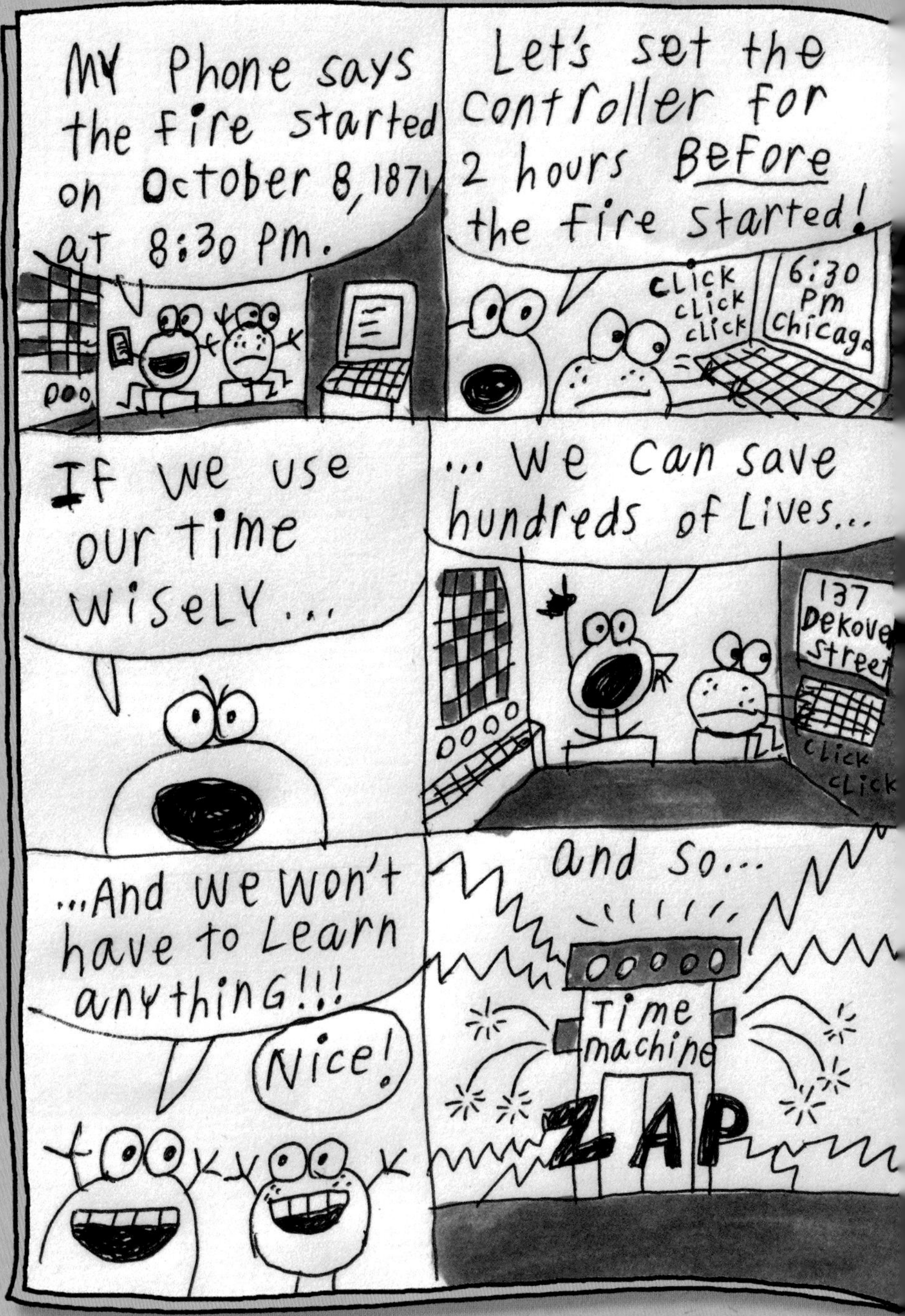
My phone says the fire started on October 8, 1871 at 8:30 PM.
Let's set the controller for 2 hours BEFORE the fire started!
CLICK CLICK CLICK
6:30 PM Chicago
If we use our time wisely...
... we can save hundreds of lives...
137 Dekove Street
CLICK CLICK
...And we won't have to learn anything!!!
Nice!
and so...
Time machine
ZAP

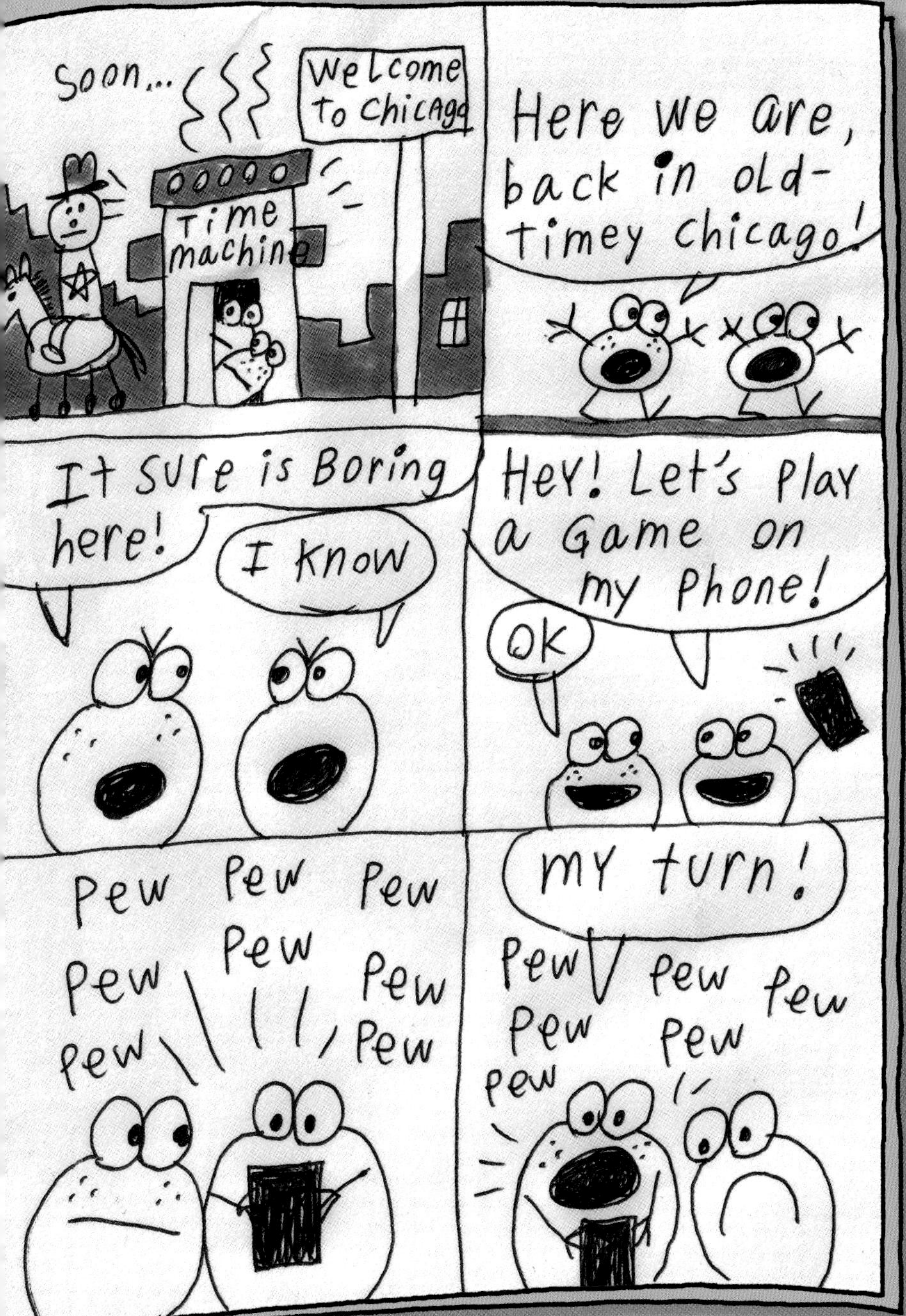
Soon...
Welcome To Chicago
Time machine
Here we are, back in old-timey Chicago!
It sure is Boring here!
I Know
Hey! Let's Play a Game on my Phone!
OK
Pew Pew Pew Pew Pew Pew Pew Pew
my turn!
Pew Pew Pew Pew Pew Pew

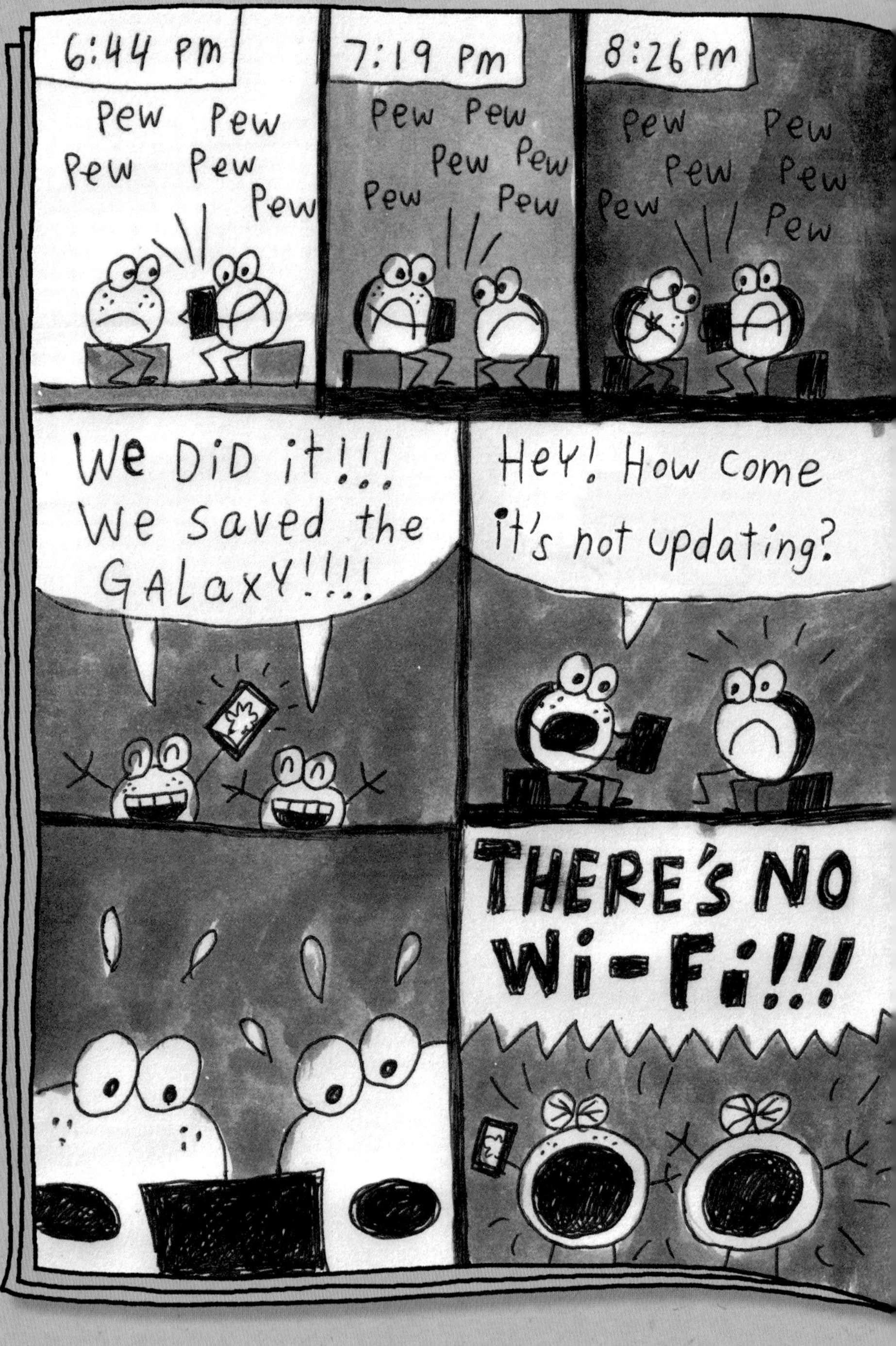
6:44 pm
Pew Pew
Pew Pew
Pew
7:19 pm
Pew Pew
Pew Pew
Pew Pew
8:26 pm
Pew Pew
Pew Pew
Pew Pew
WE DiD it!!!
We saved the GALAXY!!!!
HEY! How come it's not updating?
THERE'S NO Wi-Fi!!!

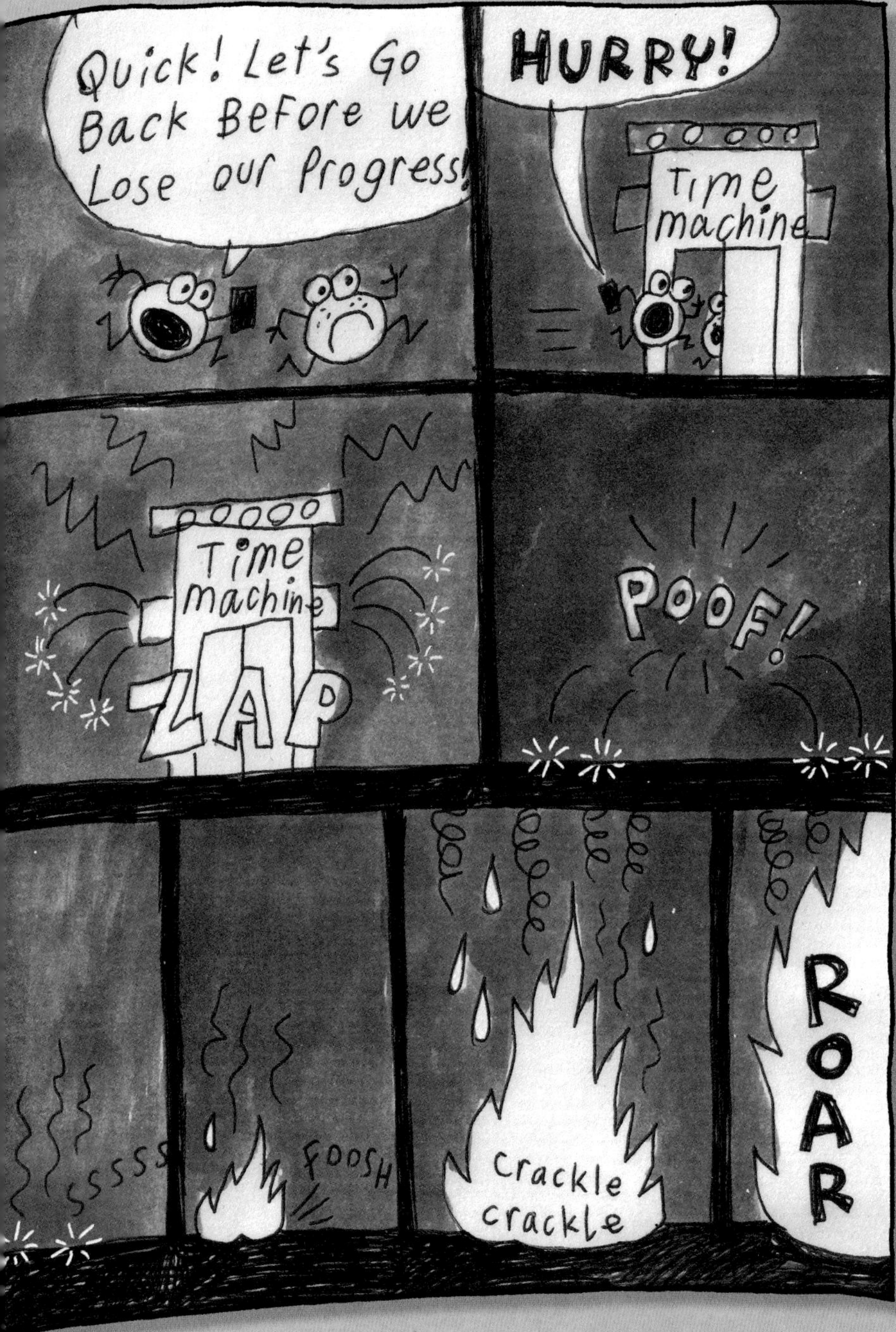
Quick! Let's Go Back Before we Lose our Progress!
HURRY!
Time machine
Time machine
ZAP
POOF!
SSSSS
FOOSH
Crackle crackle
ROAR

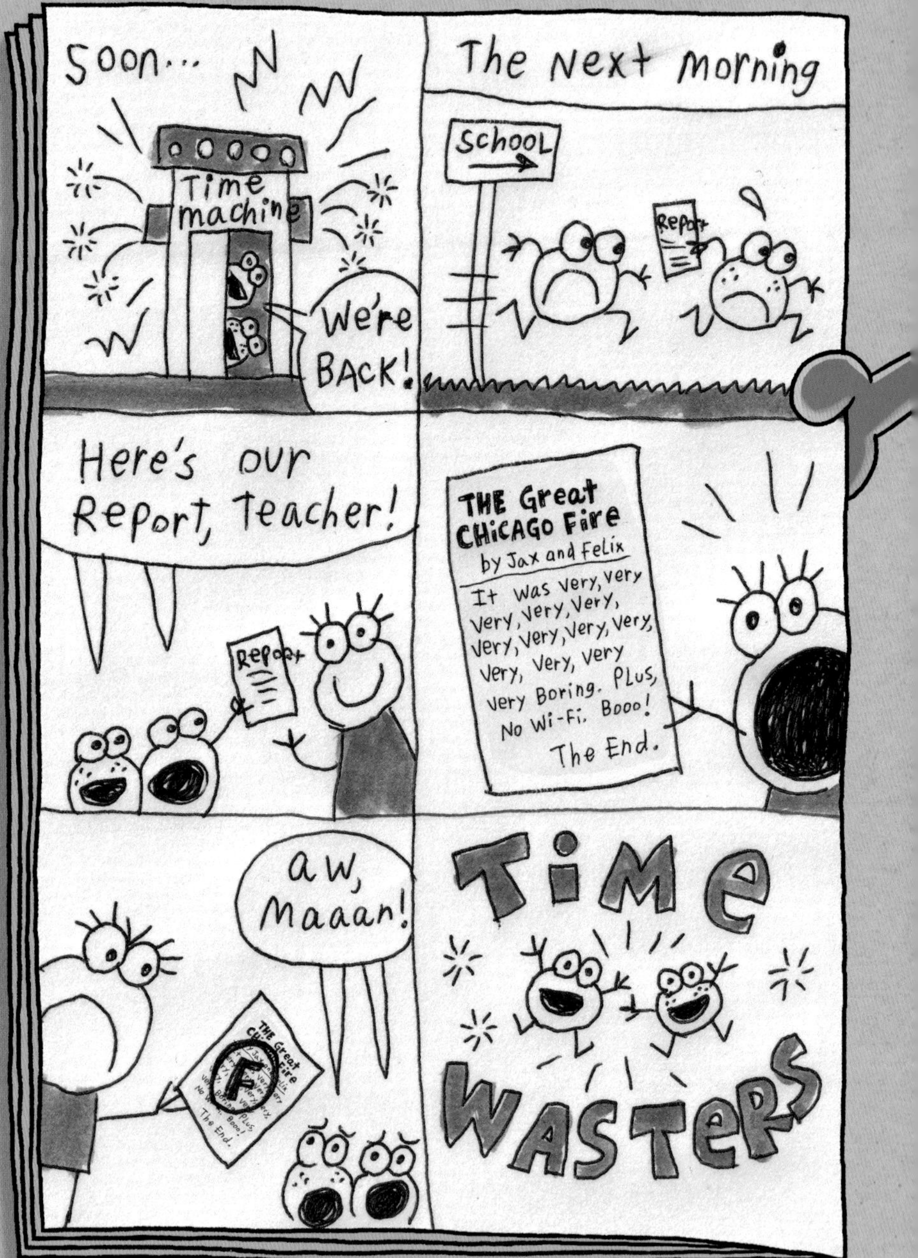
Soon...
Time machine
We're BACK!
The Next Morning
SCHOOL
Report
Here's our Report, Teacher!
Report
THE Great CHICAGO Fire
by Jax and Felix
It was very, very very, very, very, very, very, very, very, very, very, very very Boring. PLus, No Wi-Fi. Booo!
The End.
aw, Maaan!
F
TIME WASTERS

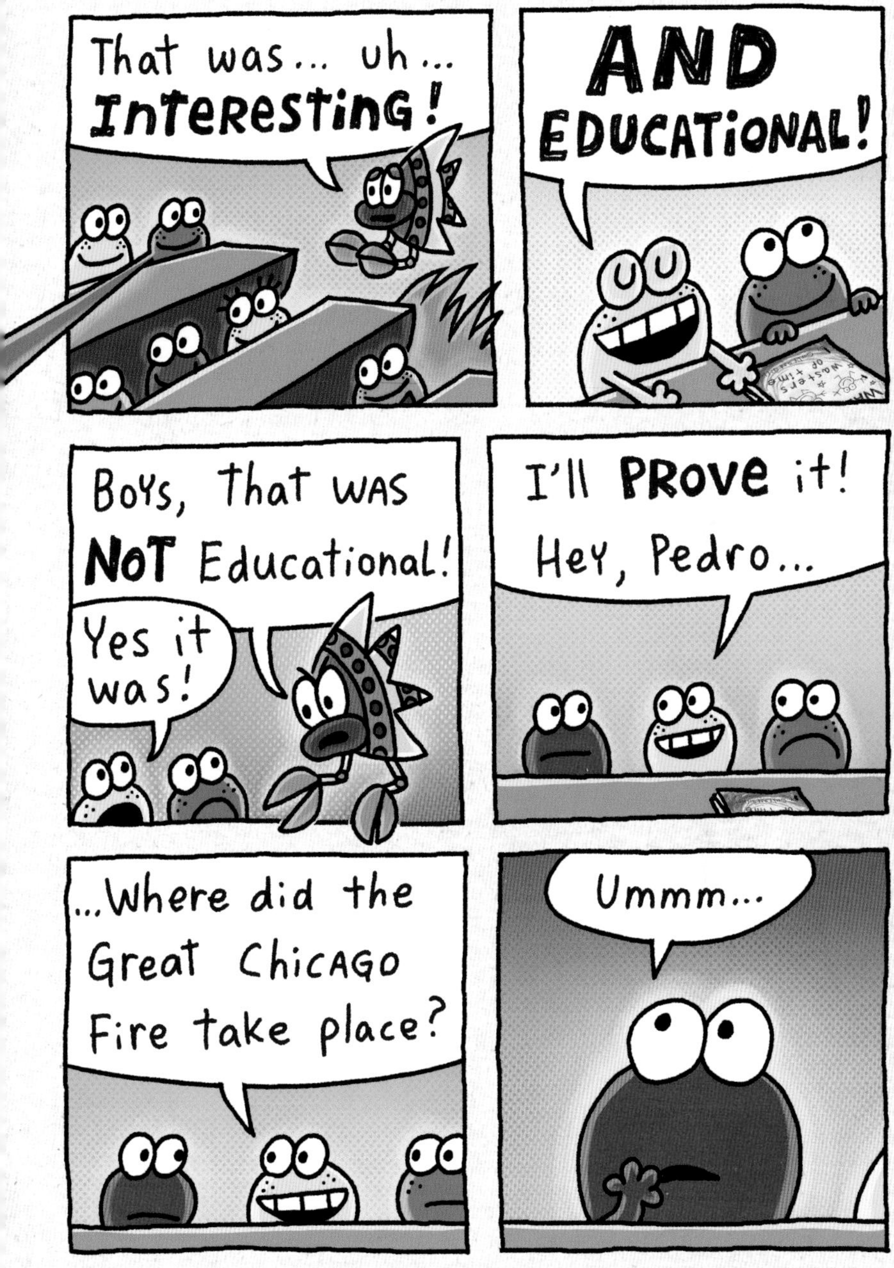
That was... uh... INTERESTING!
AND EDUCATIONAL!
Boys, That WAS NOT Educational!
Yes it was!
I'll PROVE it! Hey, Pedro...
...Where did the Great CHICAGO Fire take place?
Ummm...

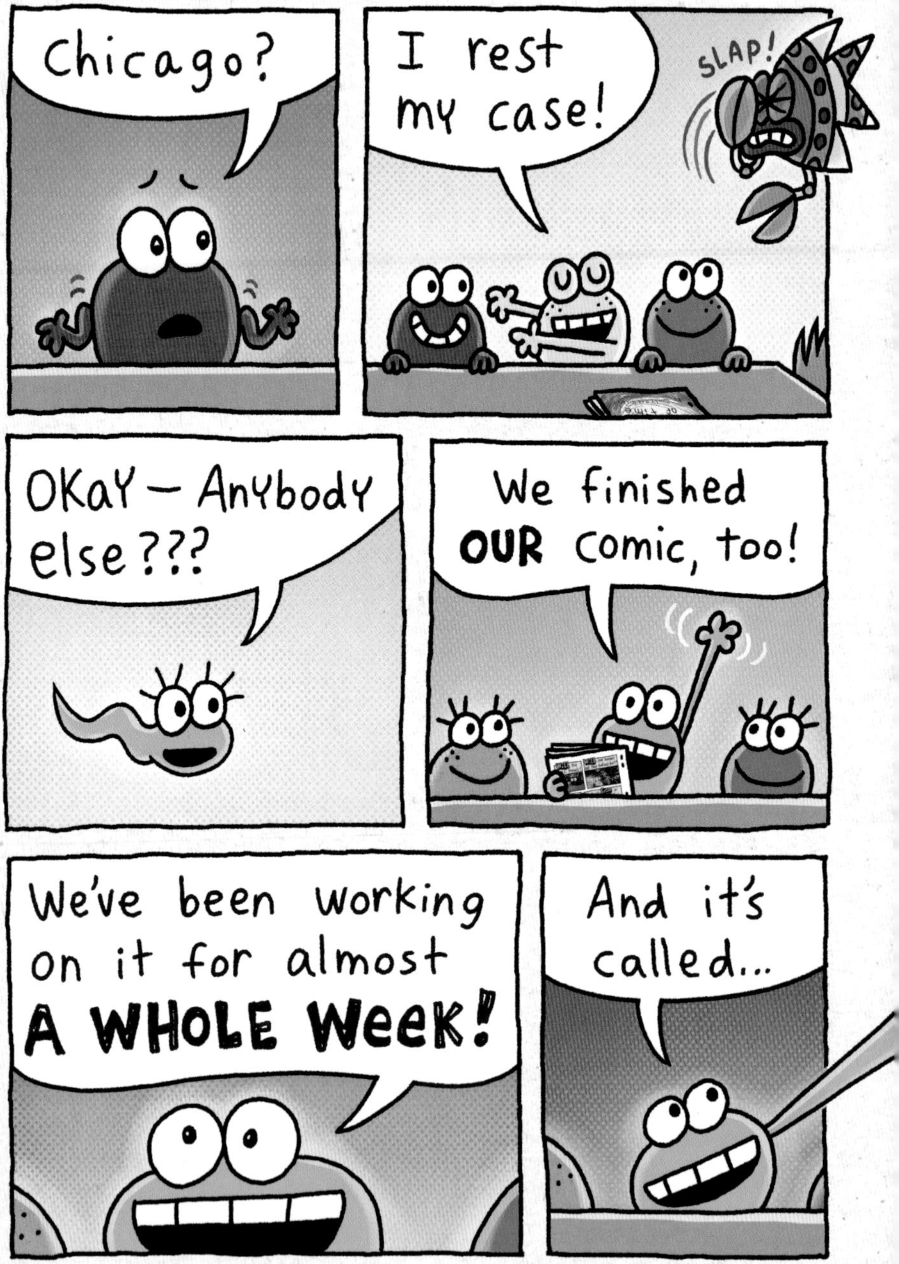
Chicago?
I rest my case!
SLAP!
OKAY—Anybody else???
We finished OUR comic, too!
We've been working on it for almost A WHOLE WEEK!
And it's called...

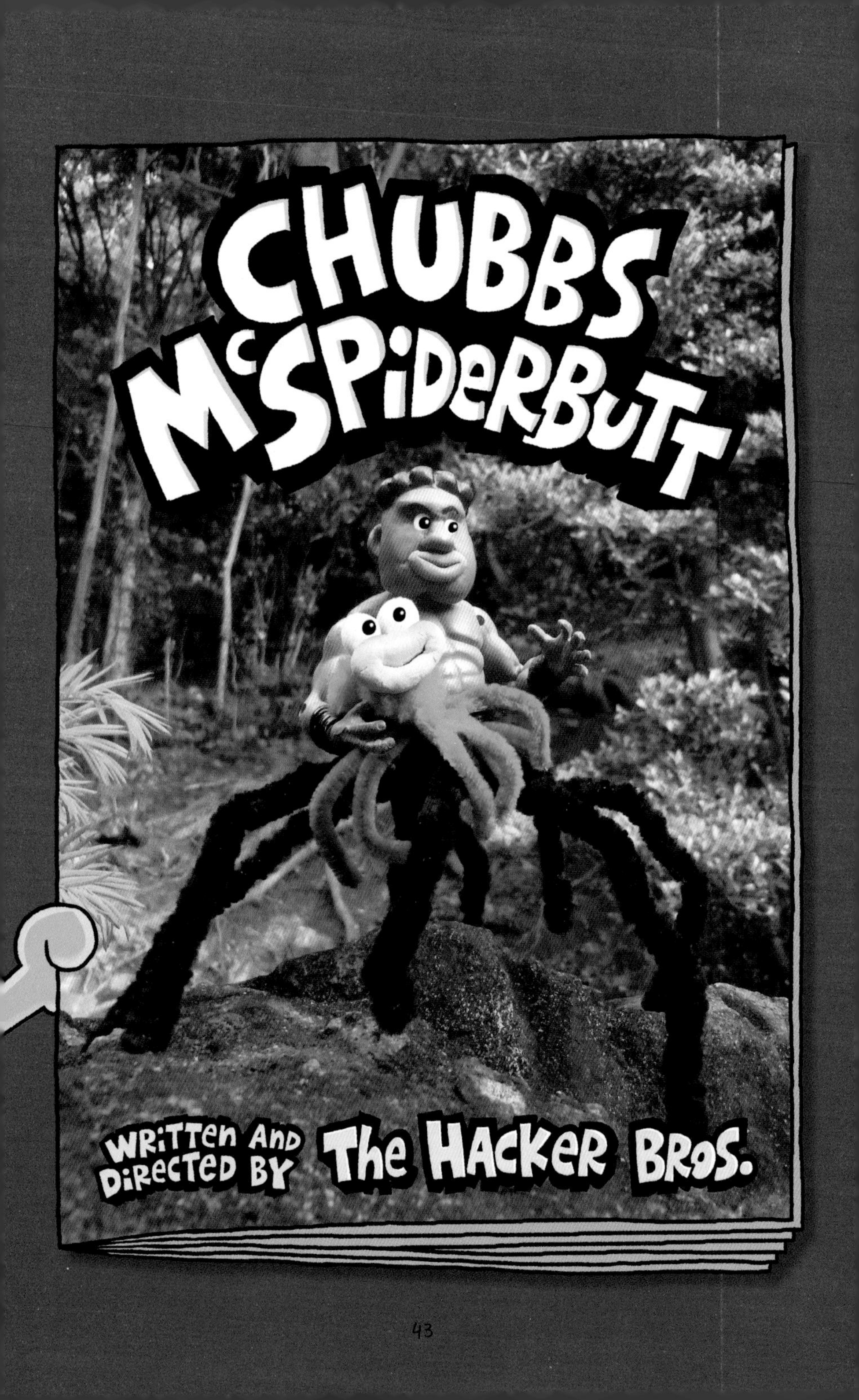
CHUBBS McSPIDERBUTT
WRITTEN AND DIRECTED BY The HACKER BROS.

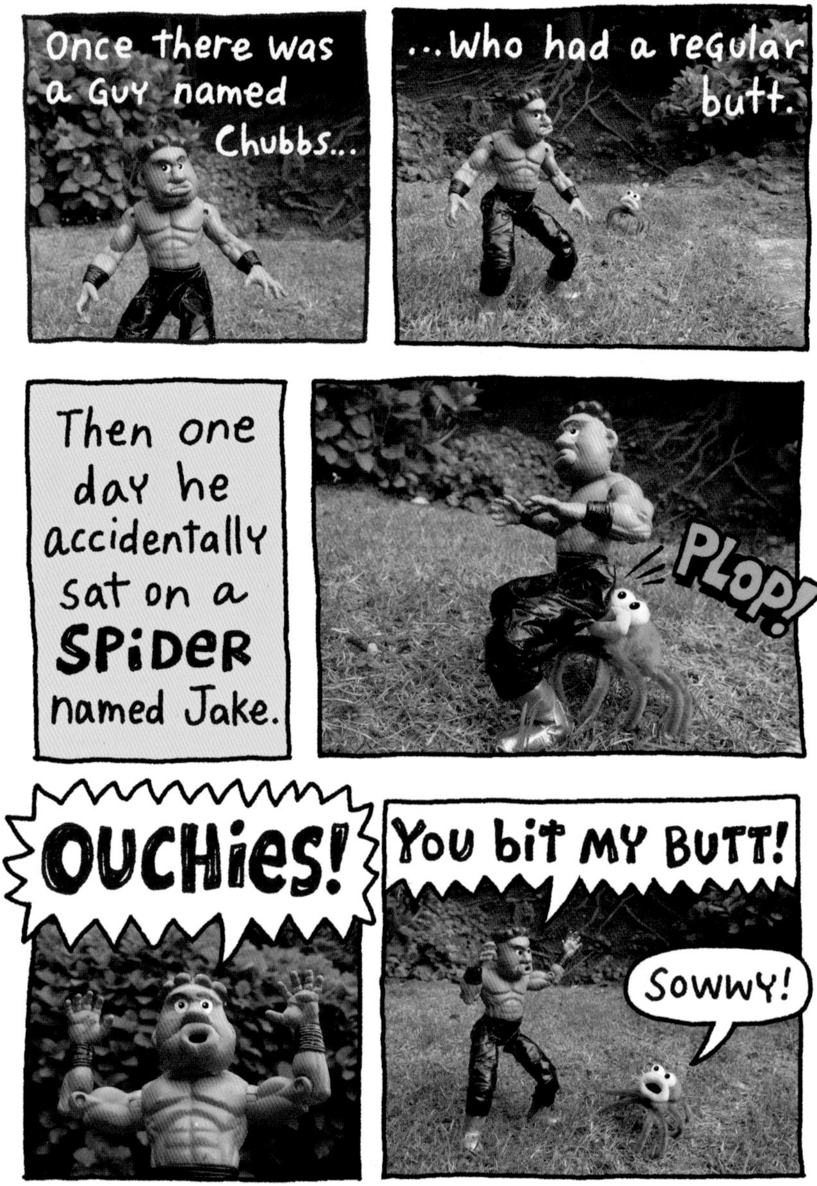
Once there was a GUY named Chubbs...
...Who had a regular butt.
Then one day he accidentally sat on a SPIDER named Jake.
PLOP!
OUCHies!
You bit MY BUTT!
SOWWY!

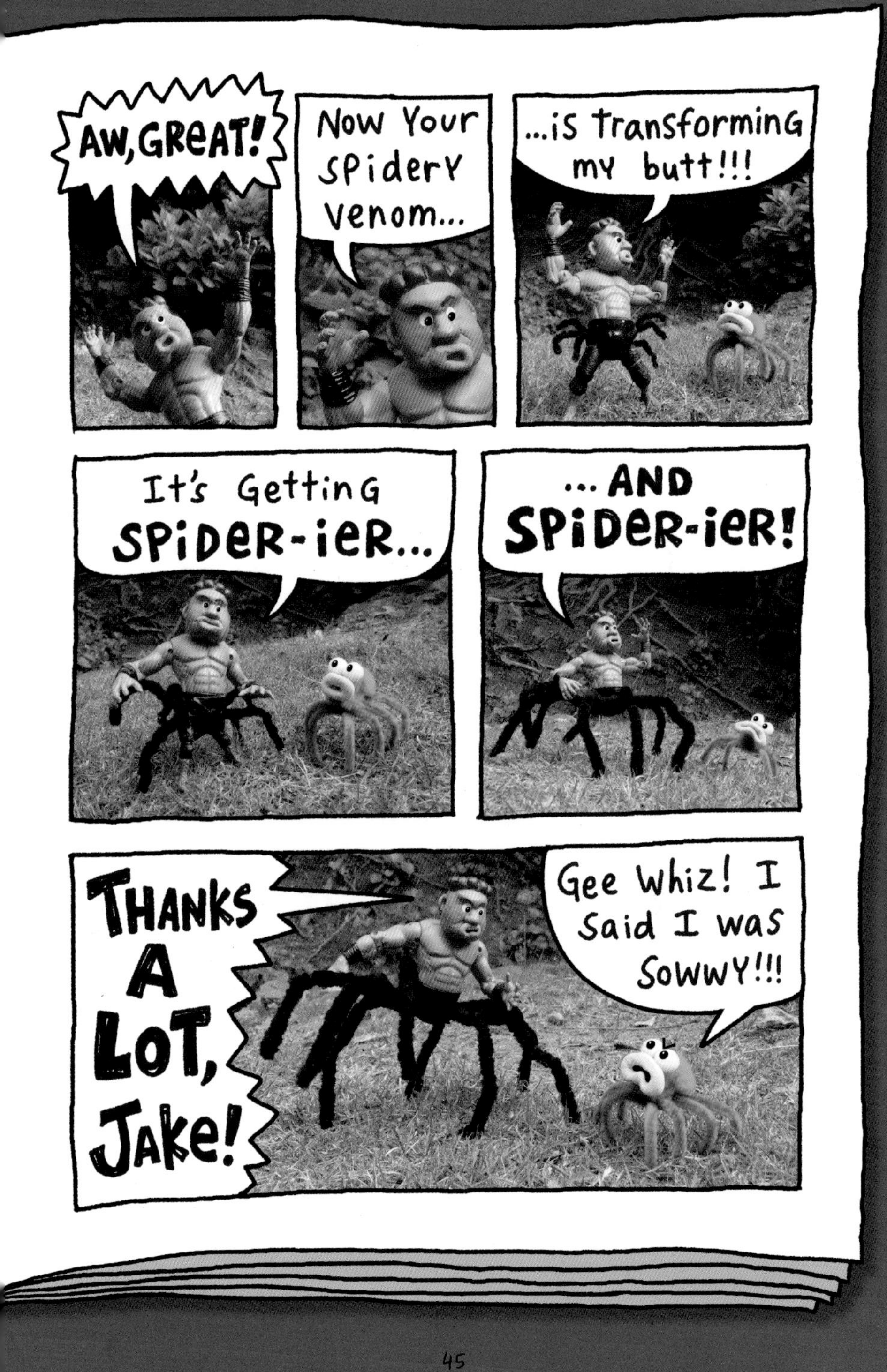
AW, GREAT!
Now Your Spidery venom...
...is Transforming my butt!!!
It's Getting SPIDER-IER...
...AND SPIDER-IER!
THANKS A LOT, Jake!
Gee Whiz! I Said I was SOWWY!!!

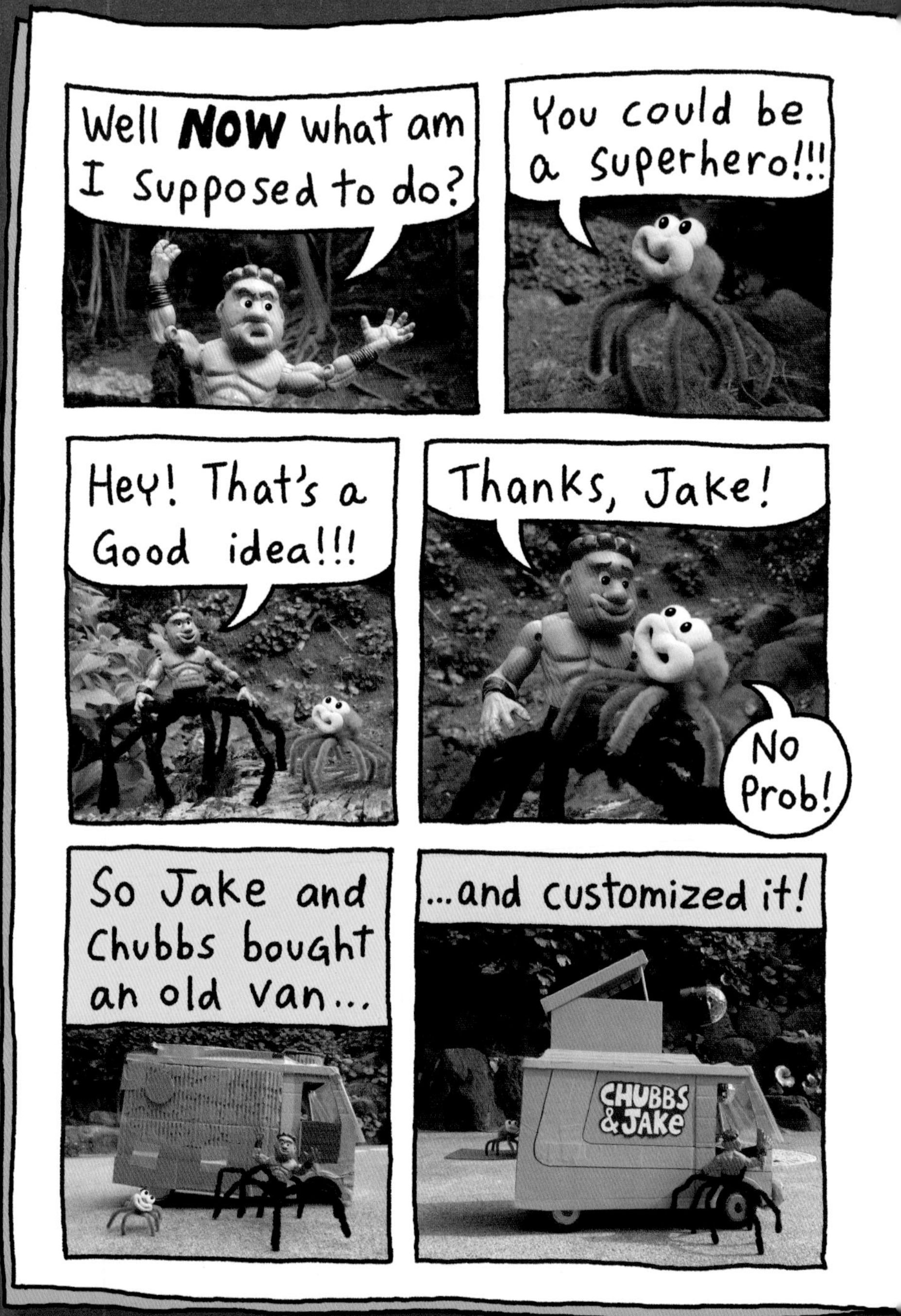
Well NOW what am I supposed to do?
You could be a superhero!!!
Hey! That's a Good idea!!!
Thanks, Jake!
No Prob!
So Jake and Chubbs bought an old van...
...and customized it!
CHUBBS & JAKE

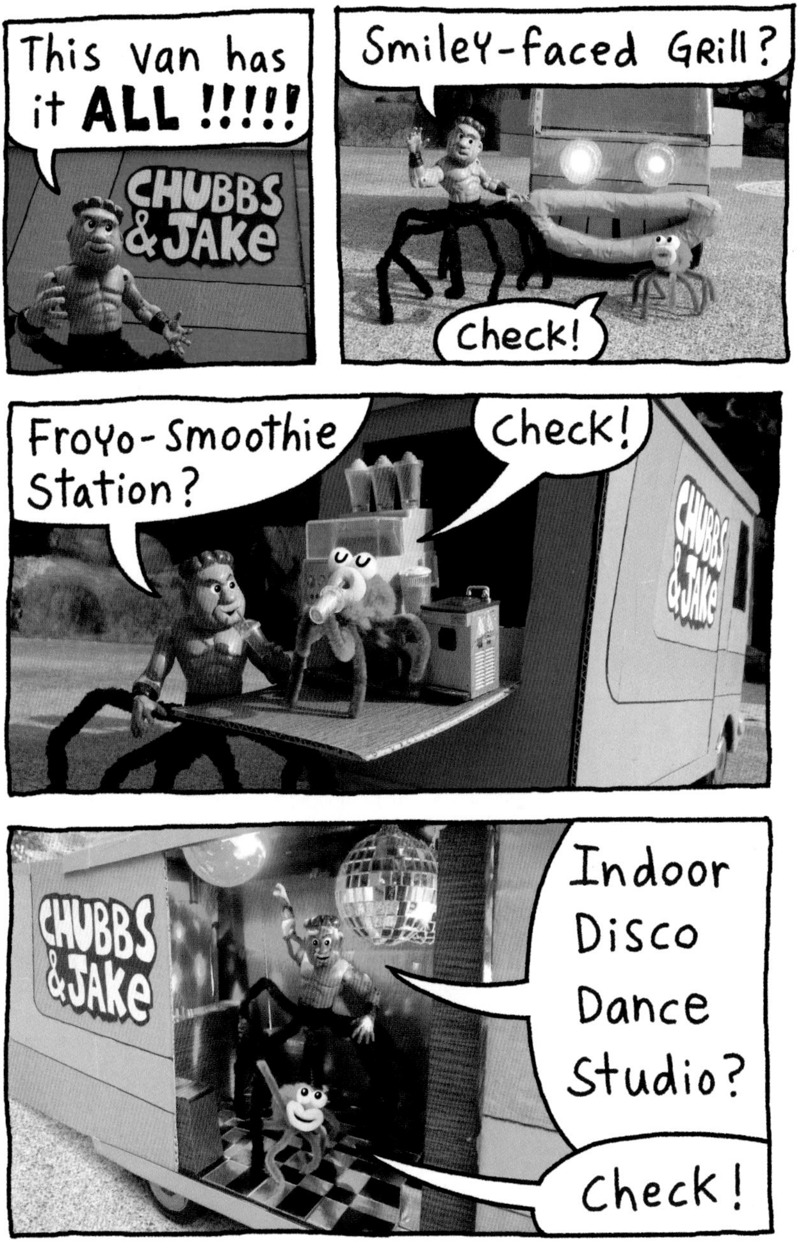
This Van has it ALL !!!!!
CHUBBS & JAKE
Smiley-faced GRill?
Check!
FroYo-Smoothie Station?
Check!
CHUBBS & JAKE
CHUBBS & JAKE
Indoor Disco Dance Studio?
Check!

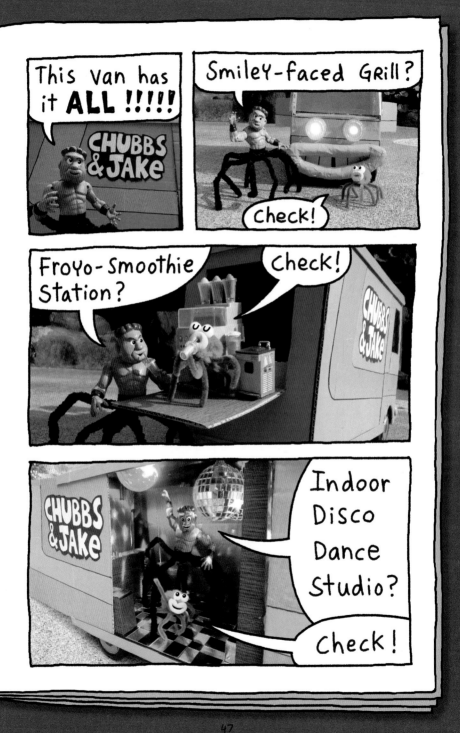

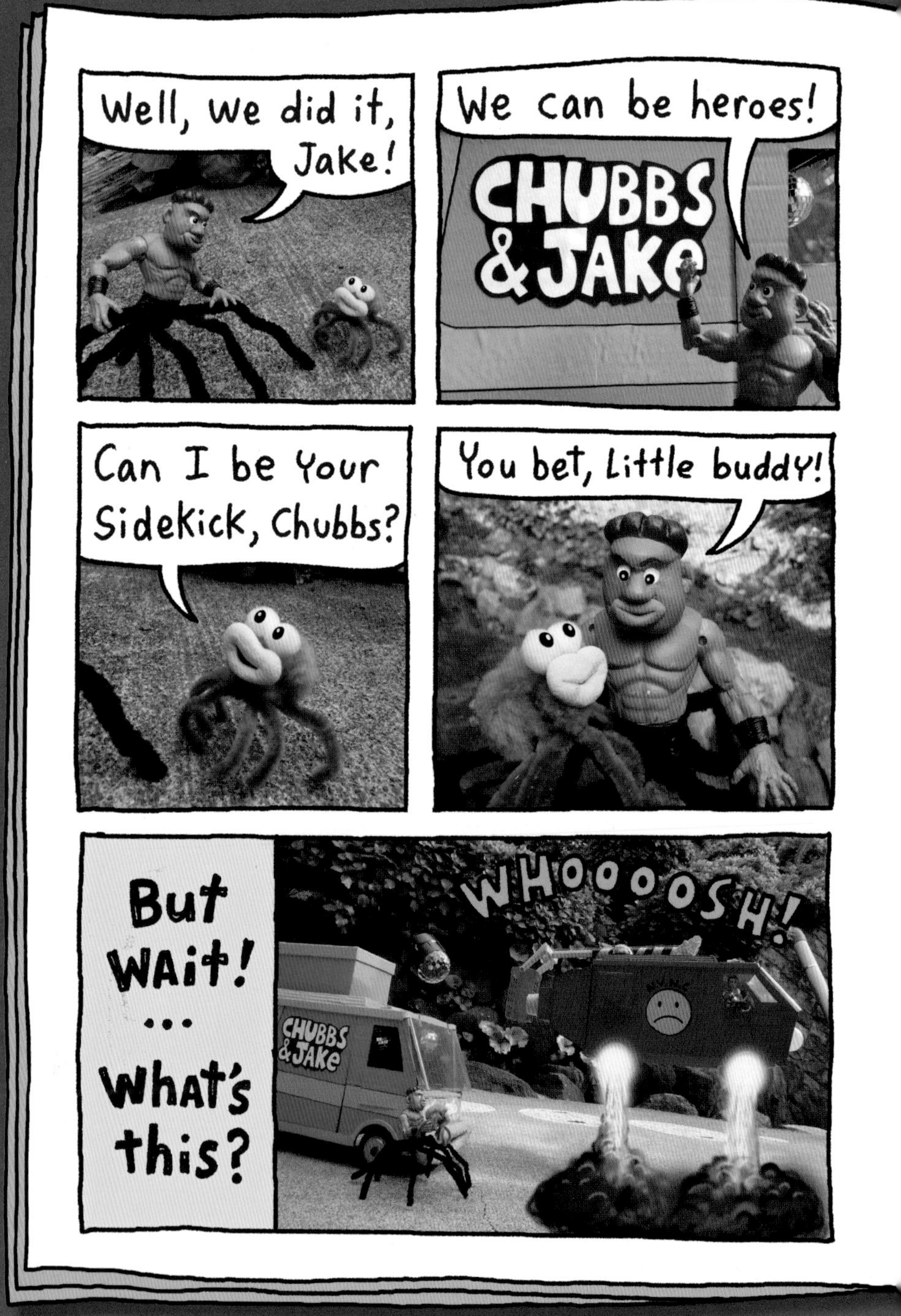
Well, we did it, Jake!
We can be heroes!
CHUBBS & JAKE
Can I be your Sidekick, Chubbs?
You bet, Little buddy!
But WAit! ... What's this?
WHOOOOOSH!
CHUBBS & JAKE

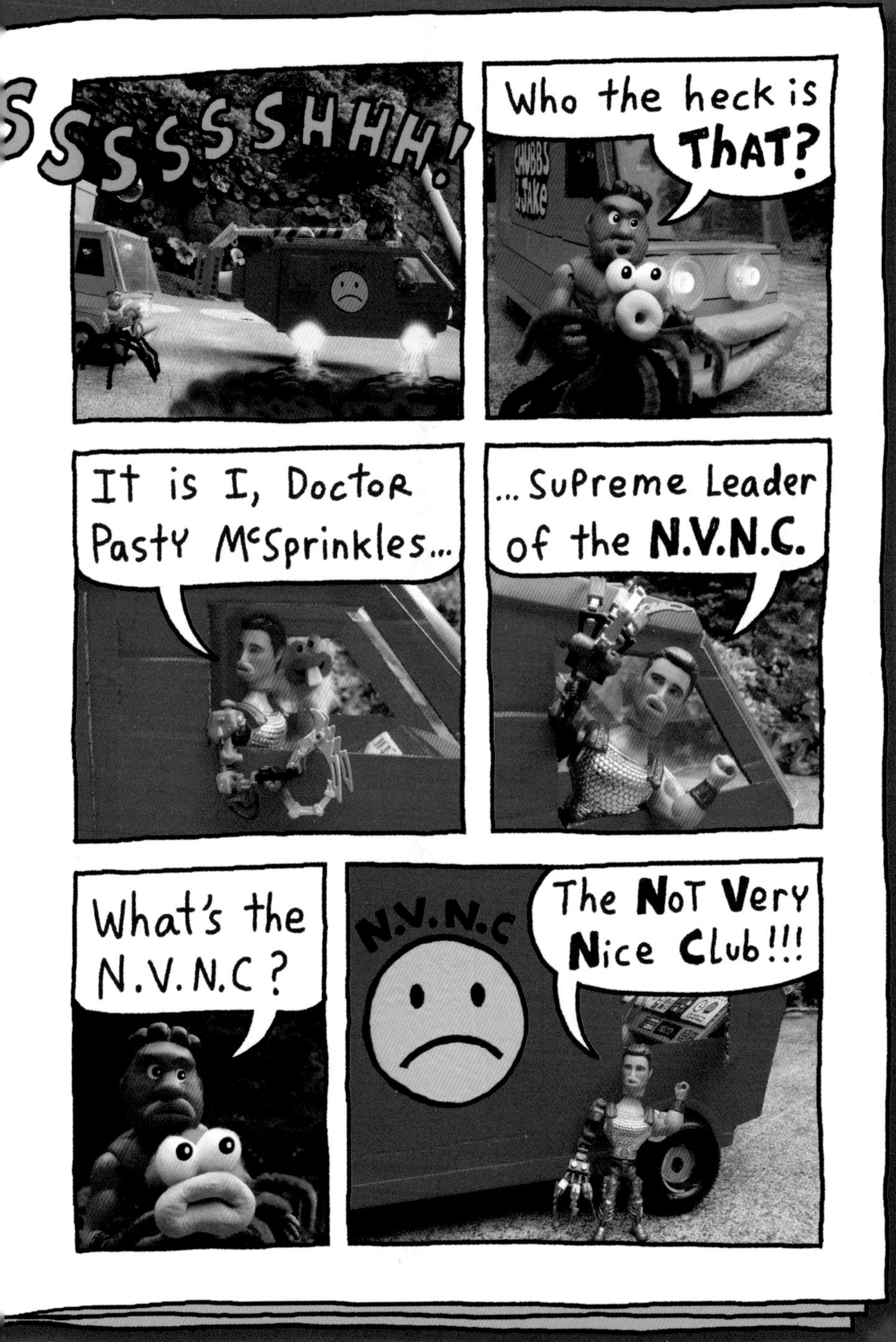
SSSSSSHHH!
CHUBBS & JAKE
Who the heck is THAT?
It is I, Doctor Pasty McSprinkles...
...Supreme Leader of the N.V.N.C.
What's the N.V.N.C?
N.V.N.C
The Not Very Nice Club!!!

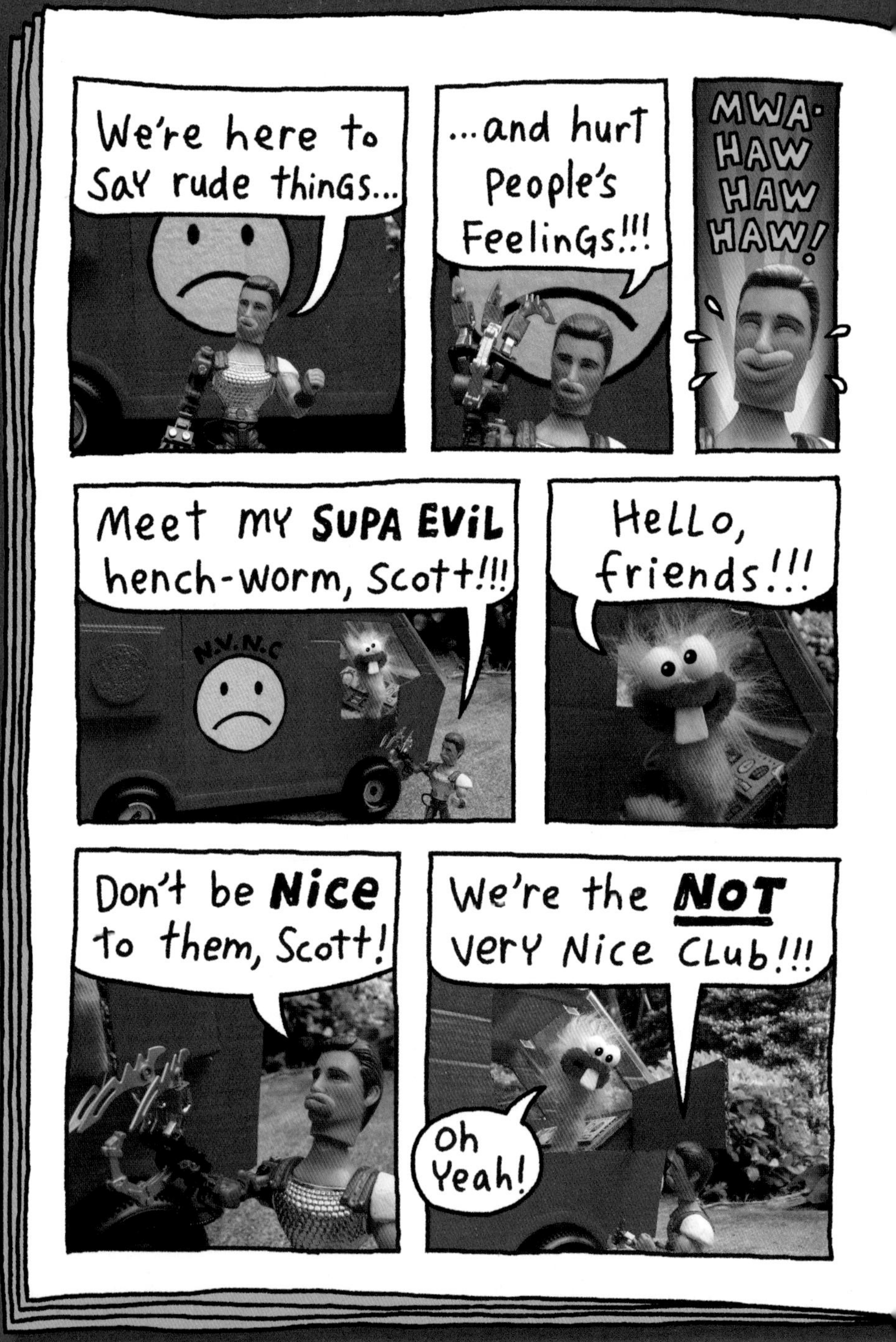
We're here to say rude things...
...and hurt people's feelings!!!
MWA-HAW HAW HAW!
Meet my SUPA EVIL hench-worm, Scott!!!
N.V.N.C
Hello, friends!!!
Don't be NICE to them, Scott!
We're the NOT very nice club!!!
Oh yeah!

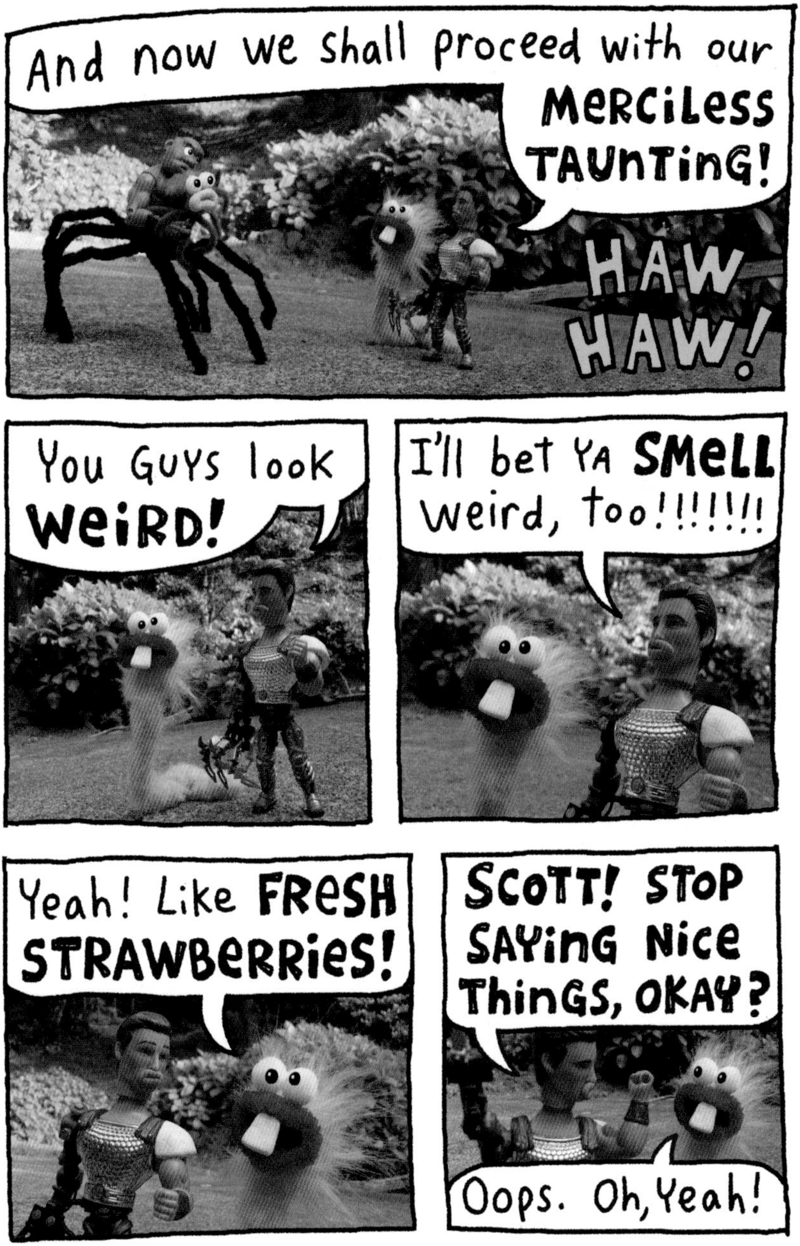
And now we shall proceed with our MERCILESS TAUNTING!
HAW HAW!
You GUYS look WEIRD!
I'll bet YA SMELL weird, too!!!!!!!
Yeah! Like FRESH STRAWBERRIES!
SCOTT! STOP SAYING NICE THINGS, OKAY?
Oops. Oh, Yeah!

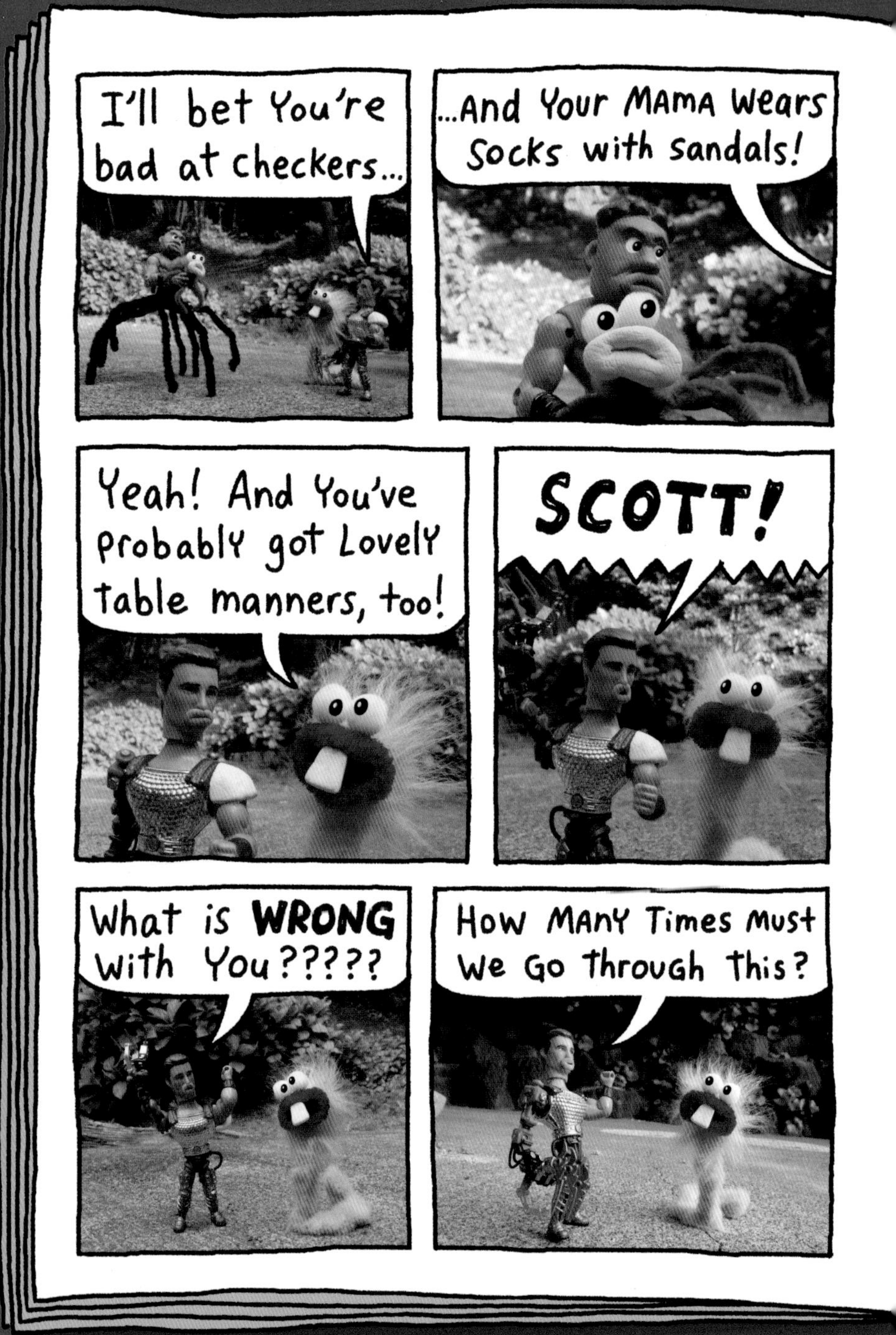
I'll bet You're bad at checkers...
...And Your MAMA Wears Socks with sandals!
Yeah! And You've probably got Lovely table manners, too!
SCOTT!
What is WRONG With You?????
How MANY Times Must We Go Through This?

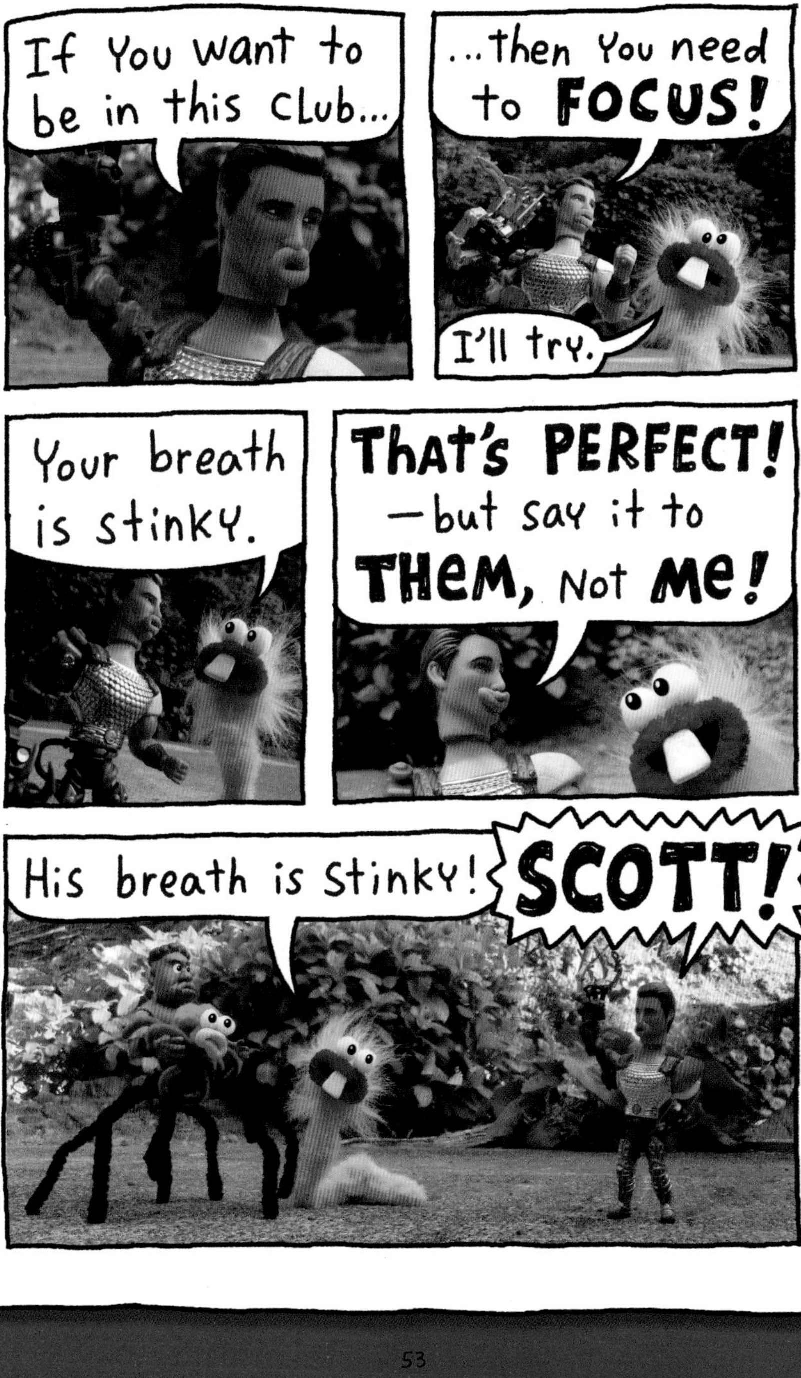
If You want to be in this Club...
...then You need to FOCUS!
I'll try.
Your breath is stinky.
That's PERFECT! —but say it to THEM, Not ME!
His breath is Stinky!
SCOTT!

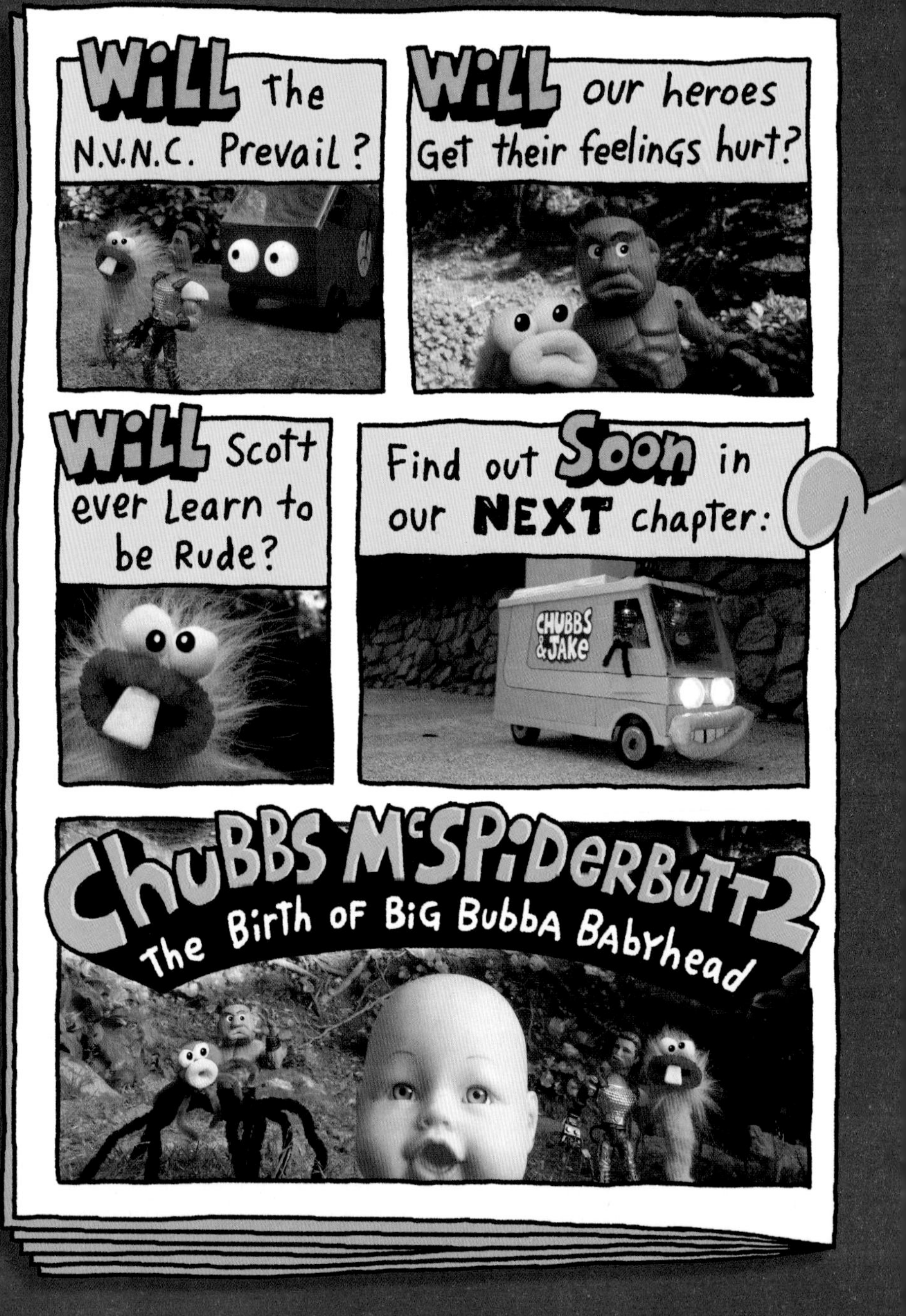
WILL the N.V.N.C. Prevail?
WILL our heroes Get their feelings hurt?
WILL Scott ever Learn to be Rude?
Find out Soon in our NEXT chapter:
CHUBBS & JAKE
ChuBBS McSPiDerBuTT 2
The BirTh OF BiG BubbA BabYhead

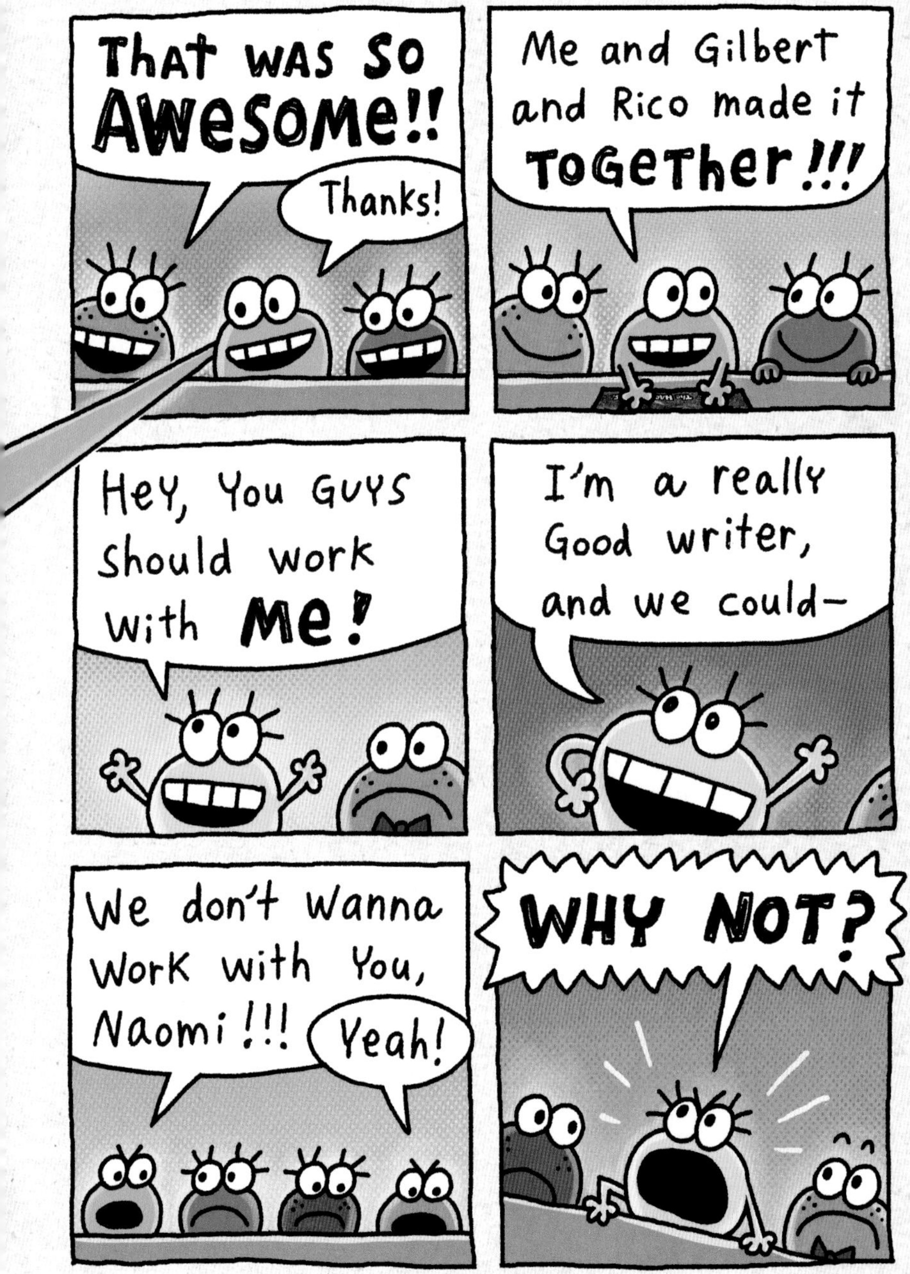
THAT WAS SO AWESOME!!
Thanks!
Me and Gilbert and Rico made it TOGETHER!!!
Hey, You GUYS should work with ME!
I'm a really Good writer, and we could–
We don't wanna work with You, Naomi!!!
Yeah!
WHY NOT?

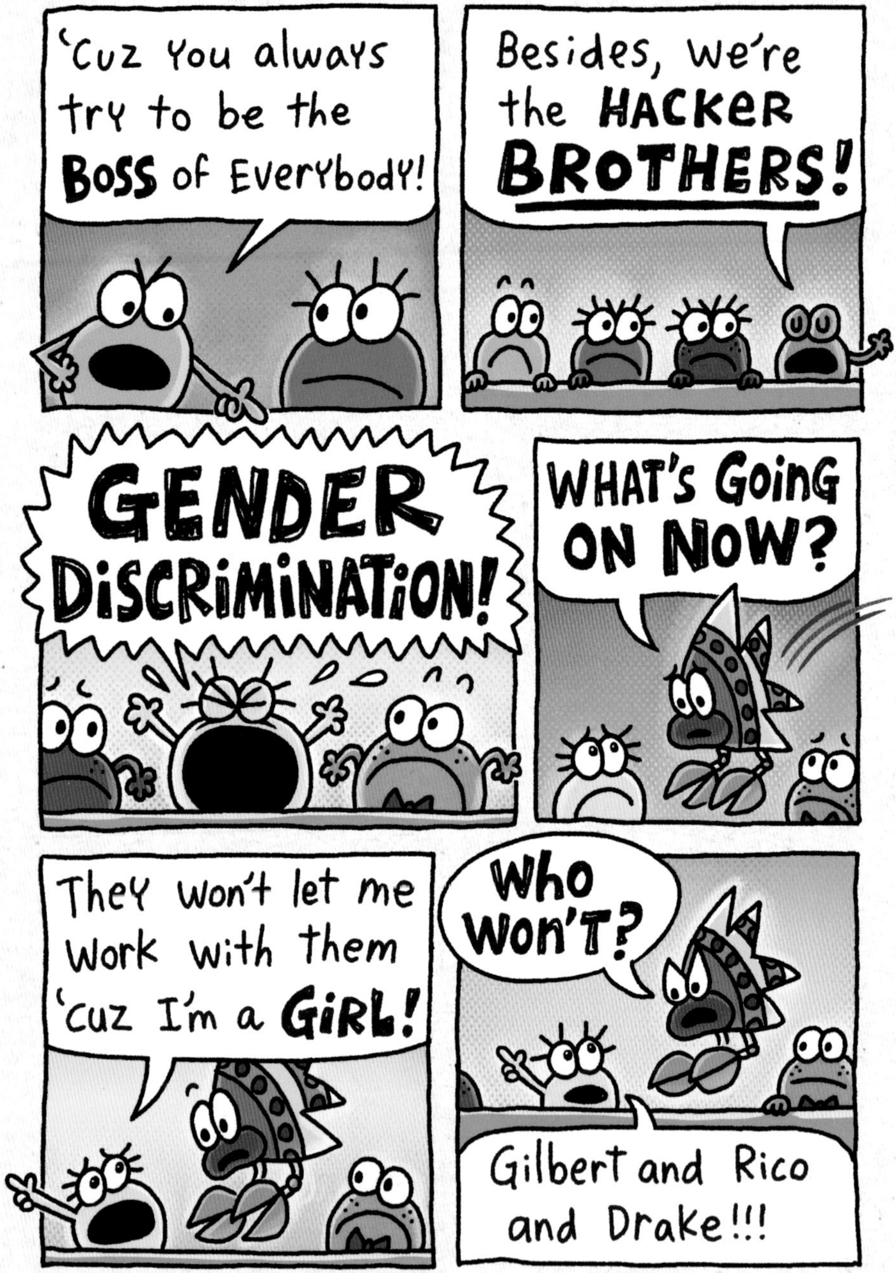
'Cuz you always try to be the BOSS of Everybody!
Besides, we're the HACKER BROTHERS!
GENDER DISCRIMINATION!
WHAT'S GOING ON NOW?
They won't let me work with them 'cuz I'm a GIRL!
Who WON'T?
Gilbert and Rico and Drake!!!

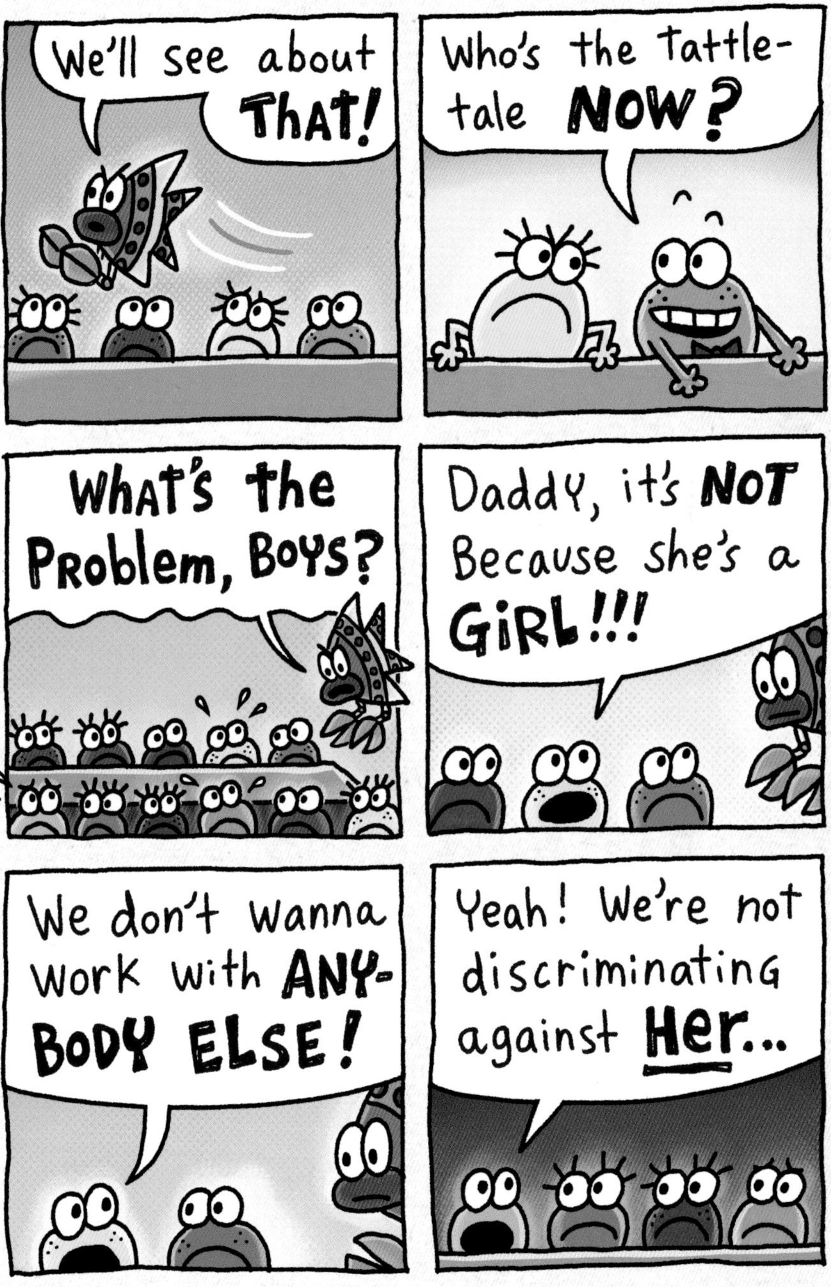
We'll see about THAT!
Who's the Tattle-tale NOW?
WHAT'S the Problem, BOYS?
Daddy, it's NOT Because she's a GIRL!!!
We don't wanna work with ANY-BODY ELSE!
Yeah! We're not discriminating against Her...

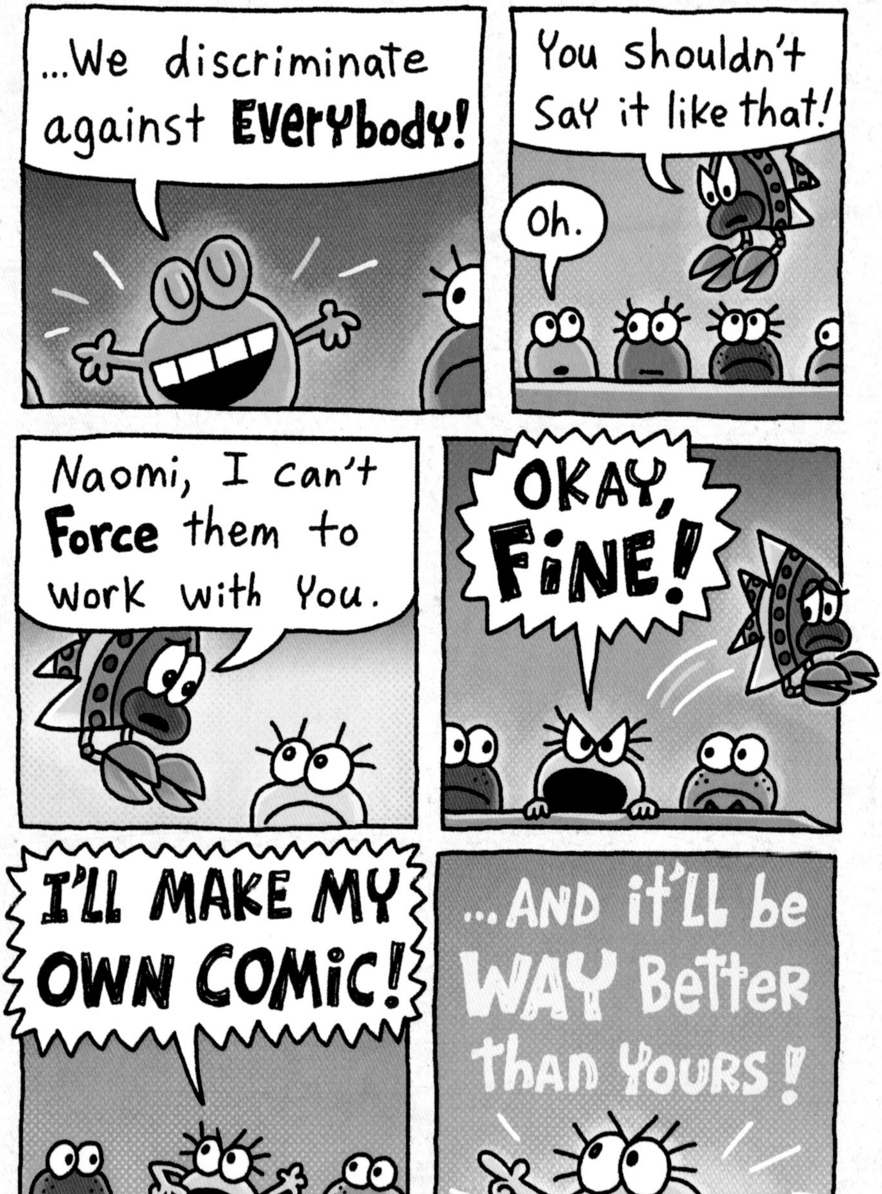
...We discriminate against EVERYbody!
You shouldn't Say it like that!
Oh.
Naomi, I can't Force them to work with You.
OKAY, FiNE!
I'LL MAKE MY OWN COMiC!
...AND it'LL be WAY Better than YOURS!

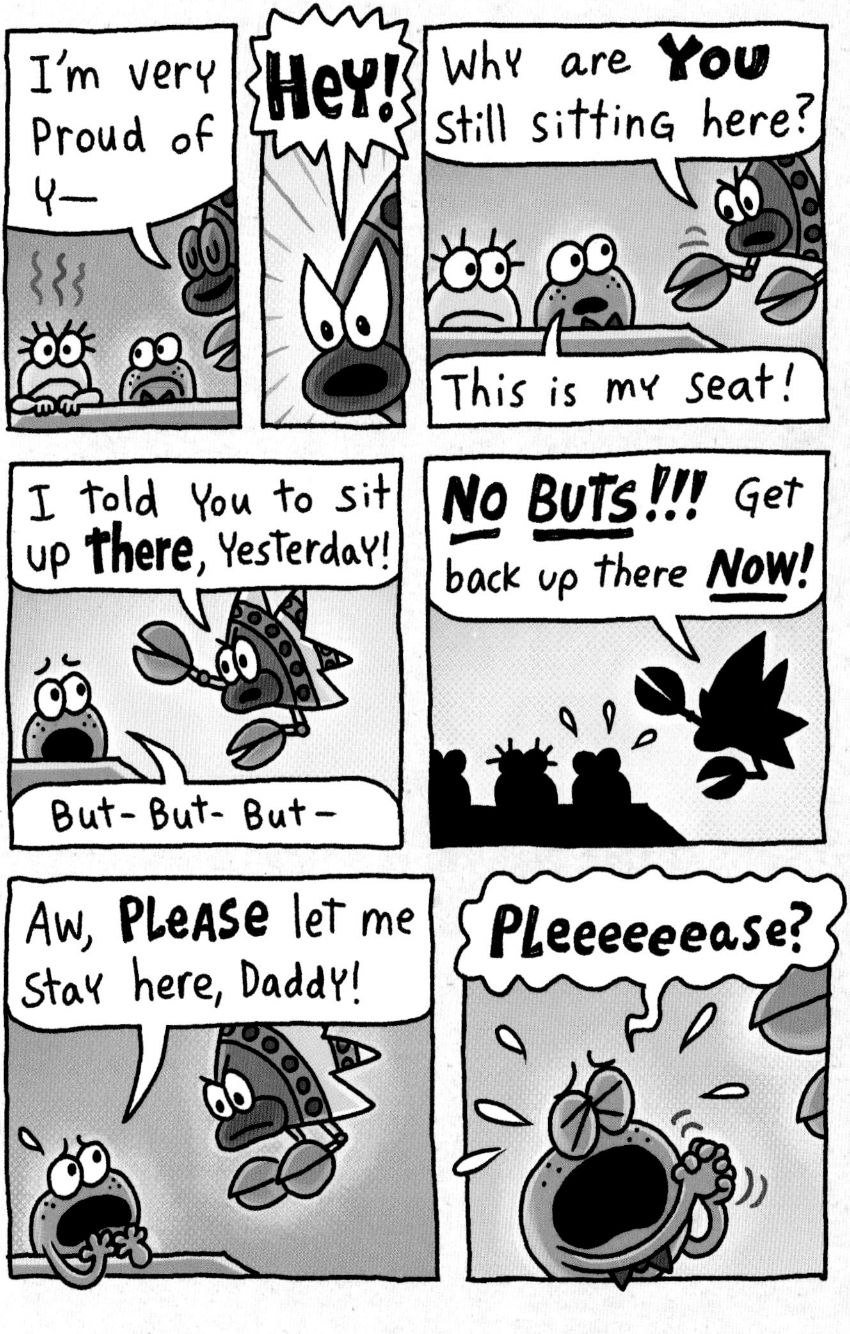
I'm very Proud of Y—
HEY!
Why are YOU still sitting here?
This is my seat!
I told You to sit up there, Yesterday!
But- But- But-
NO BUTS!!! Get back up there NOW!
Aw, PLEASE let me stay here, Daddy!
PLeeeeeease?

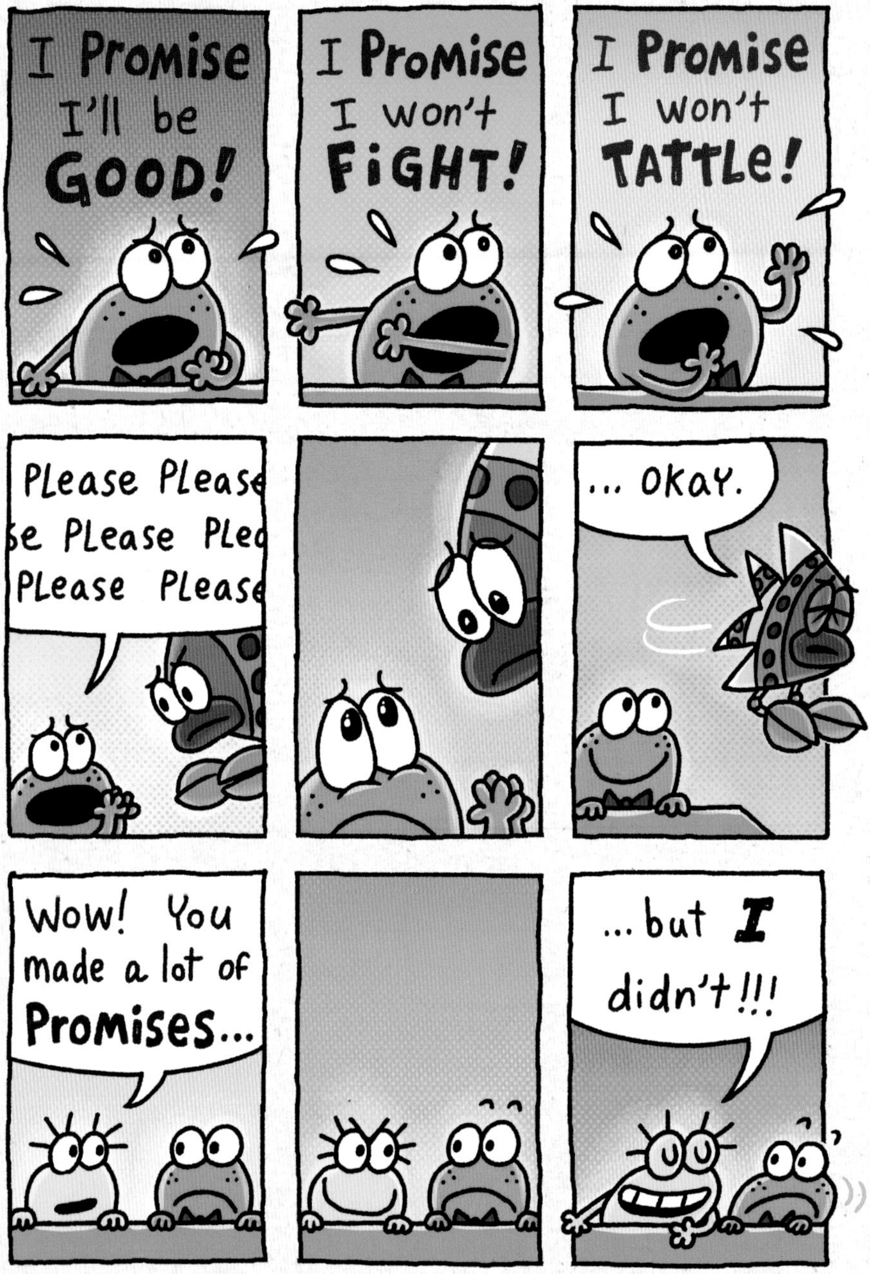
I Promise I'll be GOOD!
I Promise I won't FIGHT!
I Promise I won't TATTLE!
... OKAY.
Wow! You made a lot of PROMISES...
...but I didn't!!!

CHAPTER 3

New Day, New Perspective

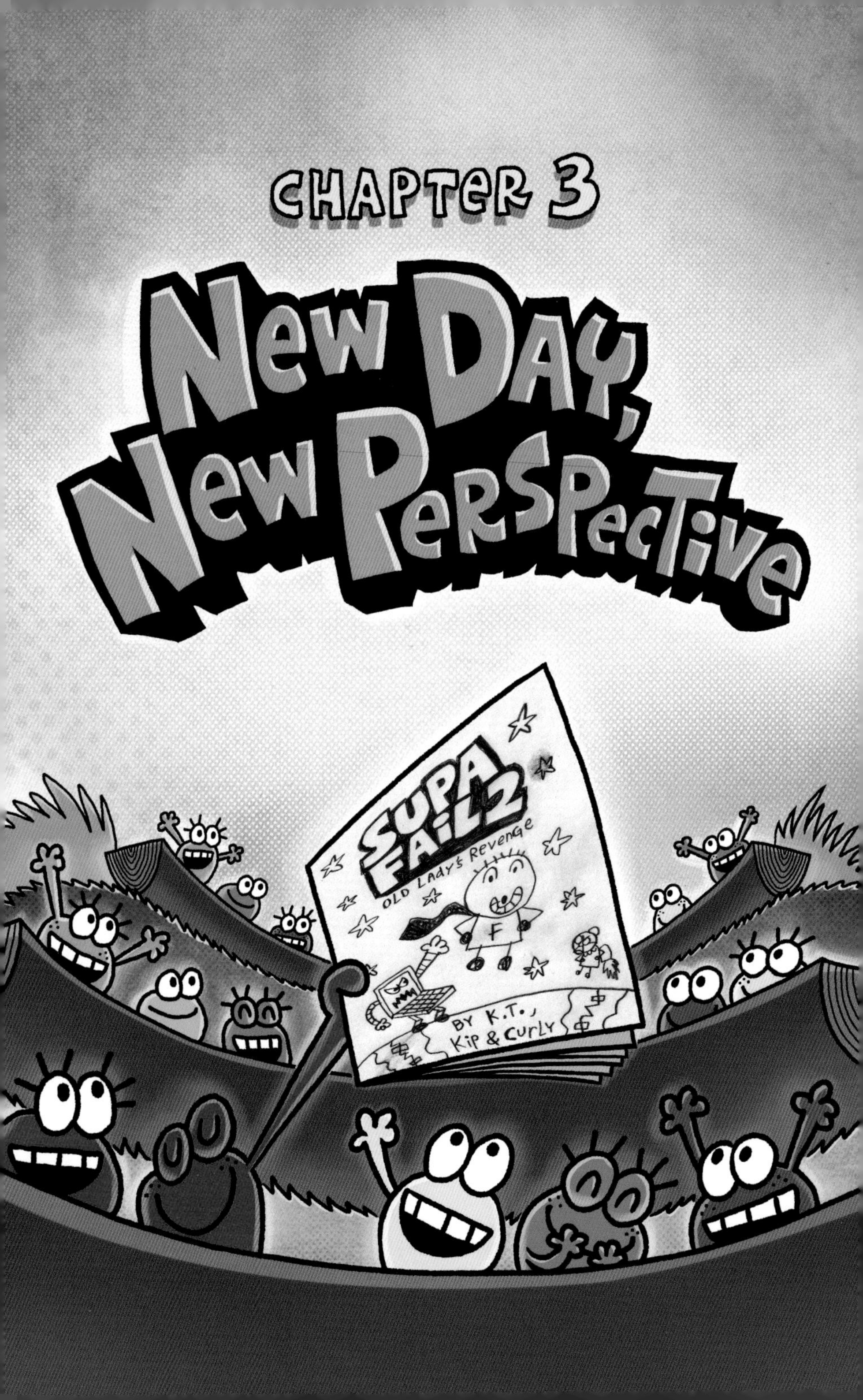
SUPA FAIL 2
OLD Lady's Revenge
BY K.T., Kip & Curly

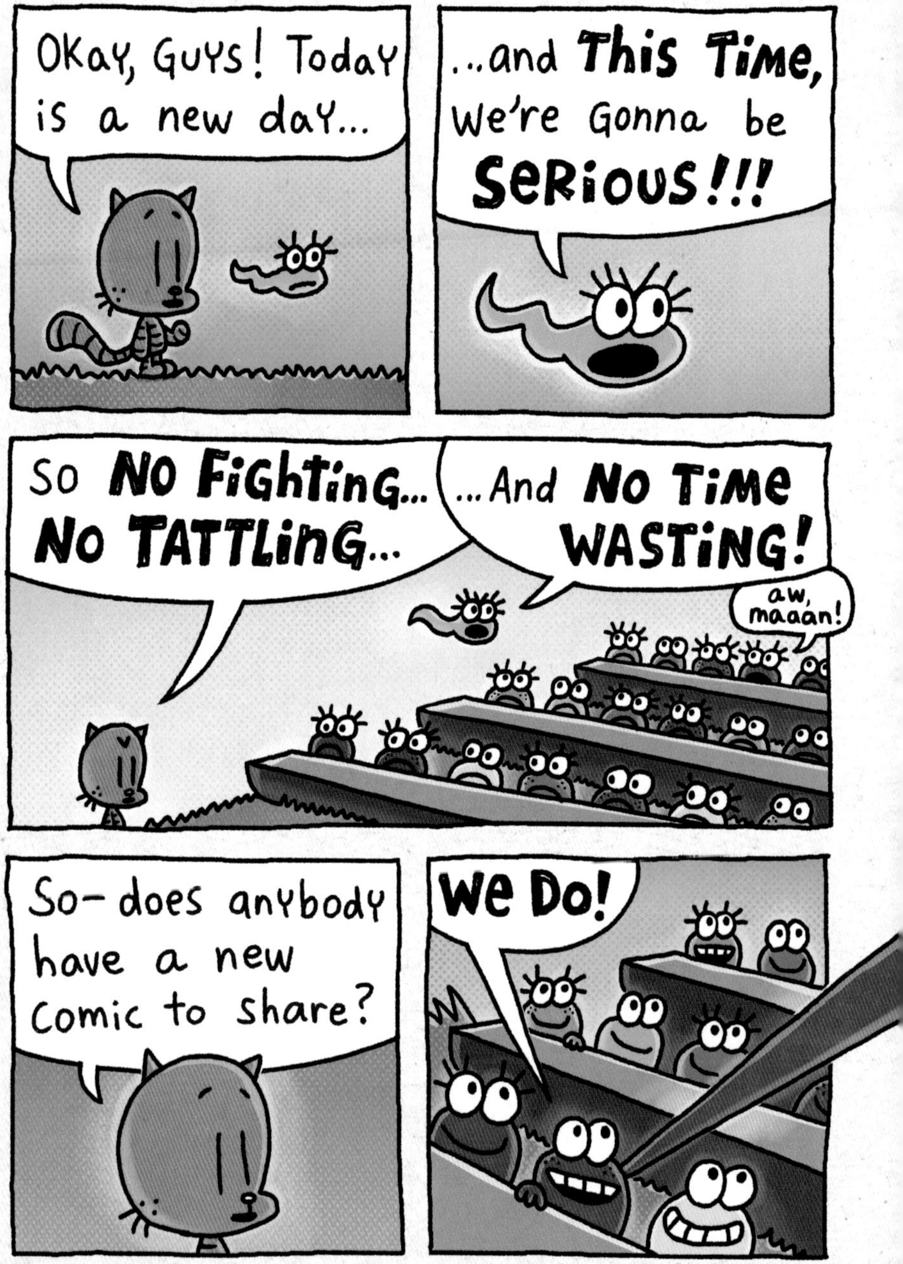
OKay, GUYS! Today is a new day...
...and This Time, we're Gonna be SERIOUS!!!
So NO FiGhTinG... NO TATTLinG...
...And NO TiMe WASTiNG!
aw, maaan!
So- does anybody have a new comic to share?
We Do!

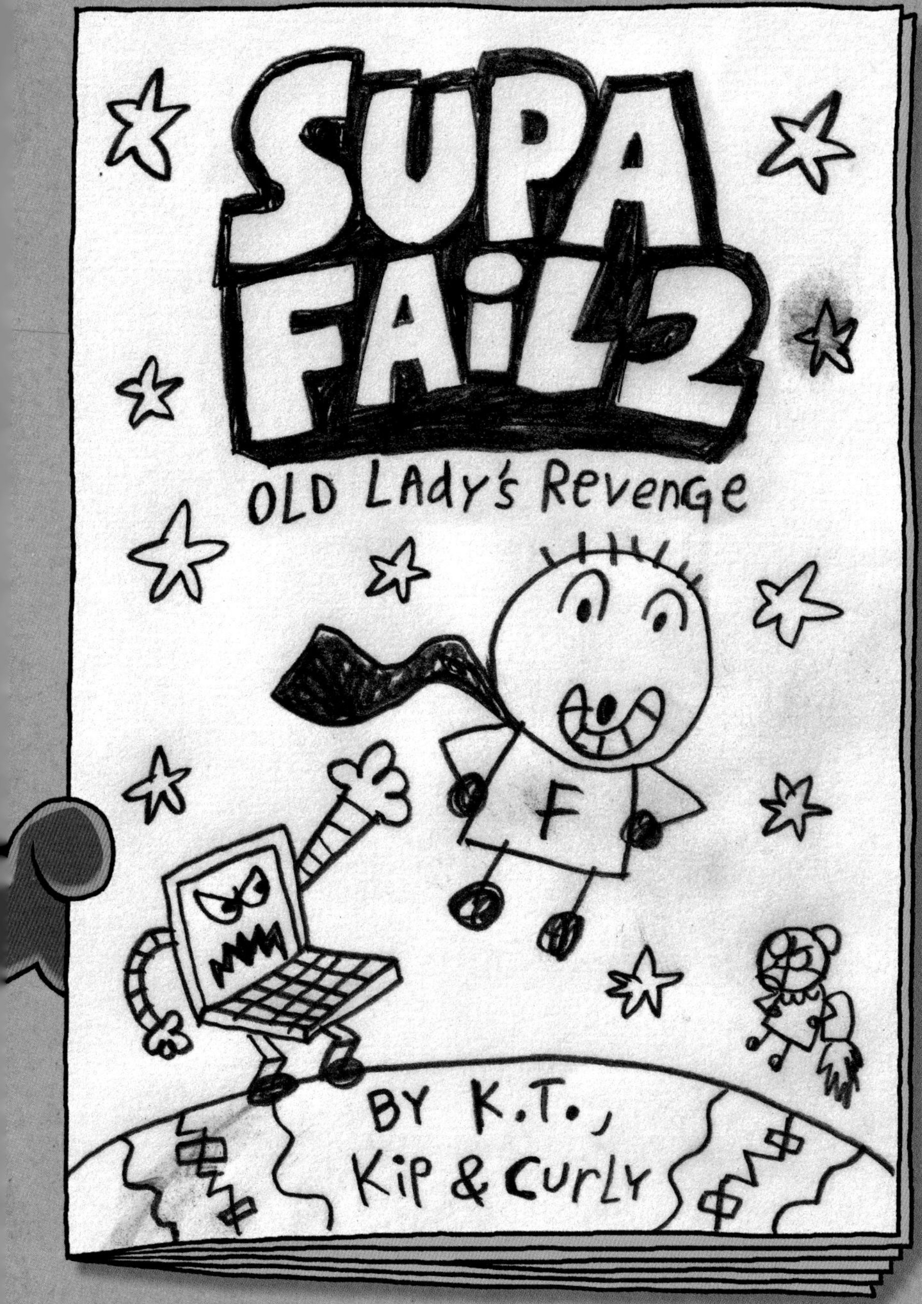
SUPA FAiL 2
OLD LAdy's Revenge
F
BY K.T.,
Kip & Curly

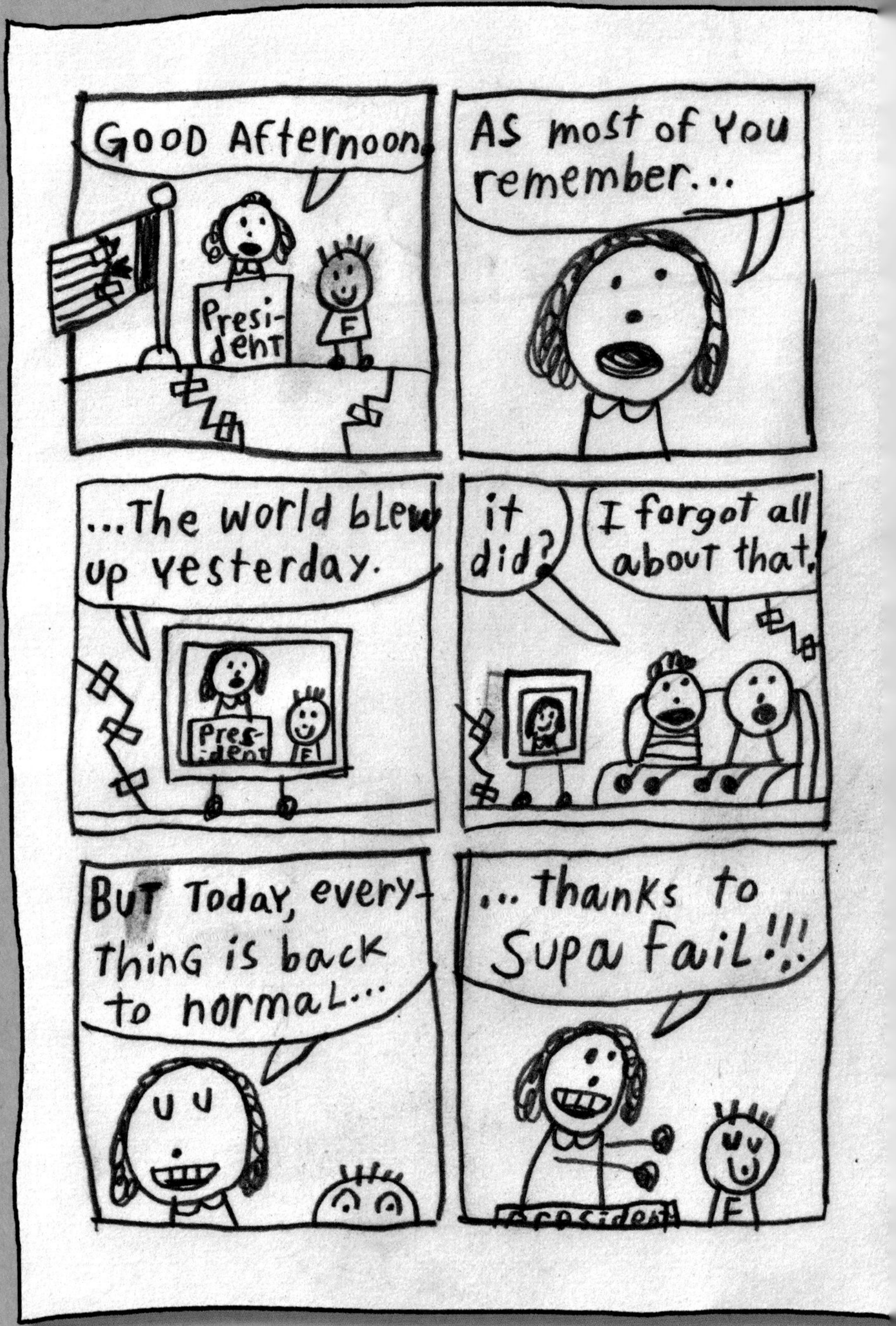
GOOD Afternoon.
AS most of You remember...
...The world blew up yesterday.
President
it did?
I forgot all about that!
BUT Today, every-thing is back to normaL...
...thanks to Supa FaiL!!!
F

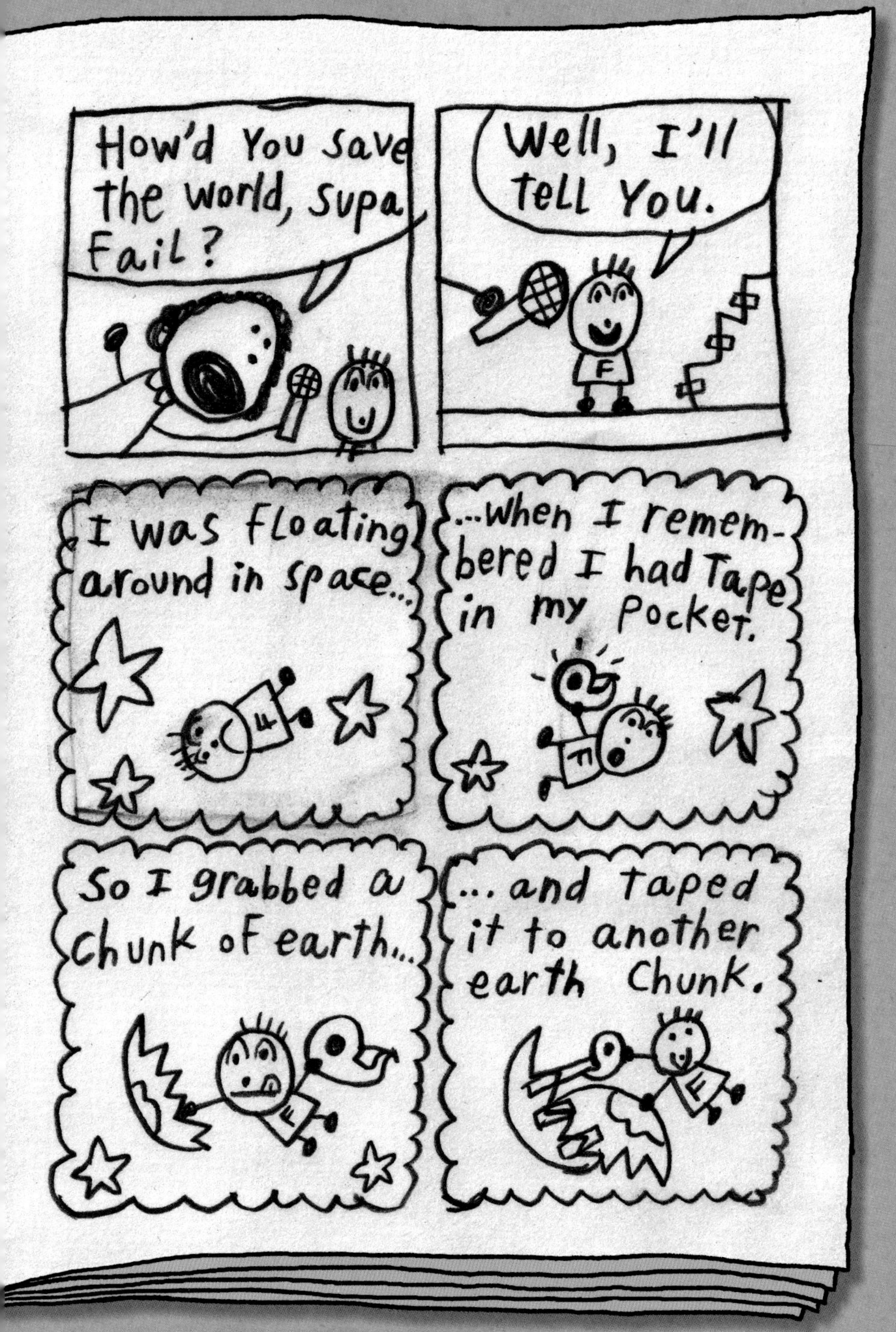
How'd You save the world, Supa Fail?
Well, I'll tell You.
I was floating around in space...
...when I remembered I had Tape in my Pocket.
So I grabbed a chunk of earth...
... and taped it to another earth chunk.

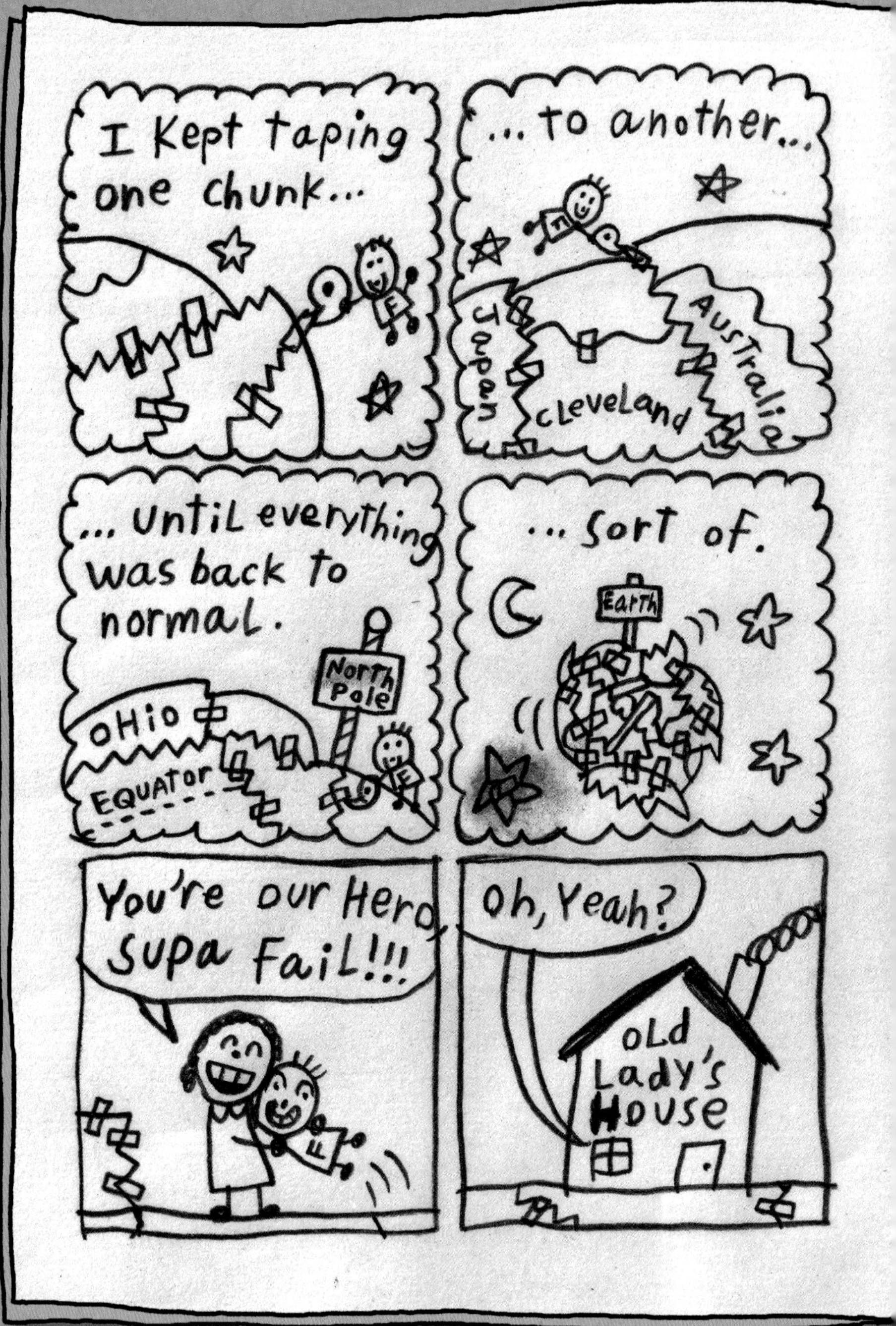
I Kept taping one chunk...
... to another...
Japan
Cleveland
Australia
... until everything was back to normal.
North Pole
OHIO
EQUATOR
... sort of.
Earth
You're our Hero, Supa Fail!!!
Oh, Yeah?
OLd Lady's House

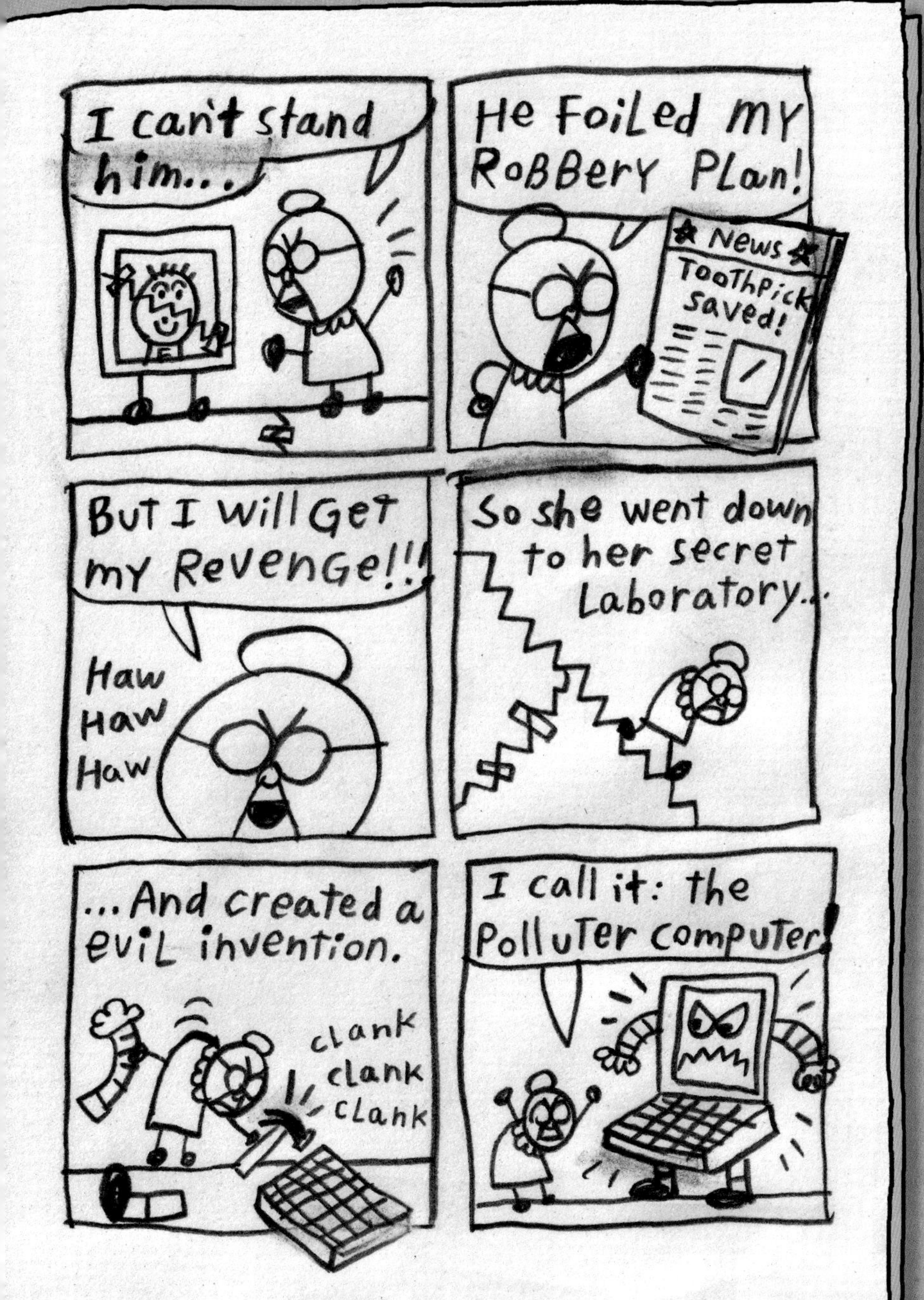
I can't stand him...
He Foiled my Robbery Plan!
News
ToothPick saved!
But I will Get my Revenge!!
Haw Haw Haw
So she went down to her secret Laboratory...
...And created a evil invention.
clank clank clank
I call it: the Polluter computer!

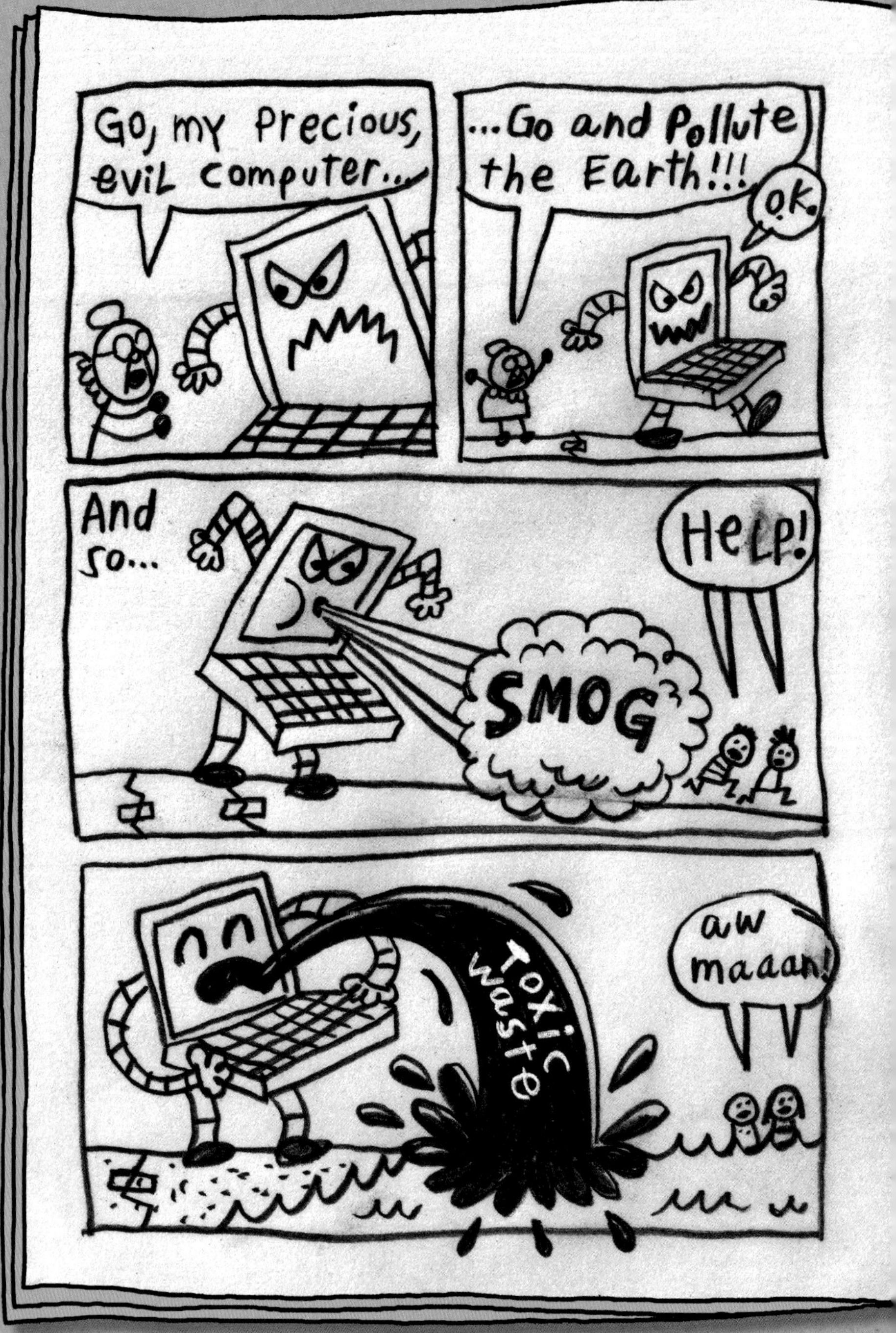
Go, my precious, evil computer...
...Go and Pollute the Earth!!!
O.K.
And so...
Help!
SMOG
aw maaan!
Toxic waste

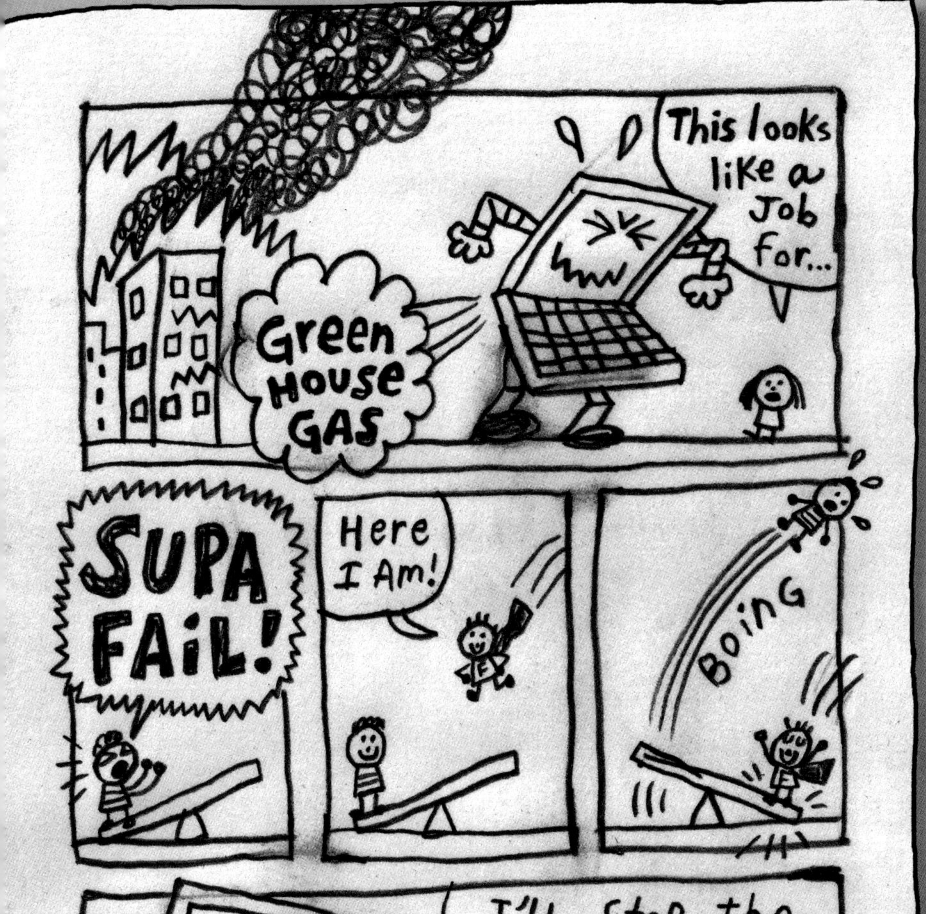
This looks like a Job for...
Green House GAS
SUPA FAiL!
Here I Am!
BOinG
I'LL Stop the Polluter computer!!!

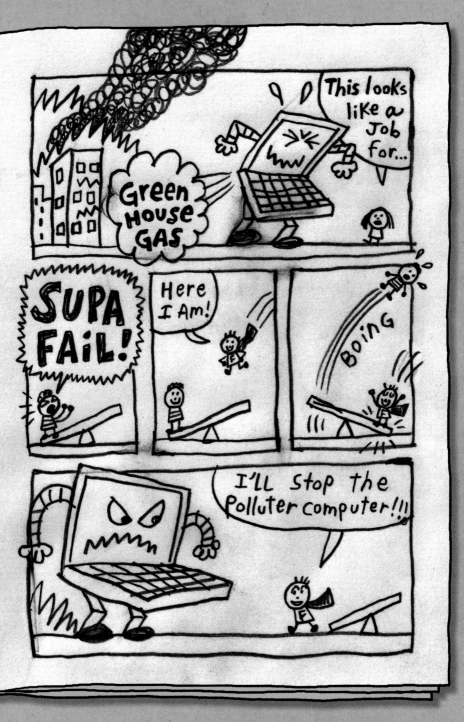

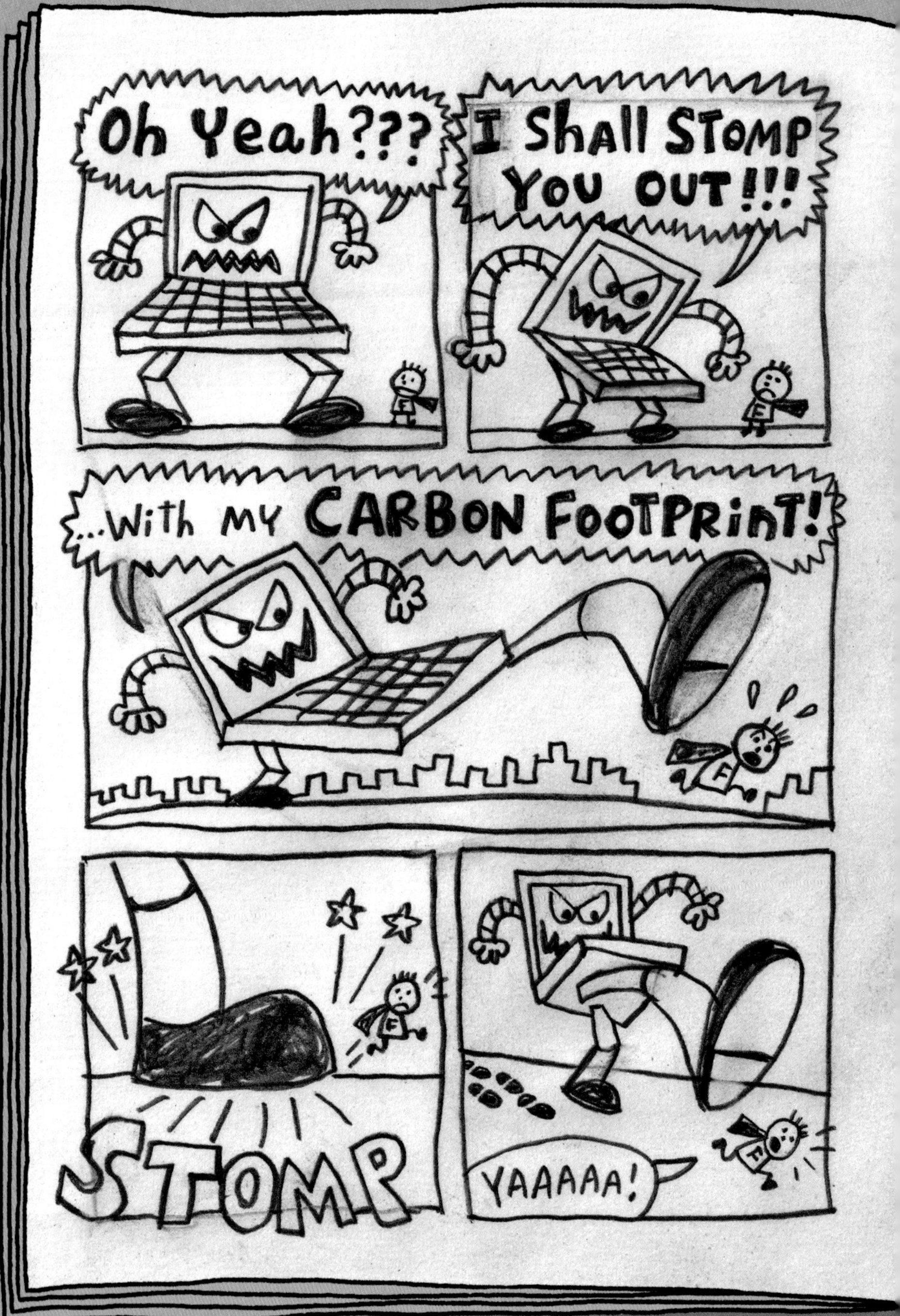
Oh Yeah???
I Shall STOMP YOU OUT!!!
...With MY CARBON FOOTPRINT!
STOMP
YAAAAA!

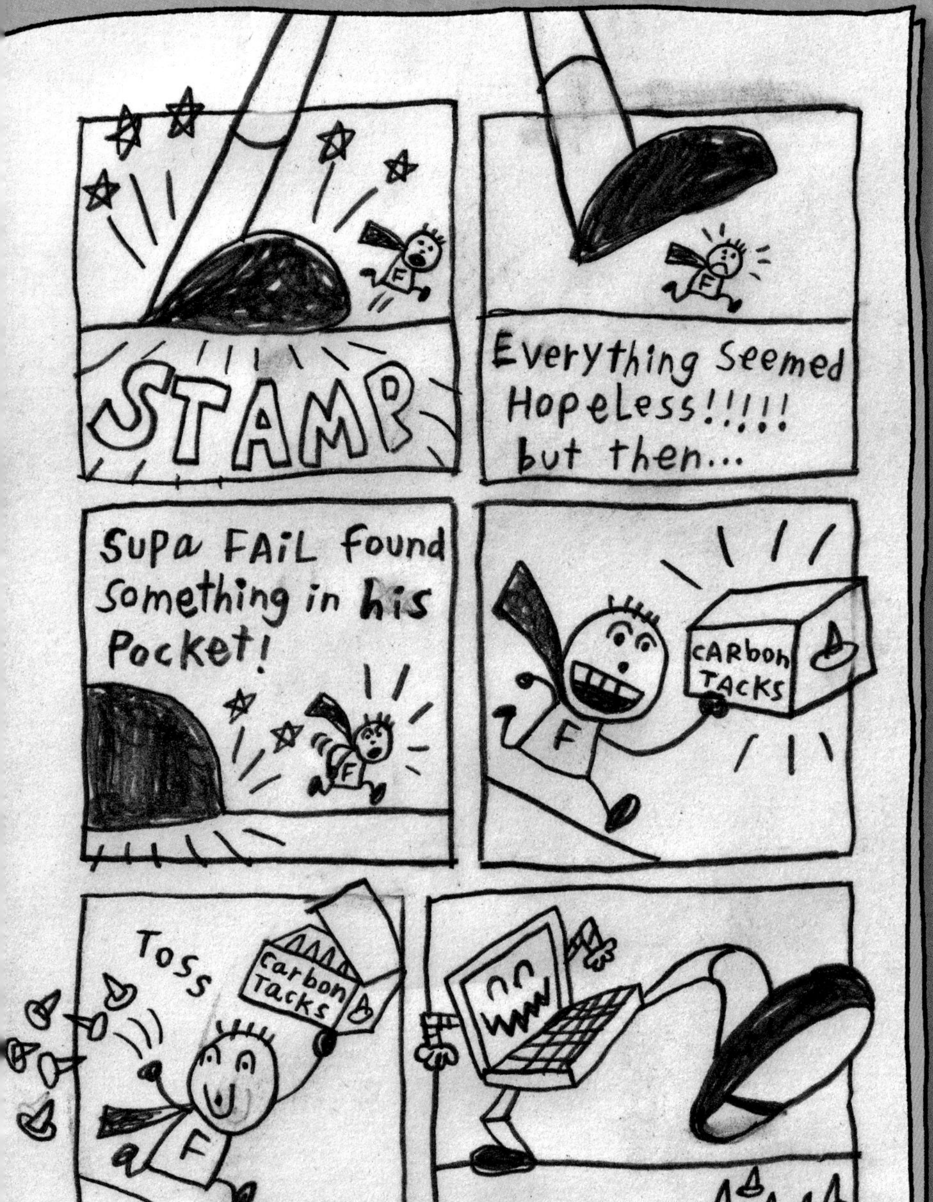
STAMP
Everything Seemed Hopeless!!!!! but then...
Supa FAIL found Something in his Pocket!
CARbon TACKS
TOSS
Carbon Tacks

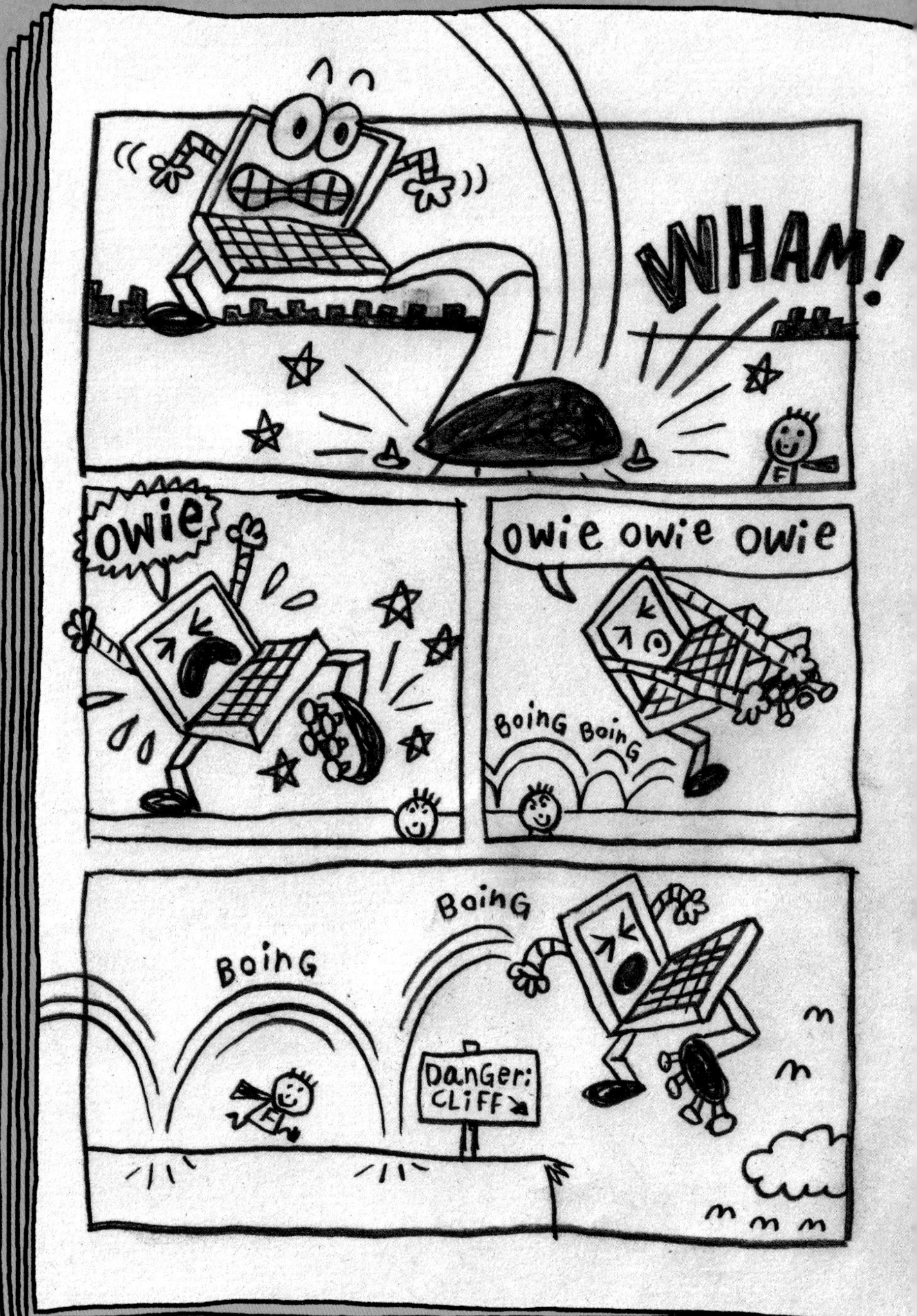
WHAM!
owie
owie owie owie
BoinG Boing
Boing
Boing
DanGer:
CLiFF

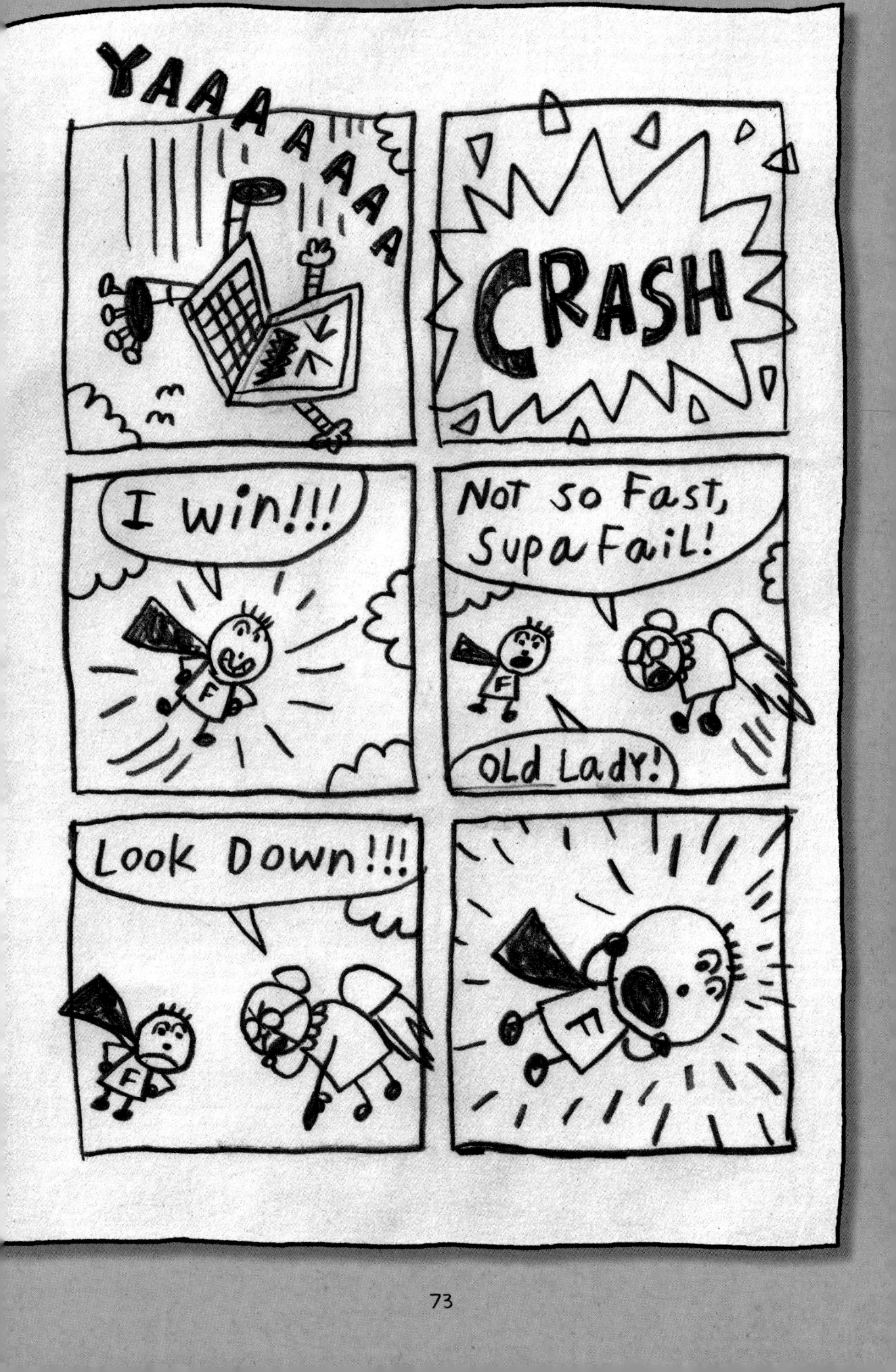
YAAAAAAAAA
CRASH
I win!!!
Not so Fast,
SupaFail!
Old Lady!
Look Down!!!

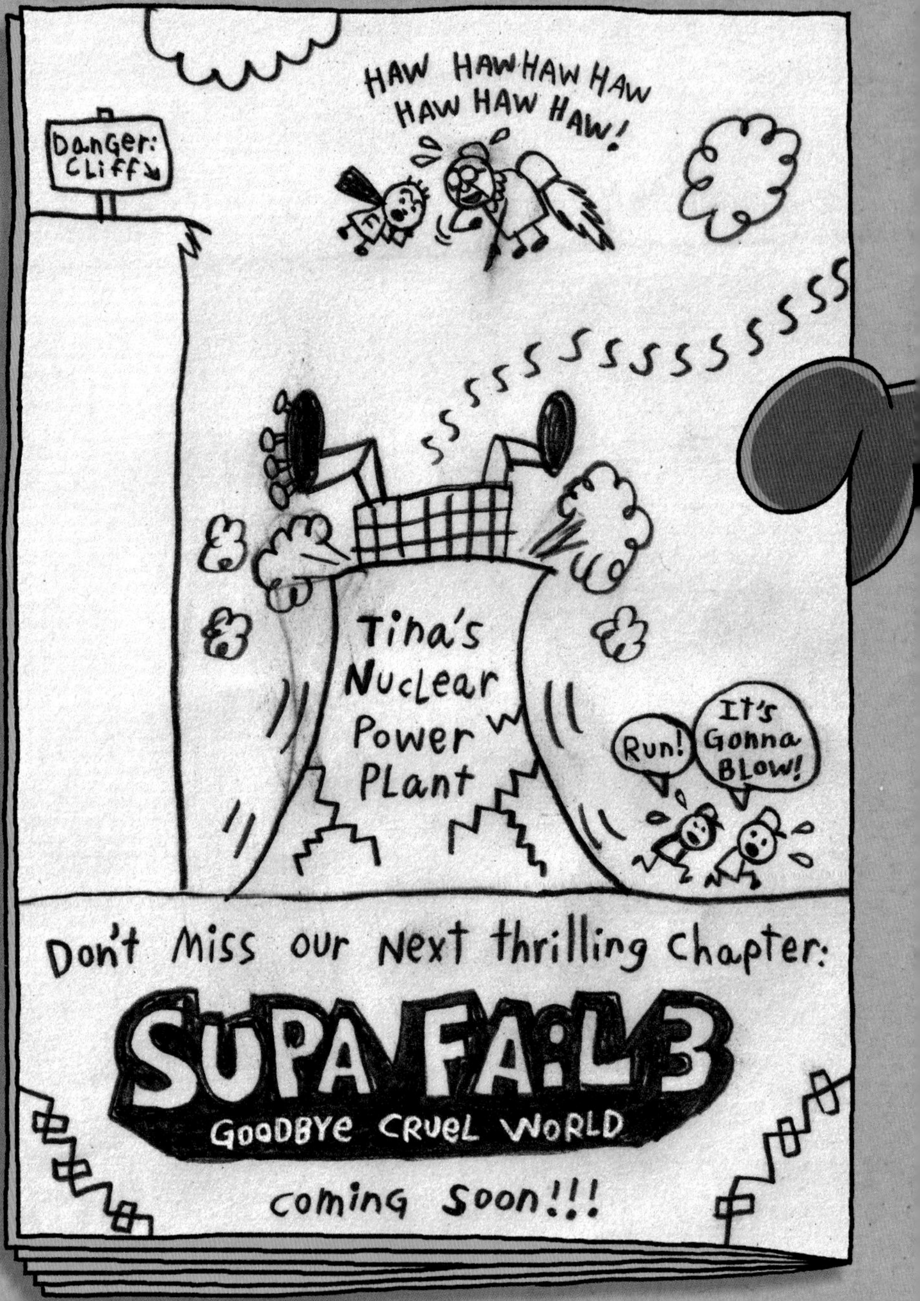
Danger: Cliff
HAW HAW HAW HAW HAW HAW HAW HAW!
SSSSSSSSSSSSSSSSSSSSSSS
Tina's Nuclear Power Plant
Run!
It's Gonna BLOW!
Don't Miss our Next thrilling Chapter:
SUPA FAIL 3
GOODBYE CRUEL WORLD
coming Soon!!!

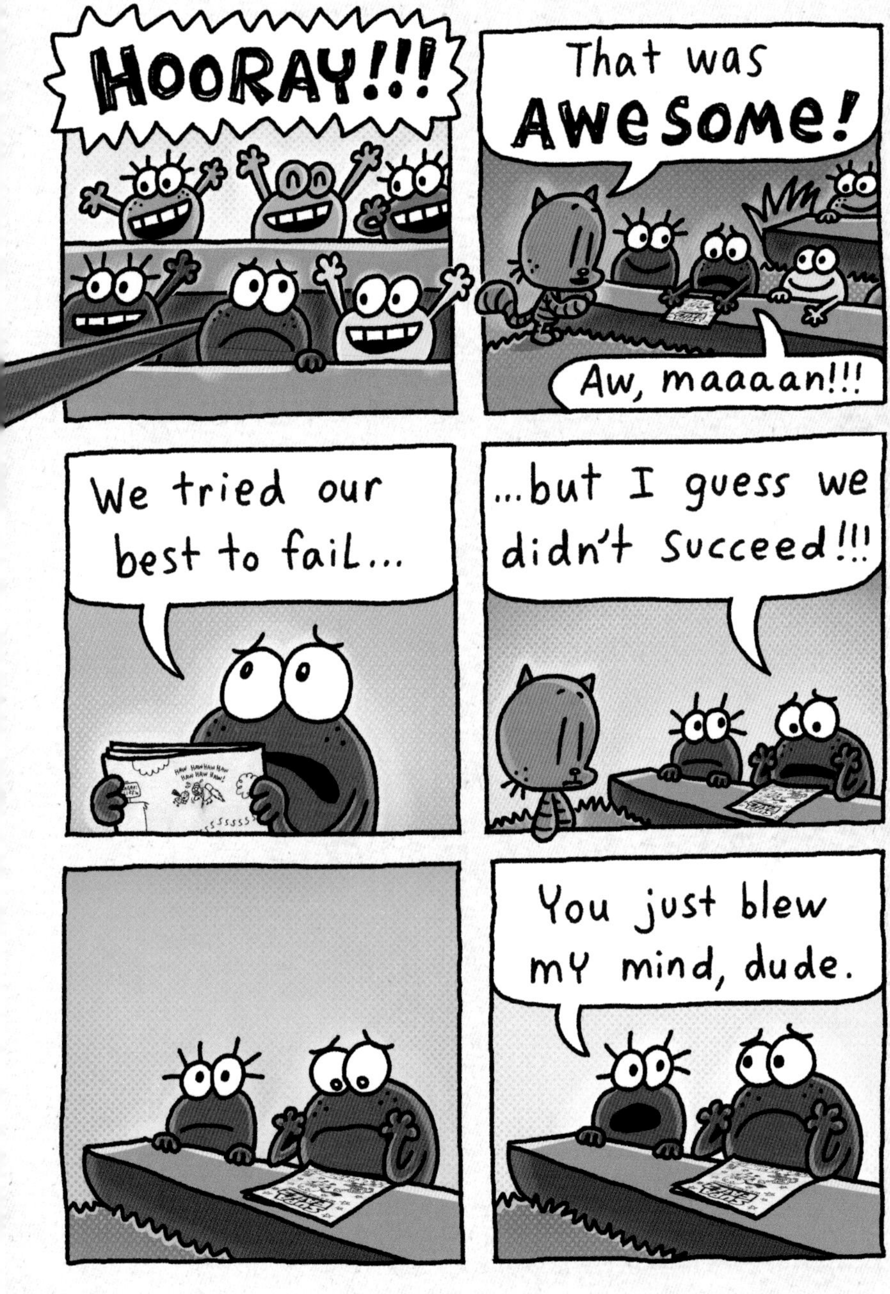
HOORAY!!!
That was AWESOME!
Aw, maaaan!!!
We tried our best to fail...
...but I guess we didn't succeed!!!
You just blew my mind, dude.

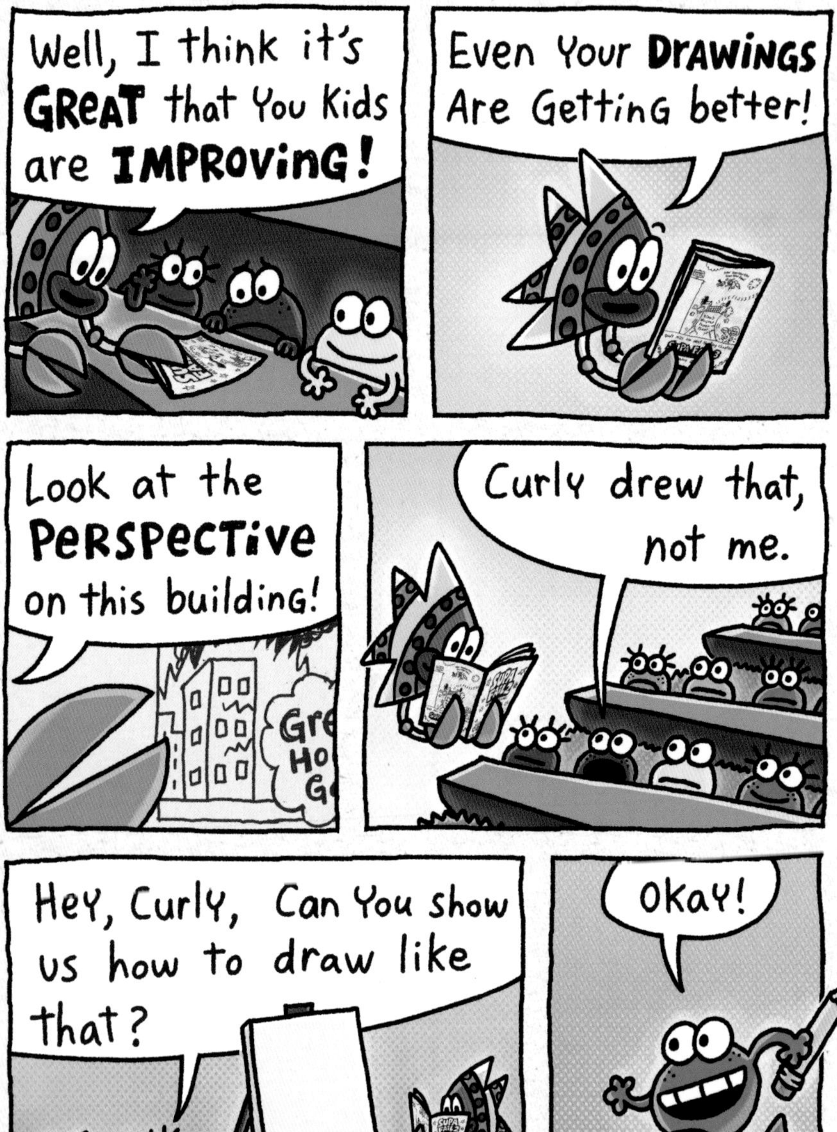
Well, I think it's GREAT that You Kids are IMPROVING!
Even Your DRAWINGS Are Getting better!
Look at the PERSPECTIVE on this building!
Curly drew that, not me.
Hey, Curly, Can You show us how to draw like that?
OKAY!

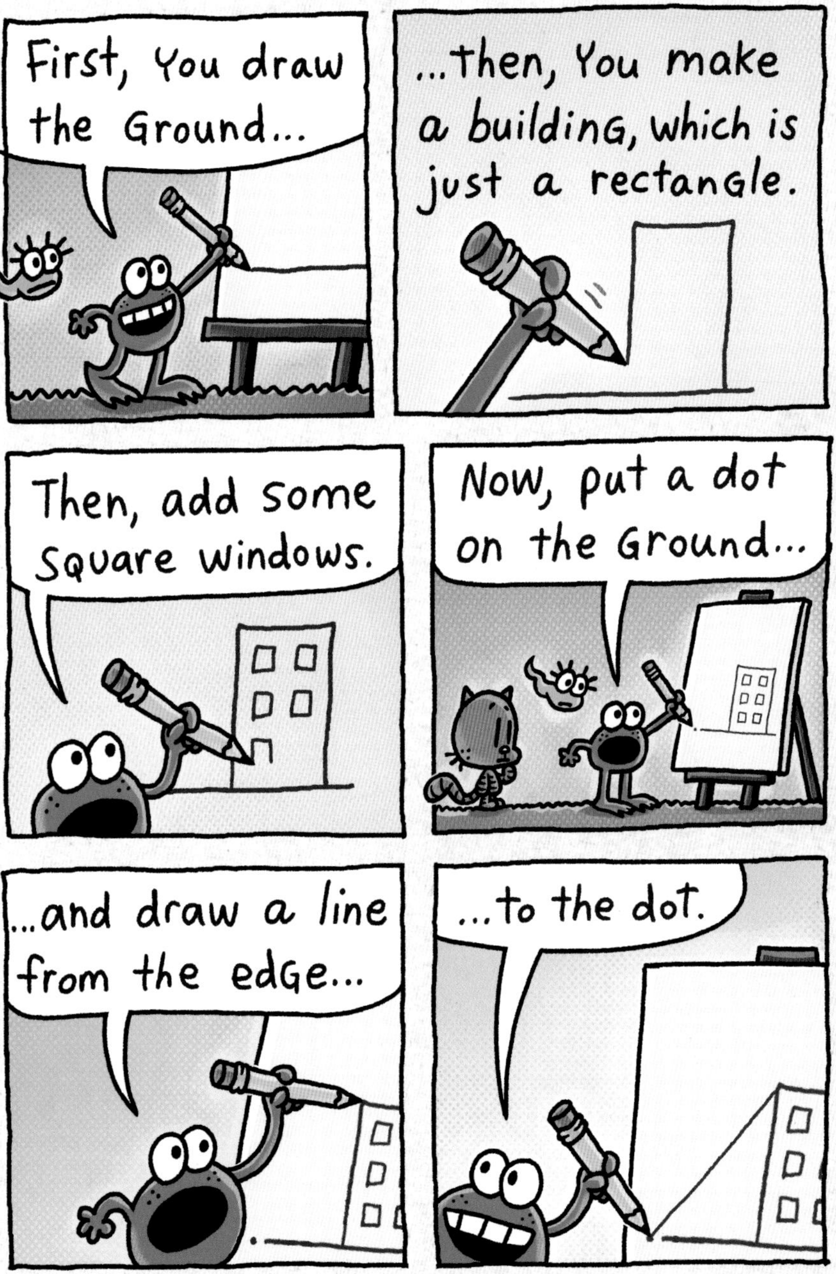
First, You draw the Ground...
...then, You make a building, which is just a rectangle.
Then, add some square windows.
Now, put a dot on the Ground...
...and draw a line from the edge...
...to the dot.

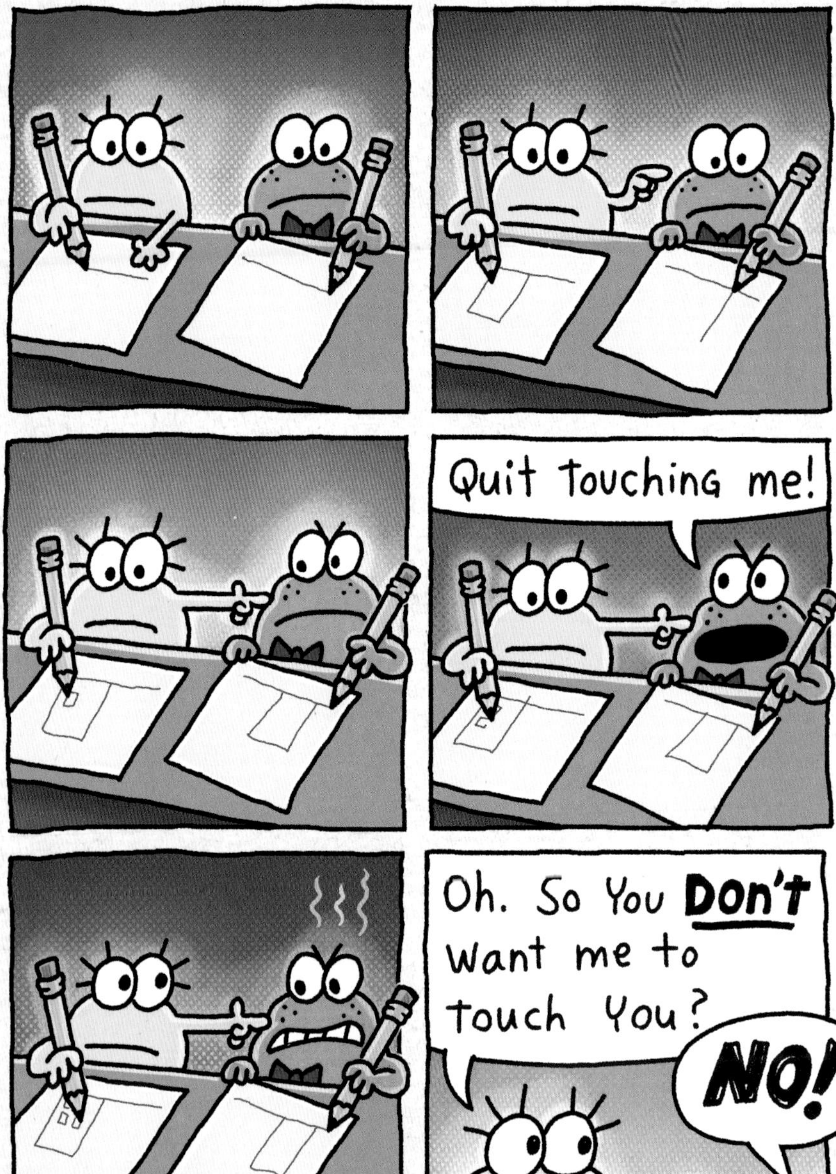

Quit touching me!
Oh. So you **DON'T** want me to touch you?
NO!

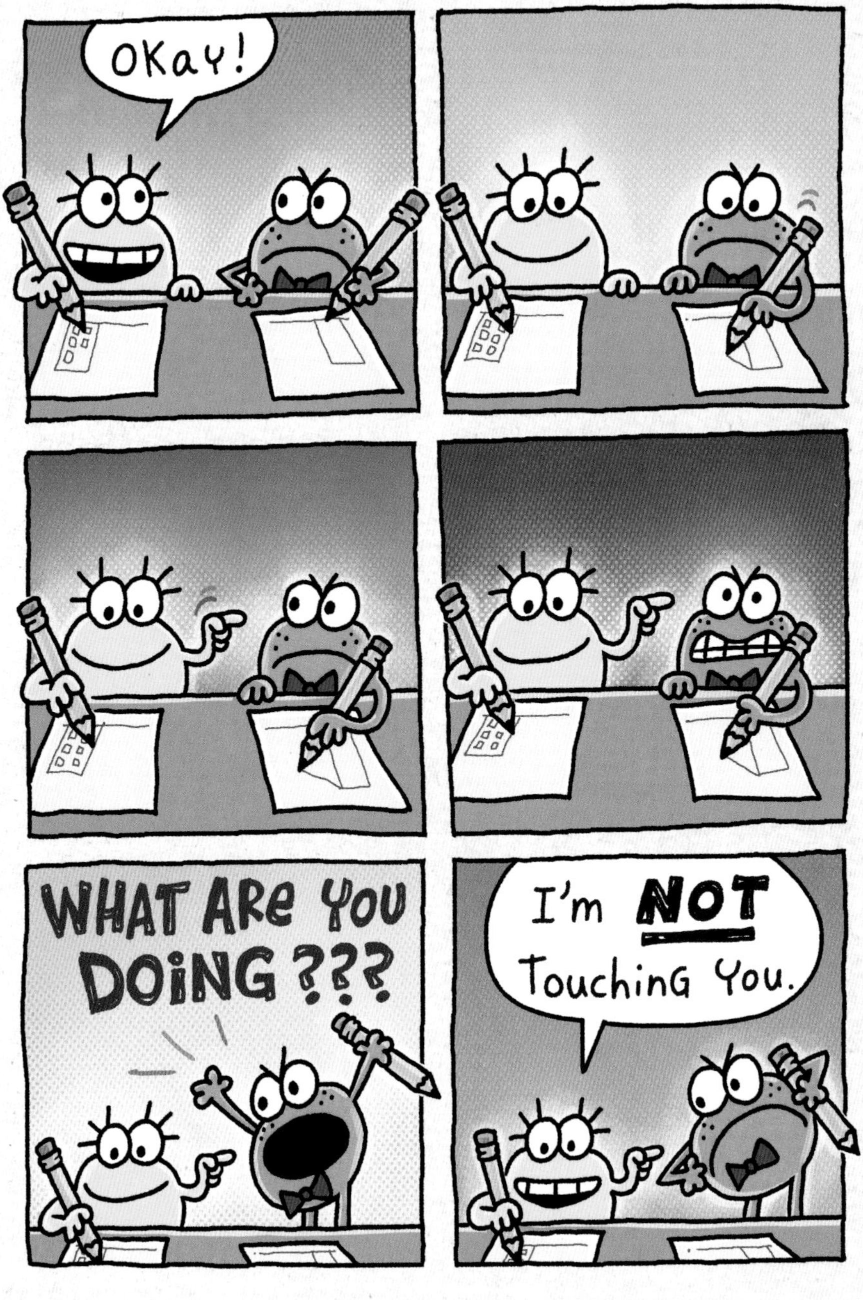
OKay!
WHAT ARE YOU DOiNG???
I'm NOT Touching You.

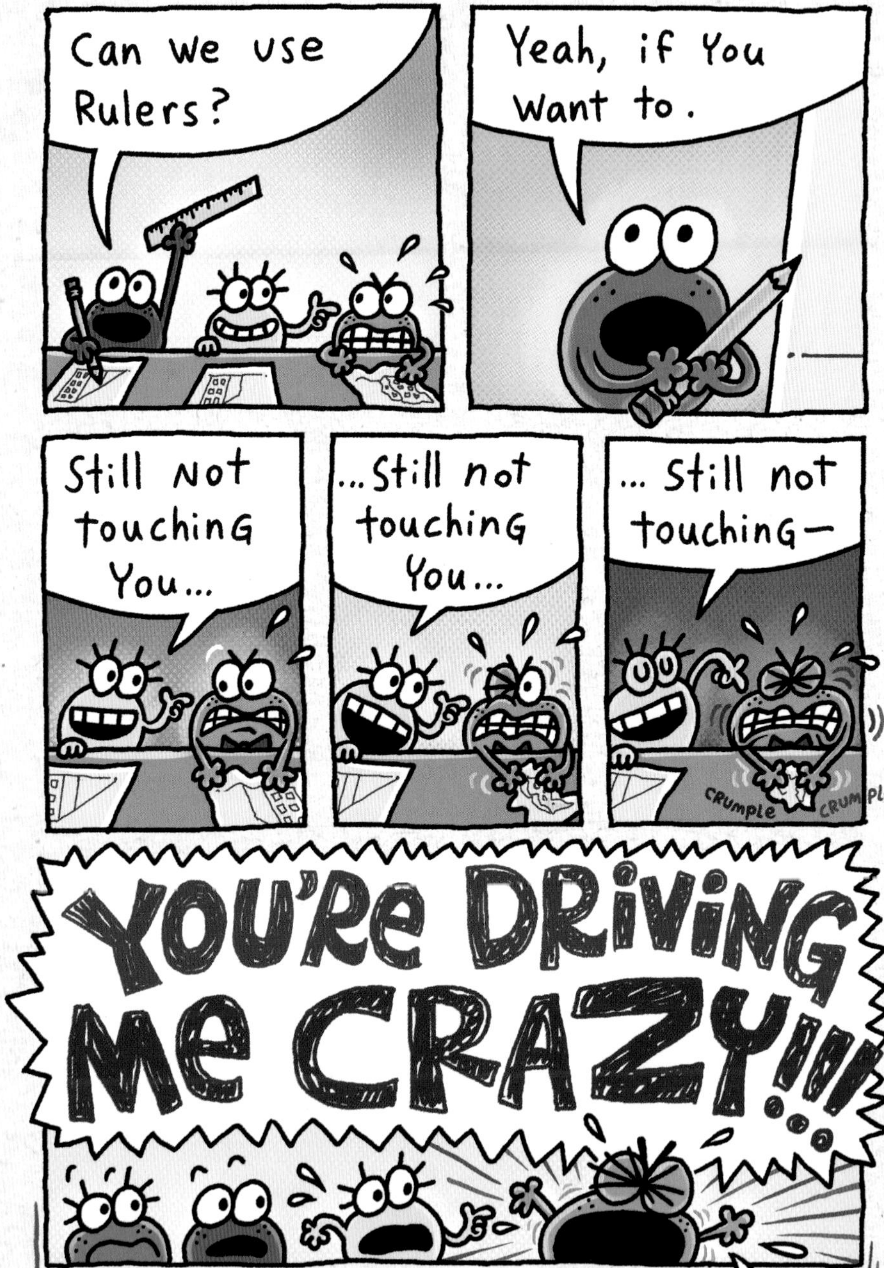
Can we use Rulers?
Yeah, if You want to.
Still Not touching You...
...Still not touching You...
... Still not touching—
CRUmple
CRUMple
YOU'Re DRiViNG Me CRAZY!!!

CHAPTER 4

Big Trouble for Little Melvin

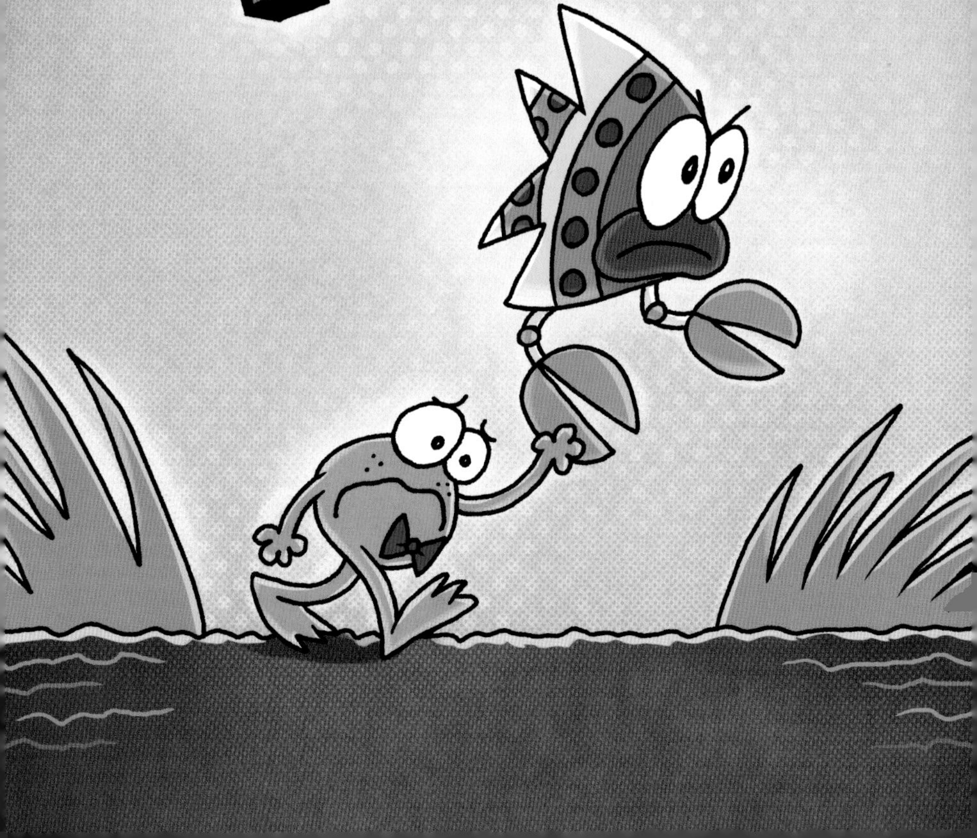

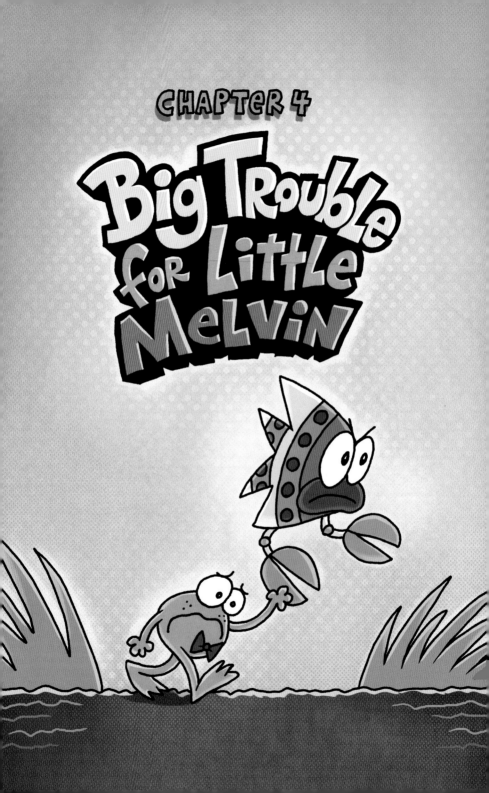

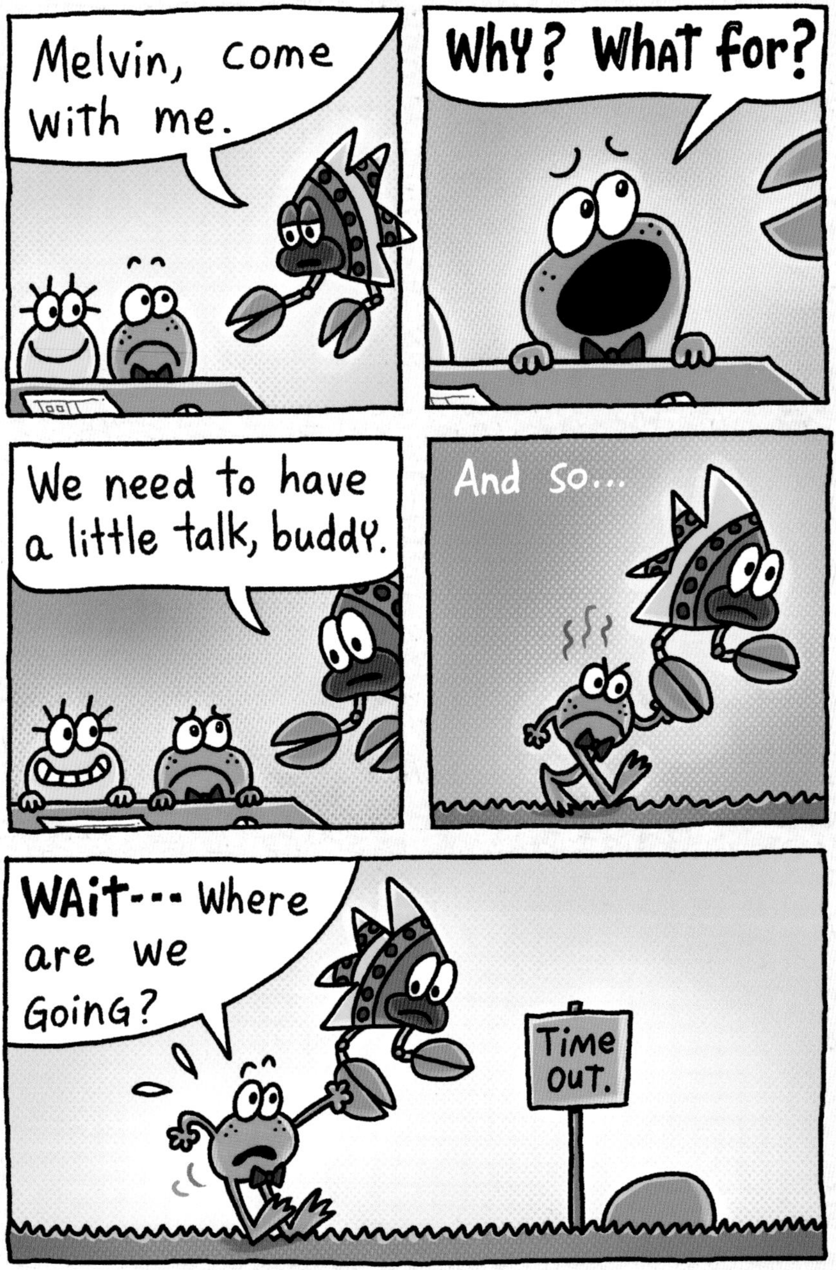
Melvin, come with me.
WHY? WHAT FOR?
We need to have a little talk, buddy.
And so...
WAIT... Where are we GOING?
TIME OUT.

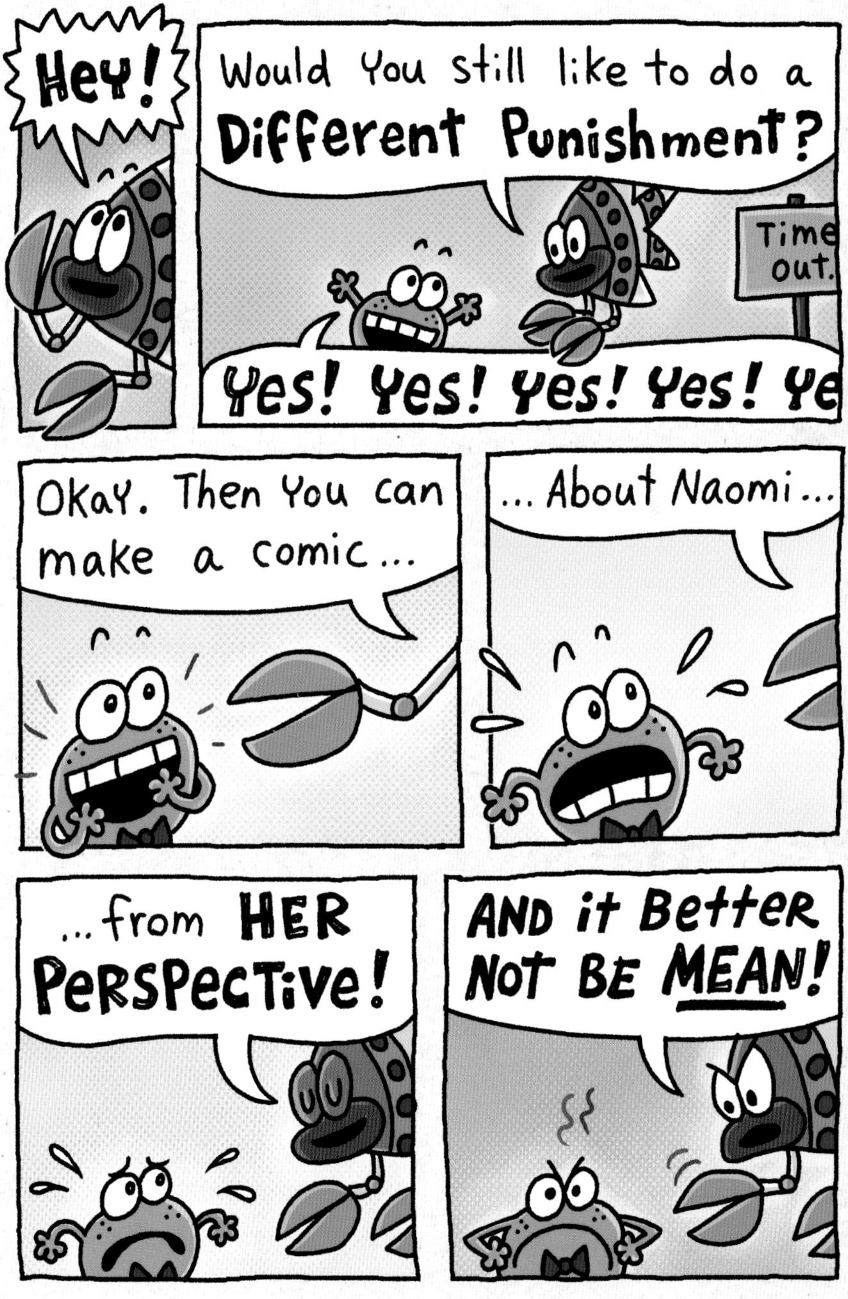
Hey!
Would You still like to do a Different Punishment?
Time out.
Yes! Yes! Yes! Yes! Ye
OKaY. Then You can make a comic...
...About Naomi...
...from HER PERSPECTIVE!
AND it Better NOT BE MEAN!

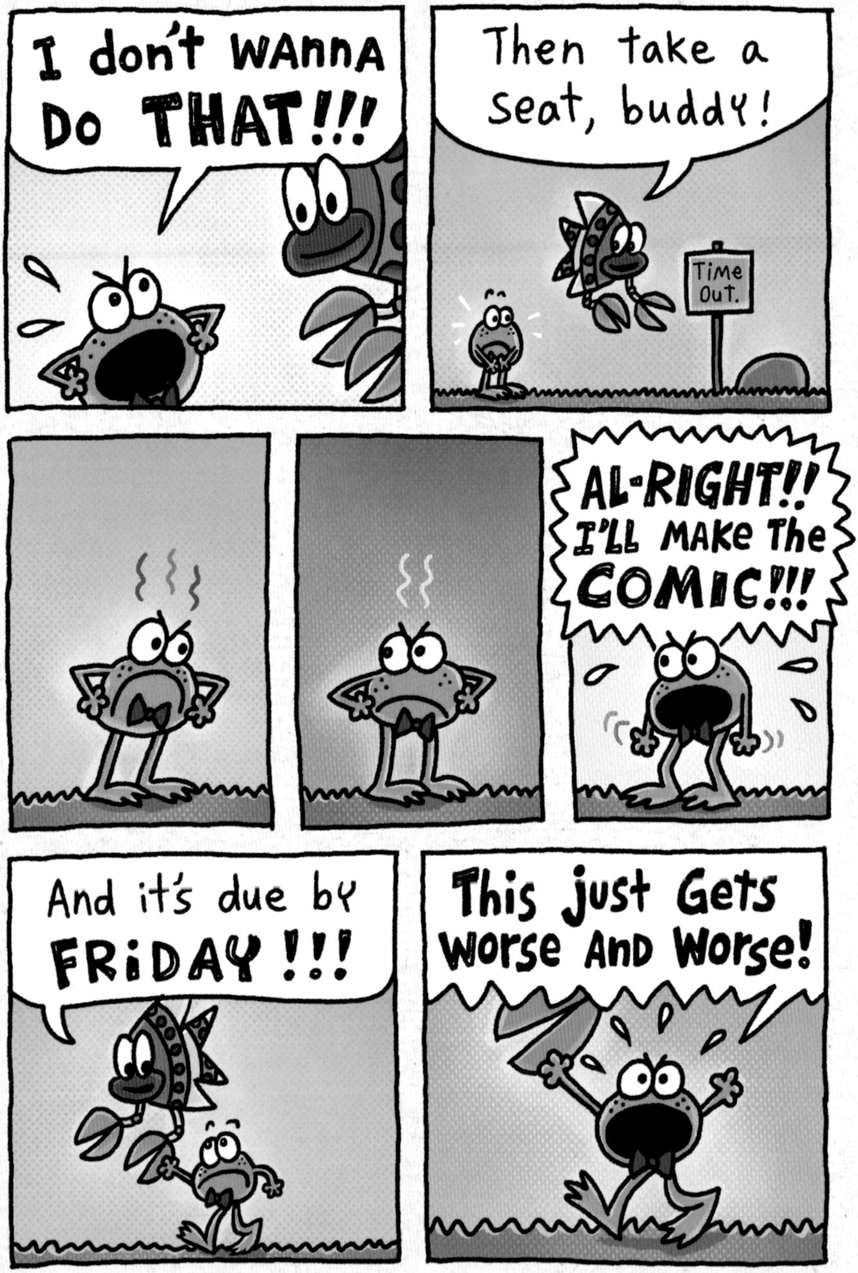
I don't WANNA DO THAT!!!
Then take a seat, buddy!
Time Out.
AL-RIGHT!! I'LL MAKE The COMIC!!!
And it's due by FRIDAY!!!
This just Gets worse AND Worse!

CHAPTER 5

The Next Day...

My Sister, Naomi

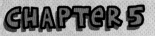

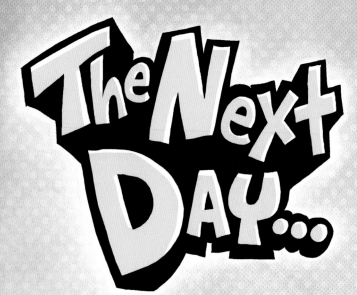

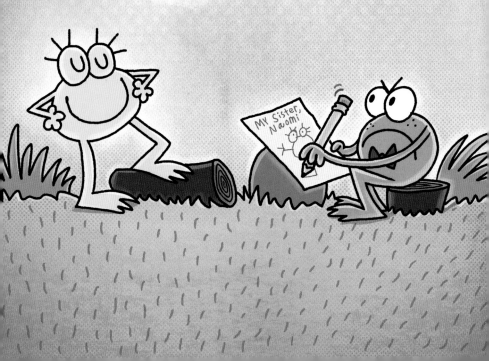

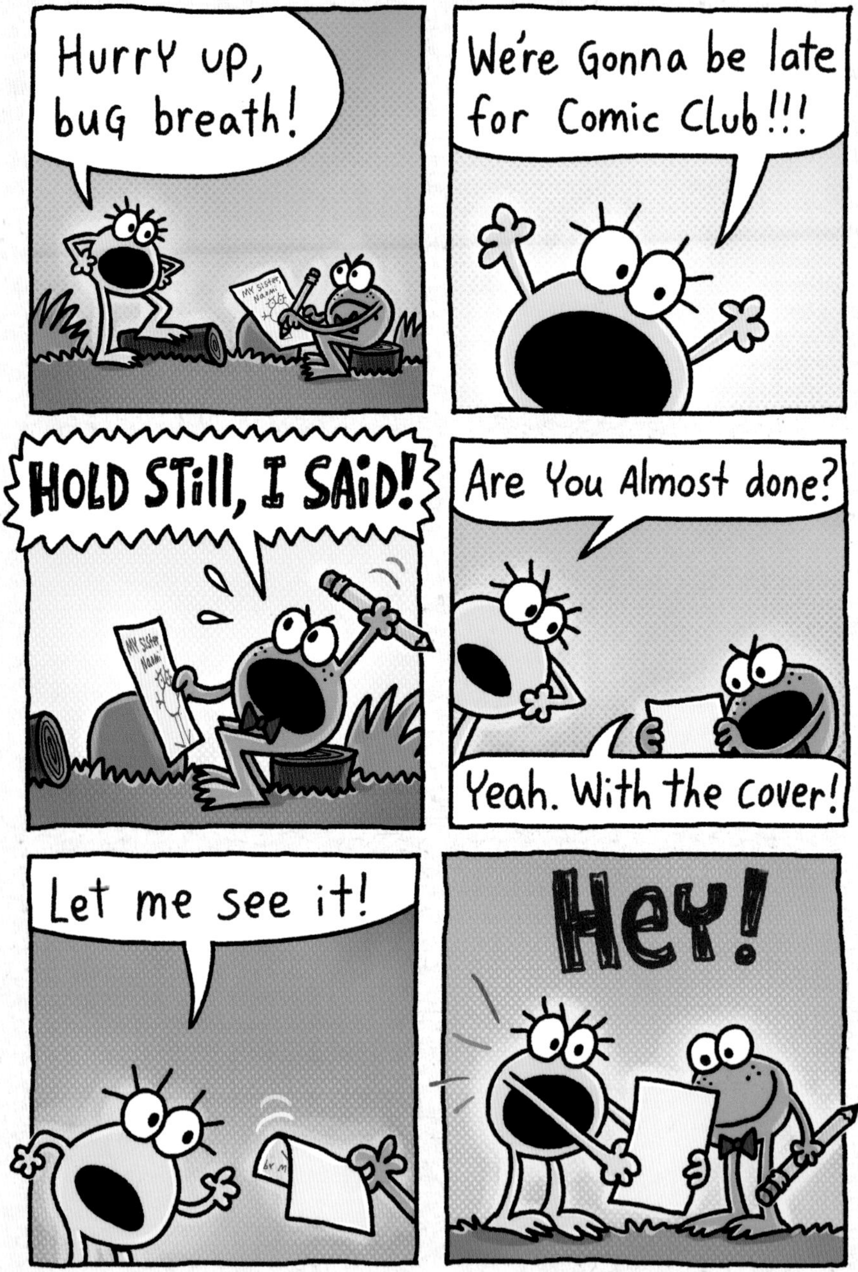
Hurry up, bug breath!
MY Sister, Naomi
We're Gonna be late for Comic Club!!!
HOLD STill, I SAiD!
MY Sister, Naomi
Are You Almost done?
Yeah. With the cover!
Let me see it!
HEY!

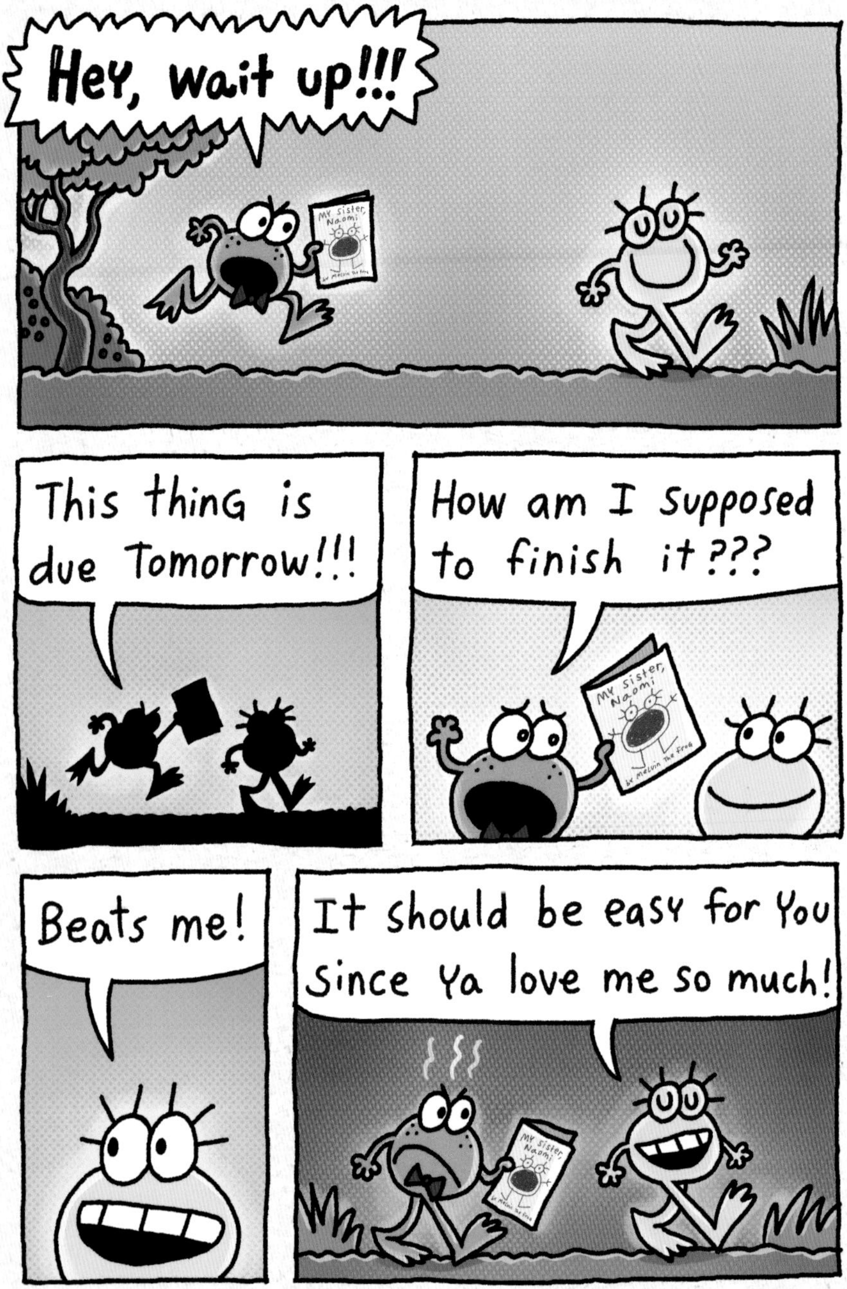
Hey, wait up!!!
MY sister, Naomi
This thing is due Tomorrow!!!
How am I supposed to finish it???
MY sister, Naomi
Beats me!
It should be easy for You since Ya love me so much!
MY sister, Naomi

CHAPTER 6

Sister Stories

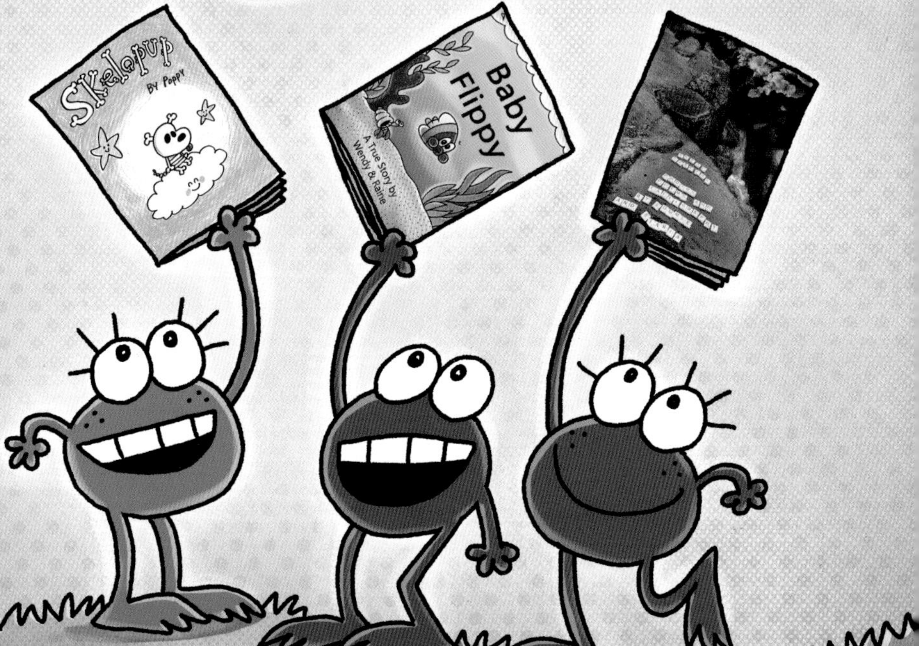
Skelopup
By Poppy
Baby Flippy
A True Story by Wendy & Raine

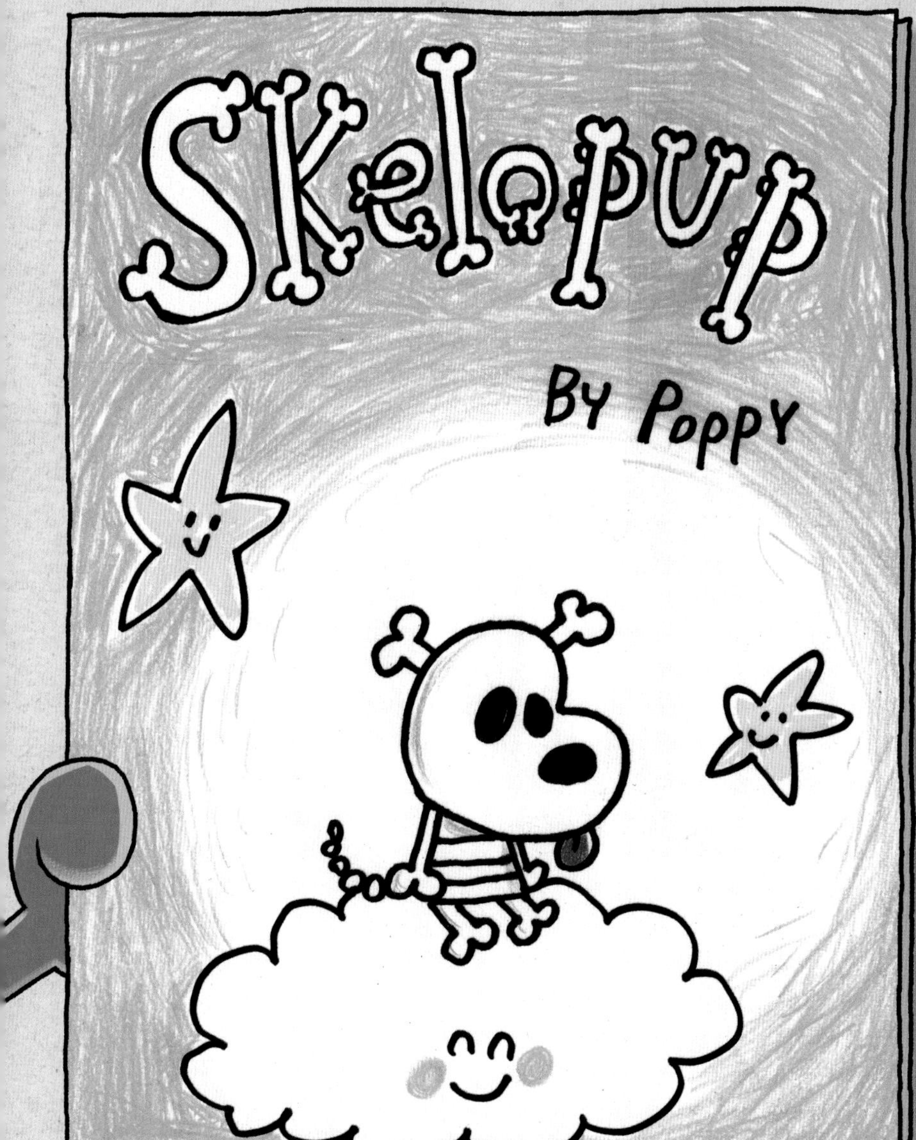
Skelopup
By Poppy

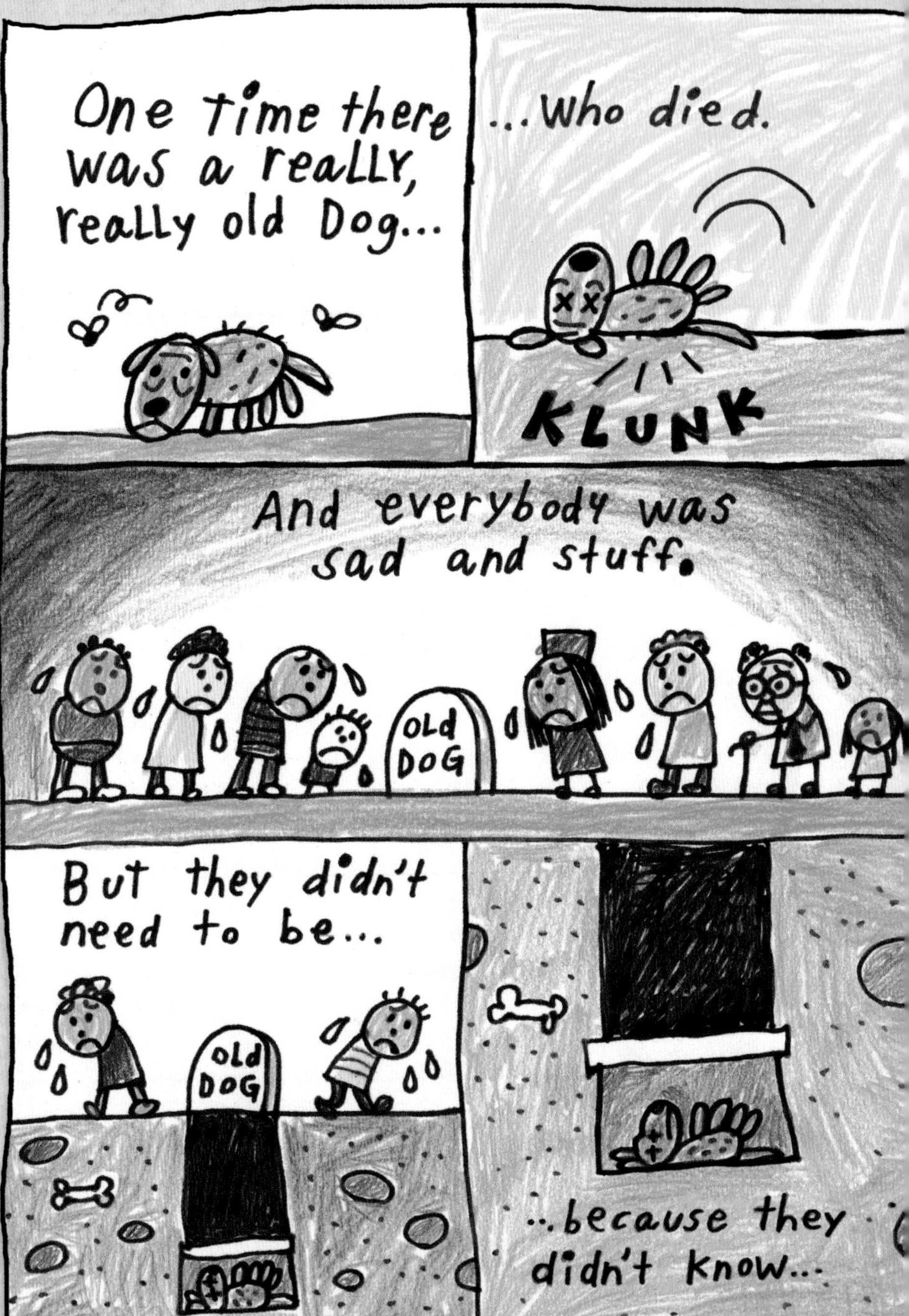
One time there was a really, really old Dog...
...Who died.
KLUNK
And everybody was sad and stuff.
OLD DOG
But they didn't need to be...
OLD DOG
...because they didn't know...

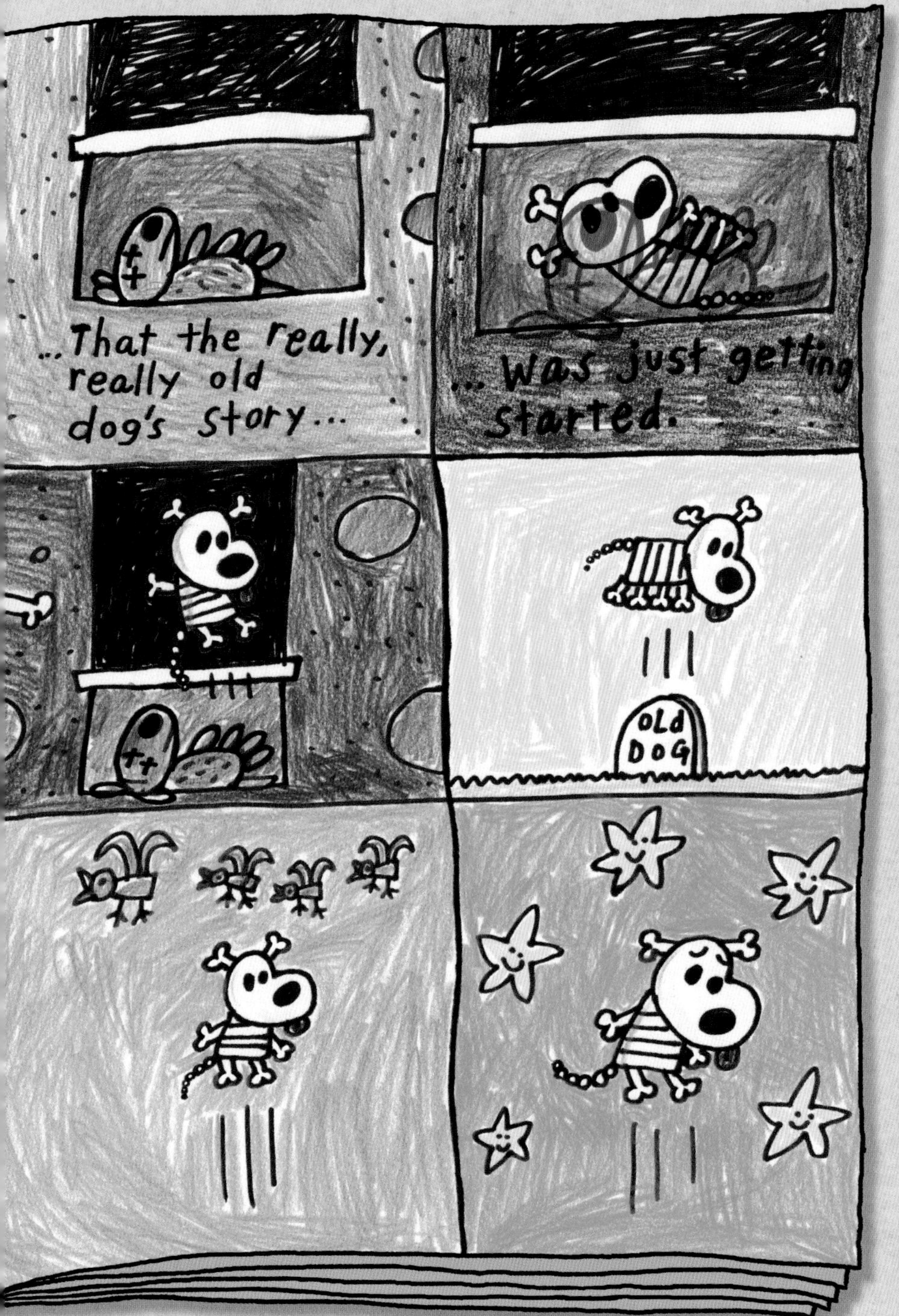
...That the really, really old dog's story...
...was just getting started.
OLD DOG

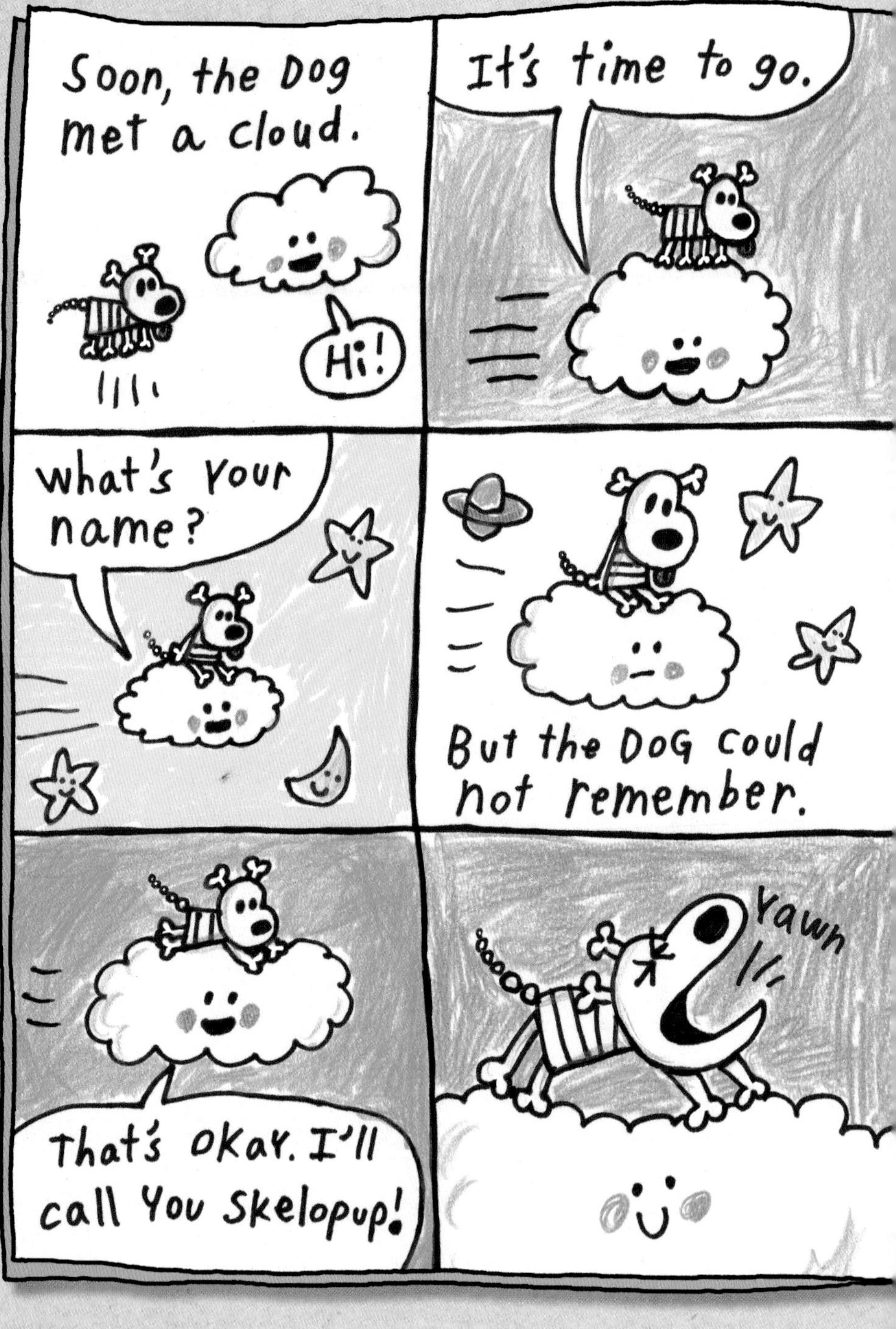
Soon, the Dog met a cloud.
Hi!
It's time to go.
what's your name?
But the DOG could not remember.
That's okay. I'll call You Skelopup!
Yawn

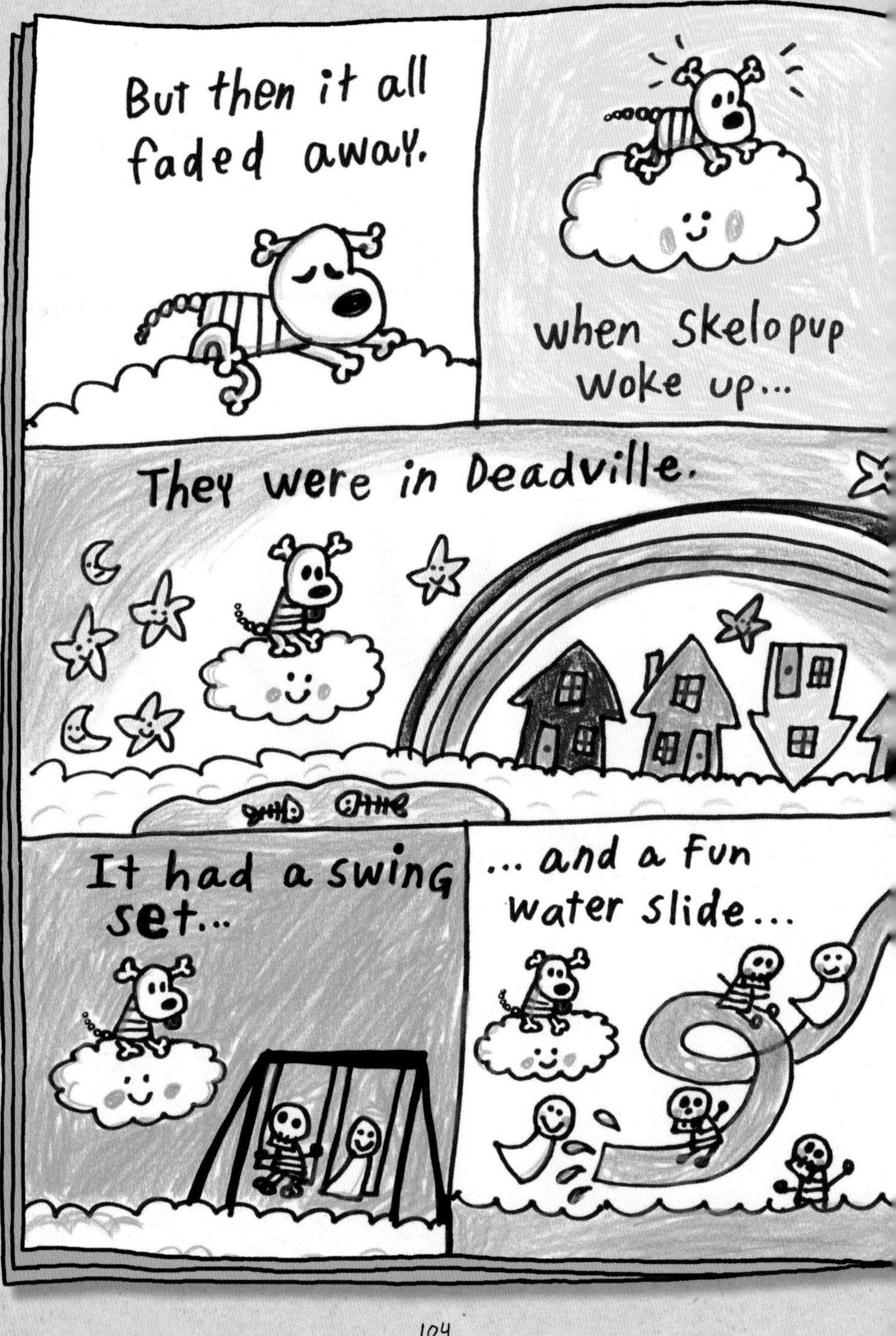

But then it all faded away.
when Skelopup woke up...
They were in Deadville.
It had a swing set...
... and a fun water slide...

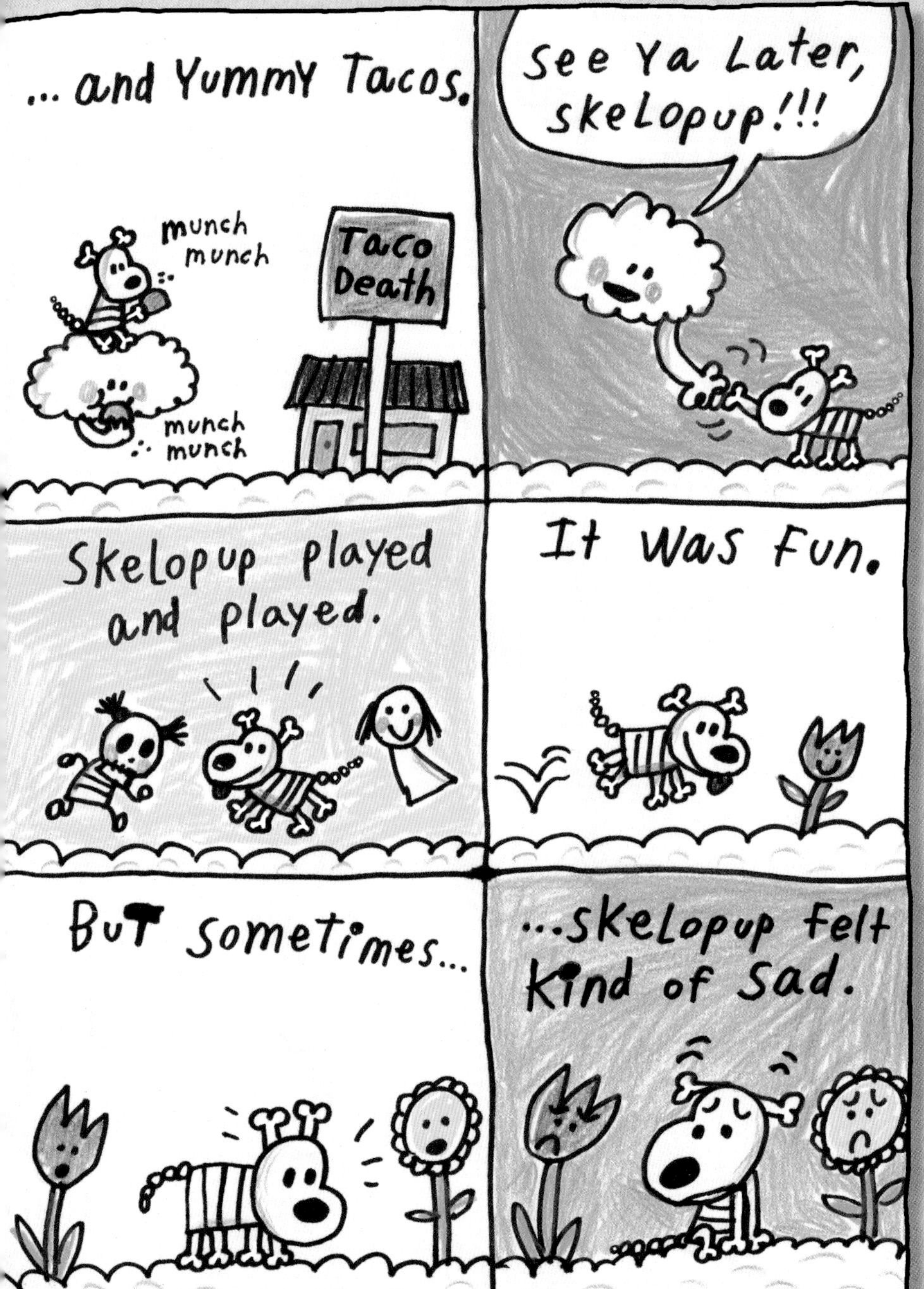
... and Yummy Tacos.
munch munch
Taco Death
munch munch
See Ya Later, skelopup!!!
Skelopup played and played.
It was Fun.
But sometimes...
...skelopup Felt Kind of Sad.

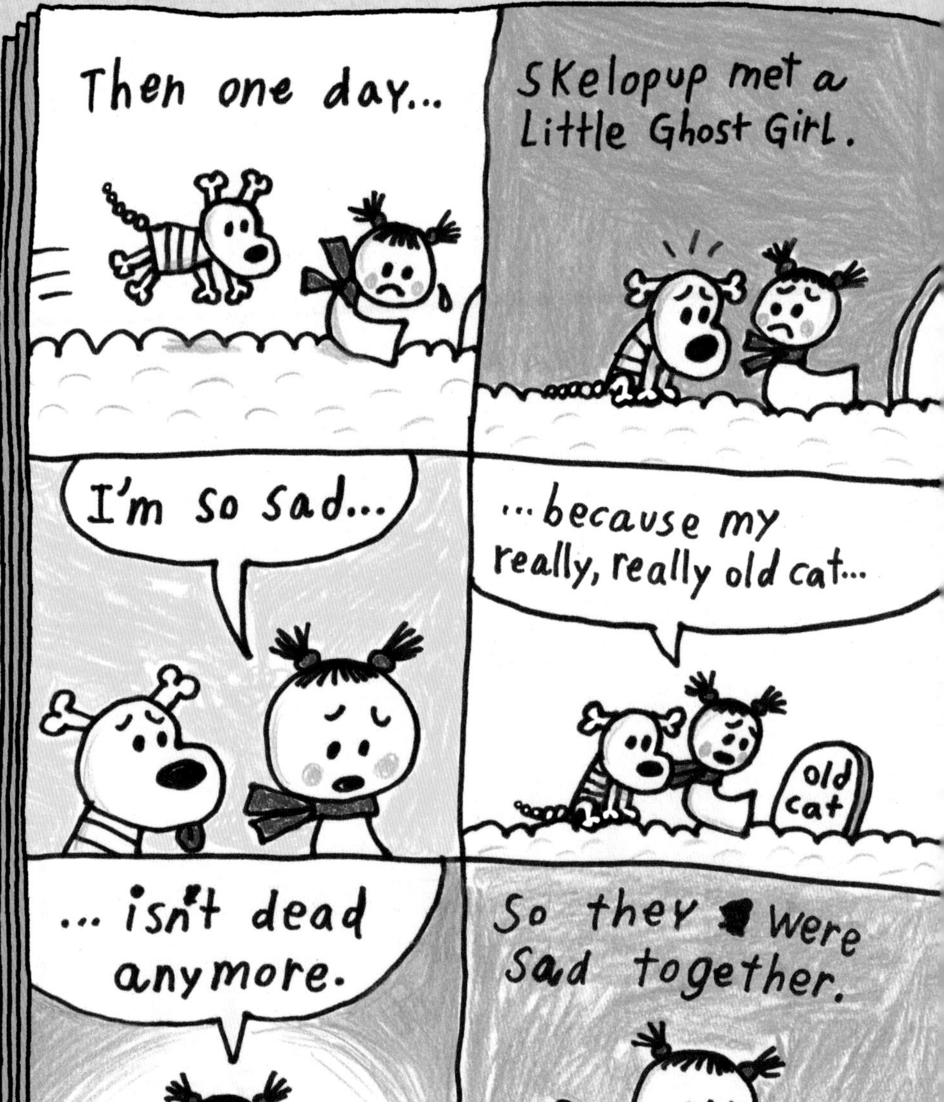
Then one day...
Skelopup met a Little Ghost Girl.
I'm so sad...
...because my really, really old cat...
old cat
...isn't dead anymore.
old cat
So they were sad together.
old cat

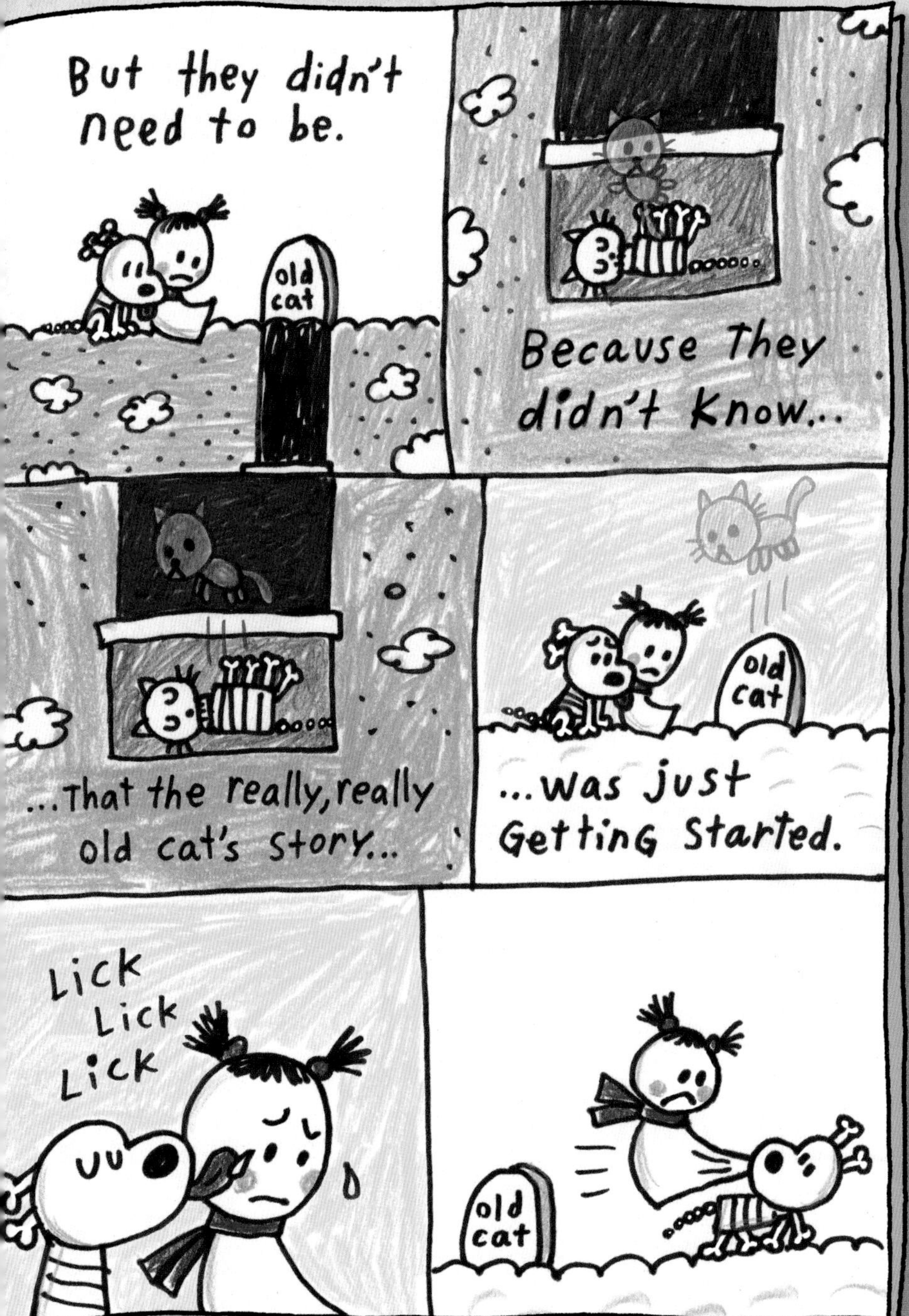
But they didn't need to be.
old cat
Because They didn't Know...
...That the really, really old cat's story...
...was just Getting Started.
old cat
Lick Lick Lick
old cat

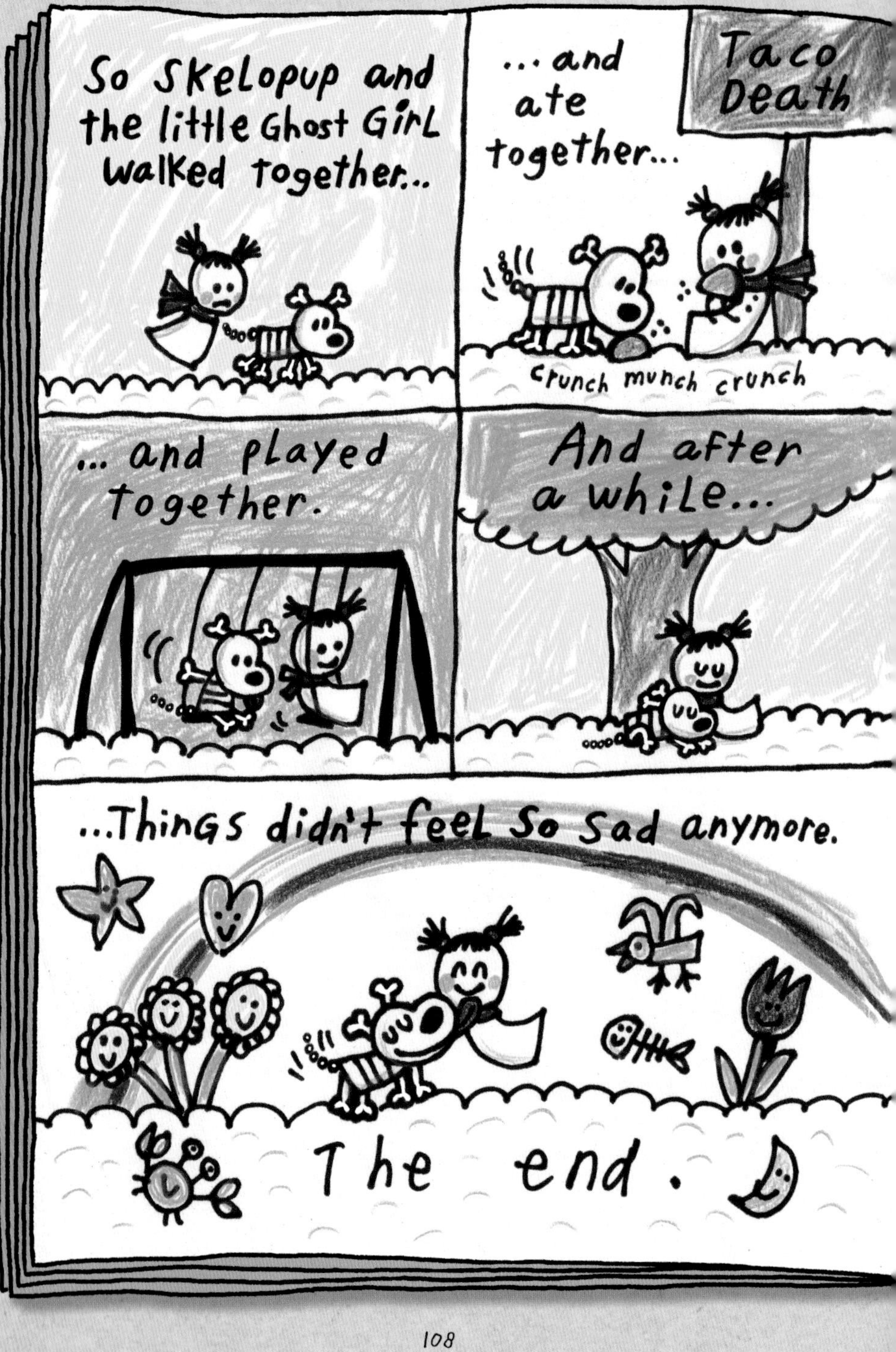
So Skelopup and the little Ghost Girl walked together...
...and ate together...
Taco Death
crunch munch crunch
... and played together.
And after a while...
...Things didn't feel so sad anymore.
The end.

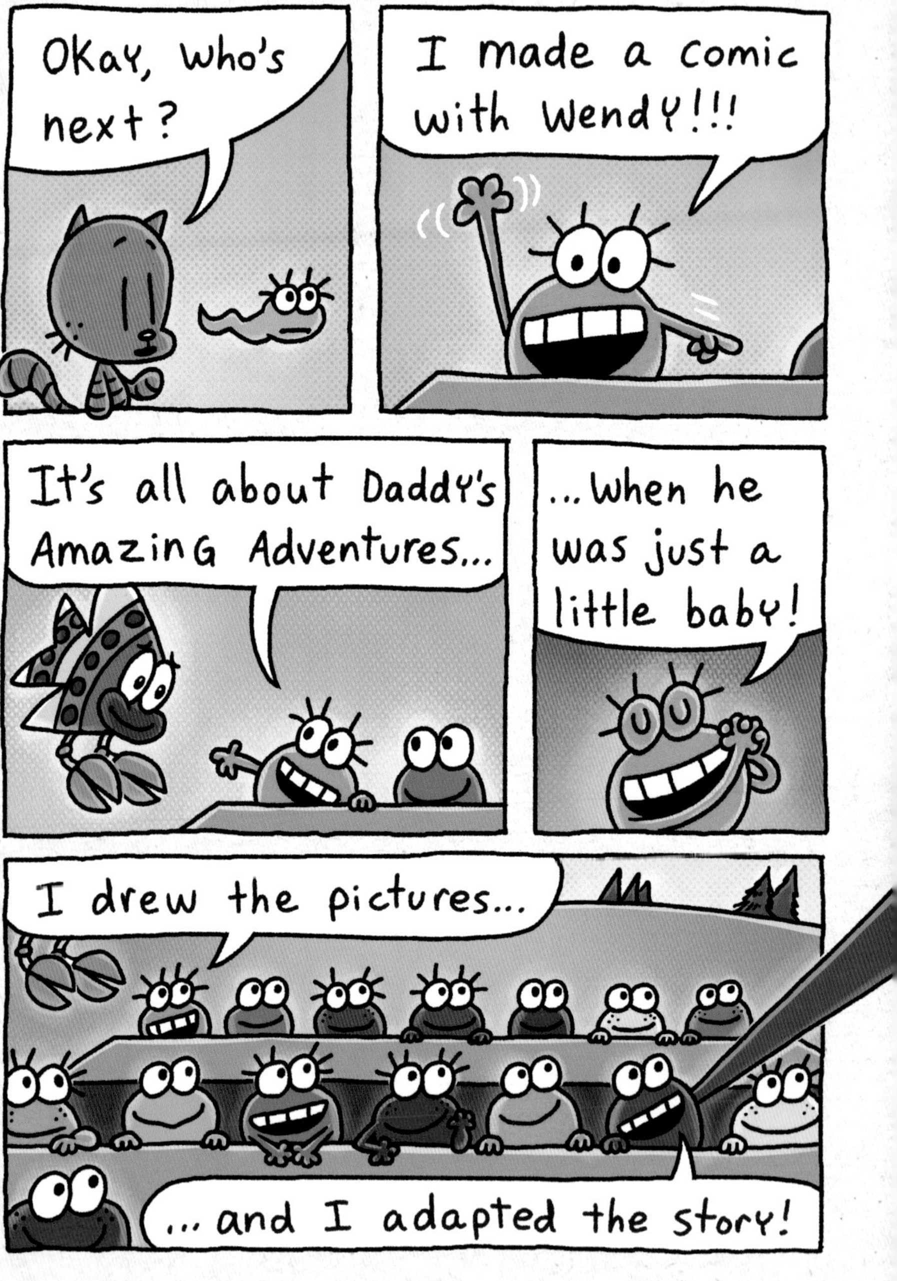
OKAY, who's next?
I made a comic with Wendy!!!
It's all about Daddy's Amazing Adventures...
...when he was just a little baby!
I drew the pictures...
...and I adapted the story!

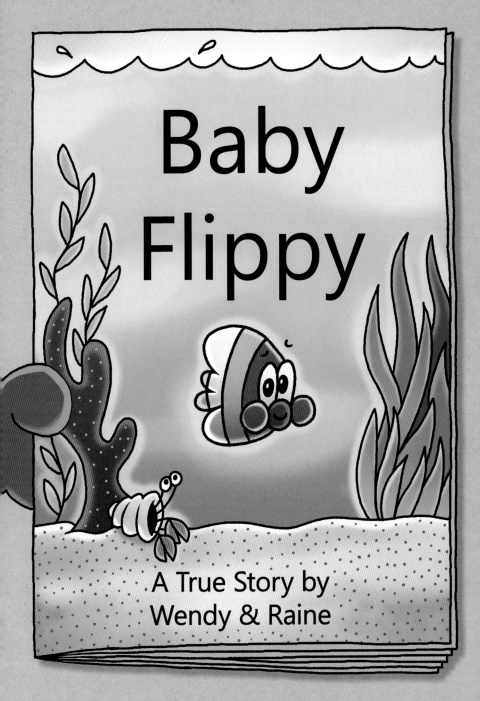

Baby
Flippy

A True Story by
Wendy & Raine

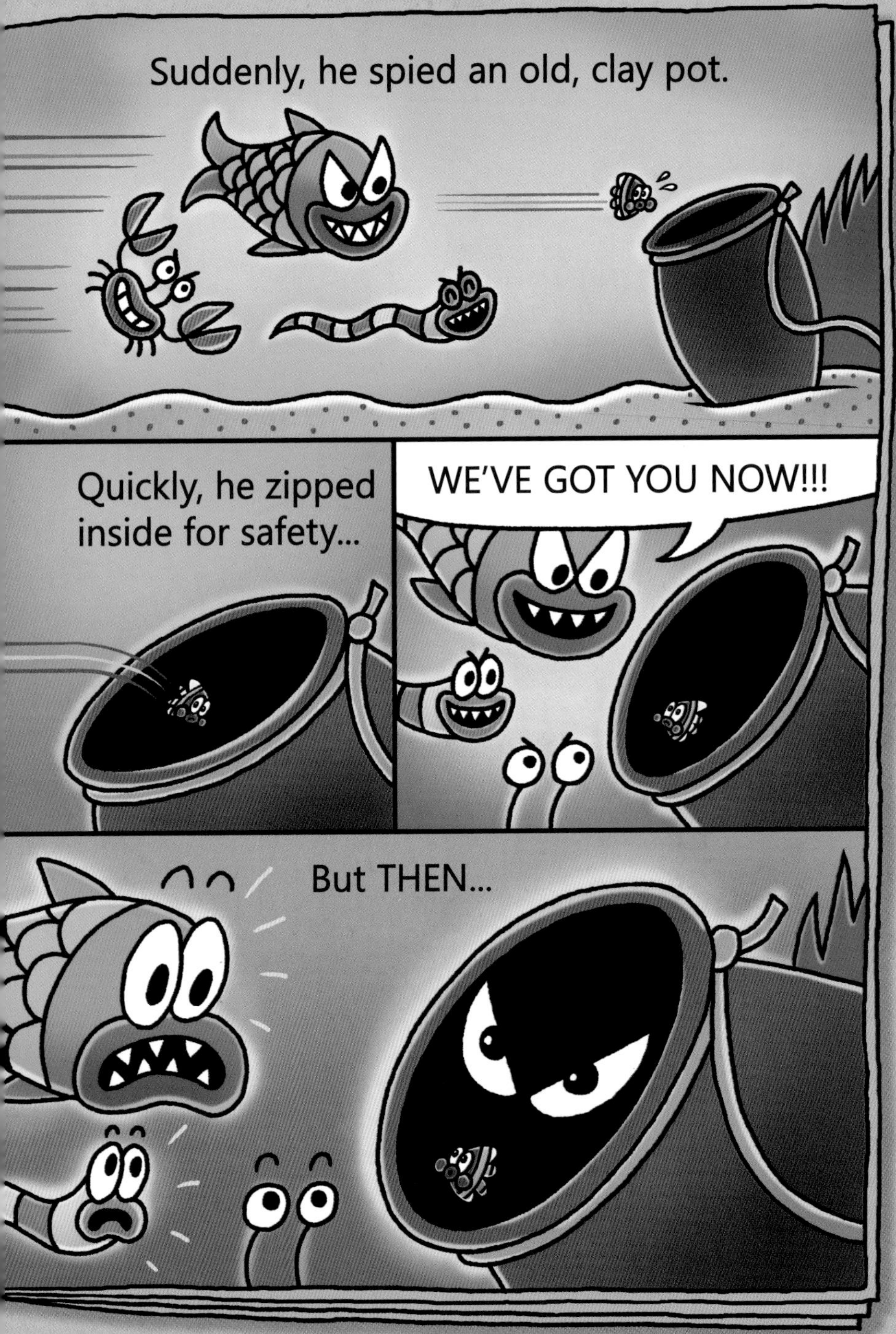
Suddenly, he spied an old, clay pot.
Quickly, he zipped
inside for safety...
WE'VE GOT YOU NOW!!!
But THEN...

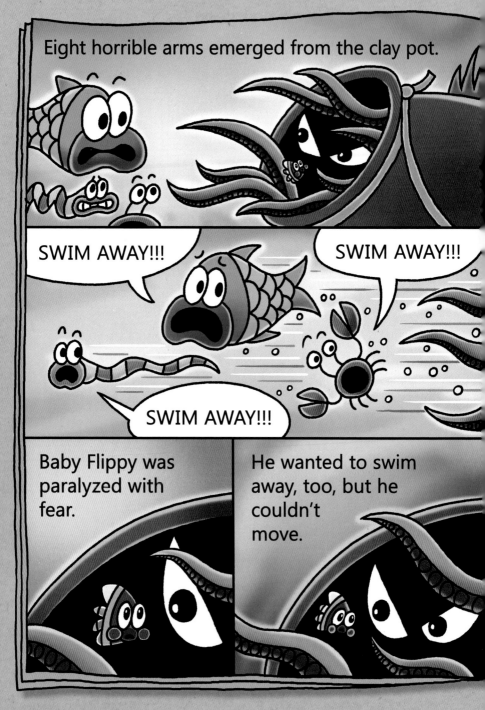

Eight horrible arms emerged from the clay pot.

SWIM AWAY!!!

SWIM AWAY!!!

SWIM AWAY!!!

Baby Flippy was paralyzed with fear.

He wanted to swim away, too, but he couldn't move.

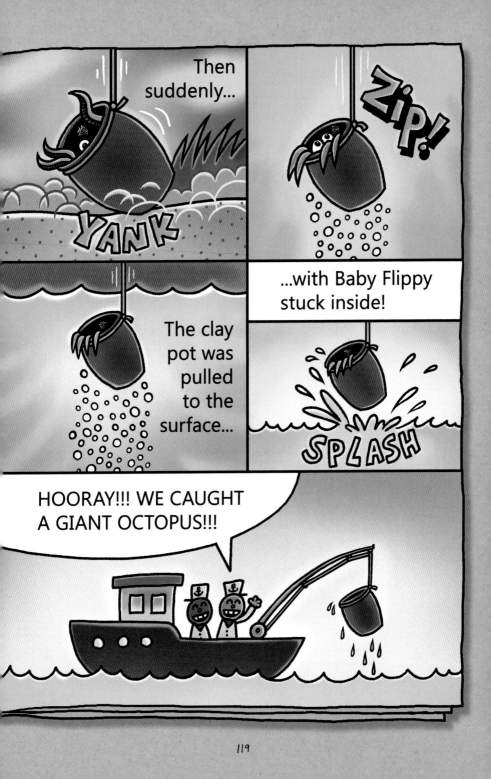

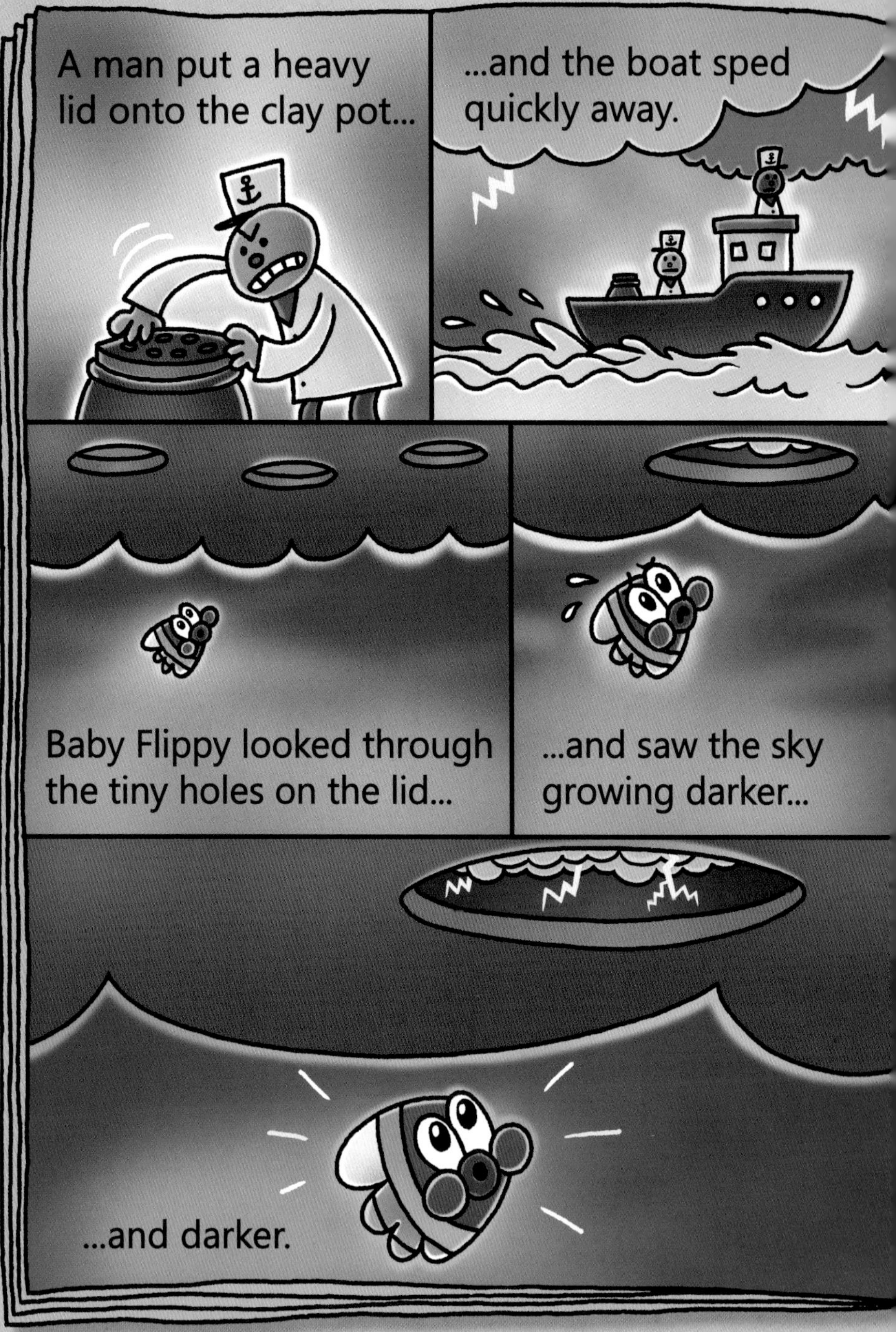
A man put a heavy lid onto the clay pot...
...and the boat sped quickly away.
Baby Flippy looked through the tiny holes on the lid...
...and saw the sky growing darker...
...and darker.

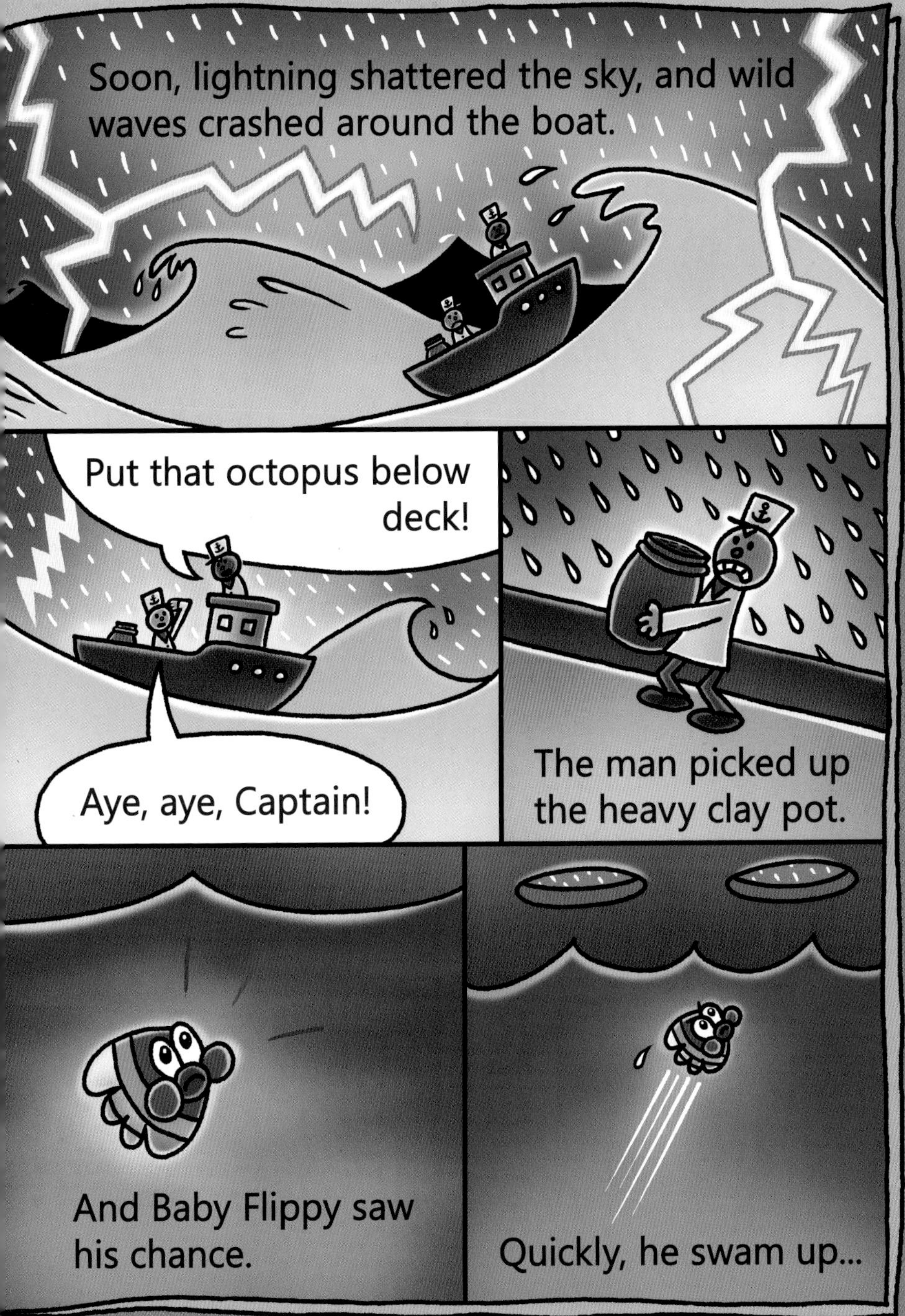
Soon, lightning shattered the sky, and wild waves crashed around the boat.
Put that octopus below deck!
Aye, aye, Captain!
The man picked up the heavy clay pot.
And Baby Flippy saw his chance.
Quickly, he swam up...

122

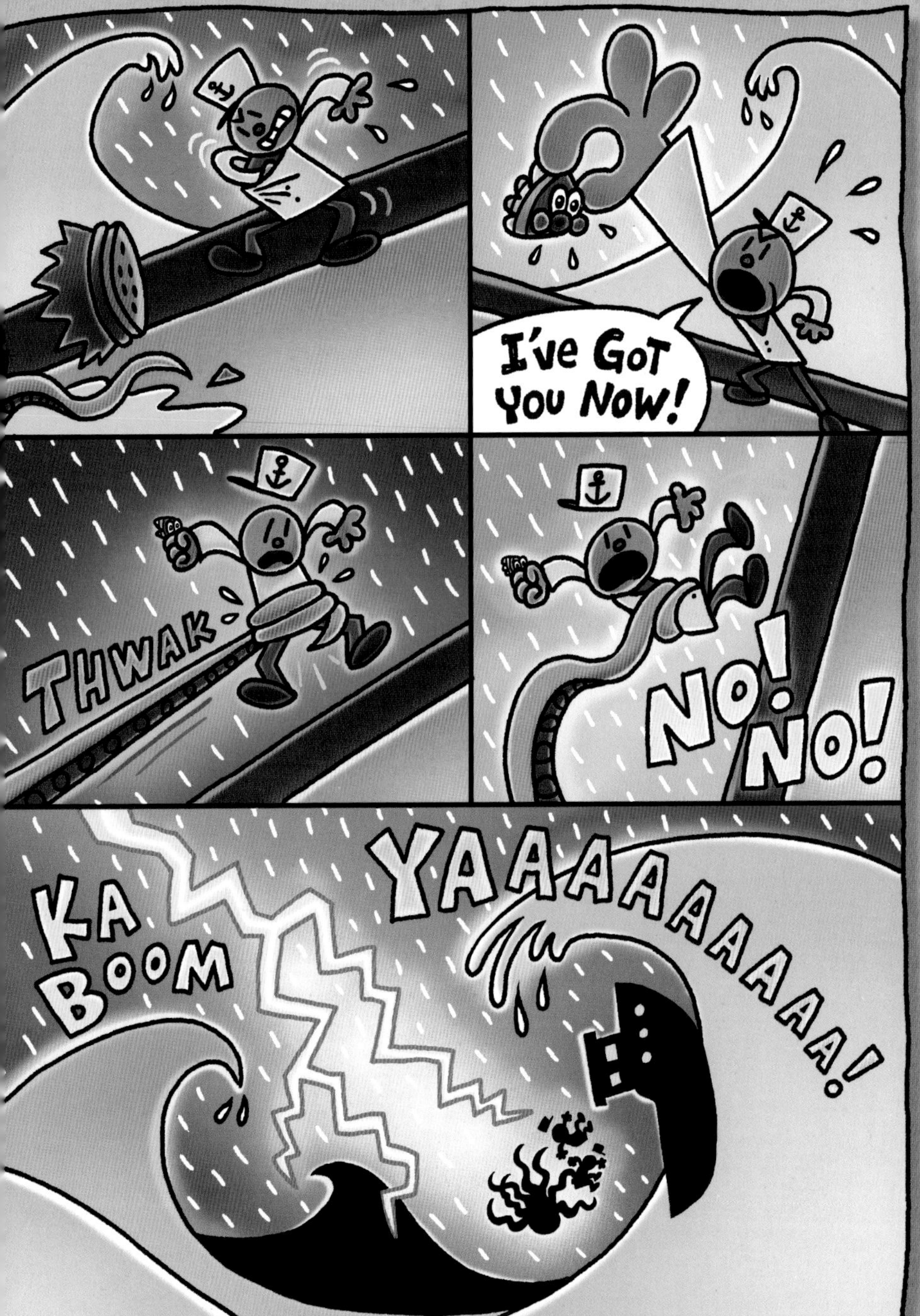
I've GoT YOU NOW!
THWAK
NO! NO!
KA BOOM
YAAAAAAAAAAA!

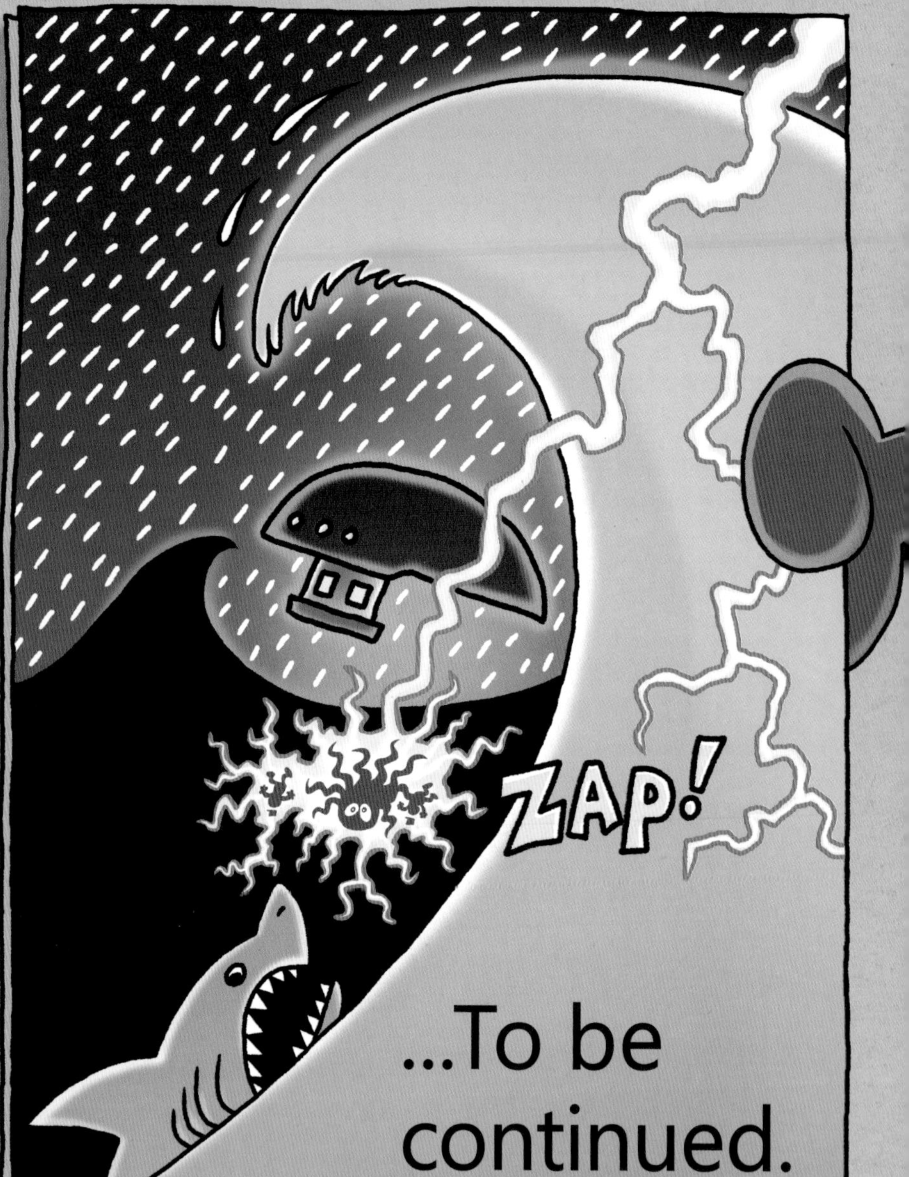
ZAP!
...To be continued.

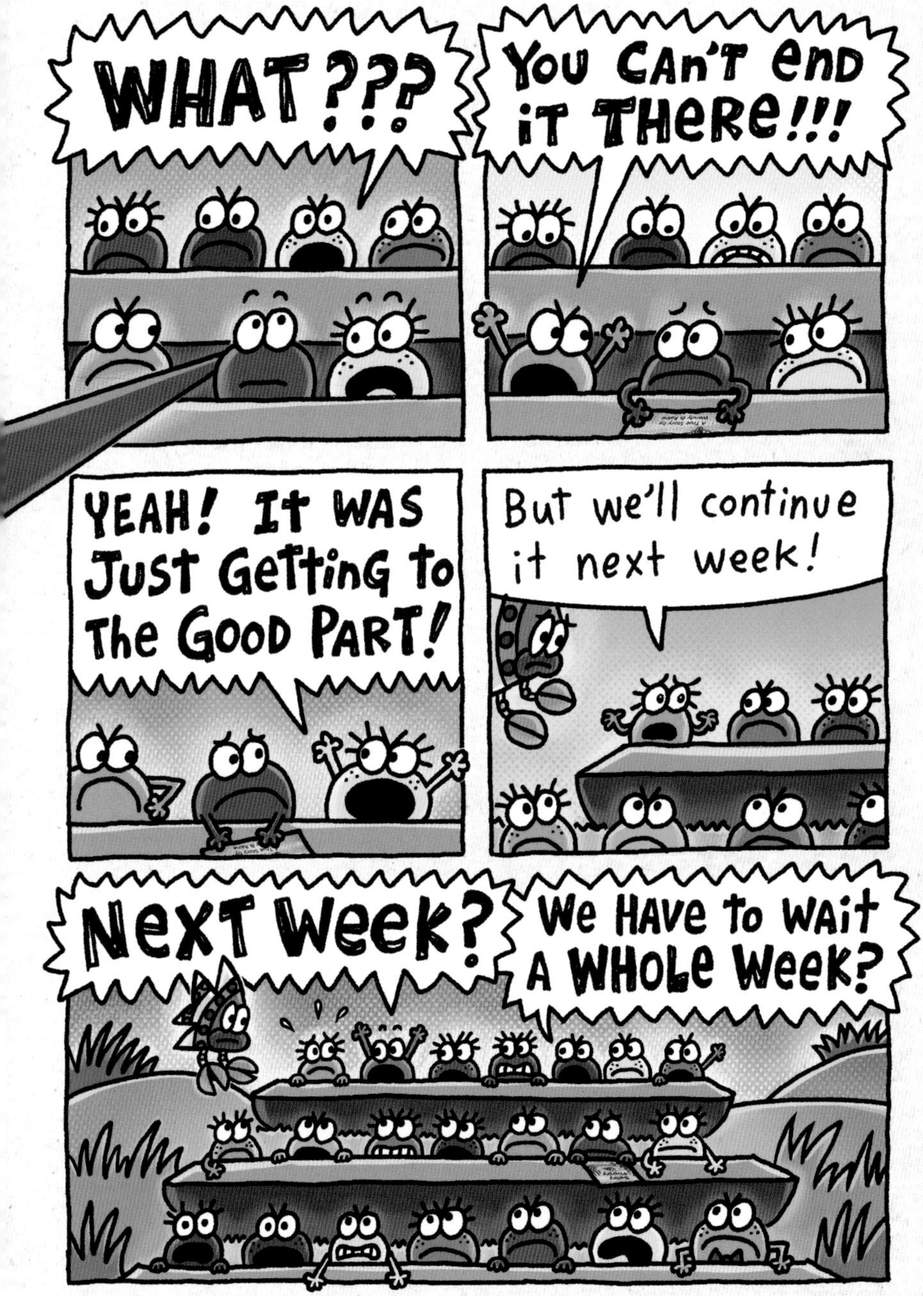
WHAT???
YOU CAN'T END IT THERE!!!
YEAH! IT WAS JUST GETTING TO THE GOOD PART!
But we'll continue it next week!
NEXT WEEK?
WE HAVE TO WAIT A WHOLE WEEK?

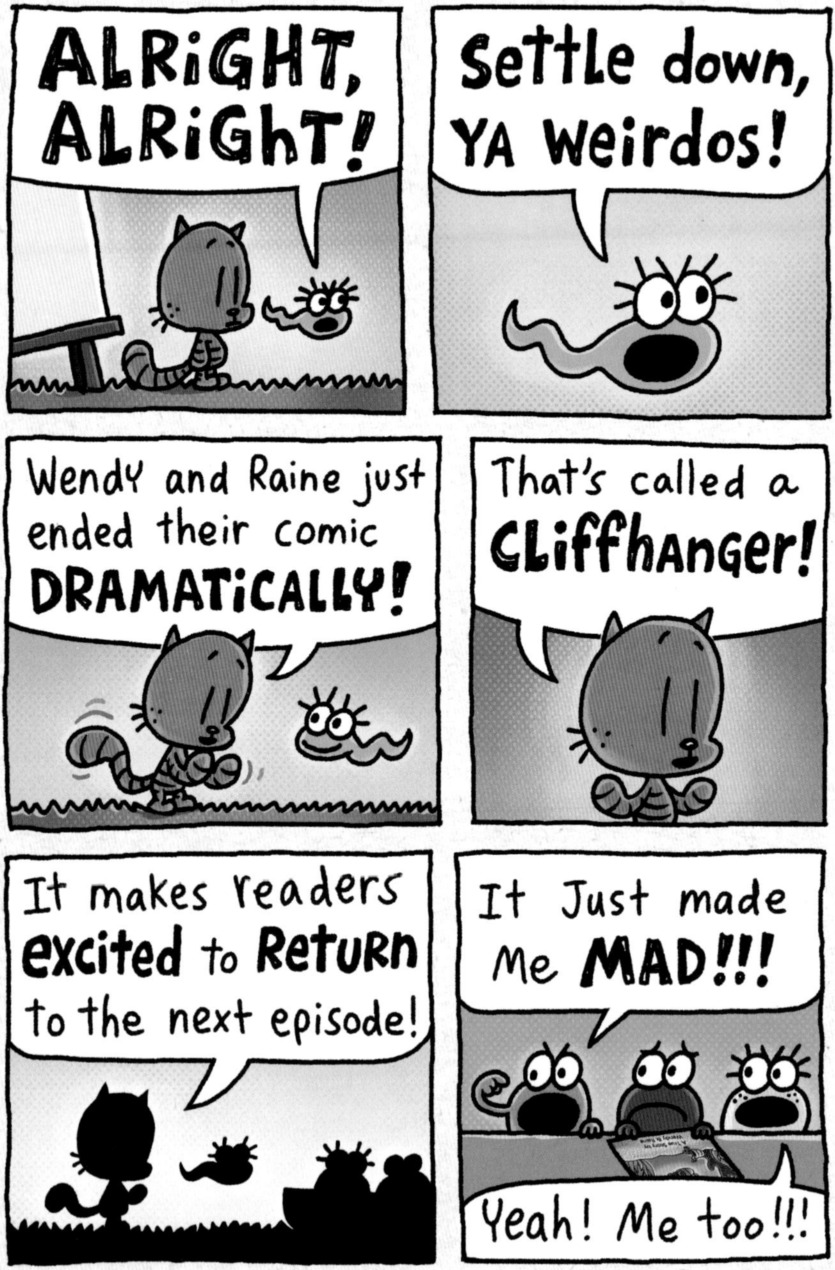
ALRiGHT, ALRiGhT!
Settle down, YA Weirdos!
Wendy and Raine just ended their comic DRAMATiCALLY!
That's called a CLiffhanger!
It makes readers excited to Return to the next episode!
It Just made Me MAD!!!
Yeah! Me too!!!

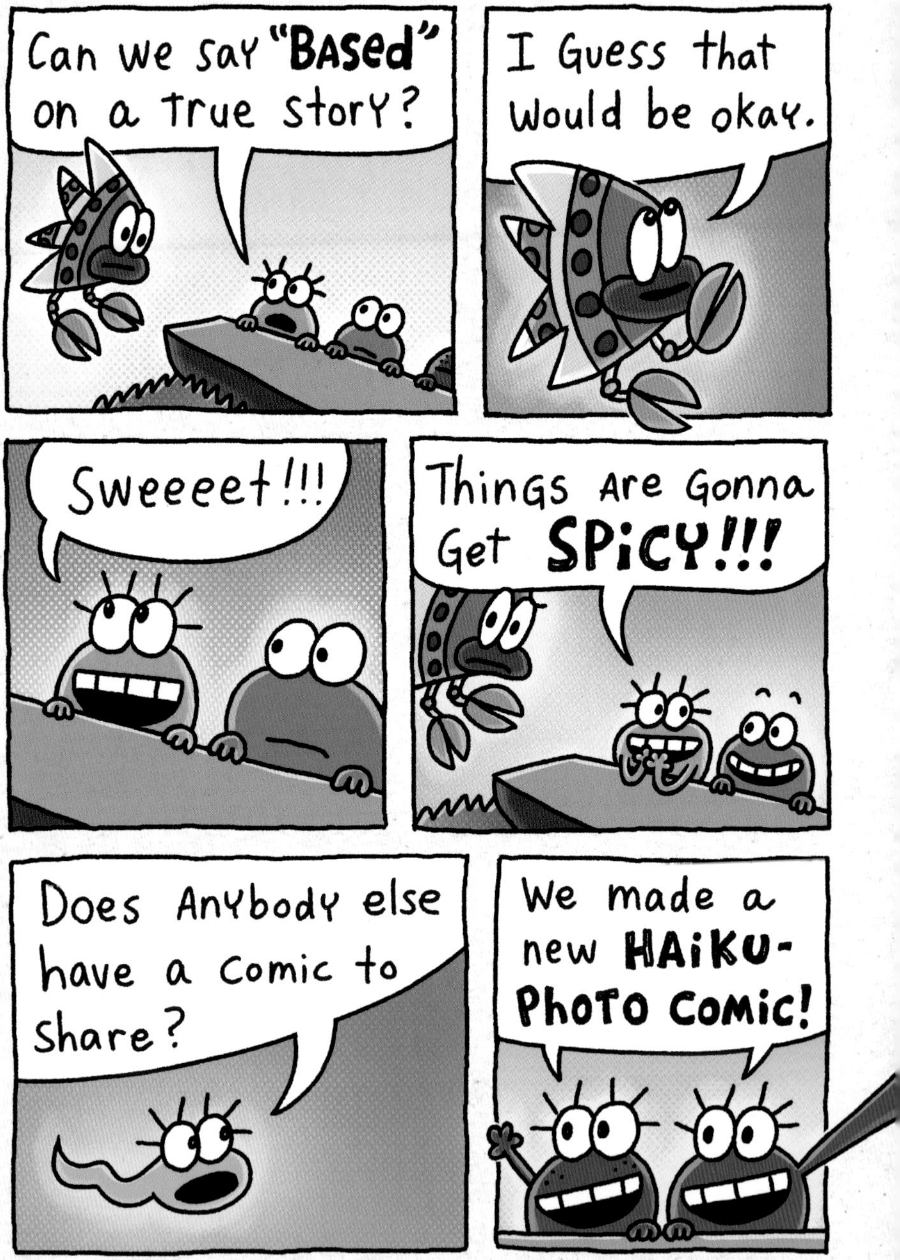
Can we say "BASED" on a true story?
I Guess that would be okay.
Sweeeet!!!
Things Are Gonna Get SPICY!!!
Does Anybody else have a comic to share?
We made a new HAIKU-PHOTO COMIC!

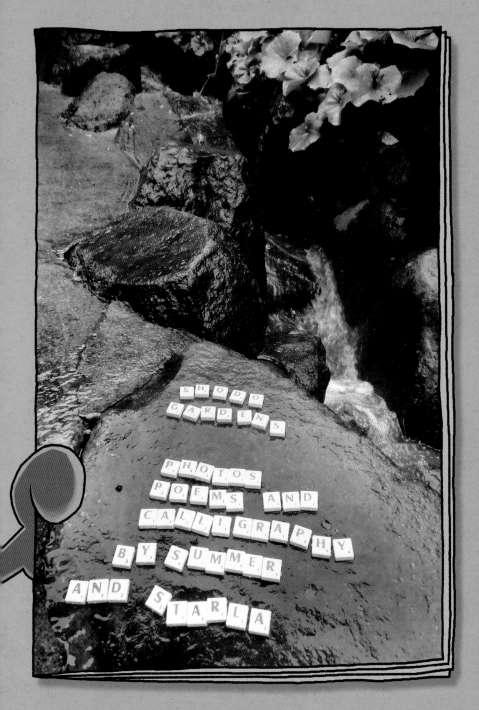

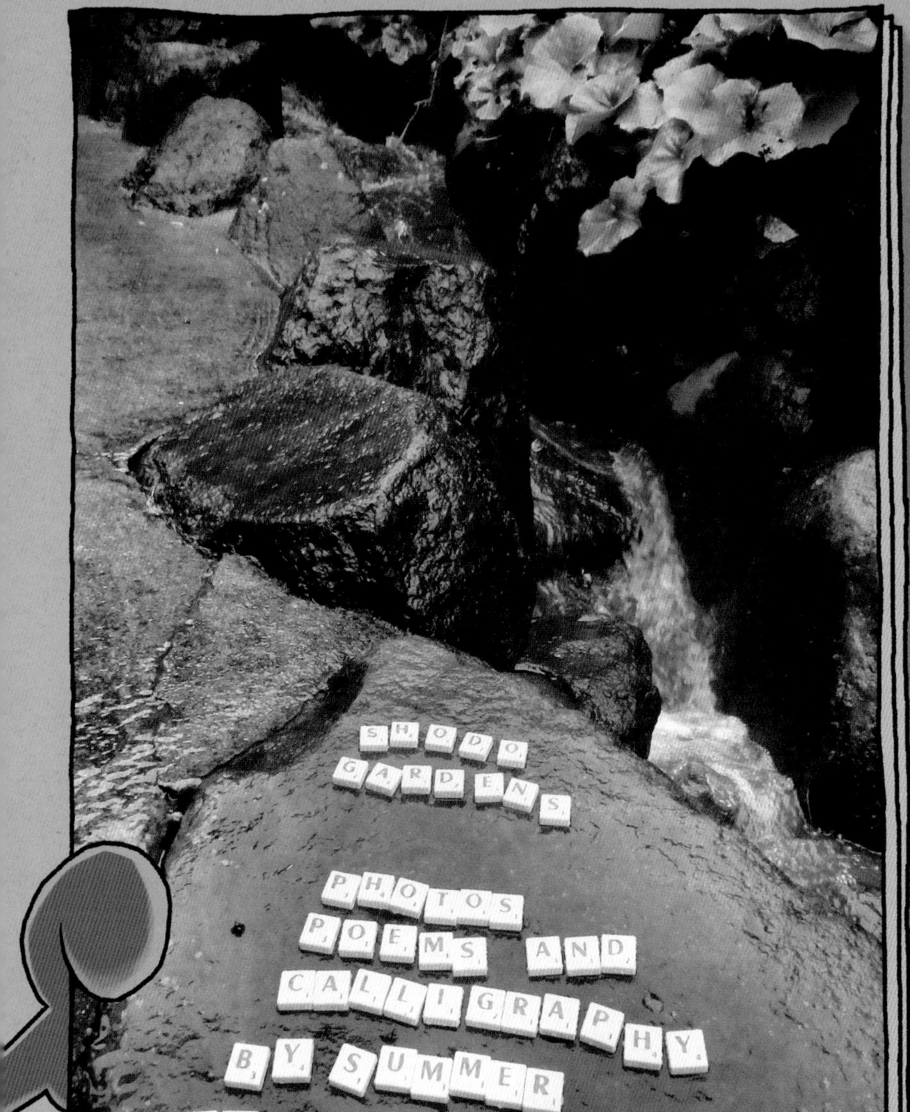
SHODO GARDENS
PHOTOS POEMS AND CALLIGRAPHY BY SUMMER AND STARLA

little blade of grass
even though the world is hard
you have found a way

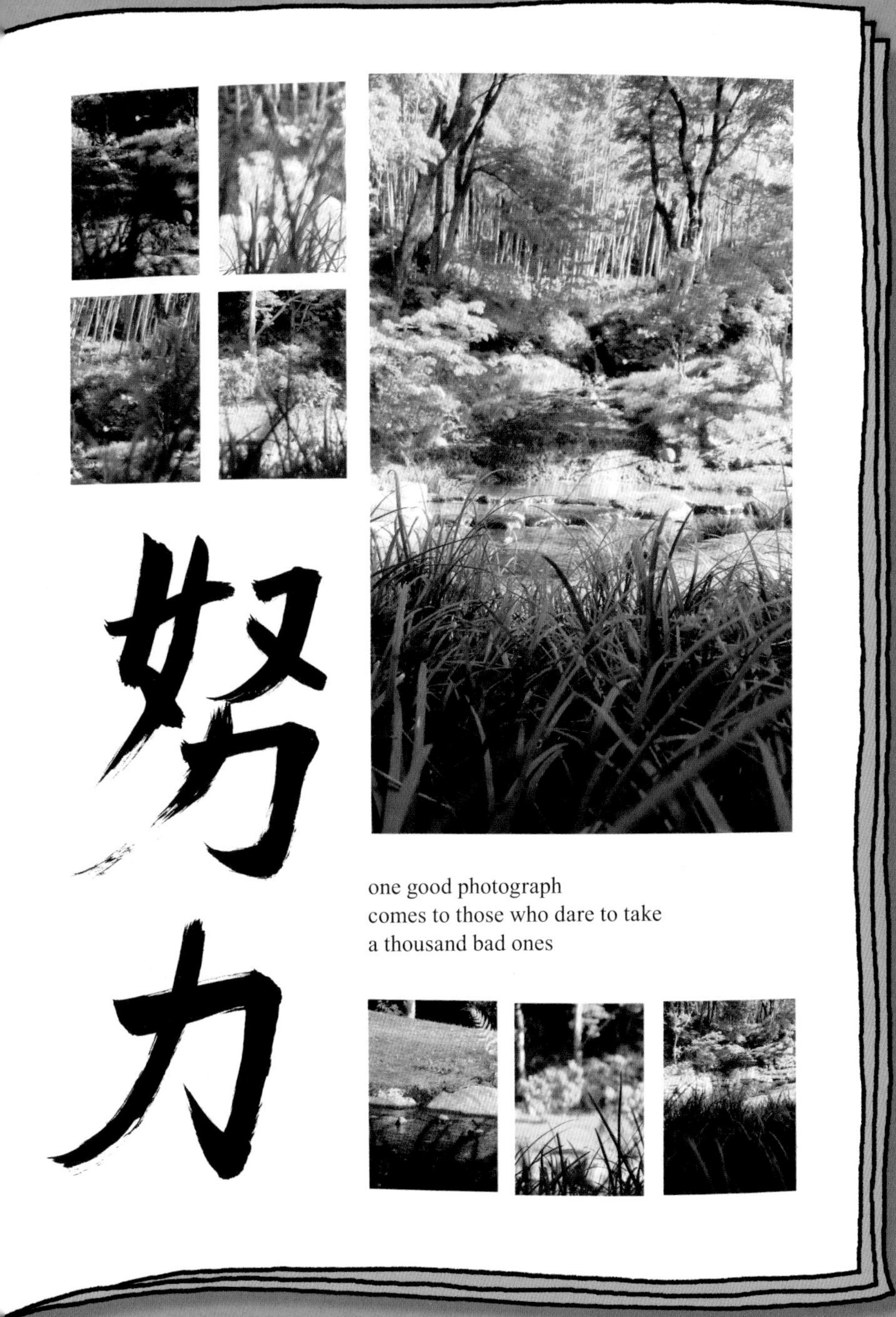
努力
one good photograph
comes to those who dare to take
a thousand bad ones

bold, black butterfly
spread your wings in the morning
and bathe in the sun

自
信

if you're the pink one
don't worry about the rest.
just be the pink one

花火

garden fireworks
bursting bright in clouds of moss
nature celebrates

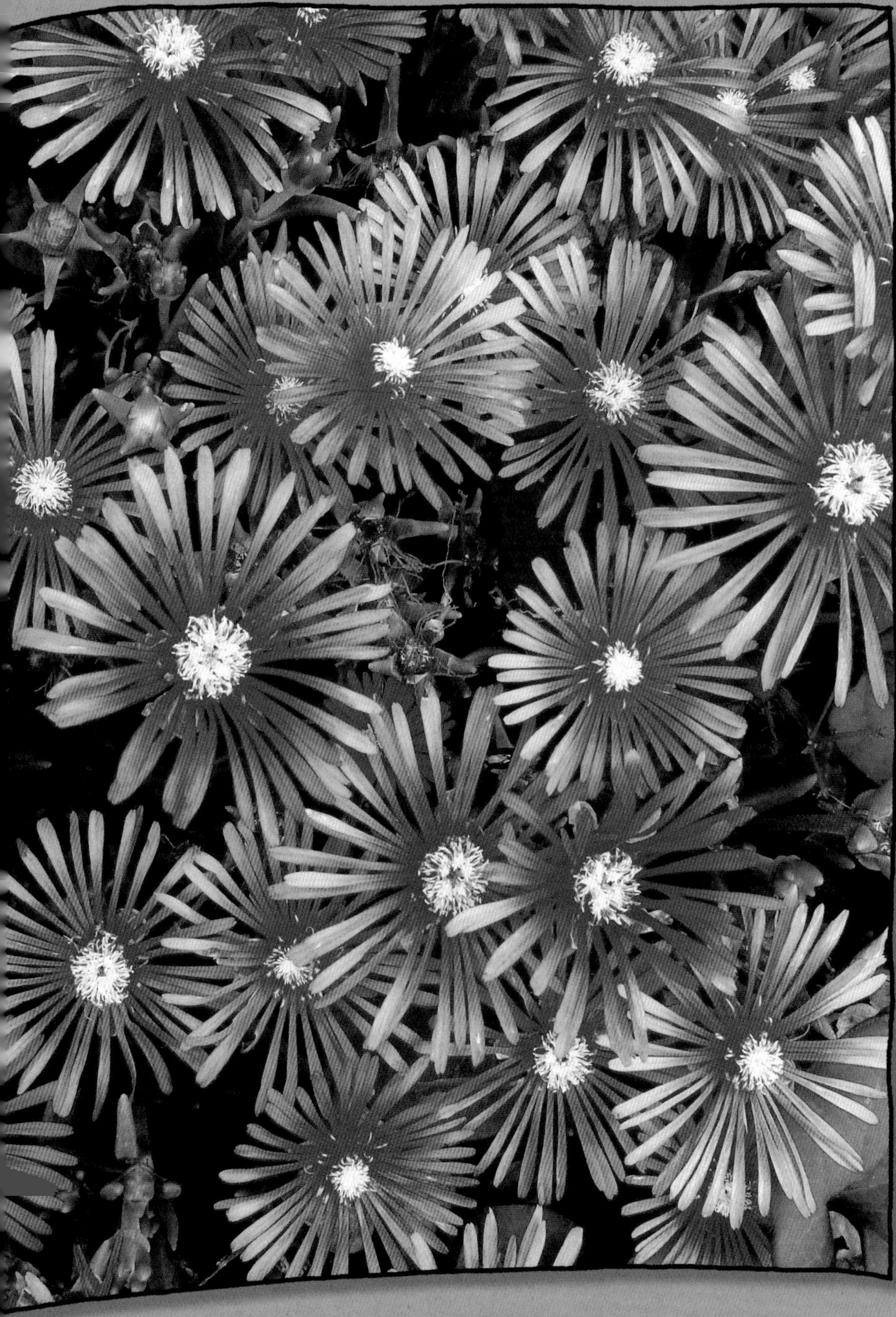

Haiku and Shodo
are types of Japanese art
with structure and rules.

but with these two arts,
feeling is more important
than anything else.

one must know the rules
in order to move past them.
learn, then step beyond...

Each Shodo character can have many meanings.
These are some meanings for the ones we painted:

道   Way, means, road

努力   Try hard + Power
= Endeavor

開   Open or unfold

自信   Self-confidence
[+ Trust]

花火   Flower + Fire
= Fireworks

Naomi Kuratani, Akemi Kobayashi, Shunsuke Okunishi, *A New Dictionary of Kanji Usage* (Tokyo: Gakken Co., LTD., 1982).

Summer and Starla would like to acknowledge and thank the artists who inspired them recently, including:

Shoko Kanazawa, who is one of Japan's most highly respected Shodo artists. She paints from her heart with giant brushes. She also has Down's syndrome.

And

Shozo Sato, author of *Shodo: The Quiet Art of Japanese Zen Calligraphy* (Rutland: Tuttle Publishing, 2014).

137

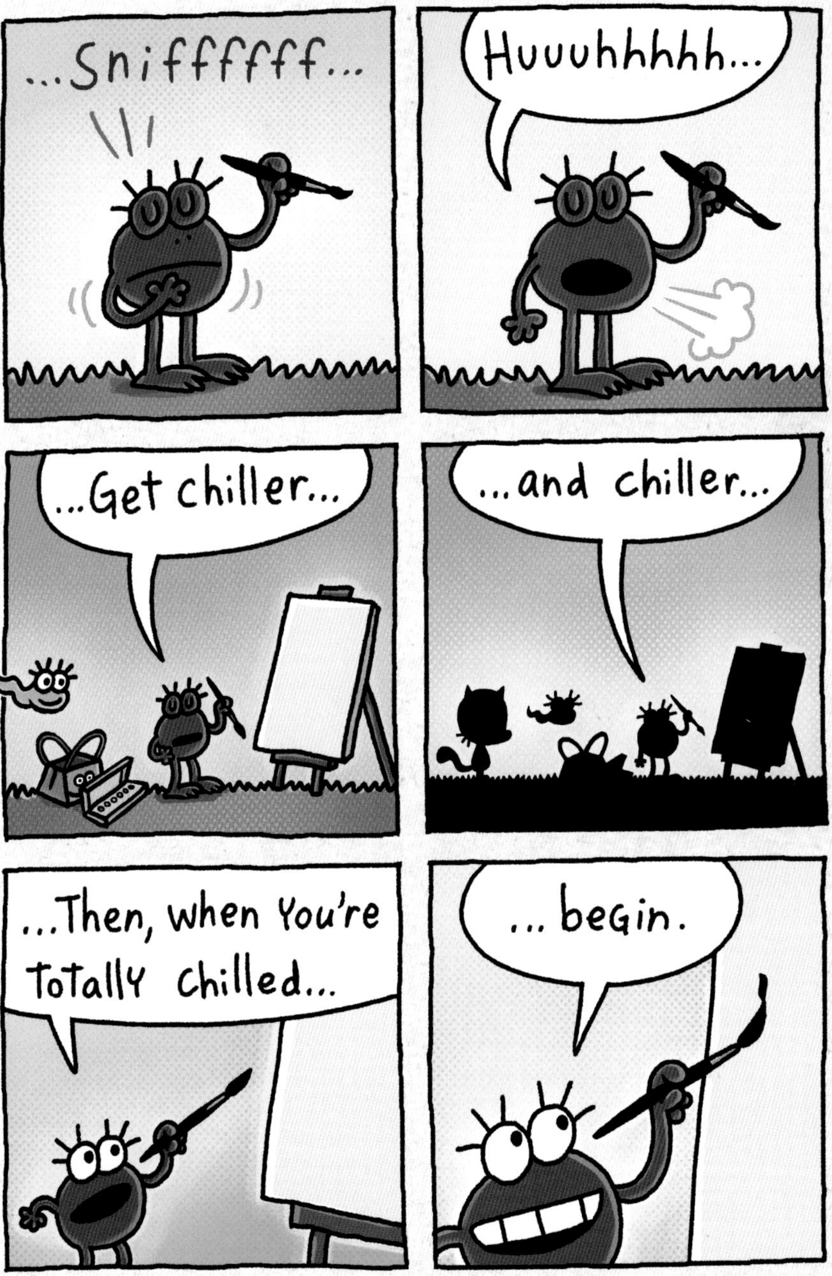
...Sniffffff...
Huuuhhhhh...
...Get chiller...
...and chiller...
...Then, when you're totally chilled...
...begin.

Chapter 7

The Inspiration

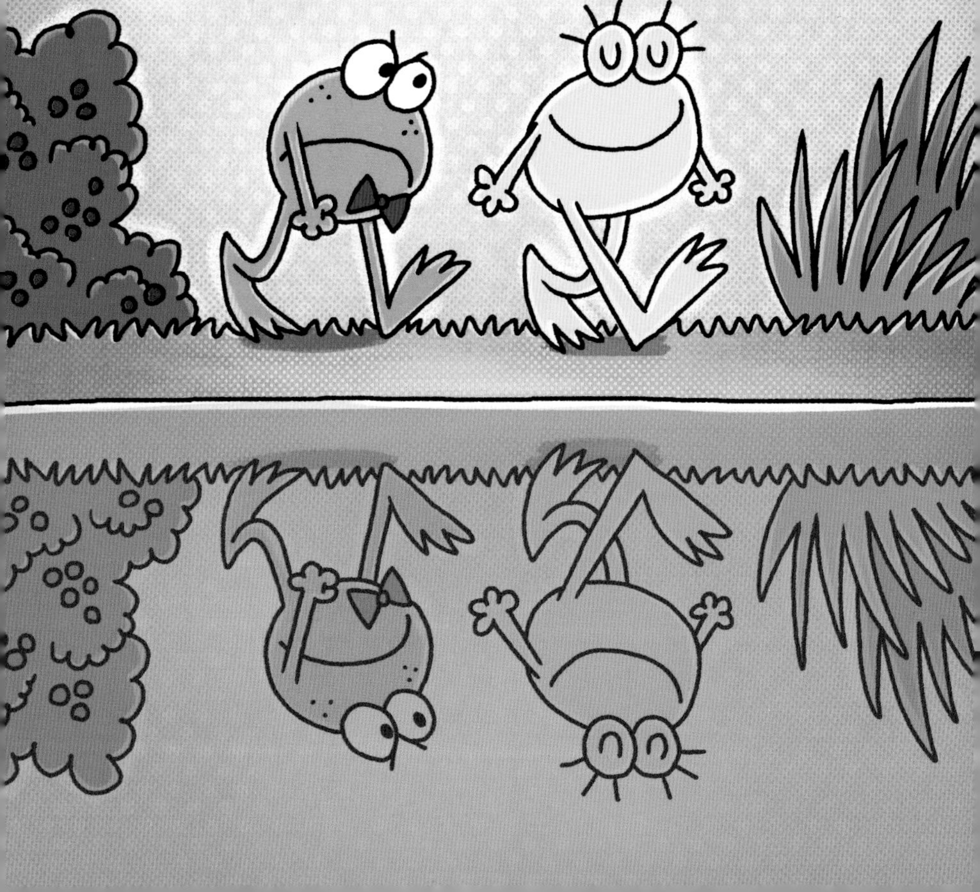

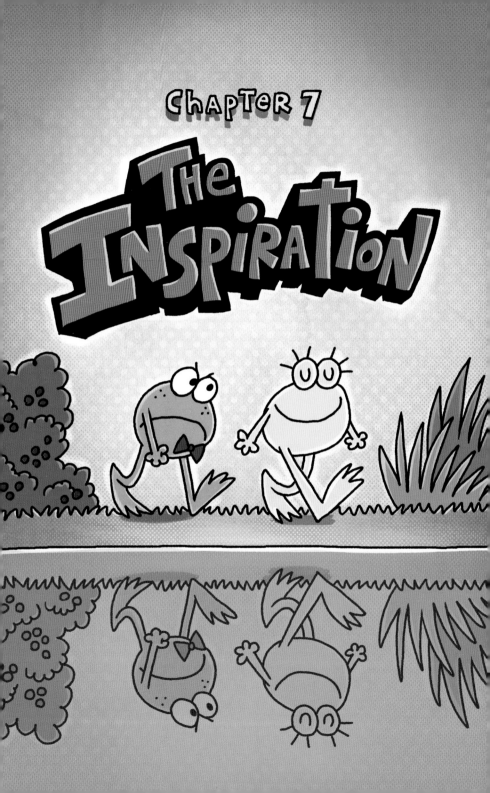

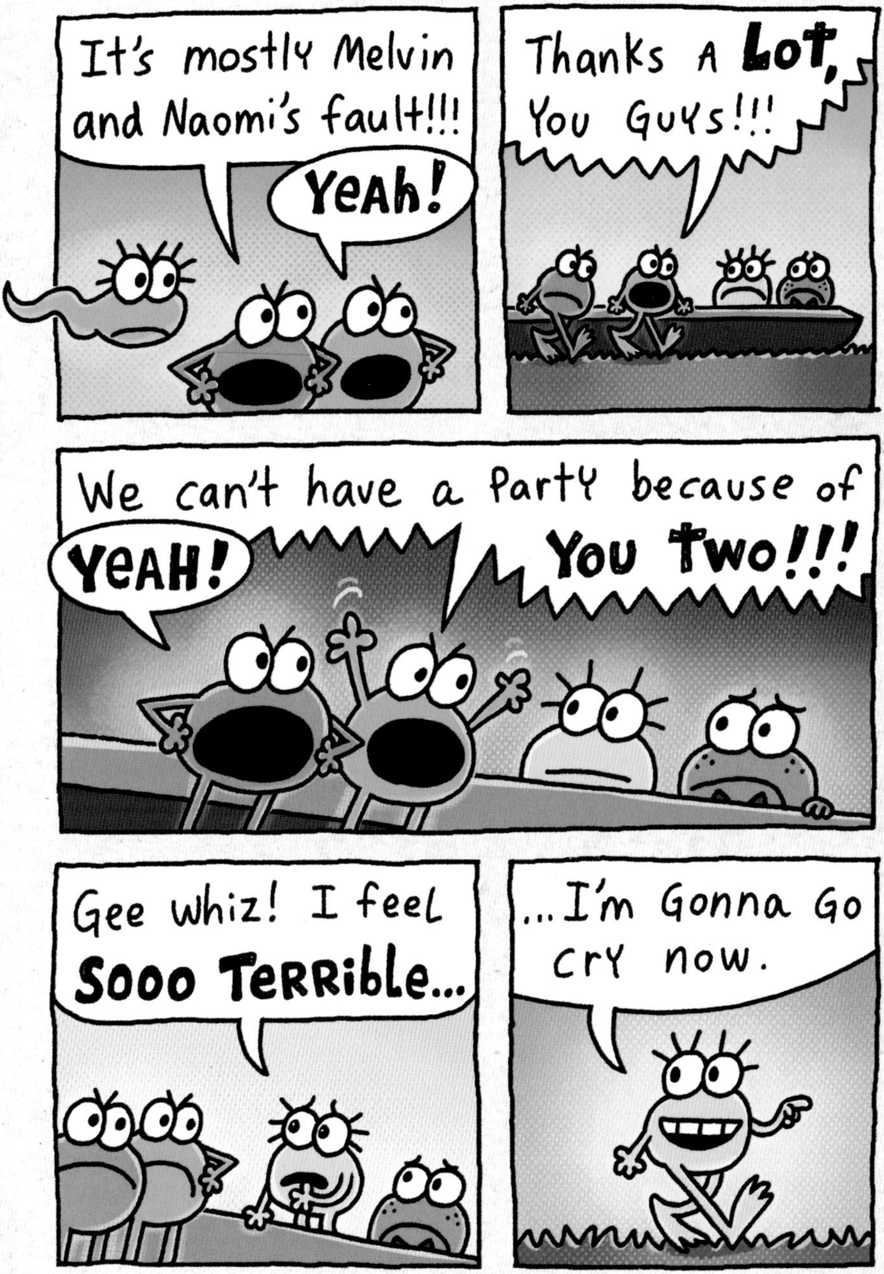
It's mostly Melvin and Naomi's fault!!!
Yeah!
Thanks A LOT, You Guys!!!
We can't have a Party because of You Two!!!
YeAH!
Gee whiz! I feel Sooo Terrible...
...I'm Gonna Go cry now.

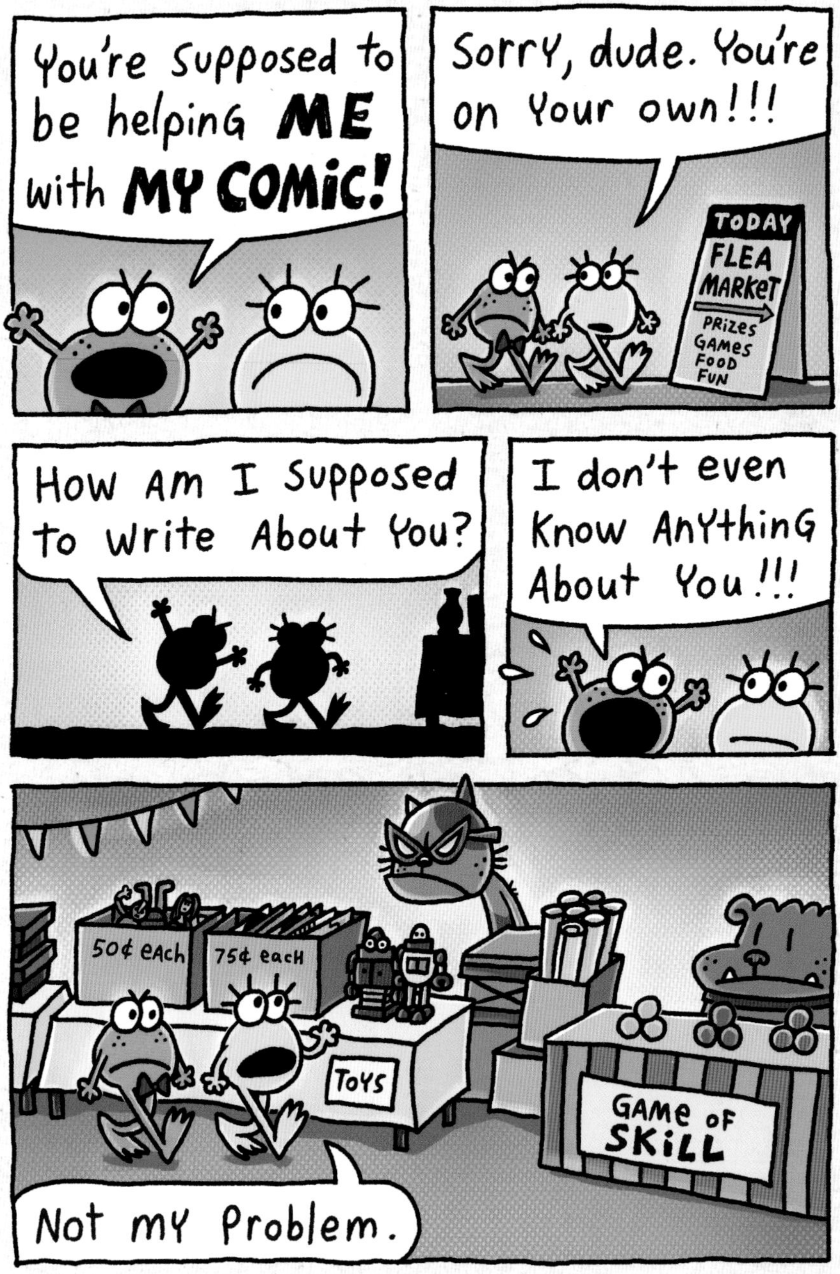
You're Supposed to be helping ME with MY COMIC!
Sorry, dude. You're on Your own!!!
TODAY
FLEA MARKET
PRIZES
GAMES
FOOD
FUN
How Am I Supposed to Write About You?
I don't even Know Anything About You!!!
50¢ eAch
75¢ each
TOYS
GAME OF SKILL
Not my Problem.

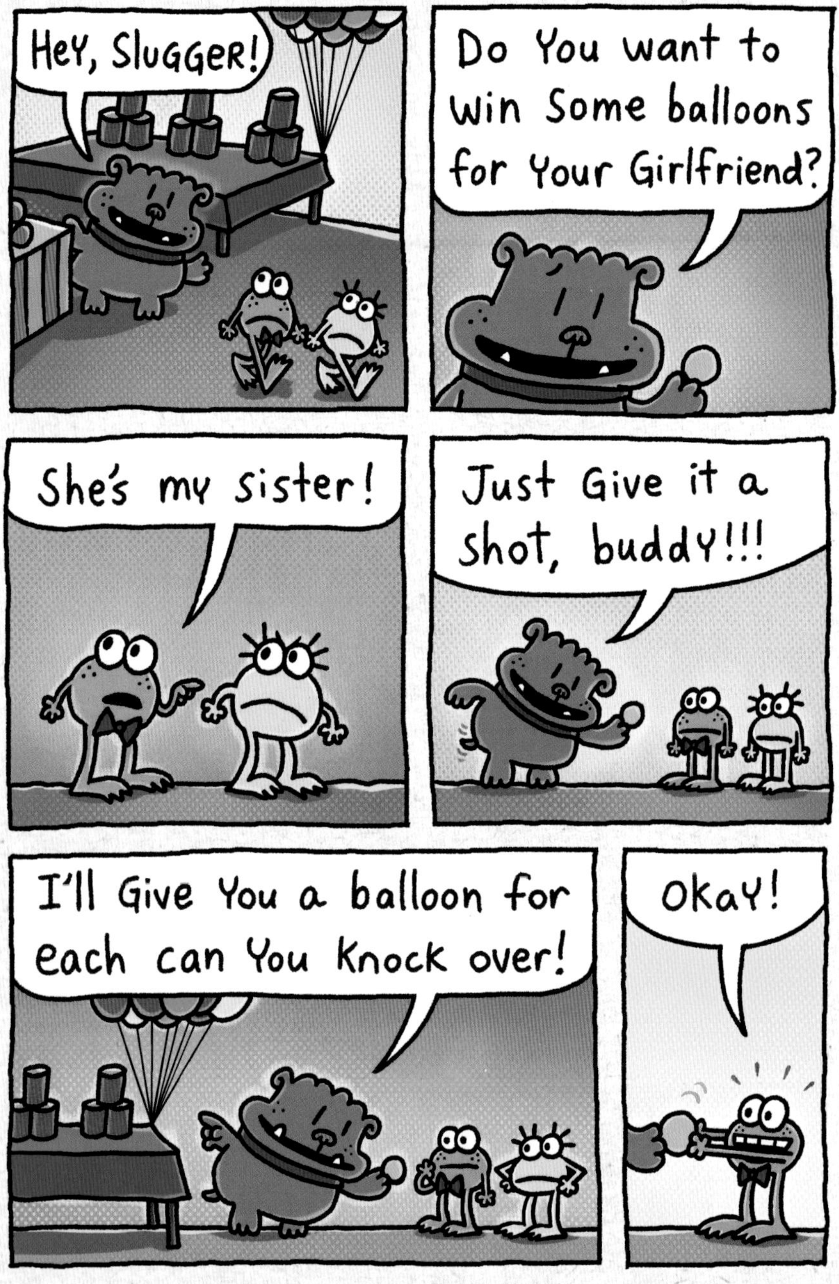
HeY, SluGGeR!
Do You want to win Some balloons for Your Girlfriend?
She's my sister!
Just Give it a shot, buddY!!!
I'll Give You a balloon for each can You Knock over!
OkaY!

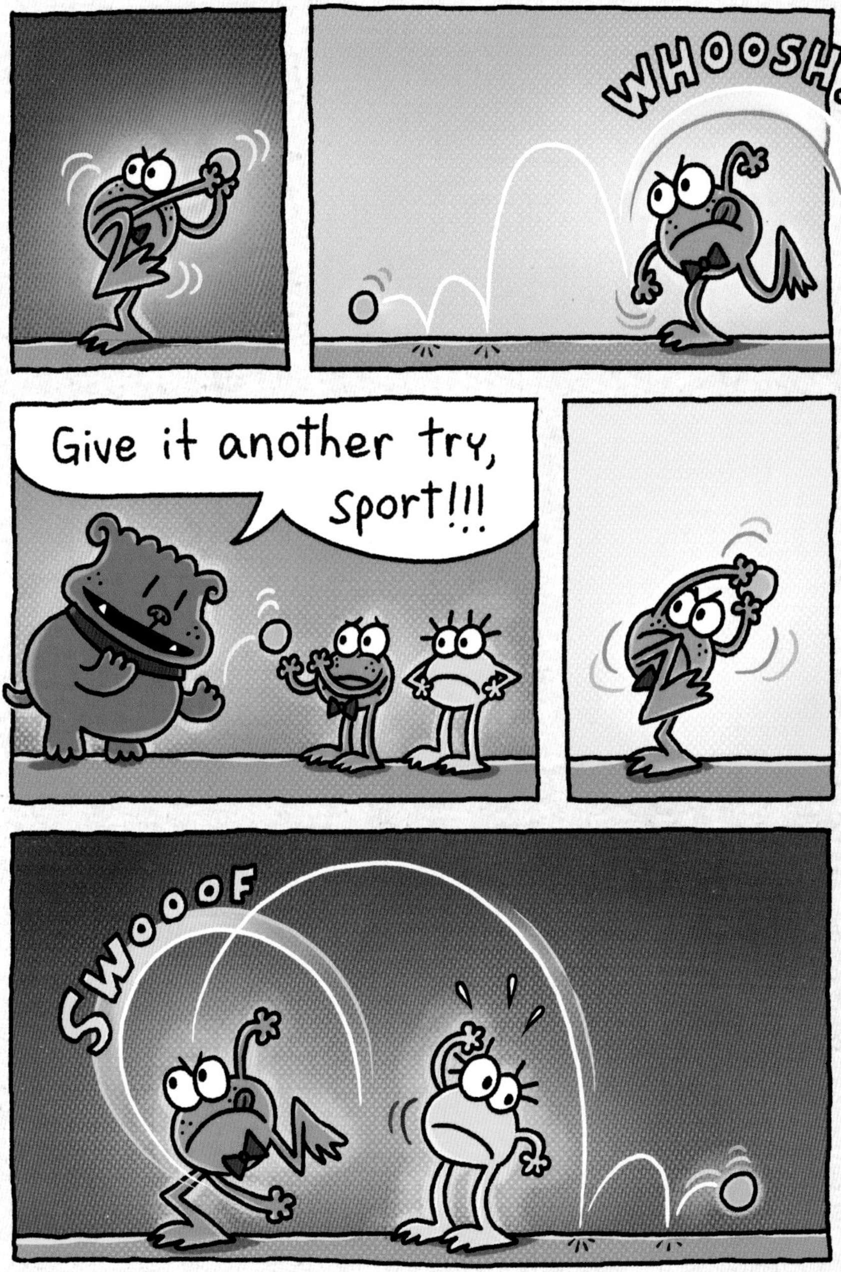
WHOOSH!
Give it another try, sport!!!
SWOOOF

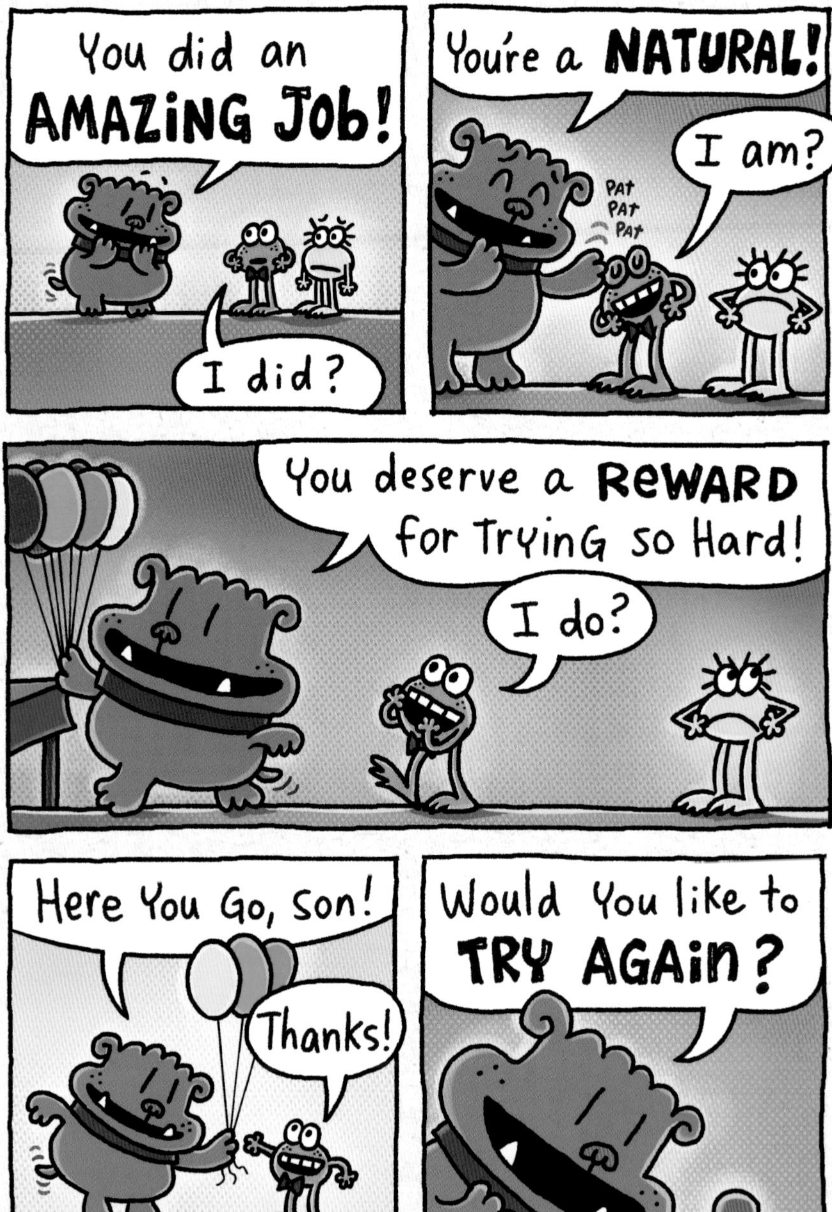
You did an AMAZING JOB!
I did?
You're a NATURAL!
I am?
PAT PAT PAT
You deserve a REWARD for TRYING so Hard!
I do?
Here You Go, son!
Thanks!
Would You like to TRY AGAIN?

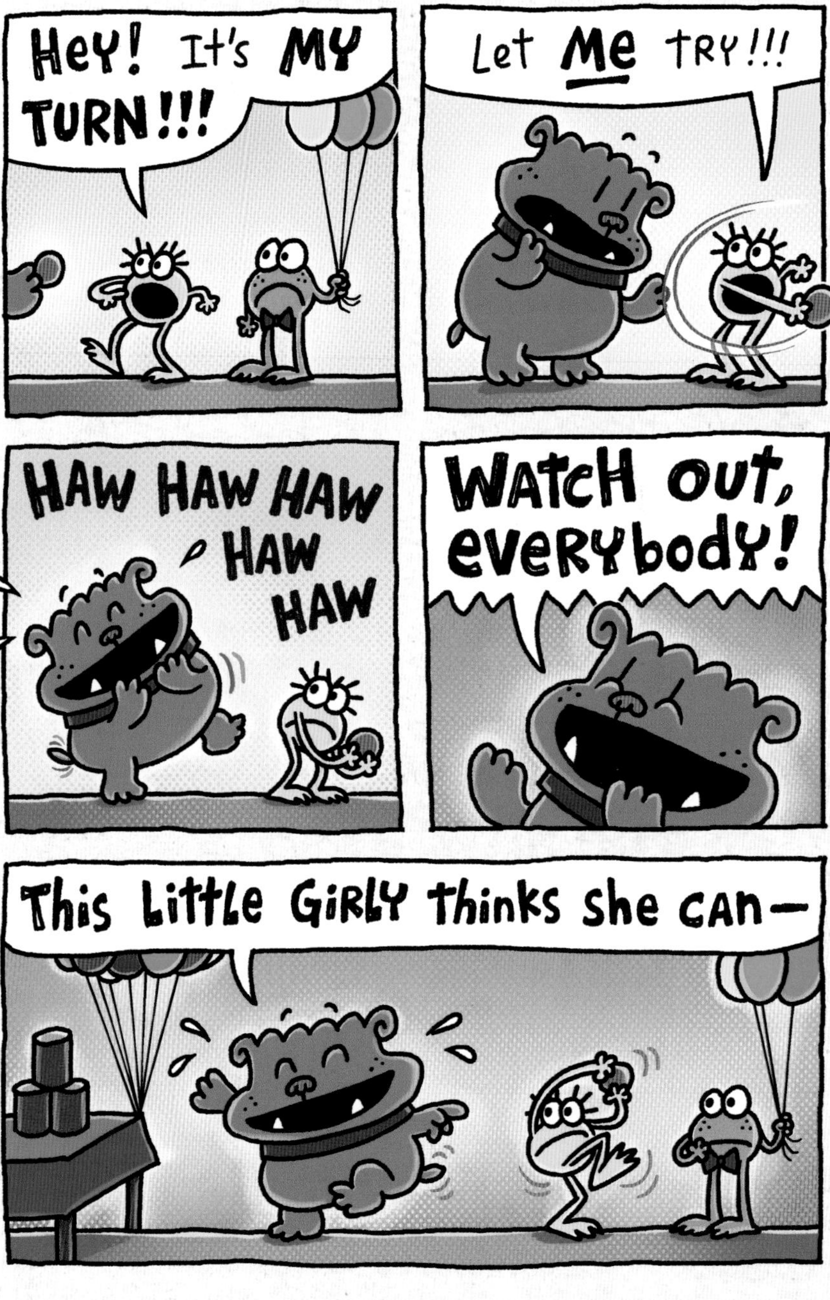
Hey! It's MY TURN!!!
Let ME TRY!!!
HAW HAW HAW HAW HAW
WATCH OUT, everybody!
This Little GIRLY thinks she can—

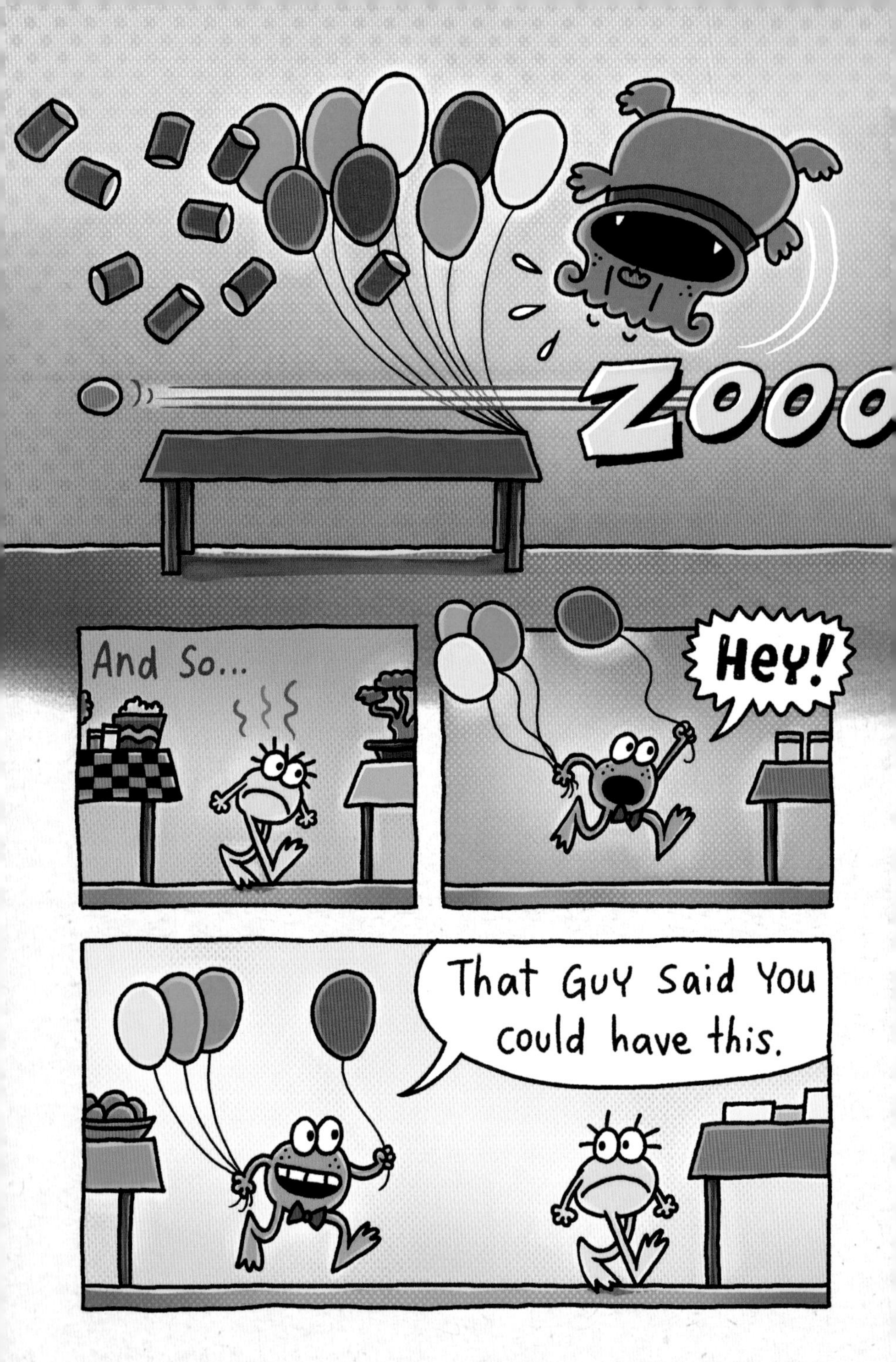
ZOOO
And So...
Hey!
That Guy Said You could have this.

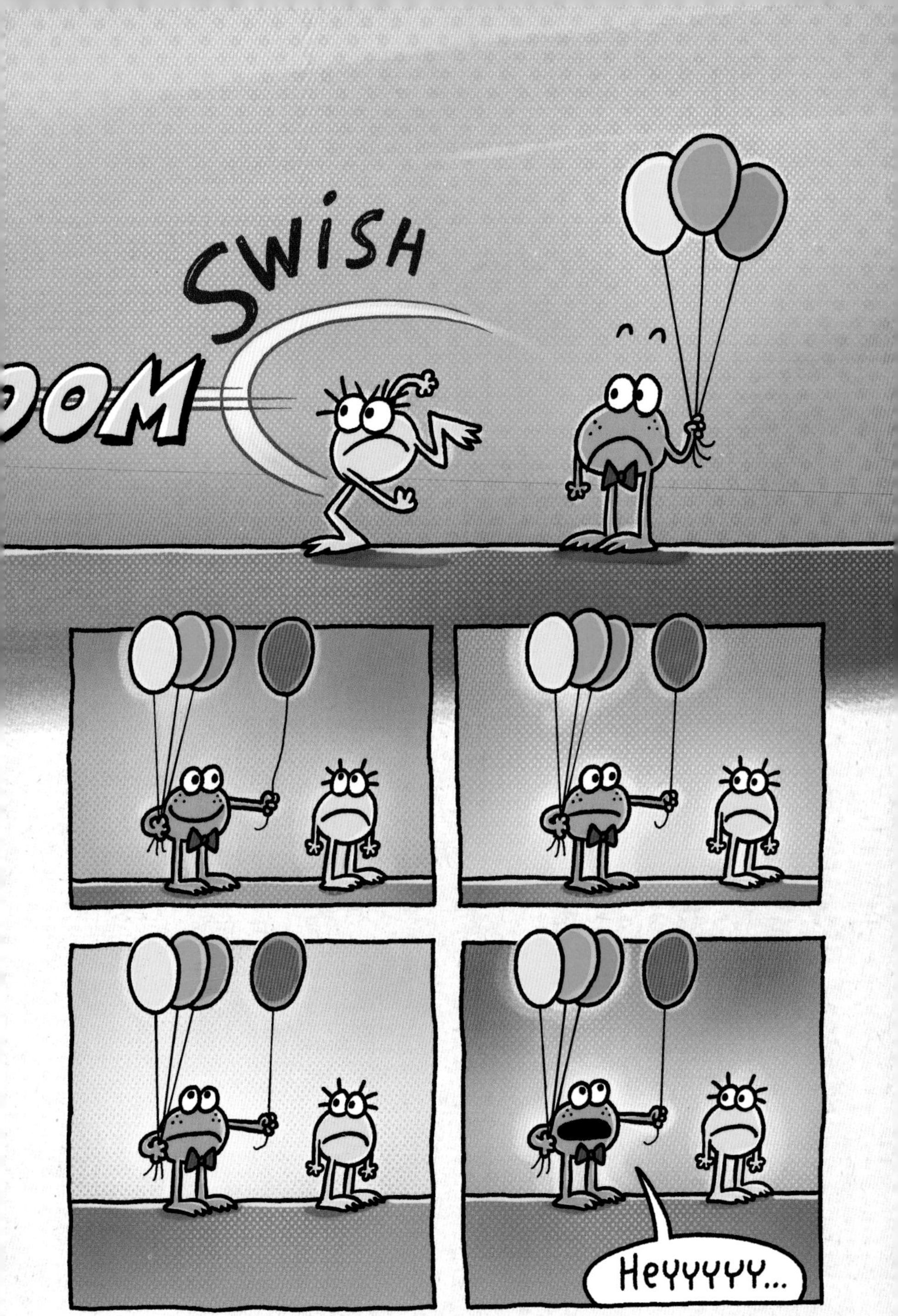
OOM
SWISH
HEYYYYY...

153

CHAPTER 8

The Saddest Friday of All Time

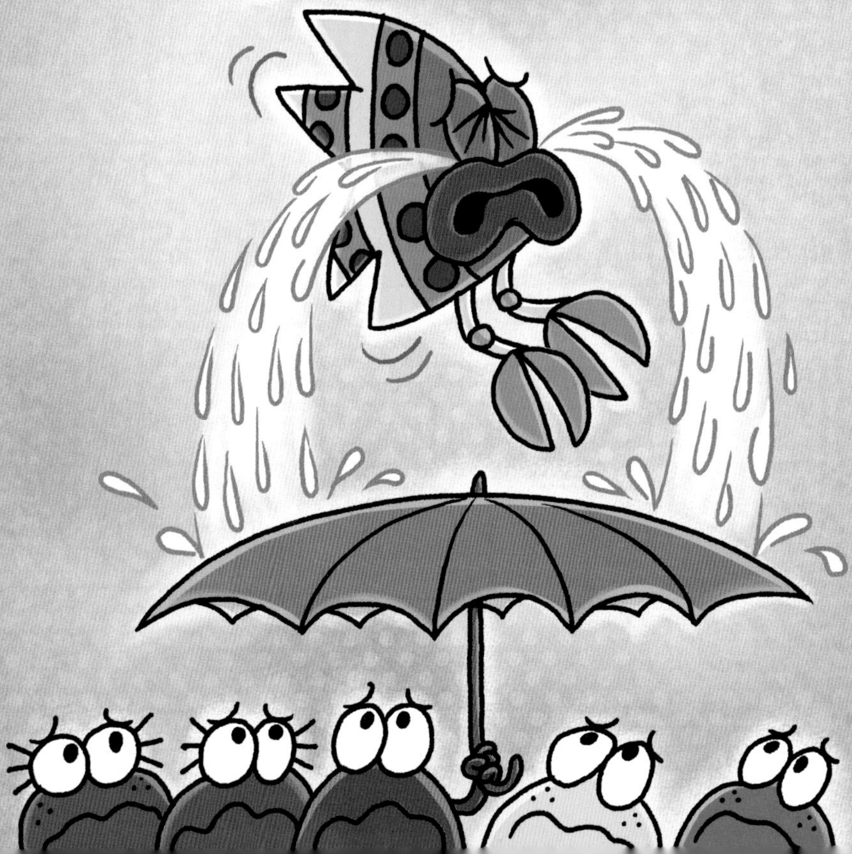

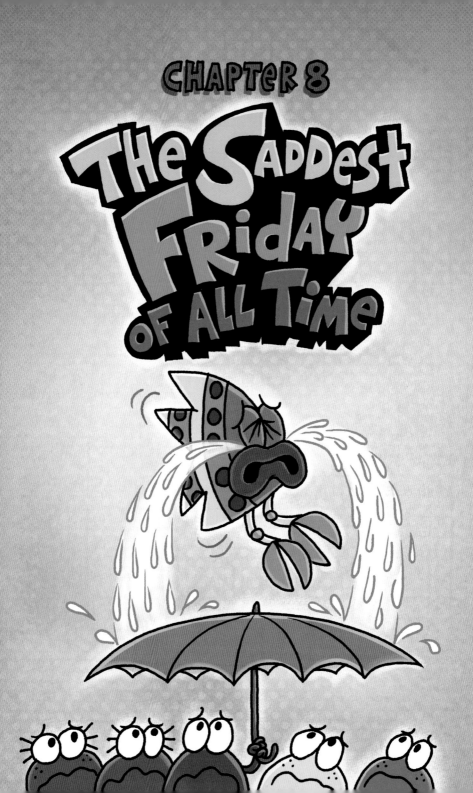

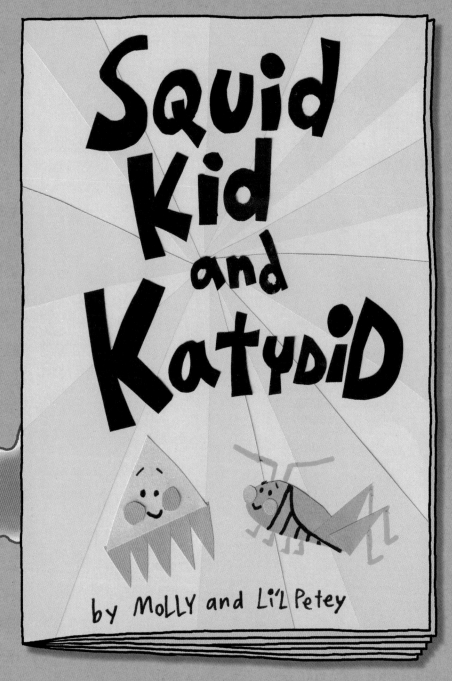

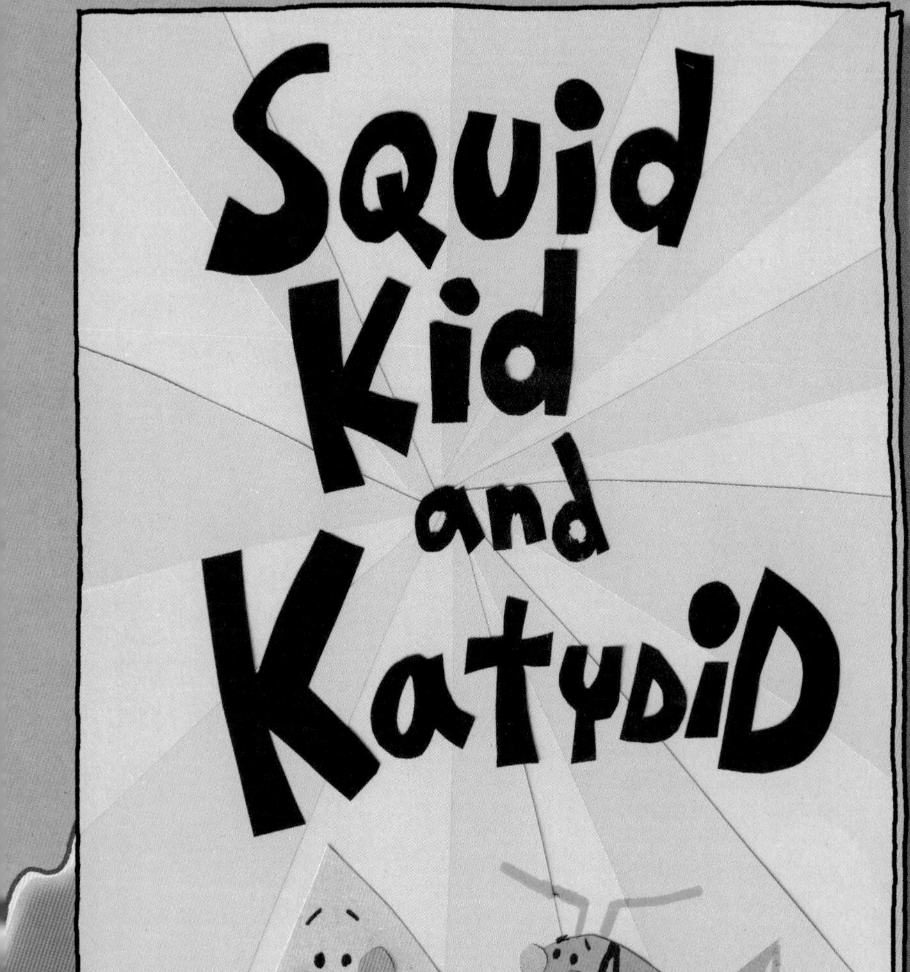
Squid Kid and KatydiD
by MOLLY and Li'L Petey

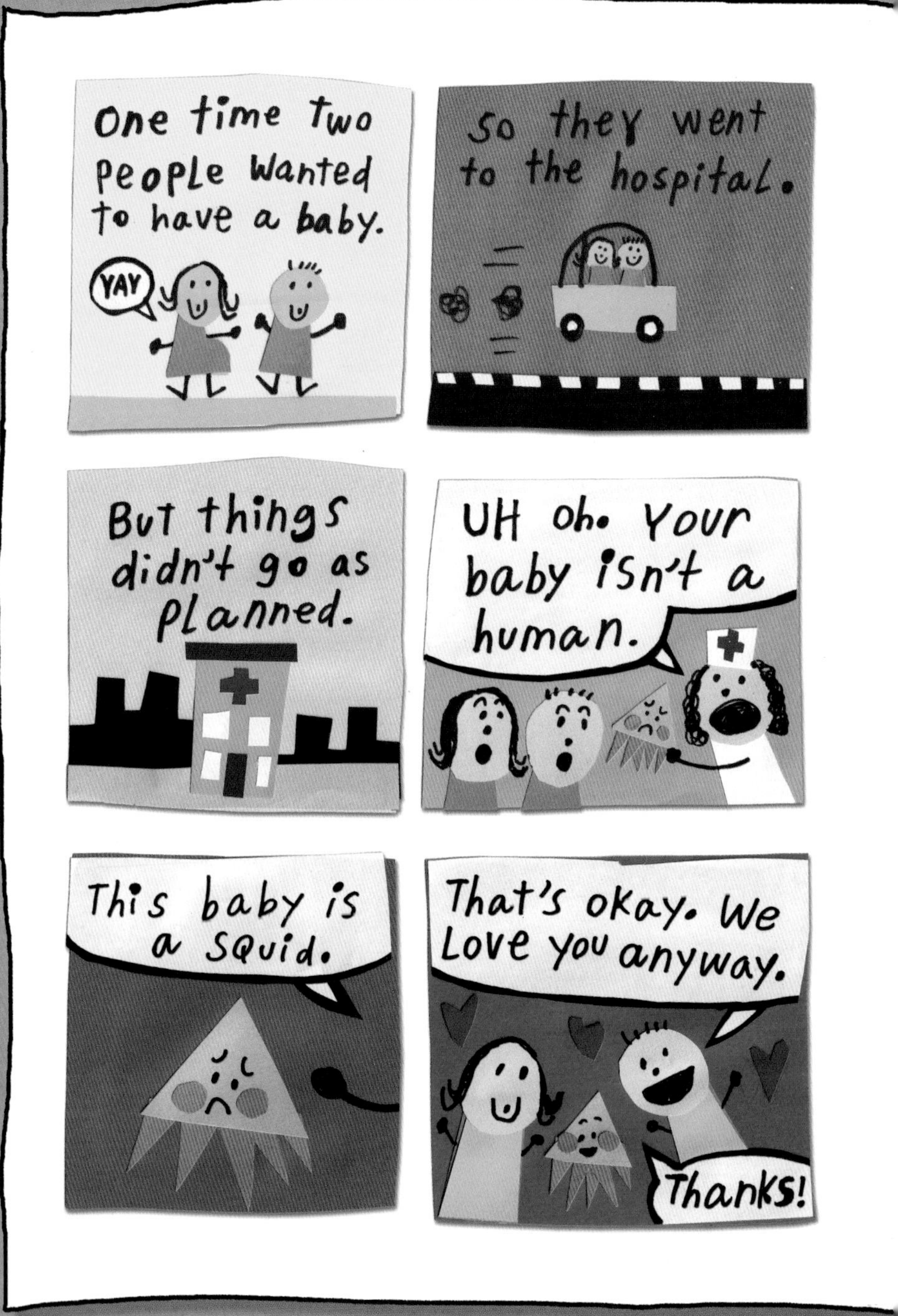
One time two people wanted to have a baby.
YAY
So they went to the hospital.
But things didn't go as planned.
UH oh. Your baby isn't a human.
This baby is a squid.
That's okay. We Love you anyway.
Thanks!

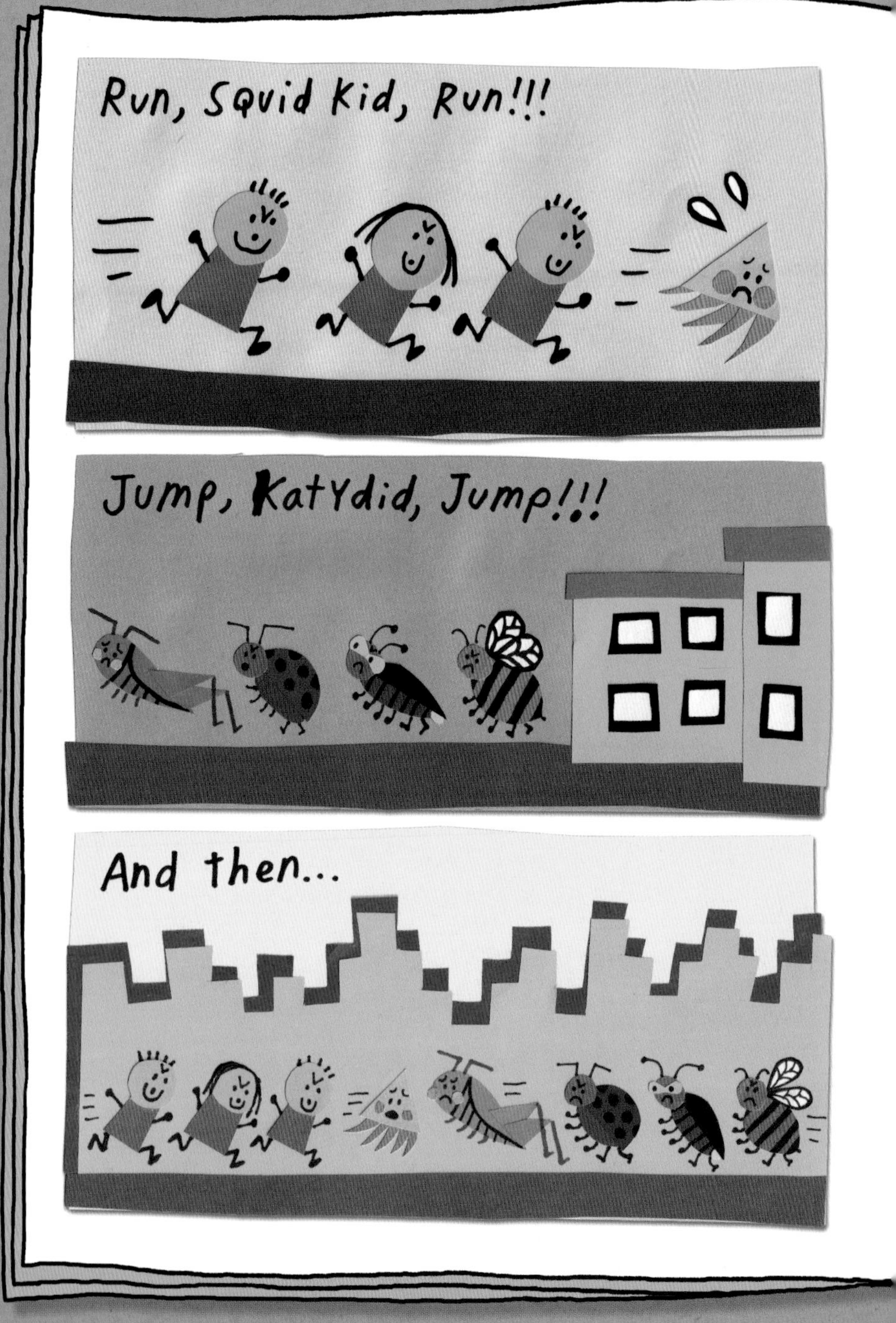
Run, Squid Kid, Run!!!
Jump, Katydid, Jump!!!
And then...

...but katydid didn't.

After a hard day of changing the world...

BOING   BOING   BOING

...They bounced to Squid kid's house.

S.K.

Squid kid's Parents made pizza.

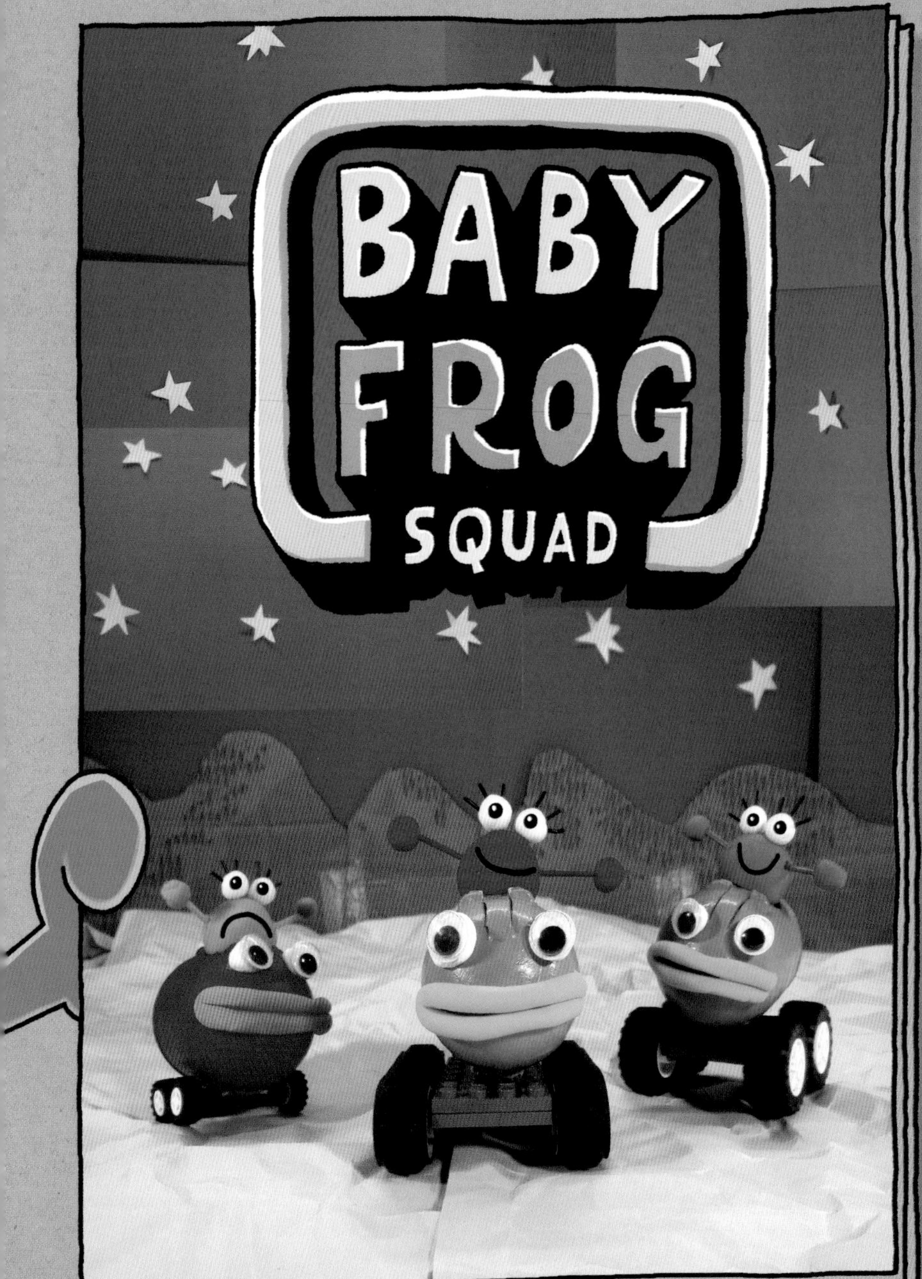
BABY
FROG
SQUAD

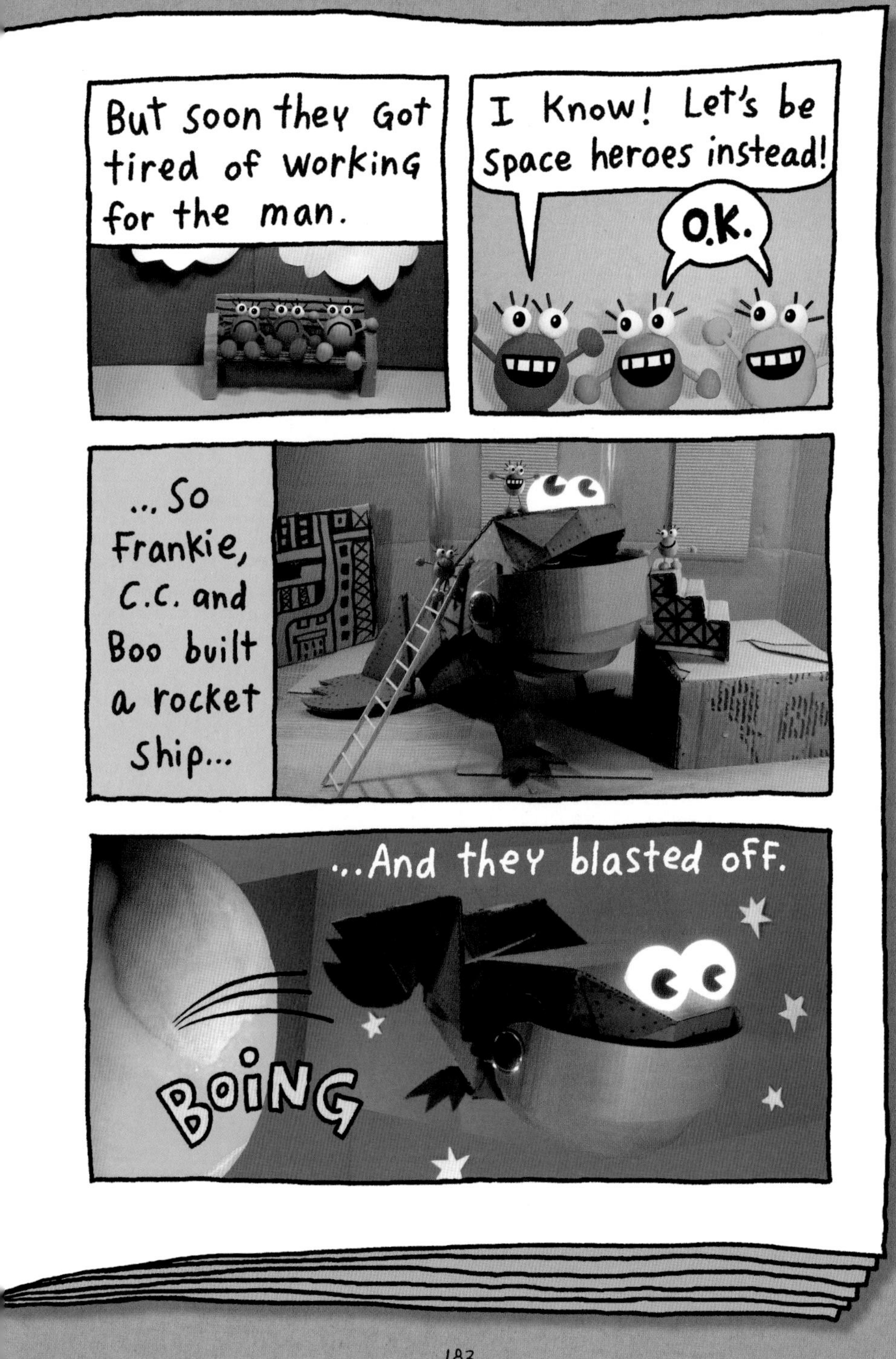
But soon they got tired of working for the man.
I know! Let's be space heroes instead!
O.K.
...So Frankie, C.C. and Boo built a rocket ship...
...And they blasted off.
BOING

189

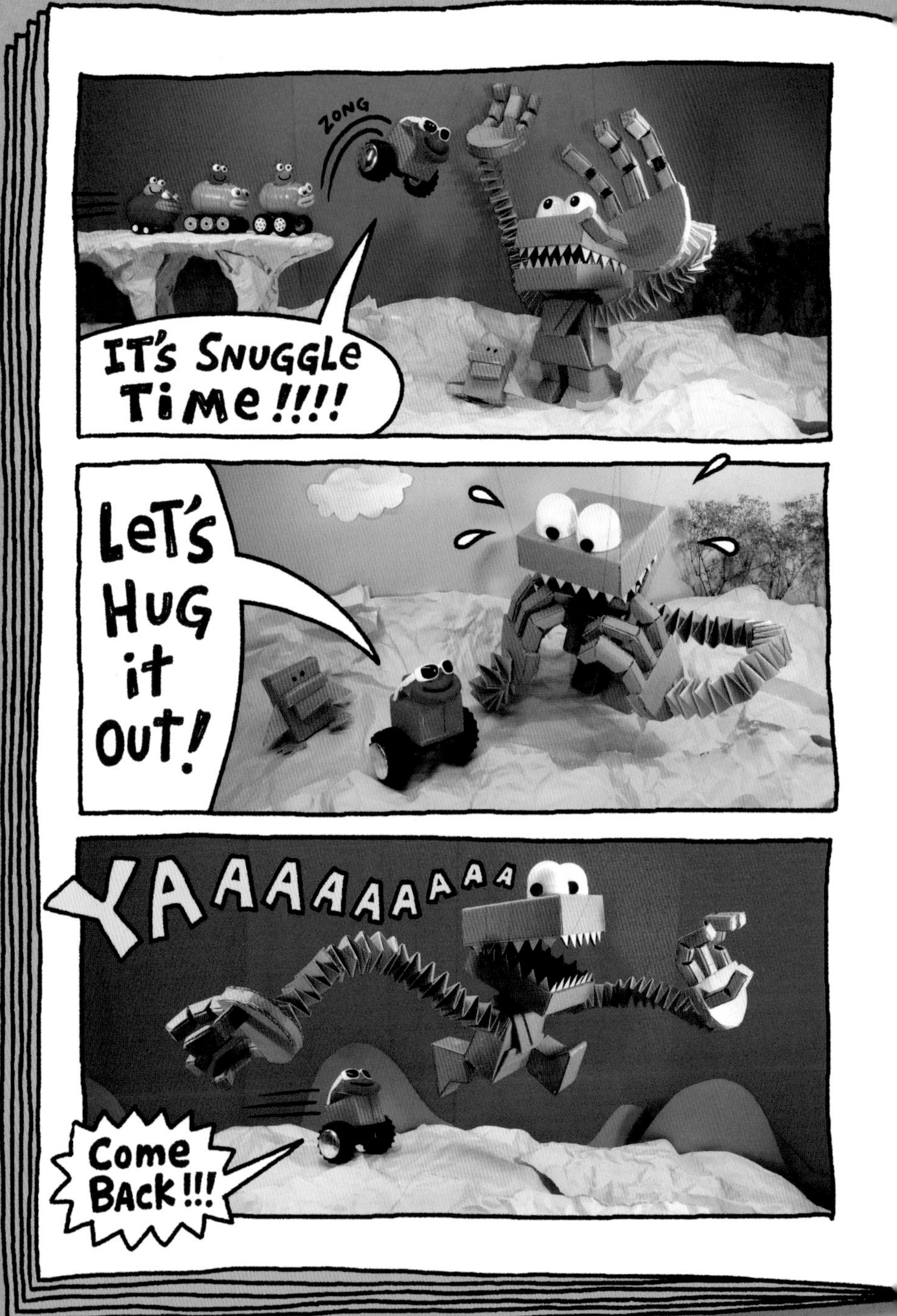
ZONG
IT'S SNUGGLE TIME!!!!
LET'S HUG it OUT!
YAAAAAAAAAA
Come BACK!!!

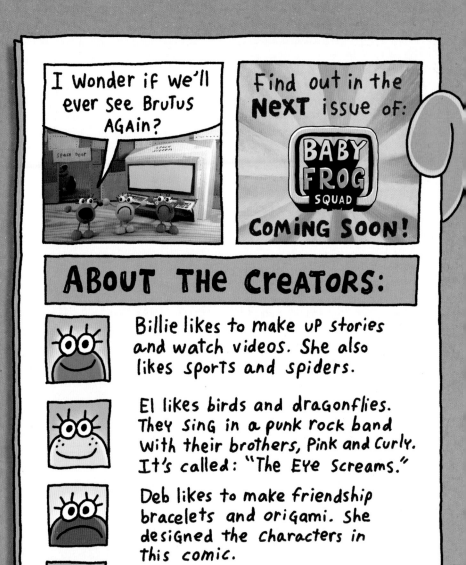

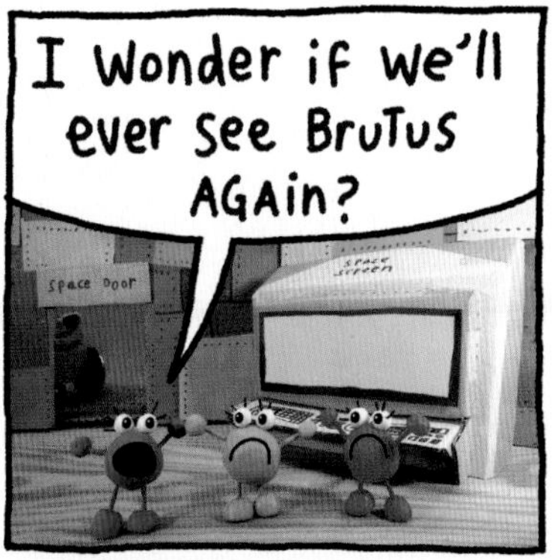
I wonder if we'll ever see BruTuS AGAin?
space door
space screen

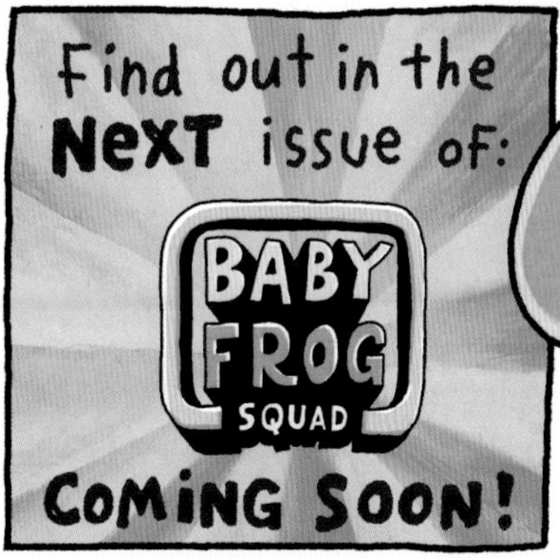
Find out in the NEXT issue of:
BABY FROG SQUAD
COMING SOON!

ABOUT THE CREATORS:

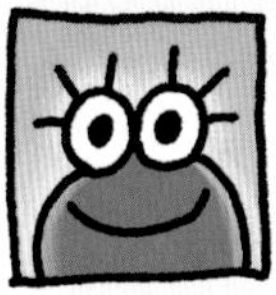

Billie likes to make up stories and watch videos. She also likes sports and spiders.

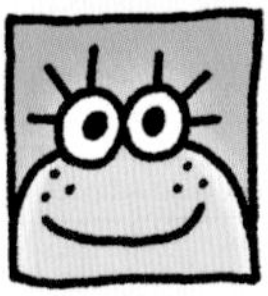

El likes birds and dragonflies. They sing in a punk rock band with their brothers, Pink and Curly. It's called: "The Eye Screams."

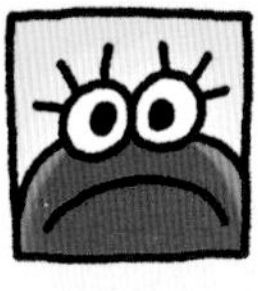

Deb likes to make friendship bracelets and origami. She designed the characters in this comic.

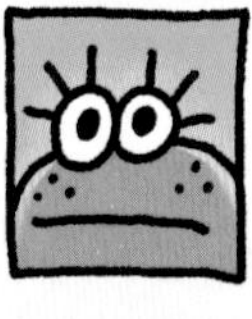

Frida likes cereal.

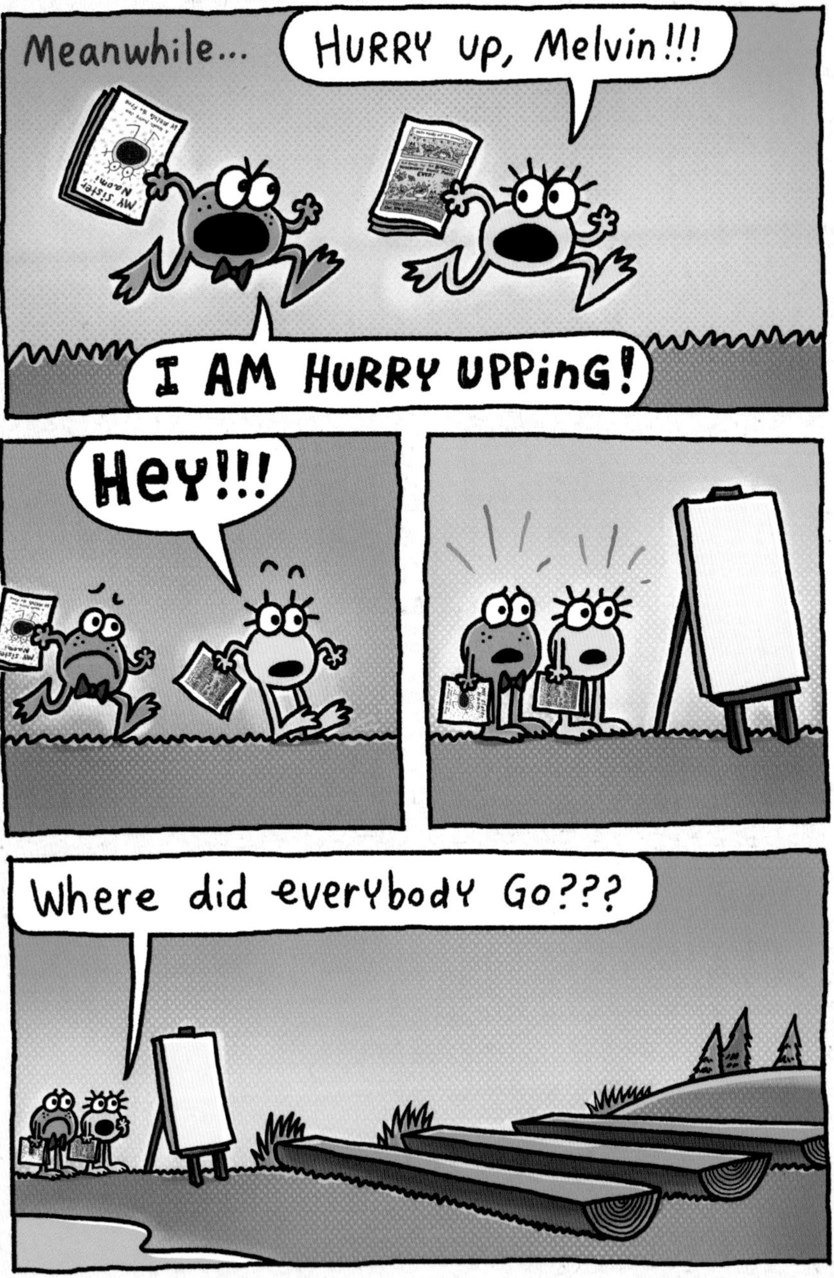
Meanwhile...
HURRY up, Melvin!!!
I AM HURRY UPPinG!
Hey!!!
Where did everybody Go???

CHAPTER 9

NAOMI AND MELVIN REDEEM THEMSELVES (SORT OF)

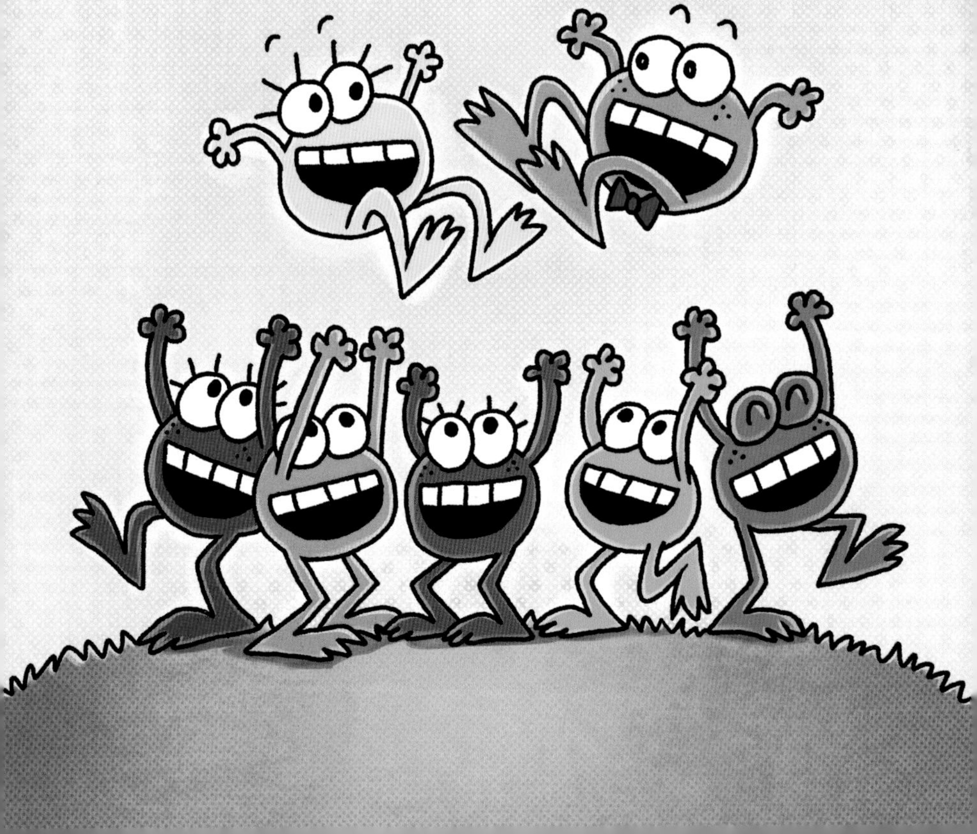

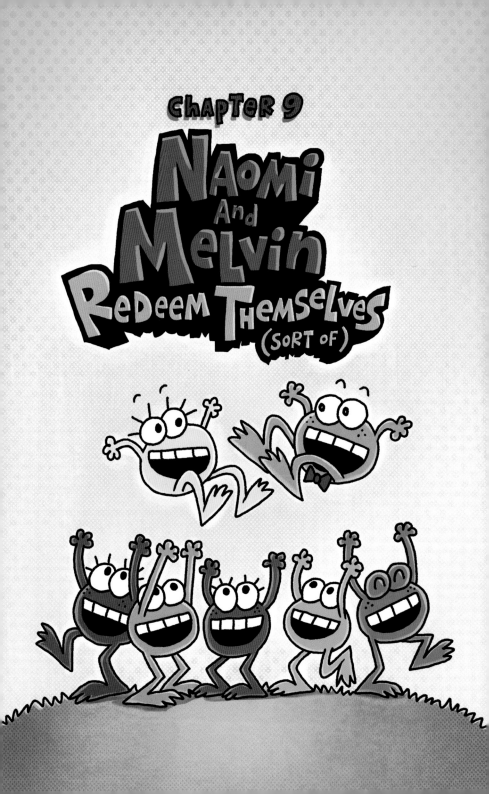

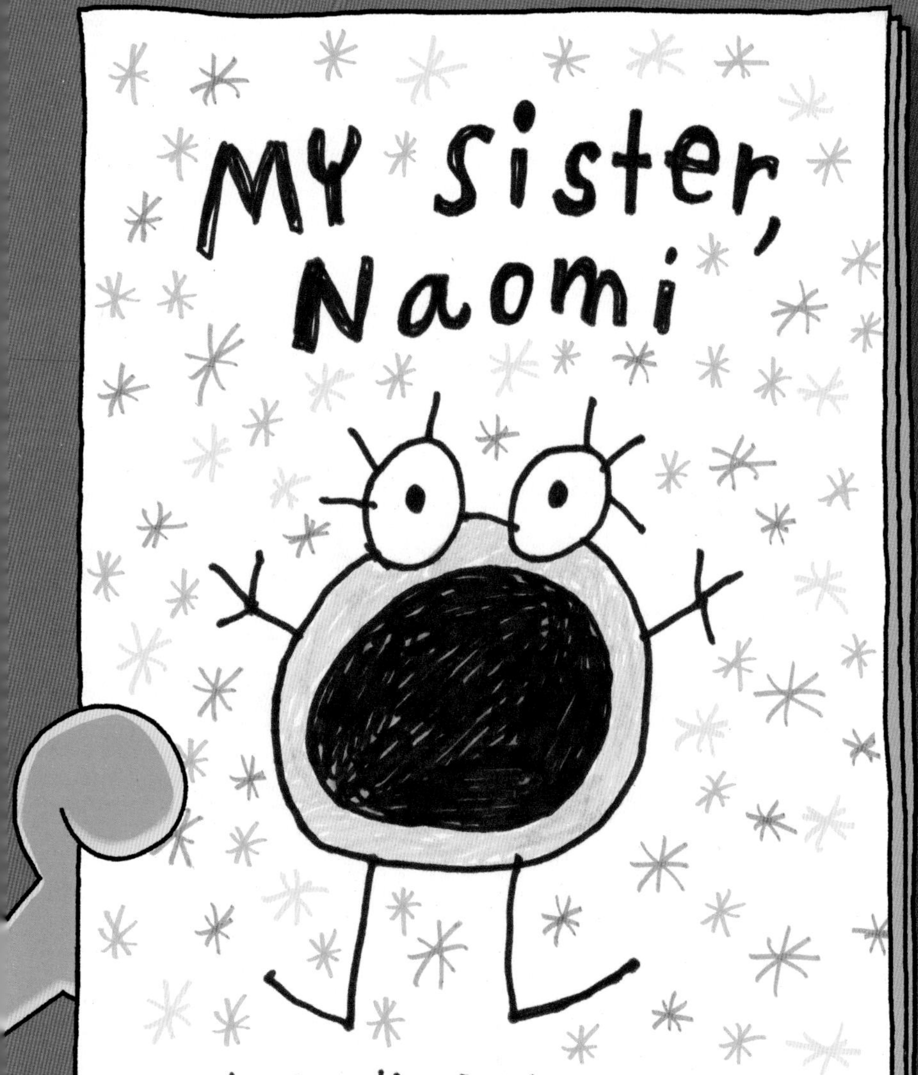
My Sister, Naomi
A Graphic Poetry Jam
by Melvin the Frog

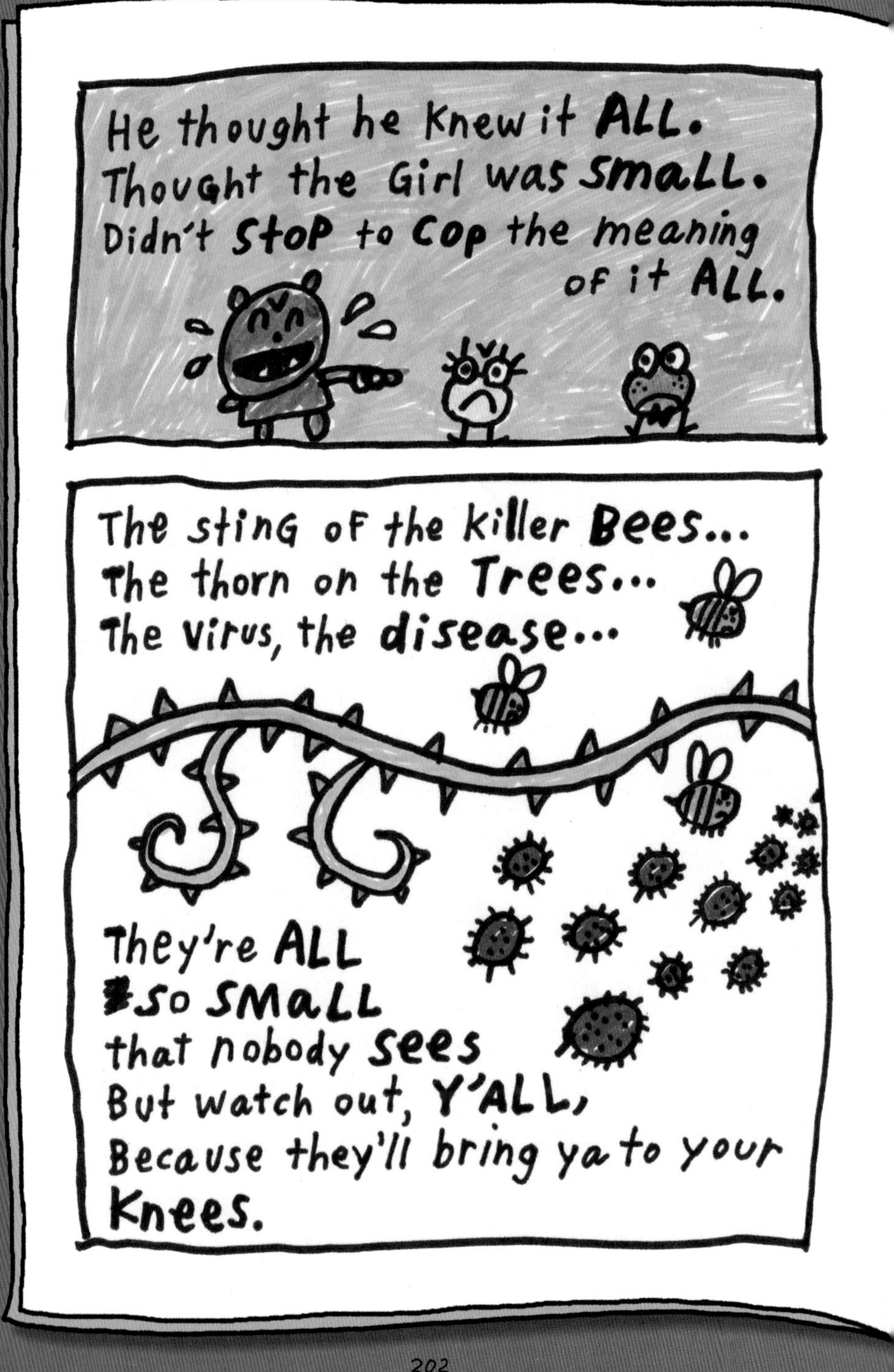
He thought he knew it ALL.
Thought the Girl was SMALL.
Didn't STOP to COP the meaning of it ALL.
The sting of the killer Bees...
The thorn on the Trees...
The virus, the disease...
They're ALL
so SMALL
that nobody sees
But watch out, Y'ALL,
Because they'll bring ya to your
Knees.

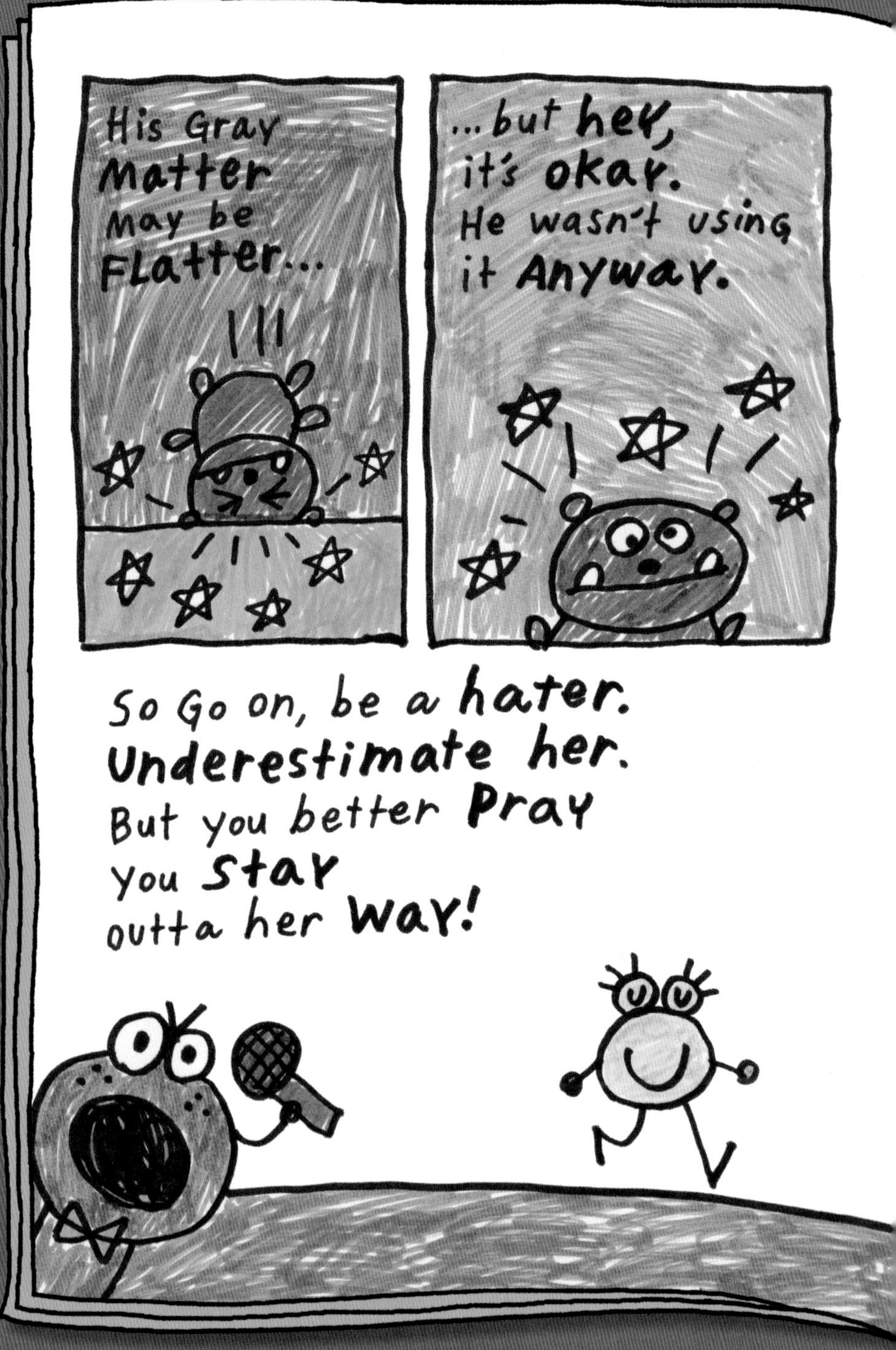
His Gray Matter May be Flatter...
...but hey, it's okay. He wasn't using it Anyway.
So Go on, be a hater.
Underestimate her.
But you better Pray
you Stay
outta her WAY!

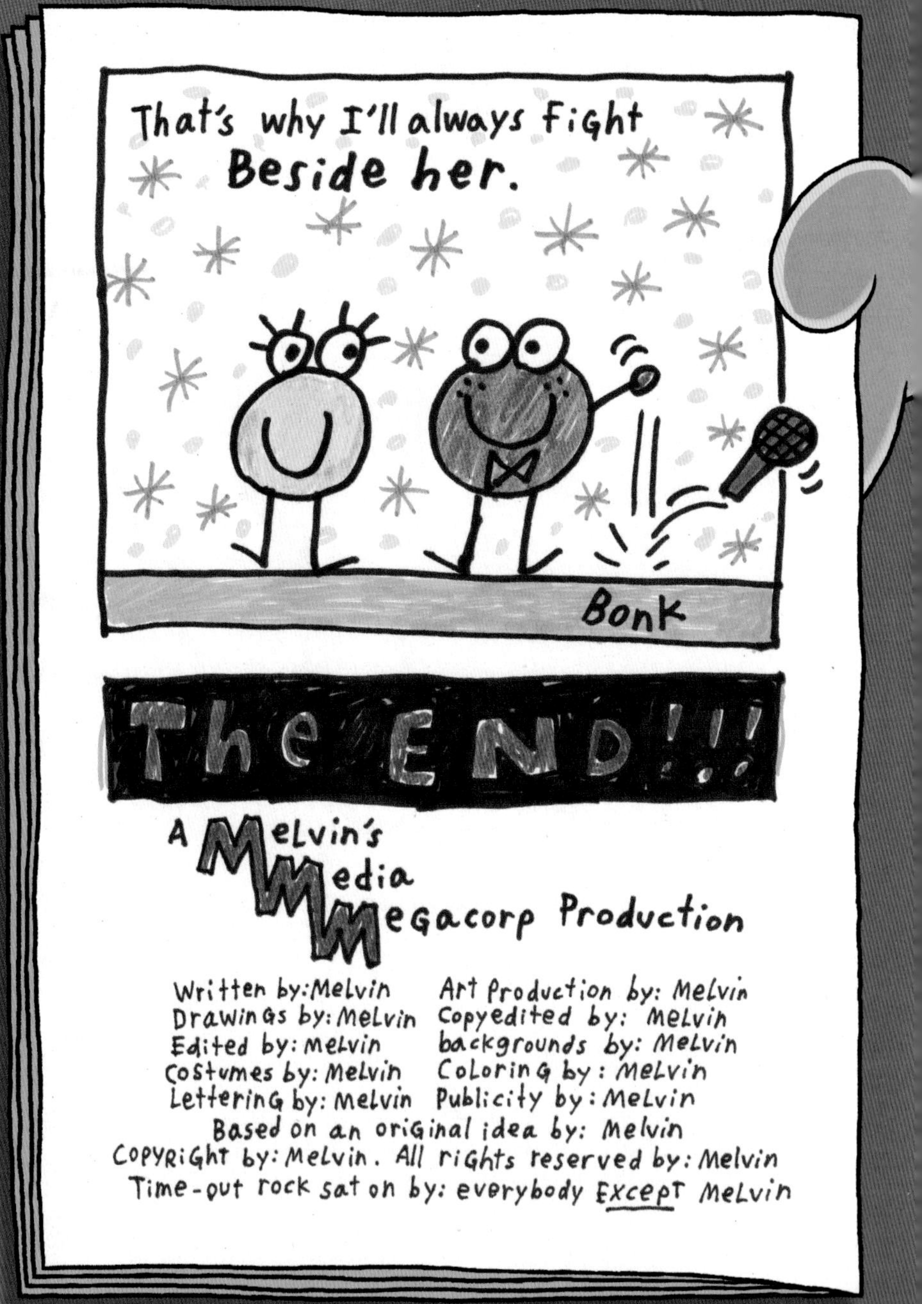
That's why I'll always fight
Beside her.
Bonk
The END!!!
A Melvin's Media Megacorp Production
Written by: Melvin
Drawings by: Melvin
Edited by: Melvin
Costumes by: Melvin
Lettering by: Melvin
Art Production by: Melvin
Copyedited by: Melvin
backgrounds by: Melvin
Coloring by: Melvin
Publicity by: Melvin
Based on an original idea by: Melvin
Copyright by: Melvin. All rights reserved by: Melvin
Time-out rock sat on by: everybody EXCEPT Melvin

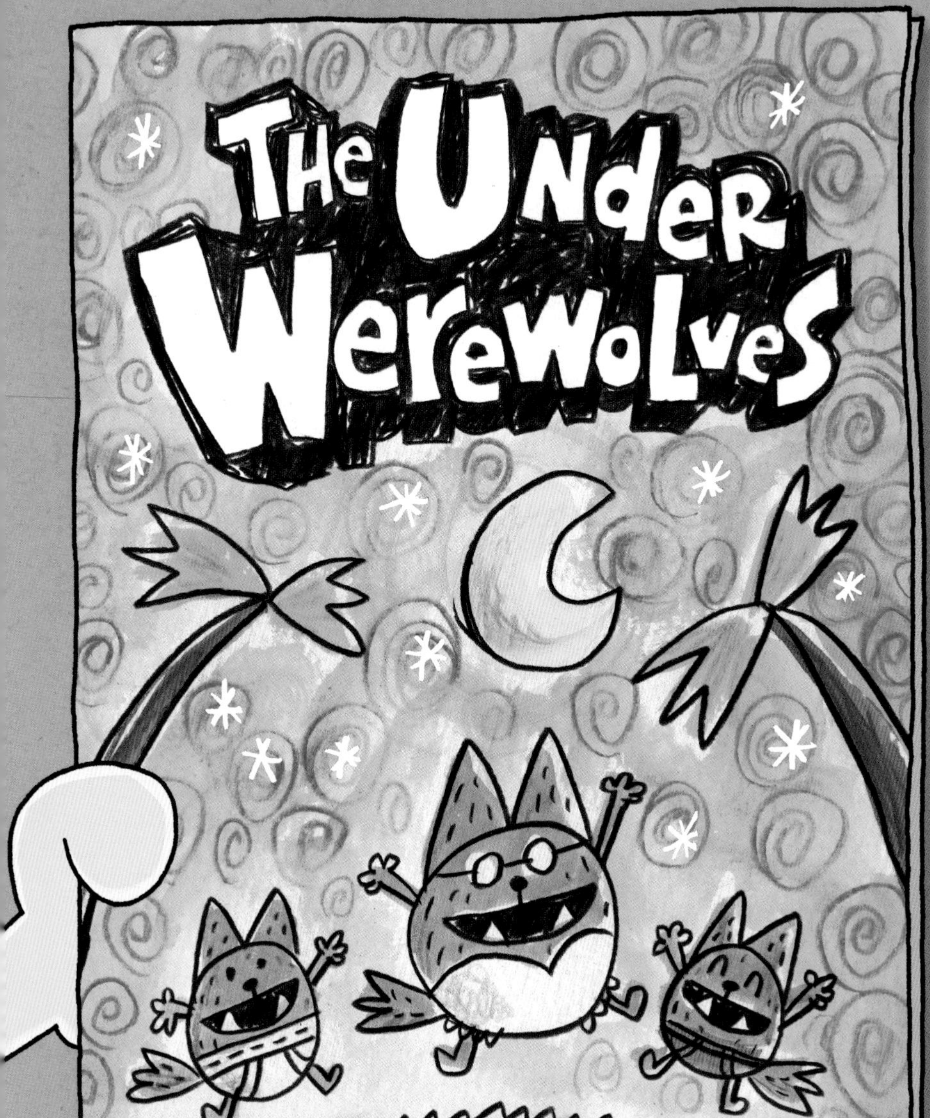
The Under Werewolves
BY Naomi the Great

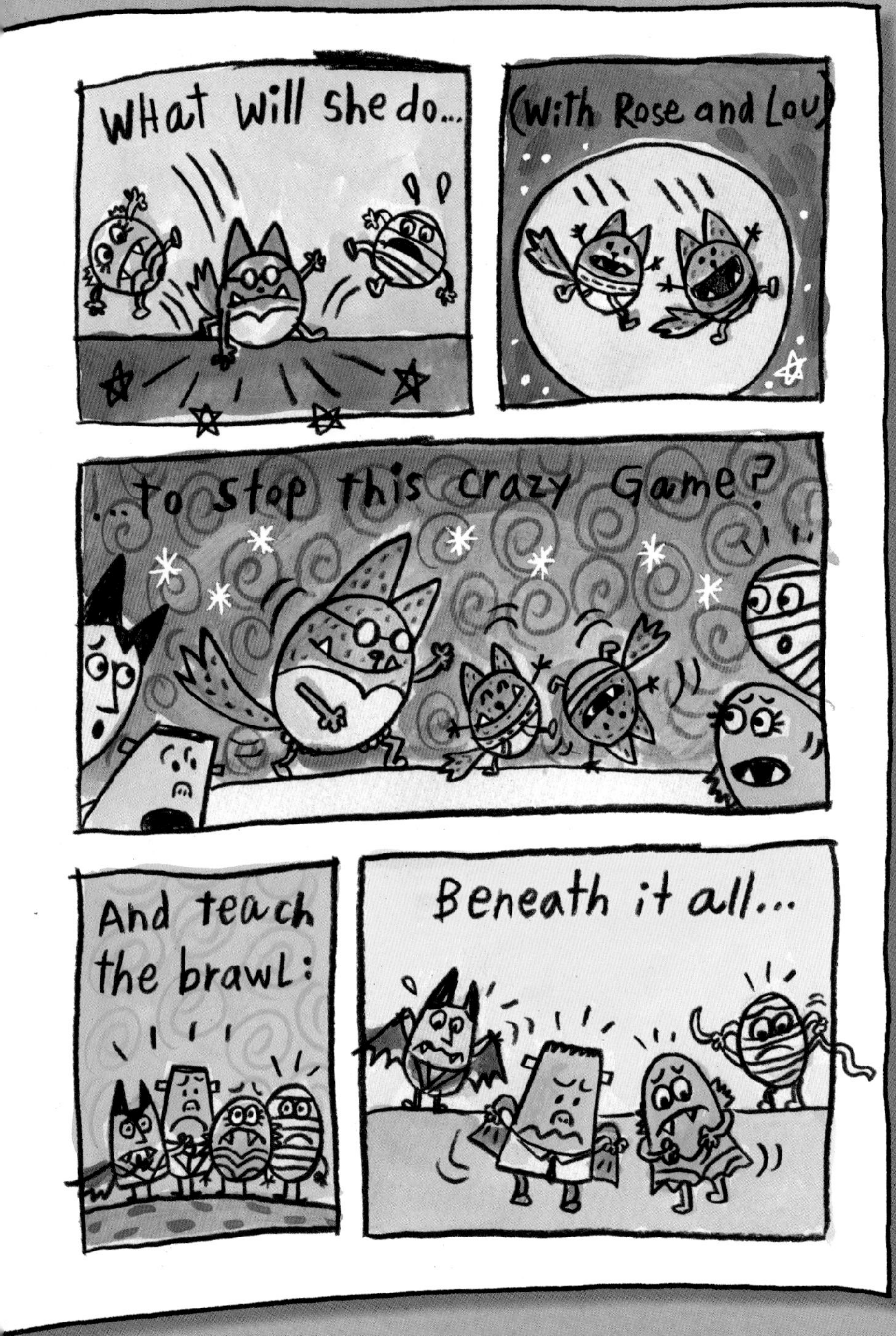
What will she do...
(With Rose and Lou)
...to stop this crazy Game?
And teach the brawl:
Beneath it all...

215

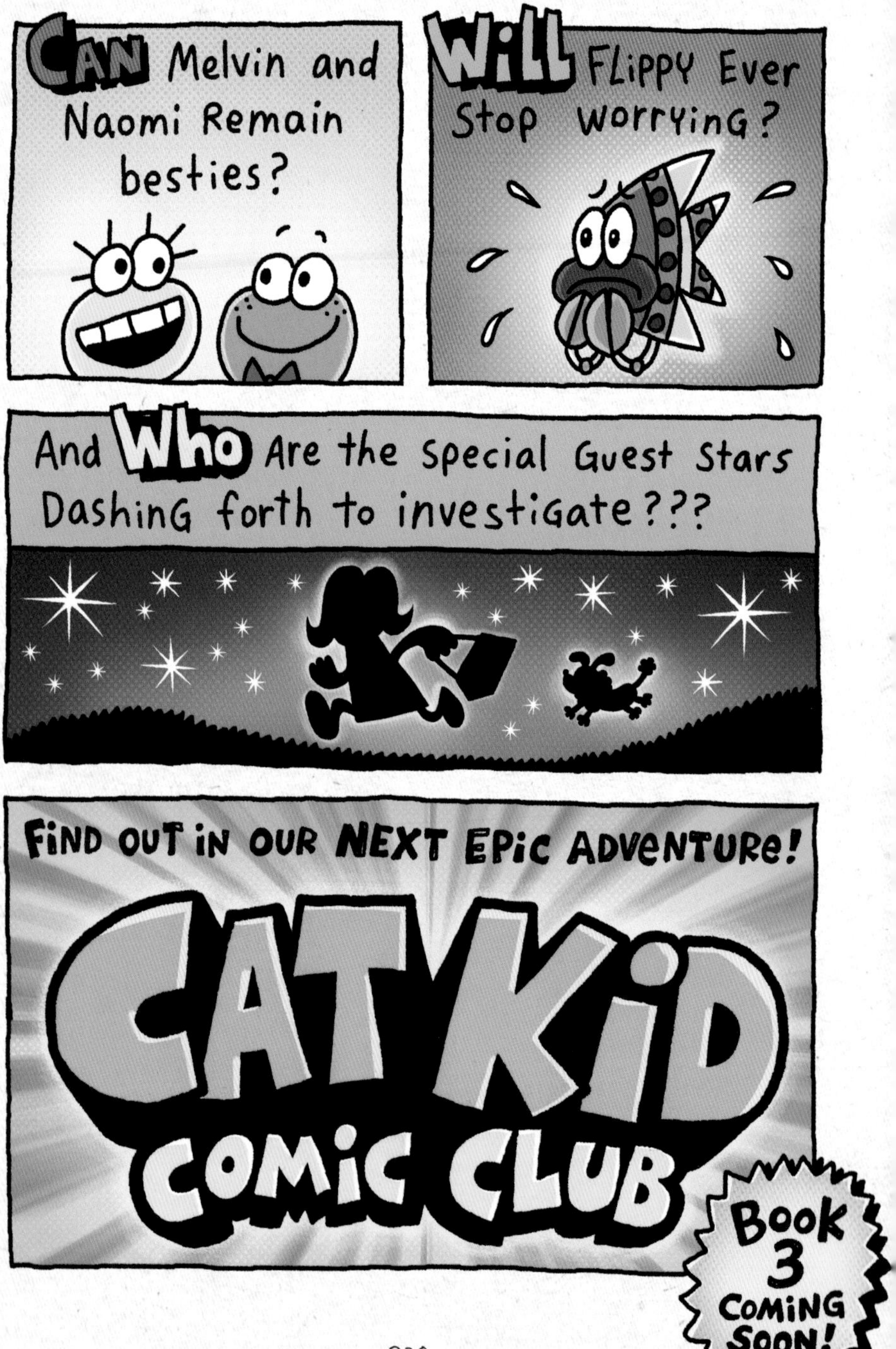

CAN Melvin and Naomi Remain besties?
WILL FLIPPY Ever Stop worrying?
And Who Are the Special Guest Stars Dashing forth to investigate???
FIND OUT IN OUR NEXT EPIC ADVENTURE!
CAT KID
COMIC CLUB
Book 3 COMING SOON!

NOTES & FUN FACTS

☆ Squids really **DO** spray ink when they feel threatened or scared. It's made of melanin, and it's usually blueish-black in color (not purple).

☆ Frankie, Boo, Brutus, and C.C. were all named after breakfast cereals.

☆ Naomi's dialogue on page 157 (panels 3 and 4) was based on a quote from Olivia Chaffin, a Girl Scout from Tennessee who boycotted the sale of Girl Scout cookies because they contain some palm oils that are linked to deforestation. Her online petition made international headlines.

☆ Chubbs and Jake's van is outfitted with an **ACTUAL WORKING DISCO** inside, including functioning stereo speakers, a mini subwoofer, 1970s faux-wood paneling, multicolored rotating disco lights, and a mirrored floor.

☆ The Baby Frog Squad's spaceship had to be rebuilt after the original one (from book #1) got sat on accidentally.

☆ The newly redesigned spaceship was made out of cardboard, duct tape, wire, hot glue, and magnets (which hold the legs up when in "flying mode"). The eyes are plastic light bulb-shaped flashlights and they really light up!

☆ The little cars in BABY FROG SQUAD were made from the tops of Japanese salt containers (taped together) with rice-dough lips and toy "building block" wheels duct-taped underneath.

☆ On page 140, Summer really **is** writing the Zen Shodo phrase, "Za Ichi So Shichi,"[1] which translates to "Sit First, dash Seven." It means: Start the day with meditation/prayer/mindfulness before dashing around.

---

1. Shozo Sato, Shodo: The Quiet Art of Japanese Zen Calligraphy (Rutland: Tuttle Publishing, 2014).

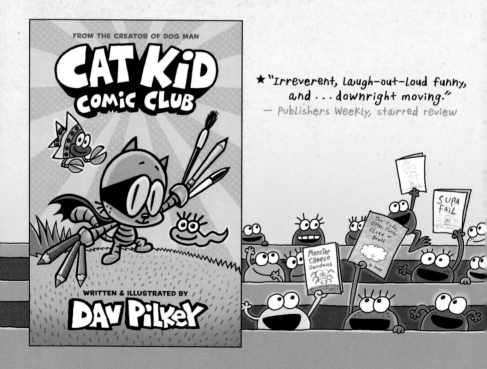

★ "Irreverent, laugh-out-loud funny, and . . . downright moving."
— Publishers Weekly, starred review

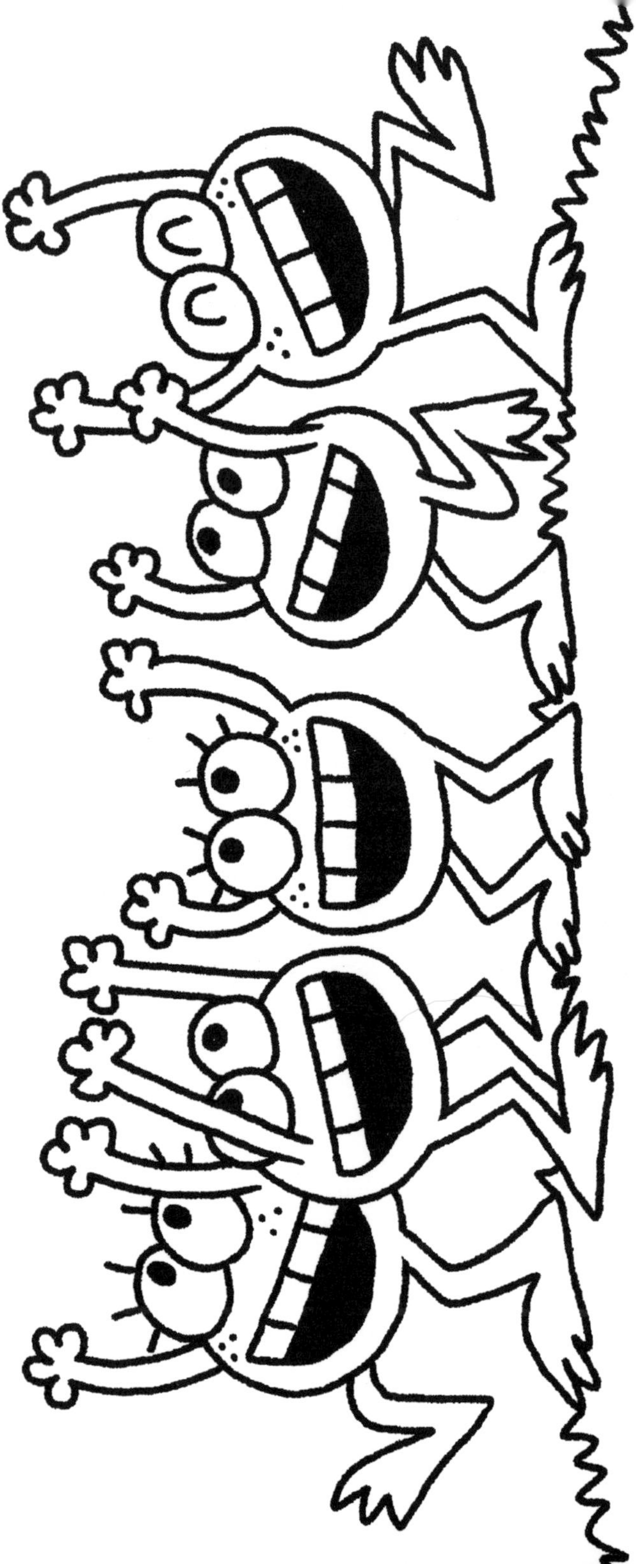

ABOUT THE
AUTHOR-ILLUSTRATOR

When Dav Pilkey was a kid, he was diagnosed with ADHD and dyslexia. Dav was so disruptive in class that his teachers made him sit out in the hallway every day. Luckily, Dav loved to draw and make up stories. He spent his time in the hallway creating his own original comic books — the very first adventures of Dog Man and Captain Underpants.

In college, Dav met a teacher who encouraged him to illustrate and write. He won a national competition in 1986 and the prize was the publication of his first book, WORLD WAR WON. He made many other books before being awarded the 1998 California Young Reader Medal for DOG BREATH, which was published in 1994, and in 1997 he won the Caldecott Honor for THE PAPERBOY.

THE ADVENTURES OF SUPER DIAPER BABY, published in 2002, was the first complete graphic novel spin-off from the Captain Underpants series and appeared at #6 on the USA Today bestseller list for all books, both adult and children's, and was also a New York Times bestseller. It was followed by SUPER DIAPER BABY 2: THE INVASION OF THE POTTY SNATCHERS, also a USA Today bestseller. The unconventional style of these graphic novels is intended to encourage uninhibited creativity in kids.

His stories are semi-autobiographical and explore universal themes that celebrate friendship, tolerance, and the triumph of the good-hearted.

Dav loves to kayak in the Pacific Northwest with his wife.

Learn more at Pilkey.com.

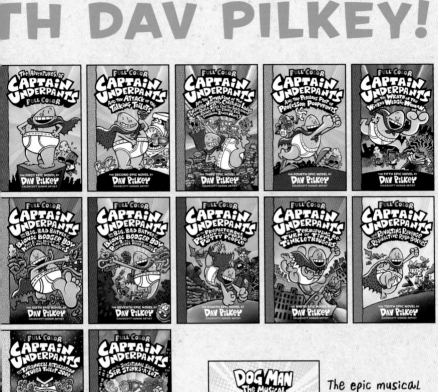

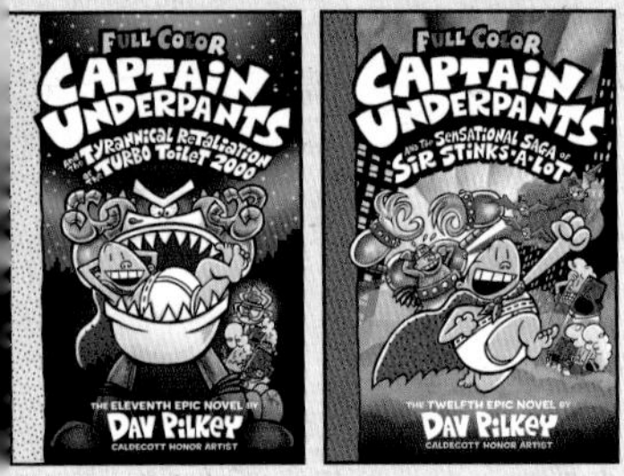